Nikki McWatters was shortlisted in the 2010 Queensland Premier's Literary Award Emerging Writer category. She has published two memoirs: *One Way or Another* (2012) and *Madness, Mayhem and Motherhood* (2018); and two young adult novels: *Sandy Feet* (2014) and *Hexenhaus* (2016). She won the Irish Moth Award (2016) and has written for the *Sydney Morning Herald*, *Huffington Post* UK and *The Big Issue*. She is currently the spokesperson for the annual Vinnies CEO Sleepout. Nikki also has a law degree in her bottom drawer somewhere.

nikkimcwatters.wordpress.com

Also by Nikki McWatters:

Saga (2019)

Liberty (2018)

Hexenhaus (2016)

Sandy Feet (2014)

LIBERTY

Nikki McWatters

UQP

First published 2018 by University of Queensland Press
PO Box 6042, St Lucia, Queensland 4067 Australia

uqp.com.au
uqp@uqp.uq.edu.au

Cover design by Jo Hunt
Cover photographs: birds by Nature Bird Photography/Shutterstock; castle by Alberto Grazioli/Shutterstock; moon by Vik Y/Shutterstock; crowd by AlbertBuchatskyy/Shutterstock
Author photograph by Zeus Eugenius
Typeset in Mrs Eaves 11/15pt by Post Pre-press Group, Brisbane
Printed in Australia by McPherson's Printing Group, Melbourne

The University of Queensland Press is assisted by the Australian Government through the Australia Council, its arts funding and advisory body.

A catalogue record for this book is available from the National Library of Australia

ISBN 978 0 7022 6029 2 (pbk)
ISBN 978 0 7022 6175 6 (pdf)
ISBN 978 0 7022 6176 3 (epub)
ISBN 978 0 7022 6177 0 (kindle)

University of Queensland Press uses papers that are natural, renewable and recyclable products made from wood grown in sustainable forests. The logging and manufacturing processes conform to the environmental regulations of the country of origin.

Although *Liberty* is based on a number of historical events and characters, some of the factual detail has been left out, smoothed over or embellished for the purposes of creating a work of fiction.

For Mia

JEANNE

BEAUVAIS, FRANCE, 1472

I walked alone, against my father's strict instructions, at high sun on the morning of the summer solstice, away from the city of Beauvais toward the neighbouring forest of oaks and chestnuts. This forest was *my* place in the world, my own personal grove of solace. It was a beautiful singing place and I came to it often, to feel the contours of the earth beneath my boots and the sound of my voice, hollow and smooth, merging with nature. I walked through the carpet of leaves and acorn husks, reaching out to touch the trees with my fingers.

I had memories of this wood that seemed to go back beyond time. It was as if the forest was within me as much I was within it. I sang as I walked. Old songs that my father told me my mother had sung to me as a babe. It was a warm day and I soaked myself in the scents of wild pear and beech. I pulled my cap from my head and shook my dark hair loose and wandered on through the woods, swinging my basket by my side, already imagining the taste of berries bursting against my tongue. In a small circular clearing, I stopped and lifted my face to the warmth of the sun, breathed deeply and watched three swallows circling above.

It was in this place that I could feel my mother. The breeze was her breath; my footsteps on the dirt, her heartbeat. As I ducked beneath a low-hanging branch and felt the tickle of a spider's web on my face, I imagined it was her kiss against my cheek. Something of her spirit still dwelled in the forest, clinging to the moss and leaves like an invisible spectre. She made this place feel safe and comforting to me, but my father would never set foot in the forest again, fearing it was a haunted and sad place. Yes, I felt her strongly. She had been only a little older than me when she'd taken her last steps in this very spot.

I needed this solitude because life within the city walls of Beauvais was stifling and it was easy to feel crushed by its bustle and noise. The people living there were wedged into small rooms, all boxed in on one another like chickens in a coop. In the quarter where I lived with my father, we had two small rooms and an attic above; the smells and sounds of our neighbours filled our ears from morning to night. Cabbages and quarrels. On the narrow streets and marketplace, voices were constantly raised to the point that my ears rang. There were fights. Robberies. Beggars. And the smells hung like an oily fog in the back of my throat.

The small forest grove was my secret place. Every small noise was crisp and beautiful. The crackling of sticks and leaves beneath some wood-creature's paws. A bird. The wind. The scents were intoxicating. I imagined I could even smell the warmth of the sunlight that fell through the tree leaves like golden sleet. It smelled like freshly baked bread. My skin, my eyes and ears all seemed to open a little more, like morning petals, to take it all in.

And I felt close to something so much bigger than myself, like I was a part of an enormous secret. I was tempted many times to bring Colin to my special place but always talked myself out of doing so. I loved Colin as much as I loved my father, but even so, deep down I wanted to keep this place for myself. Just me. It was all I had that was my own. Apart from the memories of my mother. It was 'our' place.

'Between the ox and the donkey, sleeps, sleeps, sleeps the little son, la-la-la,' I sang to the trees.

I held a good tune, or so my father had always told me, yet I sang much better with an audience of insects and birds than of people. And as the words to the old song bounced from branch to branch I let all my fears and sadness wash away. In those sacred moments there was just the music and no mourning for my mother, whose face had long been washed from my memory; no clammy terror that the fighting up north would eventually move down closer toward Paris to tread over us as the fishwives gossiped over laundry lines; no creeping discomfort about the way the Lieutenant watched me with a wolfish leer, touching me whenever I passed him in the street.

'Between roses and lilies, sleeps, sleeps, sleeps the little son, la-la-la.'

I searched the undergrowth for anything I could carry home: wild herbs, mushrooms, berries. The birds were my musicians, chirping in tune like feathered lute-players. A butterfly zigzagged past, disappearing into the shadows.

And then the birds stopped singing.

I stood stone-still, ears pricked.

Everything – the entire forest, the sky above, the earth below – seemed to become as if a tableau in a painting. Still and silent. It was unnerving. I waited. Not sure if I should move or run or remain frozen. Or just keep singing.

Something invaded the silence. I listened earnestly. It was the sound of a horse, walking slowly and steadily. The clump of its shoes against the dirt echoed out from the dim shadows of the forest. It was like the beat of a funeral drum.

All of my father's warnings about the forest came rushing at me like wild flood water. My stomach balled into a knot, my pulse quickened. The skin on my arms prickled, puckering into goose flesh. I steeled myself, trying to summon courage. Silently I begged my mother to lend me some of her own brave heart.

'Halt and announce yourself,' I called.

Still the hooves approached. *Clop. Clop. Clop.* My muscles tensed, ready and defensive. Groups of marauding men and desperate soldiers were known to roam the forest roads and deeper into the woods, looking for stragglers to rob – or worse. I turned with a graceful spin and my hand reached down for one of the small hatchets hidden in my basket. I stood, took aim and threw it, watching breathlessly as it cart-wheeled, whistling through the air.

The small axe landed with a heavy thud, the sharp blade wedged into the trunk of a pine tree. I had the other out of the basket and in my hand, ready to follow the warning shot with a more malevolent one. My father had forged the metal and fashioned the small hatchets for me, and had taught me to use them with great precision.

'A girl needs to protect herself,' he'd told me on my thirteenth birthday.

'From what?' I had laughed so innocently.

And then he had sat me down and told me the truth of my mother's death and for the first time in my life all those years of town whispers made sense. I learned that there was plenty to be afraid of in the world. I learned that I was lucky to be alive and that my father wanted me to be able to defend myself because my mother had not been able to.

I had not had cause to use my small hatchets, although I often practised with them in the forest. I had the aim of a king's marksman and a good strong arm.

'I said halt,' I called again in a loud voice, trying to sound much braver than I felt. 'I am armed and you have been warned.'

I saw the horse stagger into the clearing. Slung like a limp sack over its long stooped neck, fallen forward, was a bloodied man. I gasped. At first, I thought he was dead but he reached up an arm and lifted his head.

'Help me.'

His hair was dirty, wild and caked with blood. His unshaven face was grey. Without letting my eyes leave his face, I pulled my hatchet from the gnarled tree trunk and held the two of them defensively out in front of me as I edged warily around the horse, closer to the path so I could run if this was trickery.

'Where have you come from?' I asked, making sure he could see I was armed.

'Roye,' he gasped. 'The Bold has sacked it. We surrendered but still he butchered us. Soldiers. Men. Women. Even children.'

I looked at him. His torn jacket had brass buttons. His boots were of good quality. He appeared to be unarmed.

'Are they coming for Beauvais next?' I asked, dreading his answer.

'I can't say,' he said, grimacing in pain. As he lifted his arm again toward me I saw a gaping hole in his chest. 'But I think ... so ... yes ...'

'You are hurt badly,' I whispered. 'Can you move forward? I will ride you to town so you can warn the Captain of Beauvais. He needs to prepare for the worst.'

I could not steer a horse and carry my basket at the same time so I left it where it lay. I would return for it later. I tied the two hatchets securely at my sides beneath my outer skirts so that they did not show and then pulled myself up behind the saddle and pushed the man forward as gently as I could. He groaned. The horse did not look well either so I did not press her hard. In a gentle trot we made our way to Beauvais. The soldier closed his eyes and I prayed that he would not die before we arrived.

The horse clattered along the dusty road. We came to a break in the trees and saw Beauvais, the wonder of the whole region. There was the Cathedral, massive and magnificent, cresting the hilltop in the morning sun. The steeples and towers dwarfed the stone walls that surrounded the city. The many houses of Beauvais were cobbled together, all at chaotic angles.

As we drew closer, the gatehouse on the far side of the bridge came into view. Two round towers stood on either side of the pointed arch and in a shallow niche, a statue of King Louis XI looked down. Beauvais was a proud town. I only hoped that she would prove strong enough to resist an invasion.

We crossed over the bridge and I smelled the muddy banks of the brook beneath. I held my breath and tried to ignore the piles of refuse that had slid down into thick quagmires of human waste, rotting meat and animal carcasses. Two men, chests bared, were further down-stream, among the green grasses and reeds, hauling a barrel of excrement from the back of a cart to empty it into the water. For all of Beauvais' grand beauty as a city, her outskirts displayed all the disgusting features of a bloated glutton.

I urged the horse to go faster, hastening on to the city gates, which were open. A group of urchins with dirty faces appeared.

'What you got there?'

'Is he dead?'

'Did you kill him?'

'Can I have his boots?'

Their clothes were filthy and their faces even filthier. I ignored them and pushed on under the shadow of the gatehouse into the busy streets, making my way into the town with my sorry cargo and a heavy sense of foreboding. Charles the Bold was the villain leading the Burgundian army and was determined to take as much of France for himself as he could. With all our men away fighting with King Louis, Beauvais would be an easy town to take. I felt sick in the belly as I guided the horse past curious bystanders. I had never been one for talk of battles and politics but it had been impossible to ignore the ill-wind that had begun to blow through my beloved city over the past few months.

The roads in the merchant quarter were uneven and sodden after a week of rain. Other ponies and packhorses clopped through the town and russet-coloured peasants shouted in coarse voices.

'Hot sheep's feet, ribs of beef, many a pie!' a street vendor hollered.

Once I turned the ailing nag into the wider, sunnier streets where people wore high colours and soft fabrics, the looks my way became more repulsed than curious. I passed through the wide and handsome prospect of Church Street where some of the finest houses and inns sat, and stopped outside the Captain's mansion. I reached forward to rest a hand on the soldier to check that he was still breathing as he appeared to have fallen asleep, or worse.

A black-robed Dominican friar with a kind, round face was just leaving the Captain's house. He helped me down from the horse.

'I will call the Captain's men to take him inside,' he said and showed me to the door, ringing the bell loudly. 'You did the right thing to bring him straight here. The

Burgundians, you say? He looks half-dead or more. It seems I will be sending his soul heavenward with prayer shortly.'

Not knowing what else to do, I followed the Captain's men inside as they carried the limp, broken soldier. It was bold and foolhardy but my concern for my city and my curiosity about the interior of the house got the better of me. I felt small and meek in the palatial manor house. I had only ever delivered bread to the kitchen-maids at the servant's entrance. The main parlour room was like a dream. Soft furnishings and thick, deep floor rugs with the glint of gold, and fine glossy china adorning the smooth polished cedar side-tables.

'What the devil are you doing here, you soot-urchin?' the Captain yelled as he blustered in from the kitchens, his hair wild and his face bloated with surprise and anger.

'I found an injured soldier in the woods just beyond the city gates,' I said in a small voice, looking down at my boots. 'Before he fell to silence, he told me that the Burgundians have sacked Roye and that they may be marching for Beauvais. I rode him directly here on his own horse, which will also need some attention.'

'We have a garrison here of only three hundred men!' Captain Louis de Balagny shouted into my face as if this was somehow my fault. He looked to the ceiling. 'We must pack up and leave town or surrender peacefully.'

He seemed panicked. A far cry from the stern and sombre captain I usually saw speaking to the townsfolk in the square. The injured soldier had been taken to an upstairs room and a doctor had been summoned. I prayed that the soldier would survive.

'Sir, the soldier told me,' I ventured nervously, 'that the town of Roye had offered a peaceful surrender but Charles the Bold had slaughtered and sacked them anyway.'

Balagny turned and glared at me.

'Perhaps you heard him wrong, girl.' He frowned. 'Are you not Jeanne, the daughter of Matthew the Coward? Not really very reliable stock.' He narrowed his eyes at me. 'What were you doing in the forest alone anyway?'

'I just … I …' I stammered. 'I like to walk and … pick berries.'

'A girl wandering unchaperoned in the forest? You ask for trouble. Had that fellow upstairs felt more … um … lively, well, things might have gone badly for you. I would not tempt fate, girl. You look like your mother, uncannily so. You wouldn't want to end the way she did.'

I felt sick. I knew what he meant and wondered if I was right to pray for the survival of the unknown soldier. He might have been a horrible person.

'I did not venture too far,' I mumbled. 'And I can run fast and look after myself.'

'Big talk for a peasant girl with holes in her shoes,' he laughed roughly. 'And how would you look after yourself, child? Kick your little feet with your toes poking out? Bundle your small, delicate fists into clubs to take down a gang of thugs?'

I drifted into nervous silence, thinking of the small hatchets beneath my skirts. It was a crime for a woman to carry a weapon. A sudden panic gripped me. If the soldier awoke to tell them that he had been rescued by a girl wielding axes, I would have a lot of explaining to do. Although I'd been named for the brave and saintly Jeanne d'Arc who had been a distant kinswoman of my mother and a heroine of childhood stories told to me by my father, I doubted I could muster her courage and iron will if accused of bearing arms.

'Lagoy?' the Captain turned his attention to his lieutenant, Jean Lagoy, who had just entered the room. I looked down at my boots again to avoid his gaze, bile rising in my gullet at the sound of his name.

'He's in a sorry state,' the deep voice rumbled. 'But he'll live, I'd wager.'

'This girl is telling a story about the fellow having come from Roye claiming that the Burgundians are headed for Beauvais.'

'I said he wasn't sure,' I muttered. 'He only thought they were ... but ... he ... well ... he couldn't be certain.'

'I think we should wait for the soldier from Roye to wake and speak to us,' Lagoy said thoughtfully. 'Perhaps Charles the Bold will bypass us on his way to Paris. I could take some men and ride toward Paris, recruiting reinforcements, perhaps?'

Jean Lagoy then crossed the room to me and took my hand. 'Thank you, Mademoiselle Laisné, for bringing him to us. That was very brave of you.'

I looked up at him and my cheeks burned. His hand was clammy with sweat and his fingers massaged mine. His touch was blatantly sensuous and unpleasant. The brash and dashing young Lieutenant had pursued me for nearly a year but I had no interest in him. I found his arrogance unbearable. Whenever I was anywhere near him, he made me feel like a trapped animal. His eyes bore into mine.

'Go now, girl,' Captain Balagny barked. 'Back to your cowardly father. And see that you say nothing of this business or you will cause a panic we can ill afford. If anyone asks, tell them the man you escorted into town was a vagabond, a drunkard. And cover your head for pity's sake, girl. Have you no shame? Remember your station. Did a stint in the pillories teach you nothing?'

I fumbled in my pocket for my cap, then securing it on my head, I scurried from the room, giving an awkward curtsey and nod, cursing myself that I had forgotten to tie it back on when leaving the forest. As I stepped outside I felt a hand grip mine and I turned sharply to see that Lagoy had followed me into the street.

'Jeanne, *ma chérie*,' he said, glaring down at me with his dark, thickly lashed eyes.

'I must get home to my father,' I frowned.

'When will you come dancing with me?' he grinned.

'I am not of your station, Sir,' I replied. 'I could no sooner go dancing with you than the King.'

'Perhaps some private dancing in the stables out the back. We could go riding. I have a new horse. I think you would like him. He's quite a stallion.'

'I have no interest in you or your horse,' I snapped.

'You talk like a lady, but you dress like a peasant,' he laughed. 'You are more your mother than your father. If she'd married well you'd be the finest catch in Beauvais. I flatter you with my attention and yet you give me no love.

What's a man to do? You play a foolish game to think that you can push me away forever. If I wanted your love ...'

He clicked his fingers into my face. I blinked, put my hands on my hips so that I could feel the metal of my hatchets on either side, and narrowed my eyes.

'Do not use the word love in the same breath that you speak of yourself and me. I imagine there is not much room left for anyone else to love you after yourself, Lieutenant Lagoy. Go back to a looking glass for that is who loves you best. And my mother did marry well. For real love.'

'And look where that got her,' Lagoy laughed cruelly.

This cut me deep like a sword. I turned on my heel and hurried away through the narrow cobbled streets, down Butcher's Row, toward the marketplace to find Colin, whom I trusted more than myself. He would know what we should do. Colin always knew exactly what to do. And I could not keep this news a secret from him. Our lives and everyone's in the town were at stake.

Bells rang and children played like puppies beside their mothers' skirts. I wanted Colin to wrap me in his arms and make all the jumble of fears and discomforts melt away in his warmth. Colin was the one thing that made me feel safe in a world that marched to the beat of terror, from the tip of the steeple on the Cathedral to the empty larder at home and father's broken body and will. Yes, only Colin Pilon made me feel that there was something to live for – love.

BETSY

COUNTY DOWN, IRELAND, 1797

I was dressed in my best white dress, boots highly polished, and I had an emerald green ribbon tied into my fair hair. My da was right suspicious of me.

'Where you going, Betsy Gray?' He frowned.

'I'm nearly nineteen and a grown woman in my own right. I'm going to visit cousin Mary,' I lied. Well, it wasn't actually a lie. Mary *had* asked me to come by for tea but I'd be visiting the inn first. It was more of a lie by omission.

'You watch out for the yeomanry,' he grumbled. 'Pretty girl like you shouldn't be riding the roads alone.'

'Finn McCool can gallop faster than any English steed,' I laughed over my shoulder. 'And I'd warrant that no redcoat has better handling of his beast than me!'

'With your yellow hair out like that you look like you're off to a dance,' he grumbled as he finished his morning tea and stretched in his chair. 'Give my regards to young Mary and if you see any trouble with the English, you remind them that you are a Gray, a loyalist and my daughter. And stay off the roads south because word is they are hanging that rogue Orr today.'

I raised my eyebrows, feigning surprise.

'That's awful, Da,' I said, shaking my head. 'The poor man.'

'Poor man, tosh!' he snapped. 'You put your neck out like that and what do you expect? The rebels ask for trouble and get it. You steer clear of them, hear? George isn't meddling with them, is he? He says some subversive rot sometimes.'

I gasped, perhaps a little too dramatically. 'Why no, Da! Of course not! He's not so foolish.'

'Hmmm,' he murmured, regarding me intently. 'It's certain death to run about with rebels.'

'I know that,' I said, taking a coat from the hook in the mudroom, the satchel at my side burning guiltily into my hip.

'And young William Boal?' he called. 'He's a hot-head.'

'Oh, Will! Never!' I said, shaking my head, feeling a wee blush across my face at his name. I rushed to kiss my father on the cheek and he nodded, convinced by my act.

'Well then, ride straight to Mary's and be safe and sensible.'

'Always,' I winked at him, both of us knowing that being 'sensible' was not my strongest trait. 'Love you, Da.'

He waved a hand at me as he took out his pipe.

That crisp morning in October, as I walked outside and took a deep breath of the new day, I gazed across the plains stretching up toward the hills behind our whitewashed cottage. One tall peak dipped into an emerald green valley before rising up the flank of another slope. I took in the swell of empty boulders, squatting there like sheep turned to stone, as I crossed the garden.

The air inside the barn was heavy with the smell of hay and dung. I took a saddle from the wall peg and smiled at the horses watching me from their stalls, their gentle snorting breaths warming the stable. My darling boy, Finn McCool, was a soft-eyed grey gelding, although his coat was almost white in broad daylight. His ears pricked forward and he whinnied as I approached and gave his warm velvety muzzle a rub.

I took off his blanket and swung the saddle over him, lightly fastened the girth and put on his bridle, leading him out into the yard and closing the barn door behind me. The sun was coming up fast over the ridge as I mounted Finn McCool, urging him on through the dark hedges out toward Six Road Ends. Clouds of breath billowed from the horse's nostrils ahead of me.

Out on the gravelled thoroughfare there was a pristine stillness. I passed by sleepy farms with tendrils of smoke coiling up into the empty sky. The meadows were dusted with fallen autumn leaves.

As the sun warmed the day, more people going about their errands appeared. A cart of potatoes rumbled by with Gavin Edie driving from the stoop, his old spotted packhorse looking like it had seen better days.

'Top of the morning to you, Betsy Gray,' he called, doffing his cap as we crossed paths. 'Looking mighty grand this morning, you are.'

I smiled at the compliment and hoped that Will Boal would feel the same about me. I let one hand fall back to the leather satchel over my shoulder and knew that I was taking a great risk to be out in a public place with such dangerous contraband. I hoped the pretty dress and my fair hair and ribbons would distract any English yeoman from imagining me to be a rebel messenger.

The Hillsborough Yeomen had the meanest reputation and I would do well to steer clear of them. I'd heard the terrible rumours of the nasty ways they dealt with suspected United Irishmen supporters. Some fellows had been dragged from their beds and half-hung on gallows, beaten until they were nearly dead and then thrown back over their garden gates. But it was early and my brother had assured me that our enemy would all be across the lough, busy with their evil intent for the day, leaving the roads safe for the morning at least. Aye, they'd all be at the public hanging of Mr Orr.

I crossed a plateau where the flowers by the roadside were wilting with cold, and then rode down to Crawfordsburn. I stayed wary and vigilant for armed soldiers who might be on the lookout for rebels, but I was worrying myself needlessly because not a single soldier appeared.

At The Old Inn at Crawfordsburn, I pulled Finn McCool up at the watering station where I dismounted and tied him to a post, patting his strong haunches. I recognised my brother's dappled chestnut mare and Will Boal's gelding, so dark he looked as black as ebony in the sunlight. The paddock by the inn was busy with horses and carts.

I walked up and gave my brother's mare a pat, her soft flyaway mane grazing my knuckles.

'Hey, O'Malley girl.'

I stroked her silky coat and then gave a nod to the majestic creature that belonged to Will. He didn't let me touch him but sniffed my fingers and then gave a haughty toss of his head. I hoped, in the bottom of my belly, that his master would treat me more kindly.

Inside, the inn was already full of sombre souls. All thoughts that morning were across the waters of Belfast Lough, to Carrickfergus, where the brave rebel leader William Orr would be hanged. By way of silent protest and as a mark of respect for Mr Orr, the townsfolk had largely taken leave of the place and crossed the watery stretch by ferry to wait at Crawfordsburn until the dastardly deed was done.

I recognised the infamous Mr Brennan, poet and rebel, whose articles in the newspapers had landed him in hot water many times. He was a broad, ruddy man with tufts of silver whiskers. Behind him, over near the bar, I saw my brother, George, and the most splendid-looking young man I knew, George's best friend, and mine: Will Boal. The pair were two years older and more mischievous than me.

'Betsy,' Will bowed low as I approached. 'You are looking mighty fine on this bleak day. A little ray of sunshine at an otherwise gloomy sort of wake. You have the face of an angel.'

I felt my cheeks colour and dropped my eyes, bobbing into a small curtsey. George looked at me and ran a finger over his glass of whisky.

'Are you flirting with my little sister, Will?'

'I might be and what of it?' Will jested.

'I don't mind.' I smiled coyly and shrugged. 'Isn't it a little early in the day for that, George?' I said, pointing at his glass and ruffling his sandy-brown hair with my fingers.

'Aye, sister.' He laughed at me. 'But if you were to listen to the English they would tell you that an Irishman's sole aptitude is quite evidently for drinking.'

'I'll drink to that,' Will said, clinking his tumbler against George's. '*Sláinte!*'

'And to the godly Mr Orr,' Brennan called loudly across to us. 'A true martyr for the cause. I've written a poem for him. Those bastards were deaf to all reasonable appeals. Justice did not prevail!'

'Let's have it,' George cheered back. 'Give us a taste of this poem.'

'Oh, hapless land, heap of uncementing sand, crumbled by a foreign weight and, by worse, domestic hate.' Brennan stood, hand on chest, and bellowed out the words in a deep rumbling timbre and the men and women in the inn all raised a cheer, held glasses aloft and shouted, 'Remember Orr!'

I accepted a pitcher of fruit punch from the woman behind the bar and settled into a chair next to my brother who whispered his thanks as I pulled the wad of pamphlets from my satchel and slid them across to him. He passed them back over the bar and the small buxom woman gave a knowing click of her tongue and took them straight to the back room.

‘Hide them well, Frances,’ my brother called after her.

‘There’s an extra strong military guard over at Carrickfergus,’ Will told us. ‘But they’ll be confounded when they find that not a single Irish soul will be attending the execution. Not a one. Most everyone has quit the town. Blinds are drawn and many of the shops are shut up.’

I looked at Will. I’d known him most of my life. The three of us had grown up together, always rolling down hills until we were giddy and playing pranks on one another to the point of tears and blustering apologies. With Will and George being only a little older than me, I had for many years considered them both brothers. But after a time away at a school in Dublin, I’d come home to find that Will Boal had grown tall and broad-shouldered, his boyish awkwardness had given way to a man’s strong features. I had found myself dreaming of him nightly and thinking of him during most of my waking hours, not in a brotherly way at all. In his presence I had suddenly become more shy and reserved. For this I was mercilessly teased by George for my ‘girlish fancy’.

Will’s blue eyes were set in a handsome face topped with a thatch of unruly dark curls. He was as dark as I was fair. George was somewhere in between with his colouring. It astonished me to suddenly realise that our respective horses were similarly coloured to their riders. Finn McCool was as fair as a pearl, like me; Will’s steed was a coal-black prince and George’s pretty O’Malley was the same nutty colour as George’s ponytailed hair. In fact, her tail could almost be mistaken for the one ribboned at the nape of George’s neck.

Many of the men in the inn were wearing green neckties as a personal tribute to their condemned comrade, Mr Orr, who was rarely seen without one. I wondered if he would wear it to the gallows.

News arrived later that morning that the hanging had been quick. Drinks were drunk and ditties sung and the mourners in the inn became loud with laughter and sudden bursts of anger as many shared amusing tales of the great Orr. A quick death was a good death.

'Is that a new green ribbon you're sporting, Betsy?' Will smiled at me and I felt like I could fall into his eyes as they looked into mine.

'Why, yes, it is, Will,' I said softly, sipping at my drink, my eyes never leaving his.

'It's mighty pretty.' He winked. 'As are you.'

'Oh, please,' George groaned, and rolled his eyes. 'We're here because a man was hanged this morning and you two are making eyes at one another and flirting more enthusiastically than a pair of love struck turtle-doves. Coo-coo.'

I felt my cheeks warm, and coughed. Will leaned back into his chair and folded his arms behind his head.

'George, George,' he sighed. 'A man cannot help himself around such beauty. I come undone and have a belly of insects whenever Betsy looks at me the way she did just then. It clean took my breath away. She's a vixen.'

'I did no such thing,' I spluttered. 'What way did I look at you, Will?'

'Oh, like I was a full plate of sweetmeats.'

'I did not!'

'Oh, yes, you did.' Will laughed. 'You made me well nervous. I felt like a wee mouse being eyed off by a cat.'

'Stop it,' I said, putting my drink on the table. 'I'll not have your teasing, Will.'

'Both of you stop this game.' George moaned as if he had a belly ache. 'I don't know if you're doing this to annoy me, Will, but she's my little sister, so stop joking about.'

'Yes,' I whispered. 'It's not funny.'

We fell silent, and I nervously and shyly caught Will's eye again. He gave me the tiniest smile and a look that said a hundred words but seemed to be in another language and I could not decipher them. I returned his smile and my insides felt as if they were being kneaded like dough.

I dropped my gaze as I gathered my thoughts, trying to settle the feeling in my stomach, tracing patterns with my finger on the wooden table. My heart suddenly leapt again in my chest and my legs felt heavy with fear as the inn doors burst open to reveal a troop of redcoats, swords at their sides and muskets in their hands. A hush descended and everyone stiffened.

'We are here to find the rebels,' one yelled as his companions began to sweep through the room, rough-handling those that got in their way.

George and Will looked stony-faced as one soldier approached us. He was fair-haired and lean, with a glassy glint in his eye. He cocked an eyebrow.

'What's this then? You lads scheming rebel plans here?' he growled.

'I am the son of Hans Gray of Gransha, a gentleman,' George said politely. 'And I can assure you my father has already signed and sworn the Oath of Allegiance when you visited us last year. His oath covers our family estate, which includes me and my sister here. We are loyalists to the Crown.'

My brother's voice was wooden and dispassionate. I could tell he was lying but hoped the English soldiers could not. I felt the redcoat's eyes fall to me and I shuddered under his glare. Beneath the table I felt Will grip my wrist firmly. The man looked cruel. I was afraid.

'What's your name then, girlie?'

'Betsy. I mean Elizabeth Gray.'

He looked around the room at the revellers, who had gone quiet.

'You'll tell me what this is then, Miss Betsy? What sort of gathering is this?'

'It's a wake,' I said cautiously.

'For whom?' he demanded.

'An old woman, Molly Whitty,' I lied, because Molly Whitty had died some months prior. 'In her sleep. Rest her soul. We buried her at Gransha early this morning.' I saw a gleam of approval in George's eye at my quick thinking.

The soldier looked again at the sodden men and women in the room, many with untidy green neckties coming loose.

'We heard fiddling,' he snapped. 'And laughter. You unfortunate clods on this island have a strange way of marking death with dancing, revelling and drinking more fit for a wedding. But any excuse to drag you away from honest work into a drinking house, I suppose.'

'We have our ways, sir, and you have yours,' I said softly.

'Strike up the fiddle,' he called across to the old, weathered man with the instrument hanging by his side. 'And I'll demand a dance with Betsy Gray while my men search the premises.'

I looked to Will and George. I hoped to heaven that the pamphlets taken to the storeroom were well hidden or we might all be for the gallows. One fat redcoat came out of the back larder eating a bread roll and raised no alarm so I breathed a little more easily, sure that the bartending woman had adequately secured them.

The fiddler began to slowly string out a tune and the soldier standing at our table grabbed my hand and dragged me to my feet. My hand was torn from Will's. He and George stood up in protest as the man pulled me close to his chest. I put up my hands, balling them into fists and struggled beneath his arms. He was so close I could see the pockmarks on his face. His breath was hot and stank of ale.

'Let me go,' I muttered.

'No,' he hissed into my face. 'I will have a nice close dance and then a kiss from this fair belle of Éire. We hear all you colleens of Erin like a nice close dance!'

I managed to pull away, and slapped him sharply across the cheek.

He let me go and reeled backwards and I felt every eye in the place fall on me. The soldier's hand pulled up and away from his burning cheek and he raised it to strike me but then stopped, glaring at me.

'I cannot strike a face so lovely, although you give me good reason,' he growled and turned his attention to Will, who had taken my hand protectively. 'Who's this then? Your sweetheart?'

'I … I …' I stammered.

'*Cúl tóna*,' Will muttered a curse in the old tongue under his breath.

'What was that? You talking that savage language, you Irish dog?' the soldier challenged Will and I winced at the boy's foolishness for using the old language to aggravate the situation.

'It is the language of my father and my father's father,' Will said defiantly.

The man pulled up the musket from his side and in one lightning-fast movement shoved the handle into Will's stomach, knocking him to the ground. With another blow he brought the butt down on the crook of Will's shoulder while landing a steel-capped boot in his back. I felt my chest constrict and my breath came out in a rush.

The soldier wiped his brow, turned and marched back to the door, calling his men to follow him.

'We'll be watching you,' he shouted back into the room. 'If there are rebels among you, we will find out and you will go the same way as that scoundrel Irish Dog Orr, who, over in Carrickfergus this lovely sunny day, swung till his necked snapped. It was a beautiful sight.'

As soon as they had gone, I fell down beside Will who was groaning on the floor. I touched his shoulder, crying.

'Will, talk to me,' I sobbed. 'Are you all right?'

'I'm fine, just a little bruised,' he panted, forcing a smile. 'The whisky in my belly dulled the blow.'

In that moment, relieved that he was not gravely hurt, I bent forward and kissed him on the mouth. The room stood still as did my heart when William Boal kissed me back.

FIONA

DARLING DOWNS, AUSTRALIA, 1968

'Pie! Pie! Pie!' they chanted all around the hall.

The mood was feverish. Almost every person from Bandaroo Flats was present, dressed in their Sunday best. But after an afternoon of partying – beer for the men and shandies for the ladies – the collars were getting sweaty and high colour was pinching people's cheeks. The laughter had crept up to a gentle roar and everyone was having a marvellous time, especially the four boys lined up along the long trestle table on the stage with a mountain of meat pies in front of them.

Although a good pie-eating competition was always a winner at a function at the town hall, I found the spectacle somewhat disgusting. Almost fully grown men sitting in their church shirts, stuffing pastry, meat and gravy into their mouths like ravenous beasts, the overflow spilling down over their lightly fuzzed chins. Ugh. My brother, Murray, was the town champion, sitting on a record of seven pies in the allotted time of ten minutes. The big clock on the wall, not far from the Queen's portrait, was ticking over and the crowd was chanting 'Pie! Pie! Pie!' like a bloodthirsty audience at a gladiator slaughter as Murray and the three other young men shoved warm pies into their mouths, trying not to gag, tomato sauce running like blood over their lips. I felt my stomach turn.

The dinging of the finish bell was met with a roar and cheer as Murray stood up to be crowned the champion once again, with a result of seven and a half pies eaten. A new Bandaroo Flats record. The prize was a meat tray from Ted the butcher. Murray shot a look at Walter Leary that was filled with victory. I had to look away because it was so sad. How did poor Murray think there was any triumph in eating more pies than that horrid prig of a boy? Was that the only way he could feel avenged for the years of bullying? Walter Leary had treated my family with such disdain over the years because his father owned half of Bandaroo Flats and he figured himself as some kind of 'prince' of the district, lording it over those of us who felt the sting of a bad year of crops or the loss of livestock. My older brother had kept challenging the former pie-eating champion for a year now, beating him on the podium every time there was a town assembly. It was embarrassing and a bit pathetic. If the only comeuppance that the Leary boy got was to be the runner-up at these gastronomic events, then the world was not fair or equitable, and Walter would have to wait until the afterlife to get his just deserts for being such a vile human being.

'And now,' said Mr Jamieson, the principal of the local

primary school, 'while you boys get yourselves cleaned up, we will welcome our guest of honour to the stage: Fiona McKechnie.'

Again, the crowd cranked up a flutter of applause and I blushed as I took to the stage, feeling completely embarrassed and self-conscious. Mr Jamieson plonked a wet kiss on my cheek as he shook my hand.

'Give us a song, Fi,' someone shouted from the back of the hall.

Mr Jamieson clapped his hands for attention the way he had for the seven years I'd endured at the small schoolhouse on the outskirts of town.

'Now listen up, you lot,' he called. 'I'm so proud of this young woman. I've known since her first day of school that little Fiona was something special. A girl with big things in her future. And we're here today to congratulate her as she heads off to the big smoke of Brisbane to attend university.'

More applause as I twisted on my feet, looking down at my shoes.

'And not only is she going to university, she is going to university to study Law. Law! I'd warrant that's a first for a girl from Bandaroo Flats, perhaps the entire Darling Downs region. Yes, I'd warrant that. Quite an achievement.'

'Thanks, Sir,' I muttered.

'A few words, Fiona?' he asked and stepped back, leaving me to face all the dishevelled and partied out townsfolk.

'I ... um ... thanks everyone for coming to wish me luck. It's pretty exciting. And scary.'

All their faces were turned toward me. I felt their eyes. My face was deepening to a dusky red.

'I want to thank Mr Jamieson for making me work so hard at school and all my teachers and really ... well ... most of all, my dad.'

I looked through the sea of faces, my gaze resting on the man standing closest to the door as if he was prepared for an emergency getaway. My father was a big man, his greying rust-coloured hair sticking up and around his face like dirty fox fur, his face showing his discomfort. He had his signature pipe sticking out the side of his mouth.

'It hasn't been easy for him, bringing up two kids on his own these past few years and I'm going to miss him so much when I go ... and ... you too, Murray.' I sniffed back the tears and shot a look to my brother who was mopping the pie-residue from his white shirt and looking more than a bit nauseous. 'And Laura, my very best friend in the world.

'But I want to make you proud,' I said, trying to sound more confident. 'All of you. I want to make a difference in this world and I think that really starts with justice and the idea that we're all equally deserving of it.' I shot Walter Leary a pointed look.

'Give us a song,' another voice piped up.

'Yeah, Fi, a song!'

The crowd began a light chant and I rolled my eyes and sighed as I caught sight of Laura Bell pushing through the crowd with my battered but beloved guitar. I pulled a fake angry face at her as she handed it up to me with a cheeky wink.

'Seems like I don't have a choice.' I laughed.

'I came prepared.' She laughed back at me, flicked her dark hair over one shoulder and gave me an encouraging nod.

I draped the strap over my head and shoulder and tested the strings. I looked out at all the people urging me on, wishing me well. I hated playing to a human audience. Singing and strumming to the cows at home was where I was most comfortable. And I changed the lyrics to fit with the circumstances.

The crowd clapped. It began to feel good. Everyone was so happy. Everyone except that wide-shouldered man at the back door. He looked positively miserable.

'I'm leaving in an FJ Holden,' I sang and struggled to fit the new lyrics into the music and the crowd gave a collective laugh. I felt my belly heave as I glanced again to the back door.

Dad had gone.

The next day Dad, Murray and I sat in silence for the first part of the journey. I rested my elbow on the car window ledge and felt the breeze dance through my hair. The Holden, watched by sleepy cows munching yellowing grasses, bumped over the gravelly roads leading to Toowoomba.

Dad was quiet. I was waiting for him to break the heaviness between us.

'You don't have to go, you know,' he said. 'We could just turn around. No one would think less of you ... You don't have to prove anything.'

I gave a long sigh. I loved Dad so much but he could also be infuriating. 'I want to go, Dad. This is really important to me. I want to do it for Mum.'

He fell silent again and we drove on, turning the dust behind us, leaving the wide open expanses for the jumble of houses leading into Toowoomba, just under an hour from home. It wasn't until we started down the long, steep descent of the Range, toward the flood plains and beyond to the city of Brisbane, that he spoke again.

'She'd be so proud of you, Fiona,' he said softly.

Tears pricked my eyes and I looked out the window, letting the wind whip them away.

'She would, you know, Fi.' Murray leaned in between us, speaking softly.

Mum would have been proud of me. She really would have. And oh, how I wished she'd been there to see me head off to university. Her father, her hero, had been a barrister in Edinburgh and she had often talked about his greatest cases. The time he defended a man accused of being a bank robber who turned out to be a kindly and generous benefactor of an orphanage who'd simply had the misfortune to look exactly like the guilty party, a long-lost identical twin. And another story about the time my grandfather had accused a high court judge of corruption and been sent to prison for a month himself for his outspokenness. The judge in that case was eventually dismissed, proving my grandfather right. My mother had told me so proudly that barrister Simon Fergus was a man who upheld the principle of justice even if it meant wearing the punishment. These stories had sparked my own interest in law.

Murray started whistling and I imagine it was to distract him from the tears because I could see in the rear-vision mirror that he was very glassy-eyed. I wasn't sure if it was the mention of Mum or that he was going to miss me. Probably the Mum thing. 'It's a shame Laura couldn't come,' I said, adjusting my brand new, white-plastic frame sunglasses. 'I wanted her to see my room at the boarding house.'

'She said she was busy.' Murray shrugged. 'I dunno. She's always busy with the new job at the pub.'

'Well, you can tell her all about it, hey?' I smiled.

'Maybe it was too much for her,' Dad said sadly. 'It's almost too much for me. God, I'm going to worry about you, Fi. In the big smoke, all alone.'

Dad coughed hard as if he had a bone stuck in his throat. My dad did not cry. Even when Mum died, he just went into himself and turned to wood. Sometimes when I hugged him I could feel the splinters.

University. I imagined the scent of dusty books and polished wood and an atmosphere of intellectual vigour. Instead, my first minutes on campus saw me breathing in cigarette smoke and hot dust and feeling like I'd stepped into a circus. And it was truly terrifying. My legs shook like a newborn foal's.

I was the first woman in my family to set foot on university soil. And I'd made it here, in my squeaking new shoes, on a scholarship. There was no way my father could afford to send me and I would never have asked that of him. So the day the letter with the University logo arrived in the mailbox had been the best day of my life. It was my ticket out of the confines of my father's expectations. I had run a leaping-and-dancing lap of the farm, waving the letter and shouting great whoops of victory, making the cows look up and frown even more deeply than my father. He had made it very plain that he expected me to do nothing more with my life than find a nice man off the land and raise a head of cattle and a swarm of children. He hadn't even wanted me to catch the bus to Toowoomba to go to the high school. 'Girls don't need high school,' he'd blustered. 'It's just a waste of time when all you need to know you can learn on the farm from your mother. Find a nice fella who thinks the world of you and raise a decent family.' I'd cried and carried on until finally he relented and let me go to high school. My mother had sweet-talked him, telling him that more opportunities were opening up for girls and that I should be encouraged to use my brain. My mother knew it was my dream to chase a career in law. She had always wanted to be a doctor but that was an all-but-impossible goal. Mum believed me when I told her I dreamed of a life in the city and the chance to do some good in the world. She sometimes called me the little arrow to her bow and she said she wanted to shoot me as high and far as I could go. For Mum and the memory of her, I was determined to make my mark. The scholarship sealed the deal for Dad. He made jokes about there being something a bit 'unladylike' about a daughter who wanted to go off and study law. But I could tell by the way he told everyone in town, long and loud, that his girl was going to be a city-slicking lawyer, that he was deep-down as proud as punch.

Despite this, in my father's mind university was just a place-holder until I found a husband and he made it very clear that he was only allowing me to go because a tertiary education campus was a fine place to meet a top-quality suitor. For me, however, university was going to be a springboard into my own self-determined future and I didn't need a man to help me do that.

On my first morning at university I found the enormous campus bustling with energy and excitement. It was Induction Day. There were so many young people, all dressed in colourful, modern outfits, making me seem like a bit of a country bumpkin in my new black patent shoes, stockings and knee-length plaid skirt. Many people were also quite a bit older than me. I wasn't used to being the youngest at school.

Not knowing anyone, I pressed nervously through the crush of students flooding the walkways between various buildings on campus. I had my acceptance letter, which showed me where I was to go, and a map which I turned this way and that as I tried to navigate my way past the Student Union block toward my destination. People around me were shouting and clapping hands together in the air. It sounded like I was in the middle of some civil riot. Lots of the young men had full beards and long hair and, in a strange contrast, many of the girls had short hair, really short hair. Beatles short hair. My own orange frizz had been tamed into a neat bun at the base of my skull. I looked like a dowdy middle-aged librarian.

I walked past all the city kids with their brash exuberance, imagining pointed stares and laughter behind my back. I was wearing unfashionable, square glasses and my father had made me promise to wear stockings on my first day so that I would make a good impression on my lecturers. The day was blisteringly hot and I could feel the nylon sticking to my legs. Part of me wanted to run back to the little room at the Young Ladies Boarding House, my home away from home during school term, and hide under the terribly uncomfortable bed.

With my hair springing up and out from my forehead like loose wire in the stifling humidity, I knew I looked like the odd person out and even though I just wanted to cry, I kept walking, staring down at my ridiculously formal shoes, the ones I had been so excited to buy. Everyone else was wearing worn sandshoes or sandals. Some kids were sitting on steps, reading books in the sunshine. Others were smoking cigarettes.

My top lip and forehead were beading with sweat, turning my face powder into a paste. Dad had warned me about wearing make-up to uni. 'It might give people the wrong idea about you,' he'd said as I'd rolled my eyes. I really didn't think a little powder over my spots and a dab of pink lipstick would be noticed; looking around I saw plenty of girls wearing make-up.

I was fast learning that what was considered fashionable in my small neck of the woods was not so acceptable in Brisbane on a university campus. This Dorothy was not in Kansas anymore!

'You look lost,' said a voice at my shoulder, startling me.

I turned to see two boys and a girl who looked unlike anyone I had ever met or spoken to in Bandaroo Flats. They were like characters from a book. The young man closest to me, who I soon discovered belonged to the voice, wore glasses with old-fashioned, round steel rims, just like John Lennon. He was tall, well over six feet, had dark shaggy hair, a square jaw, and pale, smooth skin with a light fuzz of stubble on his chin and a bemused look on his face. He wore army pants and a tight white t-shirt. The other boy was sloppy but handsome-looking, almost pretty. He was shorter, blond, and was chewing gum and wearing flared jeans with peace symbols drawn on them with cracked paint. The girl was in a figure-hugging, short, white crocheted dress and had leather sandals on her feet; her rust-coloured hair was loose, catching the sun like flames. I'd spent years fending off cruel comments about being a redhead and this was the first time I had ever seen a girl who managed to make her ginger hair look glamorous and cool. She was looking straight past me and over my shoulder at the other students pushing and shoving along the covered walkway. I was intrigued. She seemed ethereal, like a thistle about to be blown away on the breeze. The girl looked back to me with a broad smile.

'I'm Agnes. Hi there.'

Her voice had the soft lilt of a Scottish accent. It was so pleasantly familiar, like my parents' voices. I'd been born in Edinburgh but arrived in Australia as a baby so had escaped a Scottish drawl.

'Hi … um … yes … I am actually,' I said with a little laugh of embarrassment. 'Lost.'

'You a fresher?' the taller man asked.

I scrambled to decipher the word. I presumed it was short for *freshman*, something I'd come across in my reading, although I was pretty sure it was more of an American term. *Fresher* must have been the local campus slang.

'Yes. Day one. All ready to fill my brain with tertiary knowledge.' I said it as a joke but realised that it hadn't come across as that; instead I'd sounded like some green goody-two-shoes. They all stared at me.

'I mean ... yes ... I need to find my way to the Law faculty.' I tried to redeem myself and gave a self-conscious cough and tried to burrow behind the fake-leather satchel that I was pressing into my chest.

'You? You're doing Law? Like an actual Bachelor of Laws?' the tall young man said and did nothing to disguise his surprise.

The looks of disbelief the boys gave me were the same sorts of looks I got back home when I told people I wanted to be a lawyer. I didn't have any interest in doing a degree that just ended up as sentimental decoration for the wall of my sewing room. And much to my father's consternation, I didn't want to marry a lawyer. I wanted to be one.

'That's so cool.' Agnes smiled dreamily at me. 'I'm an Arts student. Theatre major.'

'Yes, I'm doing Law,' I announced, trying to sound confident and controlled.

'Well, we're fourth-year Law students,' the shorter handsome man said. 'Except Agnes, of course. The actress. Second year.'

He grinned at her. I cringed.

'I'm hoping to become a barrister someday,' I told the trio.

The tall one whistled and arched an eyebrow, high and mischievous, looking me up and down, taking in my matronly outfit. 'Really, honey? I just can't see you as a barrister or even any kind of lawyer. No offence but ...'

I couldn't help myself. 'That's funny,' I said caustically. 'Because I can't see you as one either.'

I glared at him as Agnes took my elbow and led me away, frowning back at the men.

'Ha ha. That was perfect.' Agnes whistled and laughed as we crossed a grassy lawn, bordered by low shrubs. 'What's your name?'

'Fiona,' I told her. 'I've just moved here from the Darling Downs.'

'Well, Fiona from the Darling Downs.' She laughed again. 'You just served it up to the leader of the Student Alliance. The top final-year Law student who has done the degree in record time and is already being head-hunted by big firms in Sydney. He's like the king of the campus.'

'Oh dear.' I felt embarrassed and remorseful in equal measure.

'No, no!' she whispered, holding my arm tighter. 'Barton McLeod needs to be knocked down a peg or two and coming from *you* ... golly, it's priceless.'

It was a back-handed compliment but I took it anyway. As we crossed the quadrangle toward the austere sandstone building another hairy man thrust a pamphlet into my hand. 'Make love not war.' He grinned. He was part of the gaggle of people with placards and leaflets.

'Come on,' Agnes said, dragging me along.

'Who are they?' I asked.

'Just our friendly resident activists. Anti-Vietnam. Pro-feminism. Socialists. Communists. Stuff like that. You'll find out more about all that later.'

I stared, wide-eyed and open-mouthed. Socialists? *Communists?* My father had warned me about them. 'Keep away from that mob, Fi,' he had said as I kissed him goodbye outside the boarding house. 'Those red devils are out to destroy the very fabric of Australian society. Bloody commies. Hippies.'

Communists. Hippies. Beatniks. University had it all and I was beginning to tingle with the thrill of being among it. Agnes pointed me to a wide staircase inside the large sandstone building.

'Upstairs, in there and right. There will be a sign outside the lecture hall. I'm on the other side of the quad. Good luck. I'll meet you afterwards, under that tree over there, if you like. Say twelve o'clock. For lunch? Two redheads, hey? We'll make a formidable duo.'

'That would be great.' I nodded. I liked the sound of 'formidable duo'.

She waved goodbye and disappeared into the crush. As I trudged up the stairs with a sea of strangers, I made a mental note that I would pack away the plaid skirt and the patent shoes first thing that afternoon. The stockings would go in the bin. I decided right there that I would leave the red dust of Bandaroo Flats behind and become Fi, the uni girl. I was going to reinvent myself. It seemed, in some funny weird little way, like I'd joined the human race for the very first time after living in a dirt-blustered wilderness. I was a part of something big and exciting and it sent a shiver of thrill through my blood. The smell of promise filled the huge halls and the excitement and enthusiasm was palpable. Part of me felt like I was dreaming because I'd wanted this for so long and it had always felt so impossible and so far away.

I didn't have much money. Dad had fumbled a wad of cash into my hand as he'd hugged me tight, saying goodbye in a voice that told me he was trying hard not to cry. I would buy myself some new clothes. Maybe some blue jeans. And sandals.

JEANNE

BEAUVAIS, FRANCE, 1472

The streets and alleys leading to the market were a cobble-pot of shops. I passed smiths, weavers, butchers, bakers, a cloth merchant and someone selling cosmetics. The Beauvais marketplace was a festival of colour, scents and noise. A riot of wares were displayed from many stalls. Salted meats, lampreys and herrings. Woad, wine and sacks of wool. Almost anything you could imagine was there for the buying. I smiled at a furrier and let my hand float over his selection of furs. I could only dream of trimming my garments with such finery. It was only the very well-to-do who were allowed such extravagance.

The marketplace was also a place of great swindles and buyers had to be wary of unscrupulous sellers. Some bakers added stones to their loaves to make them up to the legal weight and more than once I'd been tricked into purchasing damp peppers or a sack of oats that had fresh ones at the top but was filled to the bottom with rotten ones.

I looked at all these people pushing and haggling and felt sad because not one of them knew that it was very possible that a hostile army was marching our way. I was seeking Colin and it did not take me long to find him. He was standing behind a tower of chicken cages.

'Colin,' I called as I approached, although he didn't hear me over the cackle and squawk of chicken gossip.

When he saw me, his face brightened. Colin Pilon was not wearing his coat and the wide sleeves of his white shirt were rolled up above his suntanned forearms. His fair hair was damp with sweat.

'Jeanne.' He grinned and shouted over the din, 'The hens are selling well today.'

My face must have displayed my inner fear, for his smile fell flat.

'What is it, Jeanne?' he said. 'What's the matter? You look as pale as a sheet.'

I looked around furtively. I would risk a flogging if my bad news got out into the streets. Pushing up close enough to Colin so that I could smell the scent of his perspiration, which reminded me of overripe apples, I took his hands in mine.

'Charles the Bold has sacked Roye, leaving many casualties,' I said quietly. 'There is talk that he and his men may be marching for Beauvais.'

Colin raised his eyebrows and let out a whistle.

'That is not good to hear,' he said grimly. 'All our men are away fighting with the King. How on earth did you come by this news, Jeanne?'

'I was in the forest this morning and ...' I tried to

ignore his look of concern, 'and I came across an injured soldier from Roye ...'

'I don't like you walking alone in the woods, Jeanne,' he scolded. 'You tempt fate. What with your mother—'

My frown and pursed lips told him that I wanted no more talk of my mother.

'Well, it's just as well I did go into the forest because had this man died in the woods, we might not have news that Charles the Bold is headed our way with his army.'

'Yes. That is some troubling news, Jeanne,' he whispered, his eyes widening. 'So Roye is sacked.'

'Not only sacked,' I told him. 'But sacked after surrender.'

'There's the slight chance they might just bypass us on their way to Paris,' Colin said, before he was interrupted by a person asking for a cage-full of the big reds.

'Hush,' I cautioned, but there was little danger that the swarthy man holding his coins out could have heard our talk over the squabbling hens.

We stood together without speaking, letting the sounds of the marketplace wash over us, both lost in thought. Colin lived with his sickly mother in one of the outer suburbs of Beauvais, nestled down by the river, well outside the city walls. There was no protection if the soldiers were marching our way; the outer districts would need to evacuate their homes and shelter within the city gates.

'Captain Balagny is thinking of leaving the town,' I said.

'It might save some bloodshed but this is a proud city with strong allegiance to the King. If we send for reinforcements, perhaps ...'

'But they could be here within the week, Colin.' The idea of violent Burgundians raiding my beloved city made me feel ill.

'And Colin, I was ordered to speak of this to no one so you cannot tell a soul, not even your mother,' I added. 'I do not want to end up in the pillory again.'

My thoughts cast back to my recent public scolding, punished for wearing my mother's red velvet cloak. It was the cloak she'd worn when she'd run away to marry my father, her bridal dress hidden beneath it. Some weeks ago, I'd worn it into the woods and had forgotten to take it off upon my return to the city. I'd spent half a day with my head and hands locked in place while townsfolk jeered and told me that I was lucky the Captain hadn't flogged me. Someone threw vegetable peelings at me and the general consensus was that I was a wanton girl for daring to wear a cloak above my station. Me! Pauper Jeanne, the daughter of Matthew the Coward!

'Well, leaking this information about the Burgundians might get you more than the pillory, my darling girl. And it was foolish of you to wear that coat. I hope you've put it away, along with all thoughts of wearing it in public again.'

'I wear it at home sometimes,' I said, trying not to cry. 'I imagine it still smells like my mother.'

Colin held my hand and moved a strand of my dark hair, tucking it back into my bonnet.

I wanted to hold him and sob into his broad, warm chest.

'Your mother surely watches over you, Jeanne, and is pleased at the young woman you have turned out to be. I hope she thinks of me kindly as well.'

'I'm sure she would love you, Colin, as much as ...' I stifled the rest of my thought and coughed into my hand as Colin turned away.

'Take a chicken,' he said, picking up a sack. 'For your supper tonight.'

I blushed. I did not want Colin's charity but I had nothing on me to offer to him in exchange. Only two small hatchets. Neither of which I could spare.

'Cook up a feast for your father,' he smiled and after looking around to make sure no one was looking at us, he leaned forward and planted a small kiss on my forehead at the edge of my bonnet. 'Tell him it's from me.'

'Thank you, Colin.'

I watched as he put a large hen in a sack and tied it with string, frowning as he did so. He looked at me, his pale grey eyes flecked with concern.

'I am worried about this news of Charles the Bold,' he said. 'Perhaps you should take my horse and cart and ride south, away from danger. Your safety is my first priority.'

'I'm not leaving my father or Beauvais,' I argued. 'Or you.'

Colin sighed, looking skyward. 'We need to be prepared. Balagny will not tell us anything more. Not us and not the town. By the time he announces anything it will be too late for us to make plans.' He fell silent. I could almost see the jumble of thoughts in his thoughtful eyes.

'With all the fighting men gone we stand no chance against such a huge army,' I whispered. 'But perhaps the wounded soldier may have been delusional. Maybe we are not on Charles the Bold's path to Paris.'

'I won't have you stay here in danger,' Colin stated firmly.

I looked into his face and saw the desperation. He loved me, I was sure of that. But I would not leave my father. He was frail and had no one else in the world to care for him.

'I'm not leaving Beauvais,' I said. 'If Beauvais falls I will fall with her. I refuse to step outside the walls of my home city to—'

'That's amusing coming from a girl who wanders by herself in the forest and I don't think ...' He began to speak, to argue against me but then he thought better of it and let the words fall away. I had a strong will and would not be dissuaded. Colin often told me it was a good thing, as opposed to most others who thought a strong-willed woman was worse than a stubborn donkey. But there was no way I would let him send me alone to safety down south. I did not want to leave my father but most of all I could not bear the thought of Colin being in danger, because his safety was *my* first priority.

'If we surrender then perhaps Charles the Bold will be happy to leave his Burgundian flags on the city walls and accept our allegiance and move on without harming us.'

I shook my head at him and scuffed my boots on the stones. The chicken burbled from the sack at my side.

'We have all heard told how cruel the Bold is,' I said softly, feeling a rise of bitter apprehension in my belly. 'If he comes here he will leave a mess. Our loyalty to Louis will be punished and he will fill our streets with terror.'

'Don't speak such things,' Colin said breathlessly. 'I want you in my life forever, Jeanne. You mean everything to me. The thought of something happening to you ...'

He leaned forward and kissed me deeply, gripping my wrist. I pulled away and looked nervously about, feeling myself blush. No one was looking, all too busy haggling for the best bargain. He said the word 'forever' and my face warmed and my stomach rolled over. I meant to marry Colin and that day could not come soon enough. Although he'd not said the words yet, I knew he was of a similar mind. I wondered if he would ask me or even make the suggestion right in those tense moments. I loved him and wanted us to raise chickens and children and grow to become stooped old people together. But his face glowered with the fear of what might be marching toward us. I let my romantic notions flutter away.

'If we are to be raided I will bring my mother up to stay with my sister in the merchant quarter, if her toff of a husband will allow it.'

Colin was a simple farmer, with a small leasehold of land and a crowded clutch of chickens. He was a peasant through and through but his sister had married up and rarely spoke to her family anymore. I had seen her at church some weeks prior but she had looked the other way when I waved at her. It saddened me as we had once been on very good terms. Colin and I had been inseparable friends since we could walk. I knew that his sister's disdain of her past hurt Colin deeply.

'Our city is well fortified,' he went on, almost as if he

was talking to himself. 'If we draw up the bridge and close and strengthen all the gates then they would have a hard time getting in.'

Colin pointed toward the distant high city walls and parapets.

'Yes, but we have no weaponry, Colin,' I said, shaking my head as I put the sack of chicken over my shoulder.

'All the townsfolk will join arms and use what we can. I will fight beside them.'

'But so many menfolk are away,' I worried out loud. 'We are a town of women, children and lame old men.'

'Thanks so much!' Colin laughed. 'And well-muscled, handsome poultry farmers. Don't forget them!'

I gave him a brazen wink. 'Never.'

'It will be all right, Jeanne,' he said sombrely. 'Thank you for trusting me with this information.'

'I trust no one more than you, Colin.' I smiled.

'I love you, Jeanne. We must be careful. If we discover that the Burgundian army *is* coming this way, perhaps we will find a way to stay safe. I will protect you to my last breath because you are my everything.'

'And you mine,' I smiled shyly.

Colin pulled me by the elbows between two towers of chicken cages and kissed me again. All the blood rushed to my head and I felt giddy.

I kept chanting the word 'love' under my breath, grinning like a sun-dazed lizard as I walked home. We were warming up, Colin and I, and the furnace in my chest was stoked and ablaze.

Our narrow house sat wedged next door to the tanner, whose carcasses and hides sent their gruesome stenches all the way down the street. I stepped over a muddy puddle and wiped my boots on the doormat before going inside. I had decided to keep the chicken alive. She was worth more to us in eggs than a meal of meat, although the thought of a roasted chicken made my mouth water.

'Papa,' I announced, still stomping my threadbare boots.

I took in a sharp breath of surprise. Lieutenant Jean Lagoy was sitting in the chair across from my father.

'What the devil?' I stammered, putting the sack containing the struggling chicken on the floor.

The man stood up and nodded to me, dragging a hand through his dark hair.

'Ah, Jeanne, there you are,' he said, crossing the room and taking my hands in his mauling paws for the second time that day. 'I've just been telling your father how very brave you were today, bringing the soldier and his message to us.'

I looked at my father, sure that he would be very angry to learn that I had been wandering alone in the woods, but he did not look up to meet my gaze.

'Tell your daughter the good news, Matthew.'

'News?' I asked. 'Have the Burgundians passed us by? Are we safe?'

Lagoy laughed and the sound grated on my nerves. Deep, loud and haughty. 'No Jeanne,' he said. 'I have received permission from Captain Balagny and it is all arranged. Isn't it, Matthew?'

'Arranged? What's arranged?' I asked.

My father looked up at me, chewing on his bottom lip nervously. 'Jeanne, *ma chérie*,' he said, unable to stand on his weakened legs. 'Lieutenant Lagoy has received official permission. It's all settled. You are to be married.' My father looked away from my gaze.

'To you?' I said in horror, looking at the Lieutenant as he grinned broadly.

'Yes, Jeanne,' he smiled. 'You are to be my wife.'

In that instant, the threat of the approaching bloodthirsty army of Charles the Bold lost its terror. I was facing a much greater threat. I wrenched my hands away from his and planted them on my hips.

'I think not!' I gasped. 'I have no desire to be your wife.'

'The Lieutenant will take you away from the slums,' my father said wearily. 'It's a very good marriage, Jeanne. Besides, it's not up to you. And sadly, it's not up to me either. The Captain has agreed to the Lieutenant's request. It is out of my hands, our hands.'

'No! I won't. Never!'

'Now, now! We're not going to get off on the wrong foot, are we, Jeanne?' Lagoy said patronisingly, raising a dark eyebrow. 'I will be good to you and we will learn to care for one another.'

I looked at my father, silently begging him to make this all go away, but he looked completely broken.

'I'm so sorry, Jeanne,' he said, a tear rolling down over his deeply grooved cheek.

'But Colin?' I said, the tears pricking in the corner of my eyes. 'Papa. What about Colin?'

'Colin Pilon?' Lagoy gave another boom of laughter. 'The chicken boy? Come now, Jeanne, you're a fine specimen of womanhood and deserve better than that peasant. He is just a boy. I am offering you a life away from all … this.'

He waved a hand, indicating the small, mildewy room. My heart sank. I was powerless. The Captain of Beauvais decided who married whom and most women in my position would be well pleased to be betrothed to a lieutenant, a man who might one day be captain. But I wanted my peasant boy. I wanted Colin. I looked to my father and then to Lagoy with his flashy brass-buttoned jacket. I wiped my eyes with my sleeve as the chicken in the sack began to cackle.

'Your mother would have approved, Jeanne,' my father said, noting the wriggling hessian bag by the door. 'And you are nearly seventeen after all. You won't get a better offer. For your mother, *ma chérie*.'

'That is not true and you know it, Papa,' I cried. 'She believed in love. You told me. You told me.'

I could not remember my mother's face but I carried her in my heart and I knew she would want me to be happy. But Lagoy was leering at me as if I was some small cake he would certainly devour. I knew that I might never know happiness again.

'Please, Papa,' I begged. 'Tell him "no". I will go into a convent. Anything. But you cannot make me marry this man.'

'It is not your father's decision but mine,' Lagoy said smugly. 'I meant it, Jeanne, when I said that I could have you in a finger snap. I am the Captain's man. He did consider that my choice was unusual because of your lowly station, but your mother's well-born blood means that you have potential.'

'Potential? For what?'

'For making me a happy man with a house full of healthy children.'

I wanted to be sick. My stomach was knotting and heaving. My father was rocking in his chair. He was distraught but, like me, was caught in a bind. Our poverty shackled us to powers greater than we could withstand. Despite this, my father had always encouraged me to be bold. 'Your mother had a fire in her heart and her belly and sometimes her tongue,' he often laughed, and told me that he wouldn't have had her any other way. 'Speak your mind and never let anyone force you to be someone you are not.' He had always been protective of me, after losing my mother so young, so tragically, so violently. As his health declined, he began to cling to me and had come to rely on me heavily. Now he was asking me to let this man force me to become someone I was not. I would not become Madame Lagoy.

'Please, Jeanne,' he whispered, with a frightened look in his milky eyes. 'It is best for you.'

'Because the alternative,' Lieutenant Lagoy smiled, licking his lips like a snake, 'is that your father will be thrown into the Paupers' Prison and tried for treason.'

There it was. My father had been threatened. I looked back to him and softened my face and heart. He knew that to refuse, to resist, would mean more than prison for him.

Although he had long been called The Coward, I knew that it was not cowardice driving his acceptance of the proposal. He was concerned only for me and what might happen to me if he refused Lagoy. The man was going to marry me whether Papa agreed or not.

Lagoy held my life in his hands like a fragile duckling in the jaws of a fox. I stood no chance and had no choice. For my father, who had done so much for me, I had to accept my fate. But as I stood there, the handles of my hatchets digging into the flesh of my thighs, I hoped that the Burgundians *were* en route to Beauvais and I hoped that it might mean a change, for good or bad, of the destiny that lay ahead for me.

BETSY

COUNTY DOWN, IRELAND, 1797

'You'd better be sure your da doesn't find out that you're running around with the rebels.' My cousin Mary fussed at me as she put her baby back in his crib. 'See what happened to your sister, Brigit. Your da hasn't spoken to her for ages, has he?'

'Nearly a whole year. He won't even tolerate her name being used in the house,' I replied.

'I don't know how much of that is the fact that Jimmy Ballantine is a Catholic and how much it is his rebeldom.'

'Rebeldom.' I smiled. 'That's a grand word.'

'It's serious business, Betsy!' Mary grumbled. 'I don't even like talking about it in the privacy of my own house. You're playing with fire. The redcoats flogged a boy to death the other day, right out in front of a church! Sixteen, he was. He had a bundle of *Northern Star* newspapers in his kit and they flogged him till he was a puddle of jelly.'

I pulled a face and tried to get *that* image out of my head.

'Besides, cousin,' she frowned, wiping her hands on her skirt, 'it's not ladylike to be hanging with these lads.'

'What's wrong with my brother?' I said crossly. 'Or William Boal? They are right gentlemen. And we're revolutionaries, not rebels.' I picked at the edge of my soda farl and stirred my tea, looking out the doorway to the woodpile where a cat coiled itself sinuously.

'You're not still sweet on that Boal fellow, are you?' Mary raised her eyebrows.

'Not just sweet on him, Mary! I kissed him today and he kissed me right back.'

'On the lips?' she gasped.

'No, on the sole of his foot, you foolish girl. Yes, of course on the lips.'

Mary stared at me, put her hands on her hips and blew a wisp of carrot-red hair out of her eyes. 'Well then.'

'Well then,' I mocked back. 'George was mortified!' I laughed. 'You should have seen his face. And Will blushed. He actually blushed!'

'So does he mean to make an honest woman out of you?' Mary said as if she were a woman twenty years older than me instead of my old playmate and childhood confidante.

'Are you suggesting that I am dishonest?' I pouted.

'Well, you have a wild streak, Betsy Gray. You are too pretty for your own good and your father would disown you if he knew you were running about with the rebels and—'

'Revolutionaries,' I reminded her.

'... kissing boys in public houses.'

'Ah, but that bit was fun! Remember when you kissed Michael Dyer behind the milking shed?'

'Stop it, Betsy. They hung William Orr today. This is not a game. We'd do best to put our heads down and let these fired-up men fight their own battles,' she said, her tone as dry as kindling. 'I think you are attracted to the drama of it. The excitement. You're altogether too flighty!'

'No, Mary,' I said very seriously. 'I am not some ignorant, illiterate lass who follows the boys because they want to clash with the establishment. I am a passionate, intelligent Irishwoman. And I support the cause that would see us freed from the Saxon yoke of England. I would see a Republic of Ireland.'

'Heavens be! Listen to you!' Mary scoffed. 'Next you'll be wanting to run the parliament yourself.'

I pulled out my hair ribbon and shook my hair and grinned at my stiff and proper cousin.

'Now that is something grand to aspire to. I think I'd make a fair running of it, to be sure.'

'I really don't know what they taught you at that fancy school down in Dublin, Betsy, but it's certainly given you airs,' Mary said. 'Connor says that education is dangerous for women.'

'But Connor is a lump head.'

'Betsy!' she snapped. 'Don't disrespect my husband in his own house.'

'I'm simply saying,' I sighed, 'that you don't have to agree with him in your heart. In your heart you're still a Gray. In your blood. And despite my father's protestations, he is a real Irishman right into his bones. We all must be because ...'

I heard the clatter of wheels on the gravel outside and stopped speaking, cocking my head, afraid that the dreaded Connor was arriving home.

'Ah, I have a surprise for you,' she said, jumping to her feet and all but running to the doorway, clapping her hands.

Moments later, my sister, Brigit, walked through the door. Her belly had grown large with child since I had seen her last. I burst into tears of joy.

'Oh my sweet golly goodness,' I muttered, fanning my face. 'This *is* a nice surprise. You must be getting close now, Brig. It looks like the wee babe has dropped a little.'

'Yes, love. Any week now.' She laughed.

'And you brought the cart all the way down from Antrim to see me? You treasure.' I hadn't seen my sister for some months, maybe three. How fast these babies grew!

'How's Da?' she asked, waddling across to me and hugging me as best she could around her enormous waist.

'Grumping as usual.' I smiled back at her, sniffing my tears. 'Did you hear that George took the Oath and Will is set to do the same tonight?'

'I hear them talking up in Antrim,' my sister said, settling herself onto a chair. 'Obviously Da knows nothing of this? About his son taking the Oath? Jesus, Mary and Joseph, he'd have a seizure. The dreaded Oath!'

'I don't even like you saying those words in my house.' Cousin Mary tutted. 'A man was hanged this very day for the crime of taking the Oath. Please tell me you haven't done the same, Betsy!'

'No, I have not.' I shrugged. 'George will not allow it.'

'Well, he hasn't lost all sense then.'

'Mary,' I sighed with exasperation. 'You listen to everything your husband tells you and think it to be so. George hasn't lost his senses. He's found them. And while I might not have officially taken the United Irishmen's Oath out loud, I have in my heart. The redcoats are bullies and butchers and servants of a greater evil.'

'It's you who's been listening to everything your brother tells you and believing it!'

'Come, come, girls. Get me a cup of tea and stop your arguing,' Brigit said, banging her palms on the table.

Mary went through to the kitchen and put another pot of tea on the stove.

'She's just so frustrating!' I hissed at Brigit. 'She's even beginning to talk with an English accent. Can you hear it?'

'Stop it, Betsy!' Brigit snapped. 'I've come a long way to see you and I want it to be a lovely visit. How's my old mare, Molly?'

'She's old and a little lame in her back leg but I won't let Da sell her to the butchers.' I smiled. 'I'm very fond of her. I talk to her in the paddock and slip her spotted apples. I'll say hello from you. She always knows when I've seen you. She can smell you on me.'

The baby was stirring in the crib in the corner.

'What did Mary call the little boy again? I've forgotten,' my sister asked.

'George!' I told her. 'She says it's in honour of our brother but I think she probably named him after mad King George of England. She's become such a lover of the

Crown. You know her Connor has joined the Monaghan Militia. They are traitors joining with the redcoats.'

'Hush now,' Brigit said. 'You be careful what you tell Mary. Her husband could take us all down. I don't like him all that much.'

I went to the little baby and picked him up awkwardly. His swaddling was coming loose and I handed him to Brigit after she held her arms out imploringly.

'Just think,' I said, looking down at the little face with the rosebud lips. 'You'll soon have one of these for yourself. Are you excited?'

'Oh, yes.' Brigit smiled, tracing her finger around the baby's face. 'I can't wait. Jimmy's built a beautiful crib.'

'I'm sure Da will soften his heart to you soon, Brig,' I said. 'It's a shame Ma isn't here to welcome a grandchild. She'd be like a mother hen. She'd never let you have the baby. Remember how she was with little ones? She used to smell them and say they were like fresh-baked cakes.'

'I remember! The neighbours' children were always about. The family house is quiet without her, I bet.'

'Yes, Da is quite solemn and serious and George and I are always out and about getting up to mischief.'

'Well, you take heed you keep your heads low,' Brigit said, rocking the small baby on her lap. 'Mary is a good girl but that husband is trouble. Just keep your mouth on a short rein around her, you hear?'

'But she would never betray us,' I whispered. 'Never. She's kin. She understands the cause. She's just too afraid to admit it. Her Connor is a bully. I don't suppose she really likes him all that much either.'

'Hush now,' Brigit said, trying not to laugh. 'But he is a rotten egg. Poor Mary. You must be more kind though, Betsy. Mary is just like Da. They are afraid of the English and would rather not stick their heads up to make trouble. You can't blame them. It's a survival thing.'

'But Mary loves us. Although, I do think she is happy to leave the dangerous rebel business to us.' I smiled and reached out to touch my sister's hand. 'And Da too. I think he's secretly a little in awe of people like you and Jimmy who hold so firm to your Irishness in the face of the English.'

'I doubt that very much,' she said sadly, shaking her head. 'He's more interested in keeping his estate and money. He'd see the Irish all become English so long as he stayed a gentleman.'

'Don't be so sure. He loves you still, for all your Irishness,' I said, although I don't know if I believed it. 'Just give him time. When he becomes a granddaddy, he'll go soft.'

Mary came back into the room with a tray of tea and more soda farls with butter. We spoke of other things, dragging the conversation out of the prickle thicket that was politics. I disliked pointless gossipy chatter and preferred speaking with George and Will about important issues of state. But I was well pleased to see my sister and made the effort to look interested in their conversations about babies and recipes. The only time I ever saw my sister was when Mary arranged these clandestine get-togethers behind her husband's back. That is why I worried little about my cousin betraying us – because she still helped us in spite of her husband's alliance with the English against his own people. Mary was only a year older than me but her life was so very different from mine. She had up and married early and wanted seven or eight children, one after the other. Her husband kept her shackled into domestic servitude and I had watched her go from a rosy, happy girl to a stiff, proper, frightened wife in the space of two years. I had no desire to rush into having babies. My father had status and modest wealth, which had allowed me an education and the choice to wait for a husband and babies. My uncle Robert, Mary's father, had gambled and drunk away his inheritance, leaving Mary with little choice other than marriage to Connor and all that came with it.

'So she's kissed Will Boal!' Mary announced as I finished my farl, making me laugh so hard that crumbs came out of my nose. 'On the lips. In public.'

'You never! Oh Betsy, he's so handsome. Do we hear wedding bells on the breeze?' my sister said, smiling broadly.

'Steady up, Brigit! He'll need to kiss me plenty more before I decide whether he's husband material!'

'You watch yourself lass or you'll get a reputation as a scrubber,' Mary said, pulling a face as she reached for her baby son.

'I don't care if I do.' I laughed.

'You talk nonsense.' Mary bristled. 'You've always been tempestuous. That's your Campbell blood. They say one of the great-great-aunts was burned as a witch near Glasgow. Kat Campbell. Scottish fire in the blood. I'm more cool-headed. More green shamrock.'

'More boring,' I teased.

We laughed some more and then Brigit stood up, saying she needed to visit the privy. Her face dropped as if her skin was made of molten wax and her eyes widened.

'Oh my,' she whispered. 'Betsy. Mary. I think my waters have broken.'

We looked down to see her standing in a puddle.

'Well, you're not getting back on that cart!' Mary announced. 'You can't travel after the water's gone. Quick, Betsy, we need to get her into my bed and I'll keep her comfortable while you ride for the midwife. Annie O'Neal is on Ballycreen Road, two stone houses past the dairy.'

My skin was prickling and my heart was hammering. I nodded mutely and ran as quickly as my boots would take me to Finn McCool, then I galloped him out of there as fast as his own strong legs would take him.

FIONA

BRISBANE, AUSTRALIA, 1968

The music blared in through my window. I liked The Doors as much as the next person and thought Jim Morrison was pretty cool, but after listening to it for hours, the album was starting to drive me completely mad. I was sitting on my single metal-framed bed, surrounded by textbooks, feeling more than just a little overwhelmed by my study workload. I couldn't concentrate on the terribly tedious notes about tort law because I found myself constantly singing along to 'Light My Fire'. My room was tiny and while it was tempting to pull down the heavy window, I was frightened I would suffocate or bake to death. The heat in Brisbane was stifling. The ceiling fan stirred the humid air like a spoon in tea. It groaned and sounded like it was too darn hot and uncomfortable to do a proper job.

Mrs Lotte, the stiff-lipped, grey beehived proprietor of the Young Ladies Boarding House in Kelvin Grove, ran a tight ship. There were very specific rules of conduct, all printed up on a piece of paper that was framed and glued to the back of my door and one of the rules was very clear about making noise: No music that could be heard outside of your own room and no noise after dark. I looked out the window and down to the backyard but still couldn't work out where the din was coming from.

I needed some quiet to study because this Law caper was pretty heavy going. Thick books about the nitty-gritty nuts and bolts of the law was mind-numbingly boring and took great wads of concentration to get through. And I loved music. While law was my main interest, music was my passion, but that sultry afternoon in Brisbane, the two of them did not go together well at all.

Wearing my tattered slippers, a pair of cotton pyjama shorts and an old but very comfortable t-shirt, I went out into the hallway: a long and dingy tunnel of orange carpet that had a pattern that reminded me of carroty vomit. I was determined to find the annoying source of the music. I couldn't believe that Mrs Lotte hadn't already shut it down. There were no other girls about because most went shopping or socialising on the weekends; there was a strict rule about never being allowed to have a second person in your room, so socialising at the boarding house was out of the question. There was a communal room on the ground floor where you could read or watch the small television or listen to the radio or play the piano, but few ever used it because the television reception made everything look like a snowstorm, the radio crackled and the piano was out of tune. And we weren't allowed to eat or drink in there.

I headed down the staircase, following the sound, which seemed to be coming from the back of the building near the kitchen. The dining room was empty. Four round tables were neatly set for dinner even though only a handful of us ever ate there. My board, paid for by Dad, covered my meals and I forced myself to eat the swill that was served up. Mrs Lotte was a terrible cook and very heavy-handed with cabbage. I walked through the room and into the large kitchen. The music was getting louder. At the back of the kitchen was an open door leading to another room. I stepped forward but felt suddenly very silly. What was I going to say? I very tentatively gave a gentle knock on the door. No response. I knocked louder.

'Hey there,' a male voice called out. 'What's happening?'

Mrs Lotte's was an all-female boarding house so I was taken aback and began contemplating a quick escape. I was stunned and paralysed with embarrassment when I was confronted by a young man who, for a moment, I was sure was Jim Morrison himself. A few seconds later I came back to earth and asked myself what exactly Jim Morrison would be doing in a boarding house in Brisbane playing his own record to himself all day. The fellow had no shirt on and my face was as hot as a stove-top ring!

'Hi ... um ...' I stammered. 'I wonder, if you could, I mean, I'm from upstairs. I think my room is directly above you and I'm studying ... and ...' I gave a self-conscious shrug and a half-smile.

'I'm so sorry, hey. I'm Luke.' He grinned, revealing perfect white teeth, as he flicked his long brown hair out of his face.

'I'm Fiona,' I mumbled back.

'You want me to turn the music down. I paint. Music helps. When I'm in the zone, you know? You want to see what I'm working on?' He stepped back and invited me into the room. I inhaled sharply. Mrs Lotte's rules came rushing into my brain. Never more than one boarder in a room. But I was confused because Luke could not have been a boarder because he was a boy.

'I can't ... It's against the rules. Sorry ... I ...'

'But I'm staff here,' he said. 'So I don't know if that counts. I'm the new cook.'

'Oh thank goodness,' I said, quickly, putting a hand to my mouth. 'I mean ...'

'Yeah, I know.' He rolled his eyes. 'I saw what she was cooking you girls and you will be pleased to know that from now on you will get *edible* food.'

I looked around, frightened that Mrs Lotte would walk in.

'Don't worry.' Luke laughed, reaching out to touch my forearm. 'She's gone to do the shopping. She won't be back until three.'

'Oh good.' I exhaled, relaxing a little. 'In that case, can I just say I'm really pleased someone else will be cooking from now on. To be honest, she's a bit of a dragon.'

'She's my aunt,' he said flatly.

'Oh my goodness,' I said hurriedly. 'I'm so sorry. I didn't mean ...'

'Nah.' He smiled. 'You're right. A real fire-breathing dragon sometimes. I get where you're coming from. She terrifies me.'

I couldn't believe I'd just said something so offensive about my landlady to her own nephew. I wanted to burrow into my slippers like a snail. I was also acutely aware that I was in my pyjamas and he was shirtless and only wearing a pair of low-slung jeans. He was deeply tanned and between the two of us there was a lot of skin.

'Just pop your head in and look at my paintings.' He winked. 'I'll make a deal. You look at my artwork and I'll turn the music off.'

'Okay, deal,' I answered, sounding amazingly flippant and nonchalant for someone who wanted to hot-foot it out of there like a spooked rabbit. I poked my head around the door jamb and looked into a room that looked like it had been ransacked. There was stuff everywhere. By the window that looked out over the sparse backyard was a canvas on an easel. The painting was really amazing. Without thinking, I stepped closer and put an appraising hand up to my chin.

'Hmmm,' I said, as if I were a veteran art critic. 'You're very talented. What is it exactly?'

'I call it "Acid", you know, like the drug.'

I looked at him as if he were speaking another language, showing my naiveté in all its glory.

'You know, Acid. LSD?'

I nodded unconvincingly.

'You're not a city girl, are you? I can tell.'

I gave a high-pitched giggle and pushed my glasses higher up my nose. 'No,' I said with a sigh. 'You're quite right. I come from a land of tattered shacks and bullock carts on the Darling Downs.'

Luke chuckled. 'I don't know what you just said but you make it sound primitive.'

'Primitive pretty much sums it up. Bandaroo Flats. Blink and you'll miss it. The only drug out there is a real downer and it's called boredom.'

'Well ... hey, I don't take drugs myself,' he said, suddenly quite serious. 'I don't need to. I live my whole life on a natural high. But I'm intrigued by the whole idea of the psychedelic: the music, the art. It's like a world of intense colour and sounds.'

I wasn't sure what he was talking about but I liked the painting. It was a swirling vortex of geometric shapes and colours. I snapped my attention away from the painting and realised again that I was standing in my pyjama shorts in a boy's room and if Mrs Lotte turned up I'd be in deep trouble. The music was still blaring from the record player in the corner of the room and it was kind of a sexy beat. I was blushing and folding down into myself, trying to pull my t-shirt down over my legs.

'You go to the uni?' he asked.

'Yep. Doing a Law degree.'

'So you've got brains too. Cool.'

'Well, just the one.'

He looked at me, confused.

'You know. Just the one brain. Like, you know. Regular. People.' I was blabbering and sounding like a foolish girl all tongue-tied around a boy.

'Well,' Luke said, going to his record player and taking the needle off, silencing the music. 'I think I've had enough of The Doors for one day. Sorry to have disturbed you, Fi.'

He called me Fi and it sounded so informal and friendly. I liked it.

'Thanks,' I said as I walked past him and back into the kitchen.

'Hey Fi?' he called after me. I turned around. 'I like your glasses. They're pretty cool. What's your favourite food?'

I gave a weird little snort and shook my head, trying to think of something tasty.

'Maybe meatloaf and potato chips.'

He gave a nod and returned to his painting.

Back in my room I found it hard to concentrate on the thick, wordy legal books even though the music had stopped. I managed to fill the silence with my own turbulent thoughts. I sure wasn't one of those boy-crazy girls like back at home, the ones who date every guy in town like they're auditioning husbands. I was focused and ambitious. Laura called me pig-headed sometimes. My mother had been a nurse back in Edinburgh until she'd met Dad. She had to quit her job at the hospital because married women weren't allowed to work. She'd been a great mum but I knew she was frustrated with the boredom of domestic life. She was a voracious reader and had written stories that she had shoved into a suitcase under her bed, never letting anyone read them. I didn't want that life for myself. 'The tide is changing,' she once told me as I'd sat on the edge of her bed while she plaited my hair. 'Being a wife and mother is wonderful. But you need to be something for yourself as well. You have the world opening up to you.

So reach for the sky.' Opportunities for girls *were* opening up as the sixties were inching toward the seventies and I wanted to push my foot through that opening door. Heck, I wanted to kick it down.

Despite my personal reassurances of my ambitions I still couldn't get the image of the shirtless Luke out of my mind. I turned the pages. I twirled the biro between my fingers like a cheerleader's baton and couldn't settle myself.

Too distracted to work, I decided to get dressed and go find a bus into the city to buy a new outfit. I looked into the mirror and tried to tidy my unruly hair. And maybe a haircut.

JEANNE

BEAUVAIS, FRANCE, 1472

'Jeanne! Jeanne!'

I turned to see who was calling me and saw my cousin Aimee standing by her horse with a group of women I barely recognised.

'You look terrible,' she gasped and beckoned me over.

I was in no mood for conversation but wiped the dust from my swollen, bloodshot eyes, sighed and walked over to her.

'Where are you going?' she asked.

'For a walk,' I answered. 'To take the air. This city feels like an unwanted embrace sometimes. Crushing me.'

'Well, don't go far.' She gave me a penetrating look. 'Is your father all right?'

'Yes,' I said quickly. 'As well as he can be with legs that pain him like fire pokers in his bones. He's fine. I'm ... well, I'm just needing some air.'

I didn't want to share yesterday's frightful news with

her because I knew she wouldn't understand. To girls our age, Lagoy was a fine catch. Aimee gave me a concerned nod of her head as I walked off, out the gates, through the shadows that were cast by the towers and walls, over the wooden moat-bridge. I held my breath to avoid the stench of the thick, brown, curdling sludge beneath.

The roads in summer were always dusty. Packhorses and carts trundled noisily along, overtaken by groups of travellers and the occasional messenger. But as soon as I turned off into the forest I was enveloped by the quiet and gentle murmur of the woodlands. I saw three grey squirrels in a huddle but they darted into the undergrowth as I came closer. A bird with a hooked beak sat on a branch and regarded me curiously.

'We could elope,' I called to it. 'Yes. That's what we could do.'

I kicked at a stone hopelessly. If I eloped with Colin they would track us down and kill us both, and I loved him too much to risk that. And my father would meet the same fate. I was already risking severe punishment by going into the forest, unchaperoned, again. I didn't care. I felt numb. Hiding away in the forest for even a brief time to refresh my spirit was all I could think to do that morning. A fleeting escape but better than none at all. I wanted to talk to my mother and here I felt her presence. The words 'follow your heart' flitted on the breeze but I shook them away. My father and Colin were both in my heart. But my predicament saw me having to choose between them. To run away with Colin meant certain death to my father, but to marry Lagoy would break Colin's heart.

Earlier that morning, Lieutenant Jean Lagoy had led a group of men along the road to Paris to recruit reinforcements to our garrison. He would be gone for days. I wished I could crawl up inside the wide, rotting log by my boot and hide away from the world – from Lagoy and Colin and my father. Papa should have told Lagoy that I suffered some terrible affliction like falling sickness or that I had a violent temper. But he must have been in complete shock when Lagoy arrived with his demands and threats. The previous night, Papa had spent the better part of the evening sobbing, begging me to forgive him. 'I am sick and not long for this world,' he had moaned. 'I would have refused in a heartbeat and let the rogue run his sword through my heart but I could not risk a similar fate for you, Jeanne. I let your mother fall into hands that took her life and I would not see it happen again. A miserable marriage is still better than death. He will be away fighting so much ... I'm sorry.'

I knew my father wore all the responsibility for my mother's murder. While at first it looked like he had betrayed me and thrown me to the lion, Lagoy, I understood that he was accepting the arrangement to save my life.

'But ...' he had whispered as the night shadows grew long, 'it might not work ... but Jeanne, what if I gave you the silver that the Lieutenant has promised me, you and Colin could take it and ride far away, start a new life where Lagoy will never find you?'

'But he would kill you!' I gasped.

'And I'd die happy knowing that you would have a life of happiness ahead of you. Yes! That's what you shall do!'

'No, Papa.' I had shaken my head, not only aghast at his suggestion but at my own response, which was to entertain his idea as a glorious possibility. 'No. I will not let them kill you. With the silver gone, you'd be executed for stealing from the Captain's purse.'

'At least it would be quick.' My father had smiled sadly. 'Not like this never-ending eternity of pain slowly killing me.'

'Not another word,' I'd said and put him to bed. All night, through the tears, I had imagined a new life far away, perhaps even in England.

I walked along, deeper into the forest, humming one of my mother's old songs, lost in my thoughts. Beneath my grey, hessian cape I had my two small hatchets hidden on my belt and they reassuringly banged against my thighs as I walked.

In the small sunny glade I found my basket, left there from the day before. It was damp from the overnight dew. A small field-mouse sat inside, nibbling at the remnants of the bread.

'Hello there.' I smiled. 'Oh, that you were a horse instead of a mouse. You could carry me away to some faraway place and I could …'

I stiffened. At the sound of my voice saying the word 'horse' I heard a clop like a heartbeat thudding up through the earth into my feet. Quickly, one hand on the sturdy handle of my hatchet, I fell into the shadows and held my breath. Surely the Burgundians were not so close. It was the sound of one horse not a stampede of them. The mouse darted up and out of the basket and away into the underbrush. I was well concealed, pressed against the branch of a cool tree.

'Jeanne! Jeanne? Where are you?'

At first I was terrified it was Lagoy but I quickly realised it was Colin and exhaled, stepping out into the clearing and called back.

'Here, here by the oak! Here. Colin.'

'Jeanne, you will marry that pompous fool over my dead body! I just came from your father,' Colin shouted as he rode into the open, sunlit circle of dirt.

'Don't wish it too hard, Colin,' I called up to him as he brought my cousin's horse to a halt beside me. 'That pompous fool would quite happily dispatch you with his sword. He called you the chicken boy.'

'He what?' Colin said, sliding from the saddle to stand before me. 'How dare he!'

'This is just the way it is and always has been,' I whispered, not able to look him in the eye as he took my hands. 'My father has nothing. You know that. After my mother's death he never really recovered. If I do not marry Lagoy I will be punished, perhaps put to death. I'd sooner go to my grave than marry him but I wouldn't want my father to have to weather that loss.'

'What price did Lagoy offer for you?' Colin asked angrily.

'Please don't say it like that.' I grimaced. 'The Captain gave Lagoy permission. It is done. Lagoy is giving my father a small amount of silver as a form of compensation, I suppose. Given that he would not get any sort of dowry from my father, it is generous because he is marrying beneath him.'

'He doesn't deserve you,' Colin said, looking down at me. 'It's Lagoy who is marrying up.'

'I will never love him,' I said. 'You will always have my heart, Colin. I promise you that.'

'I want more than your heart, Jeanne. I want all of you. Every hair on your head. Every kiss.'

He lifted my chin and kissed my lips softly. I shut my eyes and wished I could jump into that kiss like a bird flying up into the sky.

'We'll run away. Now. Just go,' he said, pulling back. 'Your father told me he would sooner see you loved by me and I know he has offered us the silver, when he gets it, to escape and make a new life.'

His eyes were panicked and he was flushed.

'We wouldn't get far and my father would be killed,' I said sadly. 'I love you, Colin, but I cannot let that happen.'

'If the Burgundians arrive we might all be killed.' Colin shrugged and touched a finger to my lips where the kiss still lingered. 'I can't bear to think of Lagoy's lips on yours,' he said and I could see a tear in his eye.

'Then I shan't ever kiss him.' The very thought of Jean Lagoy's lips made my skin crawl.

We led the horse to the shade and sat on the old wooden log that pressed out into the open glade like a bridge to nowhere.

'This is where my mother hid me,' I said. 'In this very log.'

I ran my hand over the rotting, mossy wood. Colin put his hand on mine.

'I come here to feel her. It gives me strength.'

The heavy sadness hung between us like an invisible fog. But at least the sun was shining. I moved away and lay in the middle of the open space, face up, on the grass and let the sun warm my skin, feeling the grass tickle my cheeks.

'I can't bear it,' Colin said, coming over to me, choking back what sounded like a sob. He lay down beside me and I let him take my hand in his. 'Truly, Jeanne. I can't bear it. We must leave and be together. Please. I cannot live if you are married to that man. I would sooner kill him and pay for it with my life.'

'Stop! Stop!' I said, cupping my hands over my ears. 'I am having a hard enough time of it without you making wild threats. Don't do that to me!'

'I'm sorry, I'm sorry,' he said softly and he laid his head upon my breast. 'I can hear your heart beating.'

'I'm not married to Lagoy *yet*,' I said softly, turning over on one elbow to look down at Colin.

'What do you mean?' Colin opened one eye.

I gave him a smile and he smiled back.

We may have been only days off war or a miserable marriage or both but on that sunny morning in my special place, there was only Colin and me. And we let the sun shine down on us and bless our sacred bond. One that no gold band or sword could ever sever.

Colin would always be my first and only love.

BETSY

COUNTY DOWN, IRELAND, 1797

I was turning into Ballycreen Road when I saw them. Three redcoats sitting on stumps by the side of the road. I slowed as I passed them, waving to show that I bore them no ill will. They looked at me and whistled, and one of them yelled something crude. Another punched his shoulder and they roared with laughter. I was nervous but I had no reason to think that they saw me as anything other than a pretty girl on her lovely white horse, out for a ride. It was impossible to tell a rebel Irishwoman from a loyalist one by the look of her. Rebels came as Catholics or Presbyterians, and were high born, low born, farmers or academics. That was the very point of us. We wanted unity for everyone, not the divisive violent unrest offered to us by the English who meant to put a wedge between every person different from the next. I kept my head high and my eyes on the road, looking ahead for the stone houses and the dairy so that I might find the midwife.

Annie O'Neal's cottage was down a long, winding path, past a drowsy mob of sheep. I found her around the back of her house in the herb greenhouse, picking snails from her garden.

'What can I do for you?' she asked, good-naturedly, her round sky-blue eyes lighting up her face, which was red from the sun. She was young, perhaps my age, but she had a matronly, serious air about her.

'It's my sister,' I said, panting with exhaustion. I stayed sitting on Finn McCool, who stamped his feet on the hard earth and shook his head. 'She's up visiting our cousin, Mary Kelly. You delivered her young 'un George some months back, I believe. My sister's waters have broken and we have her abed, ready to deliver.'

The small woman wiped her dirty hands on her skirts.

'What number?'

I cocked my head at her question.

'What number babe? First. Fifth?'

'Oh, first. Her first.'

'Right then,' she said, all business. 'I'll wash up and you can take me with you. Can someone bring me back afterwards? My husband's away with the cart and I have no way to get word ...'

'Of course.'

Annie O'Neal rode pressed up behind me, gripping her arms tightly about my waist. I felt sorry for poor Finn McCool who was carrying the extra weight, but he felt no slower for it and Annie was just a slip of a woman. We neared the three soldiers and my heart thudded as they stepped out onto the road and put their hands up. I recognised the fair-headed man as the soldier who had tried to force me to dance with him at the Old Inn.

'Whoa. Whoa there,' the rounder man cried. 'Steady up. Where are you two going in such a hurry?'

'My sister's having a baby.' I almost cried with nervous frustration at having been stopped. 'Now! And I've fetched the midwife.' I tossed my hair back toward Annie. I felt her grip tighten.

'That's right,' she said.

'Your names and places of residence?' the tallest, meanest-looking soldier demanded, his thin moustache a slash across his face.

'Elizabeth Gray from Gransha, daughter of Hans Gray,' I said, adding my father's name because he was well known to have no time or thrift for the rebel cause and was a well-regarded and landed gentleman.

'Annie O'Neal. I live on Ballycreen Road,' she said with barely a whisper.

'You live there alone?' came another voice.

'No, with my husband.'

'And his name?'

'Jack O'Neal.'

'The publican from Bangor Inn?'

'Aye. What of it?'

'Well, Mrs O'Neal, where might your husband have gone with his empty cart this morning?'

'I don't know,' the woman stammered.

I was getting impatient at their pointless questioning. Time was slipping away and I was thinking of Brigit, knowing she would be afraid, far from home and it being her first babe and all. 'My sister is having a baby. Can we please pass and be on our way?' I begged.

'Well, you see now, we've been waiting for Mr O'Neal's return,' the tall soldier said. 'Got word he's running pikes and muskets down from Antrim.'

'That's poppycock!' Annie O'Neal snapped. I had to smile at her choice of word. It was right cocky to use such a term at the yeoman. She was a brave and bold lass.

'We'll have you dismount, thank you, Mrs O'Neal.'

'She's the midwife.' I almost yelled at them. 'We need her to attend a birth. Please. Can't this wait?'

'No, lassie.' The redcoat with a missing button over his bulging belly grinned at me. 'You're free to go. There's not much to it. Having a pup. Just tell her to push and you catch it. Simple.'

I took a deep breath, shocked at his brazen and dismissive attitude. I did not like the way he looked at me.

'I'll try to make it to Mary's when I'm done,' Annie O'Neal said unconvincingly as she slipped down the side of my horse and landed with a thud on the ground. 'First one can take a while. Just make sure the cord's not wrapped around the wee bairn's neck.'

'How do I do that?' I asked, my voice wetting with tears.

The soldiers had lost interest in me and were circling Annie O'Neal like cats around a mouse.

'You see, if Mr Jack O'Neal, your husband,' the fair-haired one said, looking her up and down, 'is running arms to the rebels as we've been informed, then you, Mrs O'Neal, are an accomplice and there are very harsh penalties for supporting insurgents. We'll escort you back to your cottage and wait with you until your old fella returns.'

The leery fat one laughed, spitting something horrid onto the dirt.

I wanted to pick Annie up and ride off fast, taking her away from their questions and dark looks. But I'd identified myself and could not endanger my family. I did not look back but spurred Finn McCool into a fast trot away from them, tears falling fast over my cheeks, pooling in my ears.

'Give our regards to your father, Miss Gray,' a voice called from behind me. 'We need more good loyalists like him!'

I arrived at Mary's to find Brigit sitting up in bed with a tiny pink babe at her breast.

'I've called her Isabella after our dear mother.' She beamed and I covered my mouth in shock.

'I missed my calling!' Mary said from the doorway, her face flushed and slick with sweat. 'I did more work than Brigit here. Isabella is a right impatient one. Where's Annie?'

'Helping the yeomanry with their investigations,' I said as I rushed to my sister's bedside, covering her and her baby in kisses. 'They wouldn't let her come along with me. She may arrive yet but all the work is done, now.'

'She was in such a hurry,' my sister said, fanning her flushed face. 'Like a runaway mare.'

'You were just desperate to meet your aunty, weren't you, darling girl?' I cooed down at the pink face peering out from the blankets. 'Oh, she is grand, Brigit. Beautiful. Our mother would be proud.'

That night, before my father went down to have his dinner with the rector, I pulled him aside and told him the good news.

'Another rebel baby to cause a fuss,' he said gruffly. 'I suppose she'll be baptising it as a Catholic?'

'What does it matter? God is God,' I said with exasperation.

'Watch your words, Betsy Gray,' he said clipped me under the chin playfully. 'It's how you worship and how you behave when you're out of church that matters. I can abide the Catholics up to about here.' He smiled, pointing to a crease of wrinkled flesh on his turkey neck. 'But for rebels, I have no time. They thirst for blood instead of order and peace. If Brigit's Jimmy is still messed up with them, I have no time for any of them. Babe included.'

'She called the wee thing Isabella after Mammy.' I spoke gently and saw him baulk and take a sharp breath, but he would not meet my eyes.

'Who does she look like?'

'More like Mammy than you, thank heavens.' I laughed.

He took his coat from the peg and turned to me.

'We'll see,' he said. 'I may stop in at Mary's in the morning on my way home. Just to see the babe. It's too soon to have been christened so the poor thing is not yet a Catholic.'

As soon as we heard Da's cart rattle out down the gravel path to the open road, George and I went to work. My father would drink Reverend John McQuilton under his dinner table so he always spent the night in the Reverend's guest room. First Monday of every month. My father ran his life like a hallway clock. You could read the stars by him. And so every first Monday of the month the local chapter of the United Irishmen met at our farmhouse at Gransha. I was especially excited that night because *the* Henry Joy McCracken and his sister Mary Ann were coming along from Belfast. Henry had only just been released from prison down in Dublin, where he'd been held for his subversive views about the English occupation. Mary Ann, who was almost a decade older than me, was my heroine of all heroines. More than Miriam in the Bible, more than Deidre of the Ulster Cycle. Mary Ann McCracken was everything I wanted to be. I had heard much of her strong will and brave fight for those less fortunate than herself. She worked tirelessly in all the poor houses.

I put fresh-cut flowers on the fancy dining table that we almost never used, placed neatly ironed throws on the sofas, tidied the wood-pile and stoked up the fire. While I was in the kitchen ladling punch from the big vat into pitchers, George came into the room, whistling. He poured himself a mug of punch and looked at me.

'So you *do* fancy Will, it seems,' he said. 'Are you planning to settle with him or are you idling with him for play?'

'Did he ask you to ask me that?' I smiled.

'I won't say.' He winked back. 'But I love you both and I don't want one of you to break the other's heart. So I'm measuring your intentions.'

'Oh, George.' I laughed. 'You are so sweet. I like Will a lot. I think I always have but I'm in no rush to walk down the aisle. Brigit's babe is mighty fine but I'm not clucking for any of my own just yet.'

Outside I heard the crunch and creak of wheels on the rocky path leading from the back gate past the kitchen. I frowned and felt a quiver of apprehension.

'Is that Da back?' I gasped. 'We'll be flogged if he catches us out.'

'No,' George said, putting his mug on the window ledge. 'That'll be Jack O'Neal, the publican. He's brought down a load of pikes and muskets from Belfast. I told him to come early and we'll bury them out the back of the stables before the meeting.'

I looked at George with dismay and dropped the ladle with a clatter to the stone flagging and put my hands over my face. My heart began to race. 'Oh heavens, no!' The words gushed out of me. 'George! In all the kerfuffle and fuss with the new baby, I right forgot! Oh no, no.'

'What is it? Betsy? What is it?'

The door from the mudroom opened and I held my breath, half expecting the redcoats. But it was Jack O'Neal, a heavily bearded, stocky man. Beside him was Will Boal.

'Have you come direct from your farm, Mr O'Neal?' I asked Jack in a panic.

'No, lass,' he said. 'I've come down from Belfast and stopped for tea at the Boals' and picked up Will here. Why do you ask?'

I took another big breath and looked at the menfolk.

'The redcoats, three of them, were on Ballycreen Road,

questioning your wife.'

'When?' George yelled, roughly grabbing me by the shoulders. 'And why are we hearing about this only now, Betsy?'

'This afternoon,' I stammered. 'I was taking her to deliver Brigit's babe but they stopped us and ... they were going to search your cottage and ask her some questions.'

'And you raised no alarm, Betsy?' George shouted at me again. I could see the disbelief and fear and anger in his face.

'Oh sweet Lord Jesus, no!' Jack cried out, starting back out the door.

'You can't take the cart, Jack,' George said in a panic. 'It's full of contraband! Will, quickly go around and get two good horses and take Jack to his cottage. Betsy and I will unload the cart and bury it all out back. You get to your wife, Jack, and make sure you have no pamphlets or any evidence of your involvement with the rebels. Is there anything at your house to condemn you? Anything they might have found? Jack?'

Jack O'Neal was shaking and seemed unable to speak for a moment as he frantically shook his head. 'I don't think so. No. I must go to Annie!' He started to follow Will out the mudroom door when George held out a hand to stop him.

'No, wait!' George said firmly. 'Let's think this through. It might be a bad idea for you to go. They have you on a list if they are searching your property. But we need to get there fast and send folk who won't be suspected of being rebels. We need to rethink this.'

'I'll go,' I said softly. 'This is all my fault.'

'No, Betsy,' George said, shaking his head. 'I can't let you ride at night into a potential briar-patch of yeoman.'

'George,' I said, still feeling the sting of his well-deserved anger, 'it makes more sense for me to go and pretend that my sister needs the midwife. I'll say there's some problem with the baby. They saw me earlier in the day and let me go. And I am also the fastest on a horse. You know that.'

George sighed, deep in thought. The room was strung with invisible piano wires, tight and taut.

Will Boal looked back into the room. 'I've brought the two stallions, black and white,' he said, breathlessly, leaning around the door jamb.

That would be Fergus, my late mother's horse, and Finn McCool. He had chosen well. They were the fastest.

'You're right, Betsy,' George finally said, with a sigh of surrender. 'Your story is solid and Will is well thought of by the establishment. I don't like it one bit but I think you are the best choice for the job.'

'So you and me, Betsy?' Will nodded. 'I just need to finish saddling the horses and we'll be away. We'll bring your Annie back safe and sound, all right, Jack?'

Jack swooned and I helped him into a seat. I felt awful. It was my fault. What sort of rebel supporter was I that I left a woman in trouble and raised no alarm? I had been overwhelmed by thoughts of my new little baby niece.

'How could you forget something as important as this, Betsy?' George growled under his breath. 'Jack could have bumbled up to his cottage with a cartload of contraband

and they would have slaughtered him on the spot! This is no game, lass. It's life and death. I'm not wanting to chastise you but you have to understand the gravity of our mission.'

'Don't be too hard on her,' Will said to George. 'Everyone gets forgetful and makes mistakes sometimes. You, me, all of us.'

'I'm sorry, Mr O'Neal, I truly am,' I said, gently touching the man's forearm, angry with myself. 'I will make things better. I will get Annie for you. Come on, Will, let's ride like the wind.'

'*Dia idir sinn agus an tolk*,' Will murmured and patted Jack on the back.

'Be careful, Betsy!' George called after us as we made our way out into the moonlit night. 'William Boal, you take care of my sister. Any trouble and you take it on *yourself* and let her ride away. She is my first concern.'

As we fiddled in the dark with the straps and belts of the saddles, Will breathed deeply and I could tell he was nervous.

'Are you up for this, Betsy?' he asked. 'I can't believe George is letting you go and do this thing.'

'I'm not a child, Will,' I said defiantly. 'He does not tell me what I can and can't do. I want to make this right. I let the O'Neals down. I have to fix it. George knows I am capable and not some fluffy ornament.' I was pleased that my brother was offering me the chance to redeem myself.

'I don't know another lass like you, Betsy Gray,' he said. 'Sometimes you scare me a little bit.'

'Good.' I grinned into the darkness. 'Let's keep it that way.'

I put a boot in the stirrup and hoisted myself into the saddle, looking back at him with a toss of my hair.

'More to the point, Will, are you up for this?' I asked, spurring my horse on, leaving Will open-mouthed as I called over my shoulder. 'See if you can keep up.'

When we arrived at the O'Neal cottage it was shrouded in darkness. We lit two torches, searching the cottage and yard thoroughly.

Annie O'Neal was not there.

FIONA

BRISBANE, AUSTRALIA, 1968

When our timetables allowed it, Agnes and I met up for lunch beneath the big Moreton Bay fig. This magnificent tree sat in the middle of the grassy area near the space that was called 'The Forum', and underneath it our friendship was becoming more solid over the weeks as we opened up to each other.

'That must have been so hard for you,' Agnes said, putting her hand on my knee.

I could feel the heaviness tug at my jaw, sagging with a grief that regularly crept up on me when I least expected it.

'Yeah, it really was … is,' I whispered, sniffing to hold off the tears.

'My mum drives me out of my mind sometimes but I can't imagine life without her,' Agnes said wistfully. 'She's a stern sort of Scottish woman. No nonsense. But I know she's a softy deep inside.'

And then I did begin to cry, soft panting sobs that I tried to contain, unsuccessfully. Agnes shuffled around next to me and put her arm around my shoulders.

'It's good to have a cry,' she said softly. 'I don't know how you and your family coped.'

'The whole town rallied around us when she died in the car accident,' I told her. 'Everyone was so nice, baking for us, helping out on the farm. All except that bastard.'

Agnes squeezed me tight.

'Walter Leary,' I said, wiping my eyes, feeling the stab in my chest as I said his name. 'I don't know why he bothers me so much. He's the town bully. Fronted up to my brother, Murray, you know, at school the day after the funeral and made some crack about how cheap our mum's casket was. The Learys are filthy rich. And Murray decked him and because the Learys basically own the town, it was Murray who got suspended and after that he never went back to school.' I started crying again and blubbered out a soggy apology for raving about my misery.

'It's been years now but that still gets me.' I sniffed. 'That someone could be so hateful. Sometimes I wish Murray had hit him harder. Is that wrong?'

'No, Fi,' Agnes said, rocking me slowly. 'That's understandable. Hell, I don't even know him and I want to punch him.'

'He's a rich lout but at least my brother beats him in the local pie-eating competitions, hey?' I laughed, wiping the tears away. 'And I miss Mum but, you know, I still feel her. Like she's a part of me. Like she's inside me.'

'So how is your brother about it all now? Clearly he and the Leary boy aren't friends.'

'God, no!' I said. 'They haven't spoken since the incident at school. And that's hard in a small town, but I heard Walter's been drafted and is probably in Vietnam right now. My brother's never been the same since, you know, since Mum went? It kind of extinguished his light while it kind of fired up mine. Murray wanted to be a doctor, but after the accident the loss of Mum broke his heart and he gave up on his dreams. Dad's been so much more protective of me since then. I think that's why he didn't want me going to uni. Moving away. He's terrified of something happening to me.'

I watched the kids congregating on the lawns around the Forum. The activists were gathering over by the walkway to start their meetings and I could see Barton in the middle of the group, gesticulating with his hands, being the centre of attention, which he seemed to like enormously.

'I think he's kind of cute,' Agnes said, as we sat watching Barton and his fan club.

Talk of Mum had made me lose my appetite, so I picked at the cucumber and mayo sandwich that I'd taken from the dining room table back at the boarding house.

Barton tested his megaphone and all the students, who were lazing around in the sun, shielded their eyes and glanced casually his way while they ate and smoked and talked among themselves.

'Hmmm,' I said, nibbling on a small slice of cucumber. 'He's a bit intense. All this talk about Vietnam. It's a bit much sometimes.'

'These guys are making a good point, though,' Agnes said. 'If you were a boy, would you like someone to pull your birth date out of a barrel and tell you that you have to go to some random dangerous place to kill people and possibly get killed yourself? Not me! No way!'

'But there's such a thing as patriotism,' I lobbed back. 'You know. If your country asks you to do something.'

'Kill people? What sort of country asks that of its young men?'

'Um … pretty much all of them, I reckon.' I shrugged. 'I don't really know. America does it. Australia's the US's little brother, isn't it?'

'And we mindlessly do what they tell us? It's not even our war.'

I laughed at Agnes as she pulled the little angry frowning face that she did when I disagreed with her. Her slight Scottish accent always became more pronounced when she got enthusiastic about something.

'Crikey. You sound just like them,' I told her with a smile. 'Why don't you go and grab a megaphone and get up there like those peace-loving hippies and tell everyone to make love not war.'

'Hmmm,' Agnes said, looking toward Barton again. 'I still think he's sexy.'

'What's his friend's name?' I asked. 'The blond with the ridiculous dress sense. He looks interesting. And he's always giving you the eye.'

'Yeah.' She nodded. 'He's clearly got good taste. He's new this year, I think. Transferred up from Sydney or Melbourne. He's kind of like a pilot fish to Barton's shark, hey?'

We both laughed at the analogy.

'I thought you knew them well.'

'No.' She laughed explosively, her green eyes popping at me. 'Gosh no! That day I was just walking to campus and they offered me a ride. No! I'd never spoken to them before and I haven't since. I was pretty chuffed that the big man on campus, Barton McLeod, had given me a lift in his VW.'

'Oh,' I said, nodding. 'The blond – you don't even know his name?'

'Nup,' she said. 'Why don't you go and ask him? I dare you. I'll give you a dollar note if you do it.'

'They're final-year Law students. I couldn't. I'm just a fresher. They hate us.' I smiled but I was watching the blond guy sitting on the grass beneath a gum tree, reading a textbook. There was no one else sitting with him.

'Two dollars.' Agnes laughed. 'What have you got to lose?'

'What are you suggesting?' I giggled back. 'That I just walk up and say, "Hey, what's your name?" Why would I do that? I did kind of meet him on my first day, I suppose. But I don't want him to think I'm interested in him because I am totally not!'

'Just ask him a law question,' Agnes said, winking at me as she slopped her juice over her blouse. 'Go and tell him you're looking for a tutor. And you only get the two dollars if you get his name.'

'I might just make it up.' I laughed back. 'How would you know?'

'Oh, I'd find out.' She smirked. 'Let's guess. I think he looks like a Jeff. If either of us gets it right, the other shouts us both to the pictures. I want to see *Bonnie and Clyde* with that hunky Warren Beatty.'

'Fine! It's a deal, dare accepted,' I said, standing up, brushing the twigs and dirt from my new jeans. 'I'll guess that his name is ... Brian. And I'm holding you to the two-dollar bet.'

I closed in like a lioness on a gazelle and stood above him, looking relaxed but feeling nervous.

'Hey there,' I said.

He looked up at me, bored and faintly disappointed.

'Yes?' he said in an impatient voice. 'What do you want?'

'I met you on day one of term,' I said, my confidence fizzing out of me.

'Did you? I don't remember.'

The rude fellow turned back to his book, ignoring me for a moment. He gave a sigh of exasperation and looked back up at me, slamming his book shut.

'And? What?'

I shuffled awkwardly in the dirt with my sandals. Everything about the way this guy behaved pointed toward him being a real jerk.

'I'm doing first-year Law,' I said. 'And I wondered if you knew how I could go about getting a tutor. Is there somewhere you can put your name down or should I ask at—'

'Do I look like an information desk?' he said, glaring at me.

'Um, no.' I squirmed.

'What's this about an information desk?' said a deep voice and Barton McLeod appeared.

I felt a bit intimidated by Barton. I'd watched him speak and he was an amazing orator. Everyone loved him and thought he was awesome. Lots of kids and even lecturers reckoned he'd be the prime minister of Australia one day. He was like the campus rockstar. I looked back to the walkway, which had become something of a protest stage during lunchtime, to see that another young man with impressive mutton chop sideburns had taken the megaphone and was shouting about Aboriginal land rights. People were always so angry at university. They had this message of peace and love but when they talked and delivered their sermons they sounded like they wanted to do the exact opposite.

'I was just asking about some tutoring in Law ...' I said, everything coming out in staccato.

'I know you!' Barton said, almost triumphantly. 'You're that fiery fresher from the first day of term. You still don't look like a lawyer but I like the jeans. They're groovy. Nice to see you've joined the twentieth century.'

'You do sound like a lawyer when you're up there pontificating,' I said. 'But you still don't look much like one. I think it's the hair.'

As soon as I said it I wanted to put my sandalled foot into my mouth. I felt myself blushing with embarrassment.

'Nah.' He laughed dismissively. 'The days of clean-cut lawyers are over. You still reckon you're going to be a barrister?'

'That's the plan,' I said. 'Anyway, don't worry about the tutoring. I'll ask one of my lecturers. I was just ... you know ... wondering.'

Barton put a hand up on the trunk of the tree above my head and leaned toward me. It almost felt as if he was flirting with me.

'I could tutor you but I just don't have the time, what with all my extra-curricular commitments. But frankly, and I'm being honest here, to take that next step to become a barrister means you've got to have total dedication and how are you going to do that once you're married and have kids?'

'Who says I want to get married and have kids?' I said, glaring at him.

'Sounds like you should join the feminist brigade,' the blond guy said so derisively that it made my toes curl.

'You seem pretty into change and activism,' I said, my anger growing. 'Is there something wrong with feminists? I've heard you rallying about nuclear disarmament and racism and all manner of isms. Surely feminism is just as deserving. Don't you like feminists? Why not?'

'Apart from the short hair and hairy legs? They're okay.' He laughed. 'I wouldn't date one though. Not my bag.'

'Shut up, mate.' Barton clipped the blond guy's head with his hand. 'He's just messing with you. How are you adjusting to university life?'

'It's pretty cool, lots of work,' I said, twisting my head around his arm to see if the blond guy had his name on the front of his textbook because that was the whole point of me being there, not to get into a feminist debate with the campus king. I needed to find out the jerk's name and get out of there.

'My name's Fiona,' I said. It sounded a bit forward but I *was* fishing for the blond guy's name.

'I'm Barton. But it seems you already knew that.'

The blond remained silent and disinterested.

'And this is Jeff,' Barton added, ruffling his mate's fair hair.

I shot a look over to Agnes and pulled a scrunchy face. She smiled sweetly back.

'Anyway,' I said. 'Nice chatting and all but, yeah, see you around.'

'See you, Fiona the feminist.' Barton winked as he took off his spectacles and cleaned them on his t-shirt.

Completely self-conscious, I walked back to Agnes sensing Barton's eyes on my back. My face was warm and my pulse was racing. Barton made me feel flustered or angry. I wasn't sure which. He definitely had charisma. I really *could* imagine him as a prime minister one day, but presumably only after someone twisted his arm and gave him a haircut because Australia was certainly not ready for a prime minister who looked like John Lennon.

'Nice one, Agnes,' I teased her. 'So you already knew his name was Jeff. Very funny. There. I found out. You owe me two dollars but I am not shouting you to the pictures because—'

'Hey Fiona?' I turned to see Barton calling to me through his cupped hands. 'You and your friend should come along on Sunday night to the Foco Club. All the cool cats will be there.'

I gave him an off-hand wave, not sure exactly what that meant.

'Oh my God,' Agnes said, grabbing my arm and pulling me down beside her. 'The Foco Club is, like, where it's at!

Did Barton McLeod just invite us to the Foco Club? Us? You and me? It's just opened and it's the bomb.'

'Um, settle down.' I laughed. 'I'm pretty sure he didn't mean it as a date. Just a *hey everyone's going there and we should check it out*.'

'My mother has strictly forbidden me from going there,' Agnes said. 'It's totally notorious. But as my parents are away in Townsville this weekend, what she doesn't know won't hurt her. It's upstairs in the Trades Hall in the city. It's the happening place to be!'

'I don't know,' I said warily. 'I'm nearly out of this term's allowance and there'd be the tram fare and all that.'

'And I think you have to join to get in.'

'Join what?' I asked.

'I don't know,' she said. 'Maybe just the club itself or the Socialist group or something.'

'Socialist as in Communist?' I asked, opening my eyes wide and feel a tingle of apprehension, remembering all my father's warnings.

'I'll pay,' she answered. 'Instead of going to the pictures. This is way more exciting than *Bonnie and Clyde*. My shout for making you go and ask that Jeff what his name was. But it gave me a good laugh.'

I was wondering whether my new friend, Agnes McDonald, was going to be a bad influence. The guilt was pumping through my bloodstream but I was really quite excited by the idea. And torn. If I went along and if my father ever found out, he would drag me back to Bandaroo Flats in a flash and have me baking sponge cakes for the Country Women's Association until some shearer offered me a ring and a farm. The thrill of doing something forbidden was very tempting. I looked across at Barton who was now chatting to another group of young women, all of whom were gazing at him adoringly. I felt a tingle of something that I couldn't quite figure out.

'What the heck.' I laughed at Agnes. 'Let's do it. Let's be rebels!'

'Yeah.' Agnes hooted, clapping her hands. 'You only live once!'

With a sudden beat of sadness, I thought about how true that was. My mother hadn't even been granted a full life. It had been cut short. And in that time so many opportunities had been closed to her because she was a woman in the wrong era. I wanted to have the experiences that she had not had. I wanted to say 'yes' when I was offered new opportunities. I wanted to open up my future, not close it down.

Barton McLeod represented everything that my father was afraid of for me and everything I wanted for myself. 'Sunday night at the Foco Club, hey?'

'Right on, Fi!' We high-fived each other, then lay back on the grass and stared at the canopy of the fig tree overhead. I daydreamed about my long and precious conversations with my mum and I could almost hear her telling me to grab everything with both hands and to never be afraid to listen to my heart and to do what felt right.

JEANNE

BEAUVAIS, FRANCE, 1472

On Friday afternoon, I was in the kitchen making Papa and me some turnip soup for supper. In the two days since Colin and I had returned from the forest, I had kept my head down, staying at home, waiting for and dreading the return of Lagoy from France. I was grateful to my cousin Aimee for keeping our secret. We'd returned her horse to her and she'd looked at the two of us and given me a knowing wink. 'You're looking much chirpier after your spell in the forest,' she'd smirked. 'The air must have agreed with you, Jeanne.'

My father was not an old man but he was stooped and wizened before his time. Although he was so frail, he had been my strength. Since the visit from Lagoy he was much quieter and slept for even more of the day than usual; the turn of events with the Lieutenant had shocked him. I think the realisation that he could not protect me had taken the little self-esteem he had left and ground it to dust.

The sound of bells woke him. 'What is this? What is this?' he muttered, trying to sit up, his thin arms and gnarled fingers tangling in his summer blanket.

Suddenly shouts and cries came from the streets and laneways outside and I felt a leap of nerves. The huge bell in the town square was ringing.

'What's going on, Jeanne?' my father asked, confused. 'What's all this noise?'

'Papa,' I said patiently. 'Don't you remember? Charles the Bold of Burgundy is headed for Beauvais and I am thinking that this uproar is because his army has been sighted.'

'There is nothing here to stop them from taking over,' he said nervously, his aching fingers kneading themselves in agitation. 'Surely Balagny will surrender peacefully. It's the only thing to do.'

'I know he is of a mind to,' I said, remembering the Captain's first comments upon learning of the threat. 'But the people on the street are loyal to the King and they will want to defend their homes.'

'It would be foolhardy!' my father said. 'Completely foolhardy. It would be suicide for Beauvais!'

'Perhaps,' I said, wiping my hands on my outer skirts. I jumped, startled, as a heavy thudding came from the front door.

'Who could that be?' Papa grumbled.

I withdrew the bar, raised the latch and opened the door. Colin all but fell through it.

'Every able-bodied Beauvaisi must come to the town square immediately!' he panted. 'The carpenters on the top steeple of the Cathedral have caught sight of the Bold's convoy. They will be here by dusk.'

'That soon.' I sighed, feeling faint. 'It doesn't seem real. I never completely believed it would happen. Not here.'

'Take her away to safety, Colin,' my father said, trying to stand but falling back into his seat. His face was turning an awful shade of grey. 'Flee. Take Jeanne far from here and marry her and never return.'

'Papa,' I cried. 'We cannot. Lagoy would punish you with prison or worse.'

'My life is all but done, Jeanne,' the old man whimpered. 'I was a coward once and did not act to save you. Now, please. Go. Do not have a care for me. You have made my life so precious and wonderful. Colin is a good man. Please, Jeanne.' My father began to sob and choke.

'Don't get upset,' I said, going to him. 'Think of your heart. I will not leave Beauvais without you, Papa. I could not leave you to that fate alone. Anyway, with Beauvais about to surrender or be besieged, I hardly think we can sneak out of here unseen.'

'You stay here safe and sound, Monsieur Laisné, and I will take Jeanne to the square and protect her and get her safely back to you as soon as I can,' said Colin calmly.

'Be very careful,' my father said, looking helplessly at us both. 'If Lagoy sees you together, alone, he will be livid. He'll have your hide, Colin. Maybe even your head!'

'Lieutenant Lagoy is not yet back from his mission, Monsieur Laisné, so until he is, I will be looking out for Jeanne and he can thank me upon his return, because he has left her here in a most precarious position.'

'You stay here, Papa,' I said firmly. 'No matter what happens. I will knock three times and then two. Open the door to no other call. Keep the latch down until I return to tell you what our fate might be here in Beauvais. I should be back within the hour or, at worst, just after sundown. And we will know more then.'

'I can barely walk, *mon ami*, so I won't be going anywhere,' he said weakly. 'I can barely make it to the door.'

The bells were tolling loudly and Colin was impatient to leave. His nervous energy buzzed about him like a swarm of wasps. I readied myself to leave and threw on a light claret-coloured summer cape, pushing aside the bright red velvet cloak on the rack.

'Take the hatchets I made you, Jeanne. I insist,' my father added. 'I taught you to use them and I would have you do so now to protect yourself if need be. You inherited your mother's nerve, her will of steel. Two qualities that will protect you at a time like this.'

I didn't like to tell him that I kept them on my person most of the time outside of the house. They made me feel safe in a world that was often unsafe for young women.

'Be safe, Jeanne,' my father called. 'If you flee it will be with my blessing.'

Colin gave me a hopeful look but I growled at him under my breath.

'Not now, not ever.'

There were townspeople everywhere. It was a mad panic in the streets. Women and babies were crying. Men were running and over the top of all this noise came the long, resonating clang of the city bells.

'If Balagny chooses to surrender you must hide in your attic until the Bold's men have settled in and taken over,' Colin told me as we hurried through the throng that was pressing like a human sludge toward the town square of Beauvais. 'They go for the pretty maidens first! Spoils of war.'

'And if we choose to defend ourselves?' I asked, letting my hands fall to the hatchets hiding beneath my cape.

'I don't know,' he said.

Captain Balagny was standing on the raised platform beneath the bell tower. We were so far back in the swelling, sweat-soaked throng that we could not hear his words and had to be satisfied with the reports being passed back through the crowd from one person to the next, shoulder over shoulder.

'They will be here just before sundown,' one man turned and shouted back.

'There are tens of thousands of them,' cried another.

'Surrender? Balagny is calling for a surrender?' someone shouted angrily and the news was met with a roar of disapproval.

'No surrender!' became the chant and soon the gathered townspeople were speaking as one. '*Liberté! Liberté*! Beauvais! *Liberté*!'

It became a chorus so loud that the cobblestones beneath my feet trembled. I joined in the rallying cry.

'*Liberté*! *Liberté*! Beauvais! *Liberté*!'

I had tears in my eyes and was so moved by the passion of my people. We were fiercely loyal to King Louis XI, with many believing him to be the greatest monarch in all of history. Charles the Bold was a brute and a bully and not one of us wanted to bow our heads to him.

'Do you know what the King said?' Colin shouted at me over the din. 'When Charles the Bold first started campaigning against the French?'

I shook my head, barely able to hear him. He leaned in closer.

'He said that "The first place to resist him will be sufficient to undo him".'

I smiled. King Louis had visited Beauvais just once in my lifetime, riding through town on a fancy chariot as we waved and shouted joyously. I was a child then and I had thought him a god.

'Beauvais,' I whispered, nodding to Colin and together we continued to chant with the crowd. '*We* must resist him.'

'*Liberté*! *Liberté*! Beauvais! *Liberté*!'

If patriotism and community were weapons we would have had the power to squash the Burgundians like hooves on ants. But the truth was, *all* we had was spirit. We were short of soldiers and artillery. Beauvais had fire in her belly but little steel in her hands.

Colin moved his mother to his sister's home during the evacuation of all the outer suburbs into the city. At dusk, we stood together on the wide and high stone wall, looking out at the spectacle as the Burgundians set down their huge battalion across the open fields. The paddocks as far as the eye could see were filling with soldiers, horses, mules, carts and cannons. Big cannons. More arriving every minute.

'There are so many of them,' I said, overwhelmed by their numbers and impressive organisation.

We all watched keenly as an enemy messenger wearing a tall feathered hat was given safe passage into Beauvais via the small door at the side of the main gates. He cantered his well-dressed horse across the long bridge. We presumed that he was escorted by one of our men to take his message to the Captain. His message would be that Charles the Bold was seeking the loyalty and surrender of Beauvais to Burgundy. I was jittery with a mix of apprehension and excitement. Not only me, the whole city blistered with it. Captain Balagny had reluctantly listened to the people who were determined to defend the city. We all knew, after the messenger was let out of the gates with a scroll under his arm, what the message he was delivering back to the Bold would be:

Beauvais declines to surrender. Take her at your own peril.

I rested my hands on the stone wall and leaned my chin down on them as I watched the messenger disappear into the sea of armed men. Burgundy's flags were flapping from spears and poles and the noise of thousands of voices floated up to us on the cool night breeze. The enemy would be tired from their day's march and Colin explained to me that they would set up camp that evening and begin their onslaught of us the next morning at sunrise.

'I am afraid that they might come for us in the dark,' I said.

'No, Jeanne. That is not how war works,' he told me. 'There are rules of battle engagement. It is unchivalrous to attack your enemy at night. It would be considered cowardly and shameful.'

Colin came up behind me and cloaked my body with his, speaking into the back of my head.

'This may be our last hour together,' he said. 'I will be working the second shift tonight to gather anything and everything around the city that can be used as a potential weapon. We are lighting fires at dawn to boil cauldrons and collecting heavy stones, anything at all that can be thrown from the walls to repel them.'

'Those cannons,' I said, shaking my head, looking down at them. 'Boiling water and cabbage bombs are not going to stop a cannon ball.'

A child ran by, behind us along the wall, shouting. 'Lagoy has returned through the tunnels and has brought a small squad of archers.'

My spine stiffened and I stood up and backed into Colin's arms, feeling true dread, greater than that of looking upon an army of enemies. My bones felt like taut twigs and my blood went to water.

'I must go,' I said to Colin. 'He can't see us together. I will go home now to Papa and prepare him for what comes tomorrow.'

Colin stepped away, nodding.

'Get some sleep, Jeanne,' he smiled. 'We will all need strength come daylight.'

'People will die,' I said, whispering the words I hadn't wanted to utter those past few days.

'Yes,' Colin said. 'It is likely. But if we can defend our walls until Louis sends reinforcements we will stand a chance. We must stall them at all costs. If they get over the walls or through the gates tomorrow, we will pay a heavy price.'

We looked at one another for a few long ghostly moments before Colin spoke.

'Whatever happens, Jeanne,' he whispered. 'I will always love you.'

'And I, you,' I replied, then I turned and ran along the walkway toward the stairs before I began to sob.

I walked home through the bustle and business of a city preparing for war. Fires were being lit. Iron was being hastily smelted, hammers and anvils were beating. Carts were trailing through all of the streets and laneways while frightened people piled onto them any weaponry or heavy tools that could be used as such. Captain Balagny and his men were shouting orders, arranging civilian men into groups and instructing the archers about vantage points on the parapets.

I went home and slept, knowing that the first light would bring a day that might change my world forever.

BETSY

County Down, Ireland, 1798

I awoke on the first day of the new year to find that there had been heavy snow overnight and it lay blanketing the paddocks. The horses would need some dry hay from the storehouse. I would get George onto it, I mused, as I got myself ready for the party.

There were seven coming to lunch, not counting Da, George and myself. I wanted to make a good impression as Will's parents were coming. I'd met Mr and Mrs Boal at church and at the marketplace many, many times, but had not yet supped with them or had much social connection. Mary Ann McCracken was coming, and of that I was mightily pleased, although her brother Henry Joy was off on secret rebel business, not that anyone would be telling my father that. The Reverend and my father would get wise and wordy with whisky, oblivious to the fact that they were supping with a large number of people who had taken the Oath of the United Irishmen, including the Boals.

I felt equal parts guilty and smug at the thought of it. And praise be, my sister, Brigit, and cousin Mary would round out the gathering, but without their husbands, who were attending to business on opposite sides of the cause.

The new babe had softened my gruff da's heart. He was still no fonder of Brigit's Catholic husband, but he had begun to let Brigit back into our lives for the sake of his little granddaughter who was already smiling and laughing at us all.

By mid-morning I had drawn back some of the curtains, leaving others closed to protect the inner warmth of the rooms. George had piled the fireplace with turf and was busy working it into a blaze while the brass kettle sang from upon the hob. Our best crystal and pewter were neatly arranged, all polished and gleaming on the set table.

'You look mighty winsome,' Will said when his family arrived, and he kissed my hand like a right gentleman. 'And a spectacular New Year to you, Betsy, my sweet. May it be the happiest one ever.'

He was dressed in his finest suit and had oiled back his curls so they were less unruly. His face was clean-shaven and smooth. He stared deeply into my eyes and it felt like my innards turned over when he did. Will's parents looked like he'd stumbled across them by the side of the road and paid them half a shilling to masquerade as his kin – they were short, portly and fair in contrast to Will's swarthy complexion and lofty height. I was a tall girl but Will still towered over me. My da joked that our children, should that ever come to pass, would be giants, like the real Finn McCool, the first behemoth king of Ireland.

Over a delicious meal of roasted guinea fowl, Da and Reverend McQuilton entertained our guests with jokes aplenty and great gusts of laughter. I served up some barley pudding for dessert and then, because baby Isabella was wailing, I took her walking about the house, bouncing her in my arms as I told her stories about each and every room. I showed her where Mammy, her grandmammy, used to sew when I was a little girl. I hated the very idea of sewing. I thanked the good Lord my father had sent me to a proper school that taught boys and girls sensible things like mathematics, poetry and history, which is why I understood the very nature of colonialism and the need for emancipation from the English rule. America had banished the British and we could do the same. Poor cousin Mary had been schooled at home in domestic subjects like butter churning and needlepoint, which is why her wisdom didn't stretch much further from whatever blanket she was darning. Educating girls was the way of the future. People like the regal Mary Ann McCracken, who'd also attended a similar school in Belfast, were the promise of that future.

I rocked baby Isabella in my arms as she whimpered, and showed her where George slept, his walls covered in mountains of tattered books.

'No one in the whole world reads more books than your Uncle George,' I told her.

I showed her the family portraits in the long hallway and introduced her to each and every one of them, from the beautiful one of Mammy, her blonde hair in ringlets about her porcelain shoulders, to an ancient one where the paint was beginning to peel and flake like the scales of a fish.

'And this here is the oldest one.' I cooed at the baby and then looked into the dark, penetrating eyes of the red-headed woman in the painting. Her hair was fire-red and her face heart-shaped. 'Isabel Campbell. She was a wild one,' I whispered to the babe in my arms and smiled at her. 'Like us. She came to Ireland from Scotland and married a one-legged acrobat. Her sister, Katherine or Kat, was burned as a witch. Now there's a great-great-aunt I would have liked to get to know. All of these women share our blood.'

When I returned to the toasty warmth of the cosy dining room, only the women were still at the table, chatting and laughing. Mrs Boal's face was flushed and she looked like she'd imbibed a little too much punch. I was worried that I'd made it too strong.

'Have you scared the menfolk off with your liberal ideas, Mary Ann?' I smiled, passing Isabella back to my sister now that she seemed to have settled.

'Your father is right wary of me, I think.' She nodded. 'He's not too sold on my ideas that Catholic, Presbyterian and all other creeds should be accepted and be free in a united, equal and liberated Ireland. I told him that women should also run for office and take appointments. He nearly choked on his own tongue.'

'I bet he called you a rebel!'

'That he did!' She laughed. 'And I asked him what he thought was so bad about that, but you'll be pleased to know I stopped short of letting him know of my commitment to the cause and the small matter of having taken the Oath.'

'Shhh,' cousin Mary warned, looking concerned. 'My Connor is getting suspicious of you, Betsy. You and George and Will. I can't say what it is but he always looks bitter when I mention that you are visiting or I am coming here to Gransha. I know he still believes your father to be loyal to the King so I am able to soften his suspicions by reminding him of that.'

'Well, Connor should not be running around wearing a red coat!' I frowned. 'Do you know what they are capable of, Mary? Talk to poor Mr O'Neal who's not seen hide nor hair of his good wife since those three bastards picked her up outside her cottage down on Ballycreen.'

'Language, Betsy!' Mary scolded. 'Those military men have made a formal statement saying that they simply searched the cottage, found nothing and left her well and good.'

'So where is she?' I asked. 'It's been over two long months now, running into the new year.'

Mary looked sad and perhaps a little afraid. She clearly did not like talking about Annie O'Neal. My cousin seemed nervy and ill at ease and I frowned, feeling most apprehensive about the angry bruised eye she was sporting. I caught my sister, Brigit, looking at it as well.

'I pray for Annie O'Neal,' Mary said, and looked down at her hands folded in her lap.

We all fell into a pensive silence thinking about poor Annie O'Neal. My guilt over that sorry afternoon had made me sick and I slept badly every night thinking of it. I looked outside to see the men standing past the white-dusted hedgerow, looking at the damaged stable roof as they smoked their pipes in the white of the day. Their boots were sinking into the soft snow.

'What on earth do they think they are doing out there?' I laughed.

'Oh, men's business, I guess. Not for us womenfolk to know.' Mrs Boal giggled and helped herself to another mug of punch.

'Oh, Mary Ann, will you play us a jig on your fiddle?' I asked, clapping, pointing to the case on the armchair in the parlour.

'But of course, Betsy.' She laughed. 'No New Year is complete without a good jig!'

Cousin Mary frowned, perhaps worried that the music would wake her little bairn, George, and I was struck by how much she looked like our late mutual grandmother on Da's side. Sombre. Serious. Stern. And there she was, just a year older than me, and old and sour before her time.

Mary Ann McCracken, a much livelier and spritely Mary, stood up and began to tune her fiddle.

'Will there be a proper revolution like in America and France, do you think, Mary Ann?' I asked her. 'You know, we're all planning and talking and plotting and scheming but it all seems so covert. Will France really come to our aid and help us with our own revolution? Do we get to drag the English into the square and chop off their heads?'

'Heavens, Betsy.' My cousin coughed into her weak tea. 'You are speaking treasonous poison. You'd be hung if anyone heard you.'

I looked to Mrs Boal and she smiled, her eyes twinkling. She was a good loyal Irishwoman.

The men walked single file back into the room with the strong smell of tobacco accompanying them. We hushed our rebellious talk.

'I hope you knocked the snow off your boots before traipsing through the house!' I scolded.

'Aye girl, we did,' my father answered. They all took their seats except Will Boal who stood back from them like he'd seen a spectre.

'Betsy,' he said, and I gave him an inquisitive smile.

'Yes, what? Will, you look drunk. Are you all right?'

'I wonder, Betsy,' he stammered, 'if you would do me the honour of being my wife. *An bposfaidh tu me*?'

I laughed. Oh golly, I didn't mean to. It just up and walloped me like a slap across the cheek. At first, I truly did think he was joking, playing a New Year prank. But he looked stricken and I realised, as I looked around at all the other faces, that he was deadly serious and that they were all in on it. That's what he'd been doing outside. Asking my father for permission for my hand.

'I, uh, well.' I smiled and tried to wipe the ridiculous grin off my face. 'I am taken quite by surprise, Will. But ... yes. Yes. A big yes.'

I was laughing again because I couldn't help it. I was happy and embarrassed and a little dazed by it all. It was as sudden as a summer thunderstorm. I went to Will and wrapped my arms around him and he kissed me long and deep as everyone in the room cheered and clapped.

'To your good health and the merging of the Grays and the Boals!' my father said, raising a toast as he pulled out a ceramic jug of Cruiskeen whisky from the sideboard and began filling the good glasses.

I felt my face flushing. I was in no rush to settle down to the drudgery of married life but Will Boal was a good catch and I loved him so. The thought of being his wife so soon made me a little giddy. The thrill of it all washed over me like a wave of forest fire.

'Oh, Betsy, you will have to hurry to start a family so that Isabella can have a cousin close in age.'

'Oh, wait up, Brigit!' Will laughed. 'I haven't put a ring on her finger yet. There's time enough to talk of that later. I was thinking a summer wedding.'

I smiled and nodded at Will, already imagining the day. Yes, a summer wedding would be wonderful and it gave us plenty of time to prepare so that it would be the most beautiful day of my life.

'Let's celebrate properly,' Mary Ann said, starting up her fiddle.

The music began and George pulled out his uilleann pipes to accompany her. It was an up-tempo jig and Will grabbed my wrist and pulled me into the open space of the parlour where he began to dance and I joined him, kicking up my heels with glee. As he romped and stomped and swung me about, I threw my head back and laughed hysterically. Everyone clapped and tapped their feet until my father took Mrs Boal's hand and the two of them danced beside us. Only the two young mothers stayed at the table with their babes in baskets by their feet.

As the tune ended, Will took me in his arms and kissed me again.

'All right, all right,' my father scoffed. 'There'll be none of that until you've made your vows in the church.'

'Oh Da.' I laughed. 'Will is my fiancé now and I'll kiss him all I like.'

'You're a wild one, Betsy Gray.' He smiled back at me, shaking his head. 'You'll need to keep her in check, Will. It will be a weight off my shoulders getting rid of her.'

I slapped my father gently on his shoulder and laughed out loud.

'Not even Will could keep me in check, Da.' I grinned and flicked my long hair over one shoulder as I looked at my tall beau with his fierce blue eyes and his dark curls. 'You're a brave man, Will!'

'I like a challenge.' He winked at me. 'Perhaps marriage will settle you down.'

'Will, Will,' I said playfully. 'I don't think you'd like me too settled. You like my wildness, I suspect.'

'That I do! I love you just the way you are, my treasure,' he said and came close and put his arms around me again.

'You two!' Brigit laughed from the table. 'I do think it would be best to marry you promptly. There seems to be way too much fire between you to have to put it on a simmer for six months or so.'

'The only cure for love is marriage,' the Reverend piped up and everyone laughed.

Will and I excused ourselves and went for a walk outside to get some air and allow ourselves some privacy to discuss the issue.

'You are happy, aren't you, Bet?' he said, a worried crease in his brow. 'You weren't just saying so? You do want to be my wife?'

'Of course I do, you dunderhead.' I laughed incredulously. 'I adore you, Will and while, yes, it was a shock to me, it is a very pleasant one.'

His shoulders slumped with relief. We walked on and my boots sunk into the soft fall of snow. I picked up a gloved handful of the crunching white ice and levelled Will with a knowing look.

'You'd better run!'

He took off, awkwardly sinking up to his ankles as he ran toward the greenhouse. I threw the snowball at him and it exploded against the back of his moleskin jacket. Will laughed and hooted and grabbed a fistful, turning the tables on me as I ran back in the other direction. We were making so much noise with our laughter that I did not hear the approach of the galloping horse until the rider was almost upon us.

He came at an alarming rate down through the open gate and I feared he might barrel straight over me, but he pulled up in time and his horse gave a whinny as it came to a halt. The rider wore a broad-brimmed, low-crowned hat and sat atop a chestnut mare. As he took off his hat, I realised it was Connor Kelly, cousin Mary's husband, the one we called traitor.

'What can we help you with, Connor?' I asked as Will came up close to me, looking up at the man. 'I thought George was taking Mary home later in the wagon and—'

'I've come with some news,' he said, interrupting me. 'I've heard it at the barracks up at Newtownards. Your sister's husband, Jimmy Ballantine, has been arrested and charged with treason. He's apparently taken the United Irishmen's Oath and during a raid the fellows found a stack of pikes under the hay in his stable.'

Will and I shot one another a look of concern.

'Brigit is here with us now,' I said. 'She knows nothing of this, I swear, Connor.'

'Well, I know your da is a loyalist to the King and I'm sure that will help, but they'll be wanting to talk to your sister in the next few days.'

I shut my eyes and felt my heart cool in my chest. This would come as a terrible blow to Brigit. What with the new bairn less than three months old.

'I don't need to remind you that it's a hanging offence to be hooked up with the rebels.'

I looked up at Connor's eyes as they bored into me. I wasn't sure whether he was telling me this in relation to my brother-in-law, Jimmy, or warning me personally.

'I am duly aware of that, sir.' I nodded sombrely. 'I'm sure they'll see that Jimmy was keeping such things from his wife. It will come as a terrible shock to her because Brigit is as loyal to the King as my da.'

'And you, Betsy? And you, William Boal?' he asked us, leaning forward, fixing us with a penetrating stare.

'You won't find any United Irishmen around this farm, Connor Kelly,' Will said firmly, lying through his teeth. 'And we thank you for risking your own hide to come and tell us the grave news.'

'Would you like to come in for a dram of whisky?' I asked, feeling that I could do with one myself.

'No,' he said flatly. 'Tell your brother to have my wife and son home before sundown so she has time to prepare my tea. And don't give her any punch. I don't allow her any liquor.'

As he took off back toward the road, his horse kicking up plumes of snow in its wake, I fell into Will's chest and began to sob.

'Poor Brigit,' I moaned. 'They'll hang Jimmy just like they did Mr Orr. And if they decide that she's an accessory, they ...'

The thought was too horrible to put into words.

FIONA

BRISBANE, AUSTRALIA, 1968

'Why are the police over there?' I asked Agnes, warily.

On the corner of Turbot Street, a group of six uniformed policemen stood, arms crossed, staring at all the young people approaching the solid-stone Trade Union Building. It was dusk, yet the heat was still stifling. I could feel the sweat running down my back. We crossed the road to avoid them.

'I guess they're just patrolling the area, making sure no fights break out or whatnot.' She shrugged, not looking at all concerned. 'Or maybe they are covertly photographing all these political subversives and putting them on a black list.'

'I don't know,' I said, almost to myself, my nerve suddenly evaporating. 'Maybe we shouldn't. I mean—'

Agnes grabbed my wrist and pulled me along.

'No, no, no.'

She laughed. 'I was being funny, silly! There's a band playing and they have films and stuff. It's fine. It's just a cool place to hang out. It'll be fun. Anyone can get up on stage and do anything. Mime. Music. Dance. Anything.'

'Hmmm,' I said, following her, unconvinced, my feet shuffling along the pavement. 'But if it's just a bunch of brainwashing palaver being shoved down our throats like at the lunchtime Forum then I'm leaving and we can go catch *Bonnie and Clyde* at the picture theatre.'

Inside, we had to pay one dollar to become members of the Foco Club and then another seventy cents for the night's entry fee. I got my little rectangular cardboard member's card and put it in my purse. Agnes and I walked into the club, which was fast filling up with loud and excited young people. I recognised a few faces from uni.

'How cool is this place?' Agnes laughed.

'This place' was quite spartan and not at all what I had expected. There was a big blank expanse with exposed floorboards. There were some fabric-covered boards that were being used to partition off sections where mats and cushions were scattered on the floor. Music pumped out of the big speakers in the corner and over at the designated disco area, people were contorting themselves as they danced frenetically.

'Is that Creedence?' Agnes yelled at me over the music.

'I think so,' I mouthed back at her, shrugging.

'Hey there, welcome to Foco.' A man in a loud floral shirt smiled at us and gave the two-fingered salute of peace. Agnes and I started to giggle and had to punch each other in the arm to stop from becoming hysterical and making fools of ourselves.

'Bloody hippies.' I laughed into Agnes's ear.

'This place is jumping!' Agnes replied, squeezing my elbow.

'Hey Fi!' I heard a voice call out and I turned around, confused and disoriented.

I came face-to-face with Luke, the boarding house cook.

'So great to see you here! Part of the hive mind, hey?'

'Ah ... yeah,' I stammered. 'I guess so ... um ... this is my friend, Agnes.'

'Charmed.' Luke gave her a lopsided grin. 'I do the lights here every Sunday night,' he told us and pointed to a dim corner of the room. 'People just get up and express themselves. It's a beautiful thing. Wait till you see my light show; it's totally psychedelic.'

'Cool,' I yelled and nodded over another blast of music from the speakers as Luke wandered away doing some kind of dance.

'That's Luke,' I told Agnes. 'He's the guy at my boarding house. He lives there.'

'Tasty!' she answered back and did something weird with her eyes.

'Yeah.' I grinned. 'He looks a bit like Jim Morrison from The Doors, don't you reckon?'

'Totally!'

'He's an artist,' I explained, as we found a quiet corner and sat down on some cushions. 'He paints really abstract stuff. He showed me.'

'You've been in his room?' she looked aghast. 'How well do you know him?'

'Well, let's see,' I replied. 'He was half-naked at the time.'

'Stop! Stop it!' Agnes shouted, putting her hands over her ears, her accent getting thicker.

'Nah,' I said, giving a dismissive shrug. 'I'm not interested. My study load is way too heavy to be thinking about boys! Anyway, he's a bit intense, I reckon.'

'Not as intense as Barton McLeod,' Agnes said, raising her eyebrows and nodding her head toward a raised platform as the music was snuffed out.

Barton was on a small raised dais about to start preaching to the crowd, I presumed. A swarm of kids had congregated around him, sitting cross-legged on the floor or lying in other people's laps. They looked like a sea of zombies, all mindlessly devoted to their messiah, Barton McLeod.

'Might as well go and listen to him,' Agnes said. 'And then we'll watch the open stage thingo and you should sing a song. There are other people with guitars. You could borrow one. Maybe do something by Joni Mitchell. You sound just like her.'

'I'm not going to do that! You've got to be joking.' I slapped her on the hand. 'But, oh God ... listening to the ravings of Barton is not my idea of a fun night out. Really, Ag.'

I relented and let Agnes lead me over to some spare cushions on the floor. My dad had rung me at the boarding house earlier that afternoon to check in on me. I'd lied and told him I was going to get some takeaway fish and chips and watch television at Agnes's parents' place. If he could have seen me there in the Foco Club with the smell of marijuana thick in the air, rock 'n' roll blaring into the smoky room, with a bunch of upstart political hippies, I think he would have self-combusted.

The kids all gave a roar of approval as Barton started up by welcoming everyone to the Foco Club.

'The world needs a revolution, people!'

I sat and squirmed uncomfortably because more than a revolution, I needed to pee. I looked around for a sign pointing to a toilet but decided to hang on. I didn't want to stand up and walk away while Barton was talking in case he called me out on it and embarrassed me.

'This week Martin Luther King Junior was murdered, assassinated.'

A murmur of voices reacted. It's all anyone had talked about at uni for the previous few days. It had made me really sad hearing about it. The world was becoming a messed-up place.

'Martin Luther King had a dream, my friends, and I, too, have a dream,' Barton shouted passionately.

'Oh boy.' I leaned across to Agnes. 'Now he's going to be the phoenix that rises from the ashes of Martin Luther King and proclaims himself the new king of civil rights. The poor guy isn't even cold yet and Barton's pinching the "dream" line.'

Agnes didn't take her eyes off Barton.

'I found his speech about Vietnam truly inspiring. So much needs to change,' Barton said as he strode around the stage with his microphone, gesticulating with his free hand. 'We need to stop sending our boys to a war that has nothing to do with us. Conscription is murder. The Foco Club is where we can come to have this dialogue of change.

Your voices matter. Use them. Shout. Yell. If enough of us make a noise they have to listen to us! We will march in the streets. We are the youth and we are the future.'

He went on and on and perhaps I was breathing in the fumes and getting stoned, but I found his voice more sedating than uplifting. I got comfortable on the cushions and curled up like a cat and almost fell asleep.

After Barton finished firing up the crowd with his speech, Agnes and I stood, stretched and went to buy some lemonade. I saw Barton making his way through the crowd, nodding and shaking hands with his fans. Then he walked straight over to me.

'You made it, Fiona.' He smiled.

'Did anyone ever tell you that you look like John Lennon from The Beatles?' Agnes said. There was a hint of adoration in the way she said it.

'All the time, love,' he replied in a terrible Liverpudlian accent.

'Don't you think that our government brought in conscription because it is a fair way to call up random people to go and fight alongside our allies, the Americans?' I challenged him.

'We have enlisted men who choose to fight,' he came straight back at me. 'Let them go. I'm safe from the ballot because I'm at university but if I hadn't been, trust me, I'd sooner sit in a gaol for a few years than go and shoot at Vietnamese people in their own country. I don't love my country enough to lay down my life for it. It's just dirt.'

'What if the Vietnamese were threatening us here?' I continued. 'Would you fight to defend your country then?'

'Nope.' He smiled. 'I'd ask them what their beef was and say let's go and have a beer and talk about it and I'd try to come to an agreement. Make a friend out of an enemy. War is never the answer. I'm a dedicated pacifist.'

'I agree with you on the conscription issue,' Agnes said, smiling at Barton as if she was a cat and he was the cream.

'Cool.' Barton smiled at her just as someone started waving at him from across the room. 'You birds have a funky time. Check you later.'

We watched as he was swallowed up by the crowd of students.

'I need to pee,' I announced to Agnes. I drank my lemonade fast and went in search of a bathroom while Agnes looked for a spot near the stage so we could watch all the attention seekers who were about to have their three minutes of fame.

As I made my way back from the bathroom, I saw Luke at the rear of the room with an overhead projector. A man was playing the flute and doing some kind of Pan dance on the stage. He looked completely ridiculous. Luke saw me and motioned for me to come over.

'Isn't this cool?' he whispered and pointed down to what he was doing.

On the overhead projector screen, Luke had a tray of what looked like a mixture of oil and water and he was squirting in coloured paints or some kind of dye and was swirling them around to create patterns of colour that were being projected through the light onto the far wall and ceiling of the small stage. It was quite fascinating and made the flute player look surreal.

'That's really clever,' I said and he looked quite pleased with himself.

I looked around and saw that Agnes was talking to Barton again and noticed that Jeff, the ratbag, had also joined them. He and Agnes were standing shoulder to shoulder, very close. I smiled and waved. A young girl took to the stage with a guitar, sat on a stool and began singing a folk song. Badly. I couldn't tell what was more out of tune – her guitar or her voice. Agnes started signalling to me, pointing to the stage. I was shaking my head vehemently. There was no way I was going to get up at the Foco Club in front of so many strangers. It was one thing to play to my home town as that was mostly like an extended family, but I got frightfully nervous in front of unfamiliar people and even got stage fright when I had to deliver presentations at uni. It was so alien and overwhelming compared to small-town living and country schooling.

'No way!' I mouthed at her and did a hand motion across my neck.

There were three more acts, all fairly dismal. Luke ran out of paint and the whole venue seemed to run out of steam and wound down to an anti-climactic groan. Everyone was beginning to look bedraggled and tired. I was exhausted and felt a bit spacey.

'You want a ride home?' Luke asked. 'There's just some boring movie now and nearly everyone falls asleep. And we *are* going home to the same place after all. I'll be packing up and leaving in half an hour. My car's a bit of a bomb but it goes. You'll just have to hold your breath because it smells a bit mouldy.'

Agnes joined us, looking hot and bothered.

'Barton's going to be running a movie soon,' she said. 'It's French and has subtitles and it's all about the French Revolution.'

'Yeah, I might pass on that. Far too exciting for me. Hey Ag, how are you getting home?' I asked her.

'Taxi,' she said. 'You're on my way so you can get dropped off first. Why?'

'Luke here has offered me a lift home and I'm tired and don't really want to watch the movie and as we're going to the same destination, you know, the boarding house …'

'That's fine, makes total sense.' She grinned at me and threw me a sneaky wink, pulling me close and whispering, 'Go get him, tiger!'

Luke was right. His car was a bomb and it did smell bad.

In the front foyer of the boarding house there was a pile of mail on the hall stand. I felt my belly swarm with butterflies of excitement as I saw that there was a parcel from home, wrapped in brown paper and tied with string, scrawled with my father's terrible handwriting. A parcel felt so much better than a letter. I picked it up and held it to my chest before sifting through the stack of envelopes in case there was one from Laura. I hadn't heard from her for weeks, which was highly unusual because her first two letters had told me how much she missed me and how Bandaroo Flats was boring without me. I had written back arguing that Bandaroo Flats was boring with or without me.

'Here's one for you, Luke,' I said. 'Assuming that your surname is Sheehan. And there aren't many girls called Luke living here.'

'That's me,' he said seriously, taking the envelope from my hand. 'But I don't know who'd be sending me …'

He froze, before ripping open the envelope in a frenzy. 'Shit, shit,' he stammered.

'What is it?' I said, concern rising.

He read it and shut his eyes. It was not good news. I waited for a moment, not sure if I should say something. The moment drew out long and tight like elastic.

'Luke?' I asked gently. 'Are you okay?'

I felt really uncomfortable, certain he had received some very bad news. He opened his big brown eyes and looked right at me as if he'd seen a ghost.

'It's my draft notice,' he said softly. 'My birthday got called up. I'm twenty next month.'

JEANNE

BEAUVAIS, FRANCE, 1472

The battle began at dawn. I woke with a jolt as an almighty ripping, roaring sound almost shook me out of my bed. It was like being kicked from sleep by one of those hideous nightmares that sees you tripping off the edge of a cliff. I had spent the long night tossing and trying to force myself under the veil of sleep. I must have only drifted off into a nervous light slumber before the sun began to creep up, perhaps only minutes before I was rudely roused.

Papa shouted frantically from the other side of the room as he struggled to sit up, still wading through the delirium of sleep.

'What the devil?'

'The siege is beginning, Papa,' I cried, jumping out of bed and grabbing my boots, knowing that I should have been up before the sun.

Tears were rolling down my father's deeply lined cheeks.

'This is the end,' he moaned. 'Why did we not just surrender?'

'The people of Beauvais want to resist,' I said nervously as I tied my hatchets at my hips, pulled on my outer skirts and secured them about my waist, slipped into my stockings and boots, put a tunic over everything and planted my cap upon my head while hurriedly tucking stray dark wisps of hair into it. 'The women will be running arms and torches up to the wall all day, so I will be busy, Papa.'

Still rushing, tripping over my own feet, I went to the larder and took a mug and swiped it through the cold turnip soup, breaking through the tight scum on the surface. There was no time to heat it and it tasted like cold mucous but I needed my strength.

'Blurghhh,' I shook my head like a horse. 'You have to come along now, Papa, because we are putting the old and infirm and the children into the Cathedral and surrounding houses. And our house is too close to the walls of the city and the gates. The cannons may damage us first.'

'I can't move,' he grumbled. 'How do you propose to get me to the Cathedral? My legs don't work. I have no strength. If I am to die, then let me do it in my own bed.'

'No, Papa,' I said, going to the door, unlatching it and opening it wide. 'Carts are coming down the streets and lanes to collect folk.' I could hear the cries and clatter of the wooden wheels on the stones, getting closer.

'We must dress you. I will pull on your boots and give you a blanket. You have to help me, Papa,' I said firmly. 'You have to walk to the door. Hurry. We need to move.

I'm going to go and help.'

'Stay safe, Jeanne, and defend yourself if necessary. And if you get a chance to flee, do so. I wish for you a life of love. It was what I promised your mother and I failed. I want that for you.'

I smiled and went to him and kissed the top of his head.

'I love you, Papa,' I said softly. 'I will stay safe and so will you. Now let me pull on your boots and help you to the door.'

'I should have saved your mother,' he sobbed as I tied up his laces.

I took a deep breath, and whether I spoke the truth or not, I did not know, but I wanted to make the old man feel a little better, yes, wanted to assuage his guilt just a bit. If it was a lie, then it was well intentioned.

'There was nothing anyone could have done for Mother,' I said, shutting my eyes, trying not to think of her final terror and her bravery. 'There were too many men and had you stayed with her you would surely have been cut down as well.'

'But I left *you*, Jeanne,' he shook his head. 'I left you both. And you were a helpless babe. They were right. I was a coward then. And look at me now. I wish I could fight beside you but …'

I sighed, looking down at my broken father. How could any of us know how we might react in a dangerous situation? Some might imagine they would rise bravely to a threat and yet they run, and others might believe they would run when in fact they manage to find an inner courage they never knew dwelled within them.

'I will go and do my part to redeem the Laisné name,' I said, although my hands were shaking and my breath was short as I struggled with the terror of what the day might bring.

'Your mother hid you well and fought hard,' he said, still crying. 'I only pray during the dark days ahead that you have more of her strength and less of my weakness.'

'I will strive to be the best of both of you,' I said to him. 'You have always been a good father to me. Your moments of fear so many years ago do not reflect on the father I know. You are gentle and kind and you've taught me to sing and to smile and use my axes to protect myself. You are a good man. I can see why my mother loved you.'

I realised then that, in nature, my father and Colin were alike. Kind and gentle.

I helped him to the door and onto a cart as it clattered along the narrow alley, taking its precious cargo to safety.

'I love you, Jeanne,' he called as he was taken away toward the Cathedral.

'I will see you soon, Papa.' I waved back. 'I love you too.'

As I rushed through streets filled with panicked townsfolk, toward the town square to be assigned a post, I could smell smoke in the air and the roar of unfamiliar noise. I passed carts overloaded with old people and children, jammed in like livestock, rattling through the streets and laneways. The children wailed and the elderly looked like stunned corpses. The hordes of the weaker members of Beauvais were housed within the cool stone walls of the Cathedral as well as make-shift tents set up in the cemetery grounds. It was chaos.

Looking up at the battlements, I could see our archers firing blazing arrows at the enemy below and outside the city walls. There were not nearly enough armed men to hold back an army. We had hundreds, Charles the Bold's army had thousands.

I joined a long line of women, where I was grateful to find Aimee, my cousin. She was one year older than me but much smaller and fairer. She was the closest thing to a friend that I had other than Colin. As children we had gotten up to much mischief and preferred to rumble about the streets with the boys rather than weaving with the local girls. And yet she'd softened and become more sensible since her babe had been born.

'Aimee,' I said, grabbing her elbow. 'Are you afraid? Are your mother and baby Matilda safely in the Cathedral?'

'I'm terrified,' she whispered. 'Pierre is with the men defending the gates because that is where the enemy will attack first, they think. The messengers from up in the Cathedral spires have said that there are two large battering rams on trolleys. If they breach the moat and get in it will all be over. For all of us.'

I nodded thoughtfully. The gates were our Achilles heel. The walls were as deep as a tall, grown man; their innards fortified with huge blocks of rock and iron bars. Our external barriers were as strong as a mountain. Despite the gates being triple-deep wood held fast with enormous logs and iron fittings, they would not be able to withstand a constant battering.

From the marketplace to the south of the Cathedral I could see pens of crushed cows loudly lowing, grunting pigs and towers of chicken cages. Hundreds of families had spent most of the previous day evacuating all the produce and livestock they could carry with them from the surrounding suburbs and farms in the district, from all the way down to the river. A well-defended siege could last for months. It was critical to have enough food to feed those inside the city walls or the Burgundians could happily sit out the siege, whistling and twiddling their thumbs, while we all starved to death or, worse still, came to the point of surrender. If nothing else, Beauvais looked well supplied. There were hills of corn and teetering baskets of fruits and vegetables.

'You women, step up here,' a retired, one-eyed soldier called and motioned for us to approach his table. He had a quill and parchment and had clearly been given orders and strategies as to how to divide and assign us to defence stations.

'The next five of you,' he barked. 'You and you.' And then he pointed to the three middle-aged women shuffling up behind us. 'Go to Geoffrey Britten's shop on Butcher's Road. Tanner Andre is in the slaughter paddock out the back skinning carcasses. You will be given carts of hides, both old and fresh. You must wet them thoroughly from the town drainage gullies and take them to drape on every wooden roof that you can. Anything made of flammable material such as wood or thatch must be well draped with drenched skins. You will cover the merchant quarter.'

It sounded like one of the less savoury tasks to be given to the women, but it surely couldn't have been worse than boiling huge vats of oil on the furnaces, transporting them and hoisting them up to the high battlements by pulley. That would be a chore more fraught with danger. The city was already hot and fetid.

Aimee and I, along with the other women, hurried down the street toward the detestable slaughterhouse. The stench of spoiling flesh gave us our directions. Around us people were running, rushing to help protect the town.

'Was it a cannon? That noise this morning?' I panted out the question to my cousin.

'I think so,' she said, trying to keep up with me, her skirts bunched up higher than her boots as she ran. 'From all accounts, it missed its mark and hit the moat with a great almighty splash that sent a spray of sewage and slime halfway up the outer walls around it. Made a mess, that's all.'

I stopped and pulled up straight, my jaw set tight, as Lieutenant Jean Lagoy came marching on a collision course directly toward me, leading a small group of archers behind him. He called them to a halt with a raised hand, coming to me, glaring.

'You may find safe refuge in the Captain's manor house, Jeanne,' he said firmly. 'All the ladies are there and you'll have a guard stationed outside. The house is central so it will be too far for cannons or catapulting torches to reach. You will be safe.'

'But if it's so safe, why use up any soldiers to guard it?' I asked. 'Every man is needed up on the battlements, or to launch cannon fire of their own from the square, or to work to reinforce the gates, or man the gatehouses and I—'

'I am not asking you, Jeanne,' Lagoy snapped harshly. 'I am *telling* you. You will obey me or suffer the consequences.'

I gave a shudder not knowing what sort of threat that might be.

'Yes, Monsieur.' I nodded my head and gave a small but defiant curtsey.

'You other wenches, away with you to your stations,' he said, dismissing the other women. 'I have no time to escort you there, Jeanne. The enemy has chosen, as their first bombardment, to attempt to scale the walls and take us by force that way. I must have every man on the battlements to repel their attempts. Go now, speed you away and keep safe!'

I stood back, watching the foreign archers march in their heavy boots in a rhythm like a drum beat behind the Lieutenant, their heavy crossbows under their strong arms, arrow-heads glinting in the glare of the early morning sun.

As soon as Lagoy and his band of men turned the corner and were out of view, I spun around, picked up my skirts and ran to catch up with Aimee and the other women. I might have been betrothed to the bully Lagoy, but I was not yet married to him and I still held out the sinful and evil hope that he might fall during the siege, thereby relieving me of my marital commitment. And until I was truly chained to him in matrimony, I was a girl who wanted to work alongside my fellow women of Beauvais and use every sinew and tendon in my body to protect my home, the place where I had been born and lived my whole life.

'You cannot disobey Lagoy,' Aimee hissed at me. 'You'll be flogged. But I don't understand why he would send you to the Captain's house. To serve the fine ladies tea and croissants while Beauvais is being sacked?'

'We are betrothed,' I said quietly, trying to breathe through my mouth to avoid being made giddy by the worsening stench coming up from over the roof of the meat vendor's house.

'*Sacré bleu*! You lucky girl!' she gasped loudly, her bluebell eyes widening. 'But how? I don't understand. How could you pay a dowry? You and Uncle Matthew are …'

'Paupers?' I smiled. 'Yes, but we weren't always and our mothers, yours and mine … they were well born but married down for love. Fools or romantics, I don't know. Lagoy gained permission from the Captain and a bride-price was paid. My father had no choice but to agree.'

'Oh,' she said, nodding slowly. 'I now understand why you were so upset and why Colin followed you into the woods …'

Aimee said no more but we both knew that it was common enough for a well-bred man to take a fancy to a pretty pauper or peasant girl and arrange to compensate the family for her hand in marriage. Sometimes being fair of face and fit and young were curses rather than blessings. If I had been scrawny and narrow hipped I might have been free to marry Colin.

The hefty butcher pointed us out through the back doors without a word as he took all his knives and packed them into a crate. Outside, a huge wooden frame had warm, bloodied hides stretched out thinly.

'You *putain* get over here,' the tanner called rudely.

He worked without a shirt, his leathery skin matching those he worked with. I was pleased to see that many of the hides he was preparing were old and not too fresh. He seemed to have barrels and barrels of off-cuts and leftovers and was laying them flat, in layers, into wheelbarrows.

'Take a barrow each and you, the coward's daughter.' He squinted, pointing at me. 'You look stronger than these other wastrels, you take the ladder.' He pointed to a tall ladder leaning up against the slaughter shed.

'Head down to the nearest well and fill the barrows with water enough to cover the hides,' he told us, speaking in a fast and rough voice. 'Then make your way down to Rue de Bonneterrie and head back up Rue de Lin. Climb the ladder and pass up the hides and cover as many of the thatched and shingled rooves as you can manage.'

I knew that one fiery arrow shot from a bow across the city walls could land on a roof, sparking a fire that would leap from one roof to the next and engulf a whole quarter in flames in moments.

'Even stray carts and vendor stands,' the tanner barked. 'Anything flammable, cover it. And keep coming back to fill your wagons. We will work ceaselessly, no time to break except to quench your thirst so that you do not faint from the heat.'

We stood there not sure who should go first so I strode across the courtyard to the ladder. It was awkward and heavy but I managed to wedge it beneath my arm. The other women took their barrows of skins and we pushed them out into the streets.

The nearest water station was on a corner where a town well had been dug down a deep shaft. I rested the ladder against the stone wall enclosing the well and we took it in turns to pull up full buckets of cool water to tip over the skins in the barrows until they were full and heavy.

'What of you and Colin, then?' Aimee grunted at me as we bumped and struggled our way down the narrow streets where vendors had closed up and shut their windows.

'I don't know. I love him but … alas,' I said. 'We must focus on our defence of the town now and I will think of that later.'

'The drawbridges are up,' Aimee replied. 'So they will have a hard time getting across the water. No man will brave the bog. Drowning in that mire of human waste and entrails would be a much worse death than an arrow to the heart.'

I was calmed by her words. It was true that the deep waterway that surrounded the city was a great barrier. It protected us somewhat from being besieged by heavy weaponry.

'They may get their horses to swim them across,' I worried aloud, thinking of ways the enemy might combat the stinking obstacle.

'More likely they will fill the water with rocks and logs and debris to make a crossing,' one of the other women said. 'That's what I heard they did up at Roye. Even threw the corpses of their own dead into the bog to build up a causeway.'

We were dealing with an army renowned for their brutality and Charles had a reputation for pigheaded stubbornness. When Beauvais had done the unthinkable the previous day by refusing to surrender quietly, the despot would have been incensed and we all knew he would stop at nothing to take Beauvais and punish her for her wilfulness.

'Lieutenant Lagoy said that the enemy is attempting to climb over the walls and take us that way. I wonder if their ladders could reach though, as the walls are very high.'

'They build scaffolding and climb it,' another woman answered.

Two unfamiliar women struggled past us, carrying an injured man on a wood and canvas stretcher. He was covered in burns; his flesh was raw and blistering.

'With a marriage to Lagoy in my future,' I told Aimee as I shifted the heavy ladder to my other hip, dragging it on the stones as I went, 'I have nothing to lose. I will fight to the death to save my city. They will have to cut me down because I will not bow my head to them. I am the King's woman.'

'And your day in the forest with Colin?' she asked and gave me a knowing look.

'If I never know happiness again,' I smiled shyly at her, 'I will always have the memory of that afternoon. Thank you for your silence, Aimee.'

'I love my Pierre,' she said, blowing the hair from her face. 'And I know love when I see it and you and Colin have always had it. Damn that Lieutenant to hell for standing in the way of that.'

'We cannot win. We are doomed!' a woman shrieked from behind me and began to wail hysterically.

‘While we breathe, we have hope,’ the oldest lady in our group shouted back at her. ‘We must fight, so let’s do our little bit and get these damn hides on the rooves and shut up!’

We stopped at the first house and I climbed to the top of the ladder while the others passed up the heavy sodden hides. My clothes were soon saturated and I smelled no better than a diseased animal.

We worked hard all morning until the job was done. I was bathed in sweat, my underclothes clinging to me and my bonnet sodden. My muscles ached and my feet throbbed. Many more women were busy in the other quarters, covering everything they could. Fires burned in the street and a stream of women of all ages filled carts with boiling oil, water and slop to transport them in a never-ending caravan to the base of the wall. There, men carefully hoisted the carts up to the battlements where the contents were tipped down onto the enemy trying to scale the walls on their many ladders and ropes. The ones who were not picked off by our archers must have been retreating with terrible burns. I could hear screams ringing in my ears all morning. But most of the screams were coming from inside the city as our injured men were hurried to the makeshift hospital set up in the marketplace. Women were dispensing bandages and salves for the wounded. The day was stiflingly hot and uncomfortable, and with the fires burning it was on the cusp of being unbearable. I could hardly breathe and hot embers stung my exposed cheeks.

‘You girls,’ an officer called to Aimee and me as we sucked greedily at a water gourd that someone had passed to us. 'Take these hammers to the Bresle Gate and give them to whoever is in charge there.'

A barrow of hammers had been found at a carpenter's house. My cousin and I took a handle each of the heavy wheelbarrow and made our way through the crowds of women, heading toward the western gate. As we reached the outer road, nearest to the walls, I heard a sound that thrummed in my ears. *Thwump*. Aimee screamed and through my sweat-blind and dirt-encrusted eyes, I leapt back and saw her fall to the ground, her skirts on fire.

'Aimee!' I screamed and ripped off my apron to douse the flames. I beat it desperately while she writhed and squealed like a pig being slaughtered.

I rolled her to put out the embers completely and as I did so I saw the arrow in her side.

'Pull it out,' she screamed.

I dared not. If it had found its way to some vital part inside her belly, she might bleed to death. I started unloading the hammers onto the cobbled stones as fast as I could, all the while telling Aimee to breathe deeply to control the pain.

'Just listen to your breath,' I urged.

Once I had emptied the barrow, I shouted at a young girl standing in a doorway to get someone to come and collect the hammers. I helped Aimee to her feet as she once again cried in pain. Carefully, I placed her into the barrow with the arrow pointing skyward. I gently pushed the wooden wheels over the stones as she panted and grimaced in pain. I took her not to the marketplace that was already awash with blood and blistering burns, but to

Captain Balagny's manor house. There I would beg the fine ladies to call a proper doctor to attend my cousin. I was, after all, destined to be one of them.

All around me, dirty, perspiring women and children ran through the streets wailing as if a comet was hurtling toward the earth or the final days predicted by the Bible were upon us.

'Beauvais is lost!' they shouted. 'The enemy has breached the moat. They will swarm in like hornets.'

'What are they saying?' Aimee cried at me, her bloody hands at her side. Her face was as grey as granite.

'They are coming over the walls,' I said, panicked.

'We don't have enough men up there to stop them!' she moaned.

I looked around the streets that were filled with frightened women. Women everywhere. Strong, well-built Beauvaisi women.

And I knew then that if we were to resist the soldiers who were clambering up the framework of their belfry, if we were to stop them from spilling over to slaughter our men on the wall, if we were to prevent them from coming down to raid and pillage our city ... I knew what had to be done.

We might not have had enough manpower in Beauvais, but we certainly had a surplus of womanpower. I needed to rally my own army of Beauvaisi women.

BETSY

COUNTY DOWN, IRELAND, 1798

It was nigh on midnight when my sister stopped sobbing.

'I cannot bear to live, Betsy!' She sniffed, staring at me through swollen eyelids. Her whole face was shiny and pink.

'Hush that nonsense.' I frowned at her and patted her knee. 'Isabella needs her mammy. She needs you to be strong for her.'

'They'll hang poor Jimmy and if they have a mind to, me as well. I'd sooner go and jump into the sea from a cliff than let those English dogs drop me.'

'Didn't you hear what George and Will were saying?' I reminded her. 'They'll break Jimmy out of the slammer tomorrow night. They've got a plan.'

'A foolish and dangerous idea being hatched by a pair of halfwits,' she said, looking cross. 'They'll commit their own felony and be forced to join Jimmy. Three nooses and our family destroyed. I won't have them risk their own lives to save one.'

I looked at my older sister as she lay back on my bed. She was a head shorter than me with honey-blonde hair and a button nose. Brigit had always been beautiful. Even with the snot-glazed cheeks and swollen eyes she was pretty as a picture. Baby Isabella had settled and was sleeping soundly in the corner in her basket. We had kept the two of them with us in Gransha as it was far too dangerous for Brigit to return home to Antrim. The yeomanry would have her on a list for questioning. They'd detain her – and brutally.

'Da will speak well of you,' I told her. 'If they come knocking here tomorrow, we'll tell them that you have been staying with us here for weeks and, as you feared, your Jimmy was colluding with the rebels.'

'I can't betray him so cruelly,' she moaned.

'But you *must* if they come before we can break him out and get you all on a boat,' I told her.

'Da is right angry and will never get tired of telling me he predicted this,' Brigit muttered.

'He's a grand grumbler.' I smiled. 'Too righteous for his own good. I sometimes wonder how our ma put up with him.'

'Oh, she didn't!' Brigit gave a weak smile. 'She had no time for his moods and grumps. Ma was a tough woman and would send him out to walk in the snow whenever he complained. She would tell us that a home is for smiles and laughter, and if anyone wanted to be sour they were to take it outside.'

I didn't remember our mother as well as Brigit did. I had only been five years old when our mother passed away.

Brigit had been ten. I was sometimes jealous of the extra five years she had spent with Mammy. For the last year of her life, the poor woman had been laid up on her sickbed, frittering away to skin and bones. I wished so hard that I could remember the earlier, happier days. My strongest memories of my darling mother were of sickness and pain. Her sunken eyes had stared out from a face set like a statue and the voice I remembered had been little more than a hoarse whisper.

'You must get some sleep, Brigit,' I said to her, more because I felt like my eyeballs were about to fall out of my head from tiredness. 'I have two trunks of Mother's old clothes under the window. She was smaller than me, wasn't she? More your size. I'll find you a nightdress and you can go through the rest of them tomorrow and choose some skirts and things to pack for Scotland. We have kin in Paisley who will welcome you in.'

'If I go,' she said, looking terrified, 'I might never be able to come back. Or not for years, at least. Not unless the rebels really do run the redcoats out of Ireland.'

'Oh, you can be sure we will.' I smiled and winked at her as I went to the heavy trunks to find something suitable for my sister to sleep in and began rummaging around.

The strong smell of keeping-herbs made my eyes water. My father had packed away my mother's clothes and for fifteen years the trunks sat under my window. I had placed a stack of books and a small crystal vase for cut flowers on top of them. I always found the trunks' presence comforting, although I had stopped short of going through them as I was afraid it would make me too sad and summon up too many memories. But if George and Will could pull off their daring plan to break Jimmy Ballantine out of the lock-up and spirit the little family down to Bangor to a boat that would take them to Scotland, then Brigit would be needing clothes.

'I'm sure there must be a nightdress in here somewhere,' I muttered to myself and opened the heavy latch of the second trunk, breathing in sharply.

I may have been imagining it but I felt my mother's spirit as I tried to smell her scent. I shut my eyes for a moment and let my mother's face fill the dark space. Carefully, I pushed the clothes aside. 'Hang on, Brig. What's this?'

My hand touched something hard that wasn't the bottom of the trunk. I reached down and pulled out a book.

'What is this?' I asked again, looking up at Brigit. 'I didn't even know Mammy could read.'

'Oh my Lord,' Brigit gasped. 'I had forgotten about it. It is the Sister Book.'

I took the book across the room to hold it close to the lamplight so that I could read the inscription on the front of the leather cover. It felt heavy in my hands. By the light of the oil lamp it looked almost alive, as if it were breathing.

'Systir Saga,' I murmured. 'These are strange words. And below, here, Sister Story.'

'They are foreign words. See these early markings? Runes. From up in the Nordic regions, I think,' she answered, getting off the bed and coming to stand beside me, resting a gentle hand on the hide. 'Ma showed me this when I was little and I wish I could remember everything she said. It was when she first got sick. It is quite amazing, isn't it?'

Very gently, I opened the book and looked at the words inside, all handwritten, all names. I turned the heavy pages, which felt cold and faintly oily. My name was last. Next to Brigit's.

'What is all this? All these names?' I wondered aloud, still bewildered and intrigued.

'It's a book with all our mothers and grandmothers and aunts and cousins and sisters in it. All the womenfolk that share our blood,' Brigit whispered. 'I can put Isabella's name in there now.'

I let my finger run back over the names. My mother's, scratched into the page by her own hand: Isabella Boyne, Newtownards, Ireland. And my grandmother, Sybill Joyce, Paisley, Scotland, the daughter of Isabel Campbell, and beside her name, her sister's: Katherine Campbell. The symbol of a broomstick was scratched in next to Katherine's name. The distant aunt who was burned as a witch. We were the end of her blood.

'Granny, Mammy, aunts,' I whispered and tears came to my eyes.

I could feel them all smiling up at me from the page. The names of women who had lived their lives before us. I felt myself grow taller. My heart swelled up with pride. These women were my women. I was the result of the lives and passions of these women who had gone before me. Katherine Campbell. Burned as a witch. What a price to pay for being a woman! I looked back to the beginning where the words were faded and I ran a finger over them to feel the grooves in the leathery surface. Who was this first mother? The mother that begat all the mothers, all the way down to me. I had the blood of goddesses. I suddenly felt like a part of something so much greater and powerful than just Betsy Gray of Gransha.

'Look at all of them and the places!' I marvelled.

There were some written in strange letters that I couldn't understand and places that I'd never heard of. And in the margins were notes and scribbles. Names of castles or estates perhaps. I sat on the end of my bed, tracing my hands over my grandmothers, aunts and cousins so many times removed. I stopped on one name. It was in a strange hand.

'Is that … Yes. Dear heavens, Brig, it's Grace O'Malley. Wasn't she the pirate queen? It can't be her. Can it?'

'Show me.' My sister tugged at the book and gave a coo like a pigeon. 'Oh lordy, Grace O'Malley. I've heard tell of her. She was a wild woman of the seas.'

'Pirates and witches! My heaving horses!' I laughed and shook my head, feeling overwhelmed.

'It's really something, isn't it?' my sister said. 'Look at these places. Paisley. Beauvais. Is that in France?'

'And here I was thinking we were proud Irish girls!' I laughed. 'But we are a little bit of everything. Isn't it amazing, Brig?'

My sister put her arm around me and rested her head on my shoulder.

'I remember the day Ma sat me down and read all of these names to me,' she said. 'She told me then that we had blood of iron and that I should grow to be a strong, good, right-minded woman to honour all those who had gone before me.'

Little Isabella, named for our mother, began to stir in her basket. My sister went to her, speaking to me over her shoulder.

'I'm glad you found that book,' she said. 'It has given me a new inner strength. My Jimmy is a good man who stands for his principles and we will rescue him and I will take my family to Scotland, to Paisley, where our great-grandmother and aunt lived. One day we will come back and claim our Irish blood. I will be strong for my daughter and all the daughters that will come after her.'

I closed the book and held it to my chest, my eyes closed, feeling my heart beat against it. I felt close to my mother for the first time in many years. I had spent so much of my youth missing her, missing a mother's warm advice and stern guidance. Da was a grumpy old so-and-so but I loved him something fierce. But he *wasn't* and *couldn't* be a mother to me.

'I hope I'll be a mother someday.' I smiled. 'Maybe Will and I will have ten children. Maybe thirteen like Granny!'

My sister laughed and clucked at her babe as she settled back down on my narrow bed.

'You would be driven mad.' She smiled. 'But it is lovely. I never thought I could love another person as much as I love this little girl.'

I carefully put the book back in the bottom of the chest.

'Keep it safe,' Brigit told me.

There was a knock at the door and George put his head in.

'Word has come that the redcoats will be coming for Brigit in the morning,' he said solemnly. 'If we're to bust Jimmy out it will have to be tonight. We need you to ride with us, Betsy. To be our lookout. You'll need to be ready upon our return, Brigit.'

'Oh heavens.' My sister fussed, putting the babe over her shoulder, patting her firmly. Her calmness had gone and she looked flustered. 'Be careful. God be with you all. Bring my Jimmy home safely and we'll away to the barge before sun up.'

'We'll get you safe.' I nodded to my sister. 'I promise.'

'I believe you, Betsy.' She smiled and winked at me. 'You'll have all those mothers and grandmothers watching over you. Blood of iron.'

I dragged on my riding boots, threw a shawl over my shoulders, pulled on some thick gloves and went out with George into the dark, snowy night.

FIONA

BRISBANE, AUSTRALIA, 1968

After Luke opened his draft letter, he'd wandered back to his room looking bereft and I had let him be to process the news on his own. To distract myself from worrying about him, I'd rushed back to my small room to open Dad's parcel. Now I sat on my bed, breathing deeply. I couldn't believe what I was looking at and spent over an hour touching the ancient book that appeared to be covered in soft suede; a very thin, very old animal skin. It looked like something you would see under glass in a museum, not sitting on my lap as I sat on a tattered patchwork bedspread in my shoebox of a room at a boarding house in inner-city Brisbane. When I'd opened the parcel from my father, I had expected a pack of sheet music or a new journal or maybe even some music magazines. What amazed me the most was my strange connection to the book. The skin on my face prickled like it did whenever I was nervous or afraid.

I'd stared at the final entry, beyond which were two more bare but stained pages, which were blank. The final inscription: Fiona Paisley McKechnie, Edinburgh, 1950. The name carefully written in black ink above mine was Lillian Daisy Fergus, Edinburgh, 1924. My mother's name. Still feeling my heart beating like a drum, I lightly traced my finger over all the names and places meandering through the book. Some entries had dates and others did not. There were notes added, scratched into the unlined margins like medieval chicken-claw prints. Some of the earlier entries were faded and hard to decipher but I stopped on one name, Jeanne d'Arc, and inhaled sharply. Surely it couldn't be. Written beside her name was Domrémy-la-Pucelle and my rudimentary recollection of history told me that the legendary Joan of Arc had been born in a place called something like Domrémy. And there was an ink blotch beside the name that looked like a tiny broomstick. Beside that name was Catherine Romée and the next name began beneath it. Could that have been her sister from whom sprang her family's descendants? Down to another Jeanne, born in Beauvais?

The front of the book had some scratchings that really did look like a bird had walked across a stretch of wet sand, but beneath the markings were the words *Systir Saga*; perhaps a later translation as it was in a darker, more solid ink. Beneath that was the English translation: *Sister Story*. I said the words aloud in an awed whisper. 'Systir Saga.' The words sounded like an ancient spell. Considering that all the names in the book appeared to be female names, it made some sense. The Sister Story. A sisterhood book?

Were all these women my blood relatives? Working back from my room in Brisbane, the book appeared to have travelled through much of the known world and beyond. There were place names I did not recognise and some I did. I felt like I had stepped into a fantasy.

I threw my head back and stared up at the slow-moving fan, letting out a long sigh. I shut my eyes, trying to let my brain catch up with it all.

My father's letter said that my mother had wrapped this parcel and put it in her suitcase along with all her notebooks and journals with a note that read: *For Fiona, on her wedding day*. I looked at the crimson silk scarf that Mum had wrapped the book in and lifted it to my face, trying to inhale her scent. I wondered why my mother had wanted to wait for that day to pass the book on. To warn me not to forget who I was and where I had come from? To bond us? I would never know. I wished so much that she had given it to me while she was alive so that we could have talked about it. Dad said he had found it when he was putting Mum's suitcase in the shed and he'd decided, after some thought, and without opening it, to send it on to me in Brisbane because he was getting the very uncomfortable feeling that marriage was not going to be on my agenda for quite some time.

That made me smile.

I wondered if I should take the book to the History faculty at the university to have them date and analyse it. The historical significance of such a book could not be underestimated. And yet, my mother would have known that but she chose to wrap it up, away from Dad's prying eyes, and put it aside for me. And the significance of giving it to me on my 'wedding day' was a passing on of tradition, I supposed, something her mother must have done for her. I missed my mum so much. Many days I pushed it down and out of sight so that it didn't hurt but that made my memories of her a little dimmer every time. But, holding this book, I felt as if Mum was in the room with me and I opened my eyes, looking around, half expecting her to be standing at the end of my bed. Even though my mother wasn't actually there, I realised that I still had a deep connection with her. And the thought of this came out of nowhere, suffocating me with emotion.

'Mum?' I whispered into the room. 'Are you here? Can you see me? Can you?'

And then I pushed the book away, pulled my knees up to my chin and began to sob.

There was a knock at my door, making me fall off the bed with shock. It was late. Outside an owl hooted and a half moon rested on my window sill. I was wearing my long white nightie. The knock came again. I could only assume it was Mrs Lotte coming to reprimand me for getting in late, a few minutes past the weekend curfew of ten o'clock. I wiped my eyes with the back of my hand and went to the door and opened it a touch. Part of me wanted it to be Mum.

It was Luke.

'Luke!' I whispered harshly, pulling my nightdress up around my neck coyly. 'What are you doing here?'

'I'm sorry, Fi,' he said, and as I opened the door a little wider the light fell on his face and I could see that he had been crying. 'I just … I need someone to talk to.'

'Wait there,' I hissed and shut the door.

I took my mother's book and rewrapped it in the red silk scarf, placing it carefully on the top shelf of my wardrobe. I pulled on my jeans and a light sloppy joe and some flat shoes.

Luke and I crept like burglars along the narrow hallway, down the staircase, and tiptoed into the communal living room. We shut the door, turning on a lamp, bathing the room in soft orange light.

'I'm sorry, Fi,' Luke said miserably, sitting on a sofa and putting his head in his hands. 'I have no one else to talk to. I don't want to be a soldier. I don't ever want to hold a gun or shoot anyone or get shot.'

'That's totally understandable, Luke,' I said, sitting down beside him. 'I don't think many young men who get called up really want to go.'

'But I mean I really don't want to go,' he groaned. 'Really. I am not going to go. I'm going to refuse.'

'Oh,' I said. 'Okay.'

We sat in silence for a few more minutes. I was terrified that Mrs Lotte would appear and evict me for fraternising with a boy after hours.

'I'm going to nick off and disappear,' he moaned.

'That's against the law, Luke,' I said softly. 'If they find you they'll throw you in prison.'

'I don't care,' he said flatly. 'I'd rather be in prison than be forced to shoot someone. I couldn't kill another human being. I couldn't, Fi. Not ever.'

'It's war,' I said, lamely. 'It's bigger than one person. It's not individual. It's got a greater picture, you know?

And anyway, it's the law. It's not nice but it is what it is. No one likes paying taxes or stopping at red lights but it's the law.'

'I'm not doing it,' he said firmly. 'I'm not going.'

'You could apply to be a conscientious objector. There are grounds if you meet the criteria.'

'I'd need a lawyer,' he said bitterly. 'And I'm broke. Aunty is the only family I've got left and she's not going to help me be a coward, is she?'

'Well.' I shrugged and sighed. 'I sure am a long way from being a lawyer because I'm struggling to make sense of first-year Property Law but I know a guy at uni who's fourth year and top of his class. I could ask him to have a chat with you.'

'Oh, Fi,' Luke said, looking at me with renewed hope. 'Would you? I'm supposed to turn up at the barracks in a month so I don't have long to sort this out. I guess I'd have to be a ... conscientious objector ... or a deserter or something.'

'I think the term is "non-complier",' I told him. 'You can't desert something you haven't joined yet.'

'Whatever, yeah,' Luke said. 'But if I could talk to your friend—'

'He's not really a friend,' I said quickly. 'But he does seem to know a lot or at least makes out that he does.'

At noon the next day I was sitting in a park in Highgate Hill with Luke, Agnes, Barton and his jerky sidekick, Jeff.

'We'll start the march on campus and walk from there all the way into town and end up at Roma Street. It will be a little cooler by then.' Barton McLeod sounded like he'd already arranged the whole thing instead of looking for suggestions.

'Didn't the cops go nuts and arrest and beat up protesters last year?' Agnes asked. 'It was in all the papers and on the television news.'

'Yeah, yeah.' Barton nodded. 'But freedom of speech, you know. We are protesting non-violently. Just marching for what we believe in. And at the end of the day, the end of the march, when we've got everyone's attention, that's when you, Luke, will burn your draft notice. In front of the cameras.'

It sounded crazy to me. 'Personally,' I waded in, 'I think Luke would be better off fronting up to court and lodging a conscientious objection. That way he's doing it legally.'

'But that's a cop-out,' Barton said passionately. 'We need to make a stand, not just for Luke, but for all the young men who are being forced to go and kill. Luke could get out of serving with a court order if he lied, but this is the perfect opportunity to run him in public as a poster boy for our cause. Raise awareness.'

'Poster boy? I like it!' Luke laughed, striking a melodramatic model pose.

'You really do have the matinee idol looks.' Agnes smiled at him. I rolled my eyes at her and shot a look at Jeff who was staring at Agnes like she was made of ice-cream.

'That's all well and good, Barton,' I said. 'But you're asking Luke to take an enormous risk and he might end up in gaol. That's pretty serious.'

'I obviously would rather not go to gaol,' Luke said seriously. 'But I am pretty fired up about the whole issue. I don't think anyone should be forced to kill people. And like Barton says, it isn't even our war. No one's threatening us here in Australia.'

'It's risky,' I murmured. 'For you. And for all of us. Anyone involved. I don't want it to jeopardise my future as a lawyer.'

'And what the hell is wrong with taking a risk?' Barton said, striding around waving his hands wildly as he did when he got riled up. 'Risk is thinking outside the box, taking a chance, making a change for the better. Nothing great ever happens without risk. Evolution of the human race is reliant on risk!'

Luke gave me a smile. He was so handsome that it was quite astounding. My body was blushing without my consent! I looked up to see Barton looking at me. I was so embarrassed that I wanted to dig a hole in the ground and crawl into it like a wombat.

'I'm game,' Luke said slowly. 'I don't want to go. Not because I'm a coward, or at least I don't think so, but because it feels wrong, you know? It just feels wrong that people are being forced by the government to go.'

'I'll march,' Agnes said. 'What about you, Fi?'

I pulled a face, feeling slightly queasy. I was thinking hard and the day was so warm that my glasses were fogging up. I didn't know what to think. On principle, I could see their point. I sure as heck wouldn't want to be told that I had to pick up a gun and shoot strangers. I understood Luke and Barton's point of view – that no one should be forced to kill against their will – but I was worried about how such an attitude might play out in public. How could we hope to change the law?

'People might not like the law but it is there for a reason and society would just descend into anarchy without it,' I said softly.

'You would make a terrible lawyer, Fiona!' Barton said, shaking his head like a disappointed father. 'You don't become a lawyer to play by the rules. You agitate and change the rules for the better.'

'I would not make a terrible lawyer,' I responded indignantly. 'I want to help people and I think a good lawyer would advise Luke to follow the legal path of applying for an exemption on the grounds of being a conscientious objector.'

'Okay, Luke!' Barton said in a formal voice as though he was impersonating a High Court judge. 'Are you religious? A Jehovah's Witness perhaps?'

'No,' Luke said warily. 'I'm kind of between religions. I like the Hare Krishna food though ...'

'Are you studying theology at the moment?' Barton asked.

'What's that?'

'Are you an Aboriginal?'

'No.'

'Medically unfit?'

'No.'

'That pretty much rules him out for any kind of exemption, CO or other. How about a deferment of service, son? Are you married?'

That question made Luke roll around the grass, laughing.

'As if!'

'An apprentice? A university student?'

'No,' Luke conceded.

'Then your fate, dear boy, is sealed. Here, have a gun and go kill some people. Get killed. All in the name of liberty. What a joke.'

Agnes came over to me and started sprinkling a handful of picked yellow dandelions in my hair.

'Fi,' she cooed. 'Luke would make a great statement to the cause. It's hard to find someone who has their draft notice and is ready to refuse to go and willing to burn the piece of paper on camera!'

'You don't have to march if you don't want to, Fi.' Luke smiled. 'I understand your point of view as well and not everyone wants to make a loud protest. It's cool. Really.'

'Well, just don't ask me to bail you out of gaol, Luke, because I have no money!' I grumbled. 'And if you all get kicked out of uni for it, wait a few years and then if you need a good lawyer I'll be—'

'A factory-line lawyer who works for The Man,' Barton shot back.

'Get stuffed, Barton.' I glared at him. 'You might be the big man on campus but you're just a student who thinks he's more important than he really is. You want to change the world but most of all you want an audience to watch it. This is about Luke. Not you and not "the cause". It's about Luke!'

I stood up, brushed the annoying yellow flowers off my clothes and gave them all a curt nod.

'I've got to get back to study.'

'Fi!' Agnes called as I walked away.

I ignored them and headed back to the boarding house, losing myself in a jumble of thoughts. Could I pick up a gun and aim it at somebody and end their life? I thought about Luke with his shiny brown mane of hair and his deeply suntanned forearms. I imagined him in a rice paddy in Vietnam, slinking through the mud with a helmet on. Shot dead on foreign soil.

I walked the last block back to Mrs Lotte's, passing the raised, wooden Queenslander cottages with their enclosed wrap-around verandas. Moreton Bay figs dangled boomerangs of seed pods and the scent of jasmine wafted over picket fences. There was a hum of insects playing in the air around me.

Back in my coffin-like room, I turned on the fan, stripped and pulled my nightie back on, over my head. I gently retrieved the *Systir Saga* book from the top of my wardrobe, climbed into bed and proceeded to fill in my own fantasies of my mother and all the women, sisters, mothers, daughters and aunts that came before me. I read the names aloud: Anna Maria Mueller. Joanna Jonsdötter. Jeanne d'Arc. Grace O'Malley. Katherine Campbell. Isabel Campbell. Rosa Veronica Johannes. Jeanne Laisné. Isabella Boyne. Brigit Gray. Betsy Gray. Isabella Ballantine. Names and more names making patterns out and around the pages like random tree branches, some leading to the next page, others stopping abruptly. And my name last of all. Did these women change their worlds? I smiled, feeling sure that they did.

I fell asleep and my dreams were filled with women dressed in old-fashioned dresses, speaking foreign tongues, and I was a baby in a crib like that fairytale *Sleeping Beauty*. I felt they were all my fairy godmothers wishing me the best life.

I woke with wet eyelashes and the feeling of my mother's kiss on my warm forehead.

JEANNE

BEAUVAIS, FRANCE, 1472

'They will spill over the wall like hungry maggots consuming everyone in their path until they have seized the entire city,' I told my perfumed audience.

The women were soft and anxious. I stood in the middle of a room that was panelled in scrolled dark oak beneath an ornate ceiling of plasterwork. The place was dripping opulence and the seven women on the velvet sofas before me looked little more than fancy room decorations, dressed in ermine-trimmed jackets over brocaded skirts and satin-covered shoes.

'It is better that we stay here and attend your cousin,' one heavily powdered older woman said in a prim voice. 'She is badly injured and needs our attention. Let the men deal with the enemy soldiers. It isn't our place. Men fight and women tend the injured.'

I gave a sigh of exasperation and shook my head.

'You don't understand that the Burgundians will leave

all of us in the same state as Aimee upstairs if they breach the walls.' I almost cried. 'Our men are taking arrows just like that one in my cousin's side and every man down means one less of an already very small garrison. Half of them have one foot in the grave, they are so old, and cannot even muster the strength to throw the rocks or boiling oil.'

I looked pleadingly around the room.

'Anyone?' I asked. 'Is there any one of you who can see the reason in my idea? We have thousands of women running around, bumping into wagons and draping wet hides over rooves but that won't help us if the enemy clamber up their belfry and cut down the men on the battlements.'

'None of us has ever held a weapon, let alone knows how to use one.' A woman spoke up and I recognised her as Madame de Balagny. 'My husband would punish any woman who wielded a weapon. It's unseemly. Savage.'

'Then he's a fool!' I shouted angrily. 'We will be slaughtered and you want to sit here and drink rosewater and eat croissants while Beauvaisi blood is spilled. I will die fighting for my people, not here with you cowards.'

'When your betrothed hears what you are proposing, girl, he will throw you out.' The woman tutted. 'And I'll see that my husband has you in the stocks for your wild ideas.'

I laughed maniacally.

'We'll all be dead!'

I could see that some of the younger women were becoming distressed.

'Perhaps we should rally together some of the women, Madame Balagny,' a pretty brunette suggested timidly. 'Not *us* of course but some of the stronger peasant women.'

'Our peasant arms are strong and our wills are even stronger,' I growled at her. 'But we'll not risk our lives while you play parlour games. If we go and fight, you will too. When blood is spilled it all looks the same. Yours is no prettier than mine.'

I ripped aside my outer skirts and displayed my two hatchets.

'I am going to march out there and find myself an army of women and we are going to storm the battlements with whatever we can find and we will repel the invasion. Who is with me?'

I glowered at the women and caught the eye of one fair young girl wearing a soft, frilled bonnet. She was pale but her eyes were lively and intelligent.

'I'll fight beside you, Jeanne.' She nodded, crossing the room to stand beside me before addressing the others. 'For my children. For Beauvais.'

'No, Giselle!' Madame Balagny cried. 'Don't you dare!'

'We have no time to lose,' I said to the young woman. 'Come.'

It was a grey and overcast afternoon, which felt ominous after such a thick and humid morning. The city streets were oppressive. The muggy heat and dense atmosphere of smoke was trapped by the overhanging clouds. As we walked through the streets I waved a hatchet at those hurrying by. 'All of you women who are able,' I called.

'Take up arms, hammers, swords and knives and march with me. An army of women. We will repel the enemy from the battlements!'

Many gaped at me, wide-eyed with disbelief, but others nodded and stopped what they were doing and joined us, some carrying pots, others clothes irons and some with chisels and hammers. Nearly all the new recruits were serving girls and peasant women. There was no time for any of them to learn battle skills. We headed straight into the action.

A crowd of women had gathered south of the main gates. Many were yelling up to the men on the battlements, wailing like mourners as more and more men were taken out by arrows.

'The belfry is almost level with the battlements and it is well fortified and can hold many soldiers,' someone shouted.

'They are climbing it now and others have tied their ladders together to make them longer,' another woman told us as we neared. 'We have killed hundreds but the sheer numbers are overwhelming us!'

'Come on, sisters!' I called. 'All of us. Up to the wall! Follow me.'

A shout of assent went up. Some of the older women hurried away, but the younger and stronger ones rose and we began to rush up the stairs, climbing higher and higher until we stood beside the archers on the battlements, struggling to reload their crossbows fast enough to pick off the encroaching enemy soldiers.

The tops of the towers and the upper parts of the

battlements blazed with rows of torchlight, burning stakes that were continually being replaced as they were hurled down toward the belfry. Captain Balagny was reigniting a torch and turned to see a seething mass of women storming the battlements with all manner of implements in their hands. I held my hatchets by my side.

'What is this?' he demanded.

'You are outnumbered,' I yelled over the sound of battle cries from outside the city walls. 'But no longer. The call has gone out and every woman who loves her city is here to defend it.'

His eyes left mine and fell on the girl beside me.

'Giselle,' he shouted in a panic. 'Go home to your mother immediately and lock yourself in the attic. We are about to fall to the Bold. Run. Hide away.'

'No, Papa,' she said firmly as she cast off her stole and tore at the buttons on her wrists to begin folding up the sleeves of her expensive silk blouse. 'I will fight this fight because we can win it.'

'What?' he scoffed. 'You and the coward's daughter? And your motley crew of soft women? Get away from here now, girl. That is an order.'

Giselle looked at me and began to stammer something but I ignored her and addressed Captain Balagny.

'You can throw me in the stocks later,' I said. 'But right now you need us and we are here. So stand aside and let us all come up.'

I ripped off my bonnet and dropped it to the ground, letting my dark hair fall loose over my shoulders. My eyes bored into the Captain's until he looked away.

A shout went up nearby. A flash and scream of metal cut through the smoky air. Further along the stone battlements I could see that the first armed Burgundians in their blue and white uniforms had climbed the belfry and were breaching the wall. They were emerging with swords ready and engaging in hand-to-hand combat with our men. We had no time to lose. I ran to the edge and peered over. Spread out over the fields as far as I could see were the Burgundian camps. Directly below us, the men-at-arms were clambering over the scaffolding like insects, hundreds and hundreds of them lining up to begin the ascent. Further back I could see crossbowmen arrayed in formation, aiming their flaming arrows toward us. One whizzed past my head so close that I felt the breeze of it. My heart was racing and my dirt-stained face was prickling with fear.

Nearby, I saw the armoury room, tucked into a tower, and turned and ordered the women to raid it for whatever they could find.

'Grab yourselves longbows, pikes, whatever you can find and go and chop them back. Push them, burn them, slash them! They cannot get onto the battlements or we are finished!'

I could see our men wrestling with the enemy soldiers and ran with my hatchets, yelling to embolden myself and calm my fear. Men beside me were wrenching off the helmets of the enemy as they came up against the wall. Then they rained hammer blows on their heads, disorienting them. The Burgundian soldiers were pushed back, to fall screaming from the lofty scaffolding. I watched men fall away until they were as small as ants, smashing onto the stones below, some tumbling into the filthy bog of the moat. I could see that a causeway had been built across the moat, and that the belfry was strong and covered in humans, all surging upward.

I felt as if I was moving in a dream, pushing at the enemy, struggling from their grip as they tried to cling to me. I could only wield one hatchet at a time and kept the other on my hip. Many of the women were hesitant when confronted with such brutality. Giselle was standing by, watching, her hands nervously running over a hammer. I lopped off a man's hand as it reached up, taking it clean off his arm with the glove still intact. I felt bile rise in my throat as a spurt of blood splattered my tunic.

'It's no use,' one of our archers shouted back along the line. 'They are coming too fast.'

I looked back over my shoulder and gasped. Further along, near the next tower, I saw a man in a blue and white uniform with a silver helmet covering his head rolling his body up over the stone battlement wall. There was no one there to stop him. He held the Burgundian flag.

I ran, without thought or reason, toward him. I stared, horrified, as he jammed his spear into the grouting so that the flag flapped in the breeze. A roar went up from below and all along the upper reaches of the battlements. Our people seemed to freeze, all eyes falling to the planted flag, and a terrified ripple of voices began screaming that Beauvais had fallen. I ran as fast as I could and as I approached the soldier, I swung back my little axe and with all my strength I buried it in the centre of his chest. Through his narrow visor I could see the shock and surprise in his dark eyes. He stumbled backward, resting against the wall. With a grunt, I grabbed his legs and pulled as hard as I could, lifting and tumbling him over the edge with surprising ease. I leaned over the wall and watched as he fell like a pebble to the moat below, my hatchet still embedded in his chest. I wrenched the flagpole from the stone and threw it down after him, seeing it flap like a dying bird into the grey nothingness. A huge cheer came up from the women. As one we swelled with a new sense of hope.

I snatched a torch and ran to the edge of the belfry and tossed it. I gave a cheer of relief as the wood of the scaffolding caught fire and soldiers began to leap from the lower rungs and hurry away from the higher ones, back down and across the causeway.

I felt someone beside me and grinned at Giselle as she spun another torch down at the enemy. Other women were taking our lead, seizing more torches and hurling them until the belfry began to burn. A mighty and victorious cheer went up all over the battlements and I saw Captain Balagny helping a wounded woman down the steps. He caught my eye, giving me a nod. With the belfry and ladders burning below, the Burgundians had begun to retreat back to their camps. We all knew that they would rally their forces and come at us again the next day with cannons and battering rams, but the first strike against us had failed. I felt a change in the human weather of Beauvais.

'Jeanne,' I heard a voice call, and turned to see Colin running toward me. He had a deep cut on his cheek and blood on his shirt.

'You're hurt,' I cried, going to him and touching the skin near the wound.

'It's nothing.' He shook his head. 'But you! Jeanne. Everyone is talking about you. Without the rise of the women to bolster our resistance, we would have been overtaken. Spirits were sagging. But now we are triumphant! You are magnificent. They won't call you the daughter of the coward any longer. I just heard Balagny call you Jeanne Hachette! Can you believe it? Jeanne Hachette!'

I laughed. I liked the name. My smile wilted as I saw Lieutenant Jean Lagoy marching toward us, his helmet under his arm, his brow darkly furrowed. I had the feeling that he was not going to congratulate me.

BETSY

COUNTY DOWN, IRELAND, 1798

The ride was slow as we had avoided the roads and kept to the darkest shadows of the paddocks and farmlands. Once we reached Antrim, I'd been left as the lookout on the edge of town. Alone. I was becoming afraid. George and Will had been gone a long time and I was beginning to wonder if it had all gone terribly wrong and they'd been detained while trying to bust Jimmy out. The snow had melted but the hard earth was cold; sheets of frigid mist coiled about Finn McCool's strong legs as we waited in the gloom.

'Shhh, boy,' I whispered, not wanting him to whinny or stomp too loudly.

Cold and terrified, I bristled at the sudden sound of clattering hooves and shouting, coming from the corner of Milliner's Lane and Main Street. Someone was calling Jimmy's name.

'Jimmy Ballantine! Stop or I'll shoot!'

I reined in Finn McCool tightly to stop him from rearing up at the commotion. Overhead, the moon was full and just moving away from a shelf of dark cloud. A man galloped down the street on my mother's black horse while two others behind him shouted and frantically urged their horses on.

The arrival of three mounted riders told me that my brother and Will had successfully rescued Jimmy from the lock-up. If he'd been in the prison proper it might have been impossible, but they'd been informed he was only in a holding cell, awaiting an appearance at the bench the next day. The boys had gone in, confident that neck scarves tied over their faces and the threat of a musket barrel would be enough to encourage the guard to use his keys to release Jimmy from the small lock-up.

The first horseman gestured wildly, pointing down the small laneway where I was waiting. From the rear, well behind the approaching horses, I could see a man in uniformed breeches and stockinged feet running and waving his arms. His threat to shoot Jimmy appeared to be idle as he carried no weapon.

As the horses came toward me I turned my great stallion and pressed him back into the dim grey shadows down the laneway, fleeing fast from the town toward the free paddocks and the cover of the woods.

'*Déan deifur*!' Will cried into the night and I felt the wind and the rumble of horses' legs behind me but did not turn to look back until we were well clear of the houses.

As the landscape opened up and above us a mosaic of stars twinkled in the wide-open night sky, my heart settled and slowed, along with my breathing.

'Whoa.' I recognised George's voice and we all slowed to a canter, then a trot.

All four of us were out of breath almost to the point of being winded. George and Will peeled off their dark face-scarves and shook out their damp hair.

'I can't believe it.' Jimmy panted, laughing at the same time. 'You mad bastards! You risked your very lives for me.'

'It was more for my sister Brigit, if truth be told.' George laughed back. 'Can't let you hang and leave my sister without a provider.'

We kept to the dark paths over the patchwork of farmland. The redcoats would be raising the alarm that a prisoner had escaped and while it was unlikely they'd come riding down to Gransha immediately, it was still safer to press home hard and get Brigit and her family well away.

'The guard thought we were United Irishmen from the Antrim local chapter,' Will told me as he pulled his black horse alongside me. 'They'll be asking questions around Antrim all night but Patrick Lonigan has the boat at the ready down at Bangor. If we can get your sister and her family there before dawn, they'll find safe passage to Cairnryan in Scotland and then they can make their way to Paisley.'

At home my father was up and furious. He had heard the horses leave and had gotten dressed and interrogated Brigit for hours. She had given him the bare bones of our story. He was waiting in the parlour.

'I cannot believe you've done this thing!' he roared at George. 'And you, Will, letting Betsy go along for the ride and endangering her life? What sort of husband will you prove to be? A dead one if they find out it was you behind this.'

And then he turned his wrath on Jimmy.

'My daughters have some wicked bad taste in husbands! Jimmy Ballantine! A rebel! A Catholic! And now an escaped criminal, wanted by the Crown!'

'He is family,' George said quietly. 'We did this, not for any great political cause, but for Brigit. And little Isabella.'

'Oh Lord.' Da raged as he paced about the room, his face beet-red. 'We'll be hanged, the lot of us.'

'They've no reason to believe it is us,' George explained calmly. 'As far as many people know, you are estranged from the Ballantine family on account of the Catholicism and ...'

'You're not sympathisers, are you, boys?' Da frowned at Will and George, pointing at them. 'You're not running with the rebels?'

'Of course not!' George lied. 'Not at all, Father.'

I thought he oversold it too much. There was a hint of melodrama in his voice. My father did not look convinced.

Brigit had already packed a satchel of clothes for the trip.

'Ma's clothes are a little big but I'll eat lots of haggis in Scotland and fill them out.' She laughed as I helped her get ready for the long ride. 'Thank you, Betsy, for bringing Jimmy home to me. I love him so.'

I hugged her tightly and we stayed like that, warm body against warm body, for some minutes.

'It was the boys that took the most risk,' I told her. 'I was just a lookout and no one came to stop us, so I did naught much at all but freeze my nose off.'

'I've scratched Isabella's name in the sister book.' Brigit smiled and patted my hand. 'I know Mammy was watching over you tonight. I just hope she keeps smiling on us from heaven. The book is back in the trunk. Take care of it. I looked through the other trunk and there was some jewellery. I took half to sell in Scotland to help Jimmy and me get on our feet again. The other half is on the dresser for you. There are some nice pieces. Perhaps you can wear them at your wedding. I will be sad to miss it.'

I went into my room and took the rest of my mother's jewellery and the strange old book, wrapped them in a pillowcase, and took them back to my sister.

'There is more stability and safety in Scotland,' I told her. 'Here, Ireland is perched on the edge of a major rebellion and I think the book is safer in your hands. Bring it back when you come home. I'm in no rush to provide Will with daughters and I want you to have all Mammy's jewellery. She would want you to use it to keep safe and well and you will need it more than me. Just save her wedding ring. The rest is decoration.'

My sister began to cry, nodding.

'Thank you, little sister.' She sniffed as she dug into the pillowcase until she found our mother's gold wedding band.

'You wear this,' she said, handing it to me. 'Mammy may not have beaten her sickness but she fought it bravely. The English are our sickness and you should wear it to remind you of Mammy and her courage.'

I slipped the ring onto the fourth finger of my right hand. I would not wear it as a wedding band but as a reminder ring. It would remind me of the strong, passionate, fiery blood that ran in the veins of my women.

'Be safe,' Brigit whispered as she kissed me. She tied her baby to her chest as we slipped out to the horses.

Through the cold night we rode, down the small back lanes, all the way to the ferry dock in Bangor. My cheeks stung from the cold, and my clothes smelled like sleet and the bog smoke that filled the cold night air, churning out in light-grey plumes from the chimneys. Baby Isabella was strapped to her mother's chest to keep her warm but we rode slowly so as not to disturb the little girl. We kept our horses to a quiet pace when passing houses and inns and gathered more speed when traversing empty pastoral estates.

Down on the water it was colder still and the sea breeze was bitter. The smell of brine and fish slopped through the night. We saw a lantern swinging from the deck of Patrick Lonigan's boat. It was a big, seafaring vessel and he ran it from Irish to Scottish shores regularly. He was one of the rebel messengers who secretly trafficked news between the United Irishmen and the French fleets that were promising to send us reinforcements of artillery and men once the revolution was called. He was a good man and that night, praise be, he was sober and ready to sail.

I helped Brigit onto the boat and kissed both her cheeks and those little cherubic ones on her baby's face. The little girl smelled like soap and milk.

'I'm so very glad I made amends with Da and that you and I have come so close these last weeks, Betsy,' my sister told me, holding my hand tight. 'Stay safe and keep your head low when the rebellion breaks. And send word if you hear more of what became of Annie O'Neal. That worries me.'

My heart was heavy with the memories of that day, too. Annie O'Neal was still missing. No one had heard or seen a thing of her. It was as if she had just vanished into thin air. We all knew those three redcoats had been responsible for whatever had befallen the poor woman. To keep Jack O'Neal afloat we tried to convince him that the arrival of the redcoats had simply forced Annie to flee and that she was probably lying low with some distant relatives and would send word when she could. Jack clung to that story because to think otherwise would destroy him. Will told me many times that I should shake off the guilt because I could not have known they had ill-intent.

George came across and wrapped both of us in a big bear hug.

'This business will be forgotten within months, sister,' he said gently. 'You tell Jimmy to grow a beard, adopt a Scottish brogue and come back calling himself some foreign name. Or we'll come visit you in Paisley in the summer. Send word by mail when you are settled.'

We watched as the lights of the boat grew fainter and fainter until they were extinguished like the dying flame of a candlewick, disappearing on the purple horizon. The morning star winked down from the sky, which was streaked with shafts of grey. George, Will and I rode slowly back to Gransha as the sun crept out for the day, bathing everything in a tangerine glow. I was sad to farewell my sister and my little niece, but I was happy that we had been able to give her a new start.

As we came to the gates of our farm, we pulled up our mounts and I felt my heart give a lurching thud. Two well-dressed horses were tied up near the potting shed down the end of our long gravel path.

'Will,' George said quickly. 'Take the spare horses and rein them out the back of your place. If we pull in here with them, it will be clear what business we have indulged in. We will get them some time later from you. Best to be safe.'

'What will we tell them when they ask where we have been?' I asked George, more than a little worried that we were about to be found out and punished accordingly. 'We don't know what Da has told them.'

I did not recognise the horses. George looked as terrified as I felt. Will carefully took the reins of the riderless beasts and hurried them back down the road toward his family's farm.

'Take good care,' he called softly. '*Ádh mór.*'

'Tell them we were partying at cousin Mary's,' George said flatly. 'I know that Da is smart enough to tell them nothing at all so that our stories don't clash. He'll say he doesn't know where we are and that he doesn't know when we left. I just hope Mary's husband will not betray us. He's riding with the Monaghan Men, but he's family and blood *is* thicker than water. He's no Englishman.'

I did not like to point out that Connor Kelly was only kin by marriage. He had not a drop of Gray blood in his veins. But his baby, George, did, and I hoped that would count for something if and when the time came to use him as an alibi.

What confronted us inside made my innards constrict and knot. My father was tied to a chair and his face was covered in blood. I could see that his lip was split and swollen, and one eye was completely shut and as purple and round as a ripe plum.

'What the devil?' George shouted.

'Aha.' One of the two soldiers looked at us. Both were slick with sweat and their cheeks were flushed. 'Here they are now. Your father was just telling us that he had no idea where you two rascals were.'

'Da,' I said, rushing to his side and dropping to my knees, crying. 'What have they done to you? This is all my fault.'

One soldier stepped closer to me and I felt his hot form standing almost on top of me.

'And how might this be your fault, Missy? Have you been gallivanting about with your sister?'

'My sister? I beg your pardon, sir?' I asked, standing to face him.

'We had word your sister was staying here with you in Gransha,' he said gruffly.

I shut my eyes and swallowed hard. So Connor had told them that much but how much more? I decided to take a leap and make up a new story that did not rely on Connor Kelly's familial loyalty; I doubted he could be trusted. I girded myself, looked at the soldier and lied though my teeth. I was getting quite good at it.

'Is my sister not here? I left her asleep in my room,' I said, feigning surprise.

'No, she is not, and her husband, Jimmy Ballantine, is gone. Busted out of the lock-up by two unknown men.'

I put my hands to my face and shook my head.

'Oh my!' I whispered. 'It cannot be. Two men, you say?'

The soldiers cast a look between themselves and then back at George.

'Where have you been, son?' one asked.

I interrupted and answered for both of us.

'I'm most embarrassed, sir,' I said, dropping my eyes to the thick carpet below. 'I had crept out my window to meet up with my beau and my brother came after me to haul me home.'

One soldier sniggered.

'A typical wanton Irish lass!' He laughed.

'I'll have you know,' George said stiffly, 'that my father and I have trouble containing Betsy's wild spirit sometimes but she will be locked up good and proper from now on. She'll be married off in summer, and not a moment too soon. It's a danger, Betsy, don't you know, to be out on the roads at night!'

'And you've not seen your sister or Ballantine? Not at all this early morn?' the taller man asked, still looking unconvinced.

'No,' I replied. 'Oh goodness! I hope no harm has come to Brigit. She was only staying with us because she was afraid the charges against her husband might be true. Imagine! Being married to a rebel and her not even knowing it. Perhaps he came by and stole her away, kidnapped her.

We should check all the roads for her.' I was putting on a theatrical performance worthy of the greatest actors who had ever wandered the boards of a stage. George looked uncomfortable and I guessed he thought I might have been overplaying my role.

'Well,' one said, untying my father who drooped down over his knees with relief or pain or a combination of both. 'See you inform the nearest barracks if you see or hear a single word from the fugitives. Your sister is on a wanted list as well. See that you don't join her!'

'Was it really necessary for you to manhandle my father this way?' George grumbled as he helped my father across to the long settee.

'He fell and we were simply helping him to stay upright.' A soldier laughed. 'Maybe too much Irish whisky. It's just gone sun up after all! Don't you savages stir whisky into your porridge for breakfast?'

Both left, full of mirth, while George and I tended to our father.

'Are you all right, Da?' I sobbed.

'I'll live.' He moaned and then whispered, 'Did Brigit get away safely?'

I nodded, wary that there might still be English ears at the door.

'She is safe.' I smiled and held his hand gently, trying not to grimace at his broken face. 'Oh, that I could say the same for the rest of us.'

A bitterness rose up in me like gall. I hated the English invaders more than I ever had before.

FIONA

Darling Downs, Australia, 1968

I didn't realise how much I missed home until I saw the old FJ Holden parked in the bus stop carpark in Toowoomba with my dad leaning up against it, a pipe hanging out the side of his mouth and his unmistakeable halo of springy ginger hair that seemed charged with voltage.

Dad gave me a once over. I wasn't sure if he approved or not. I was wearing a floral cotton dress and a pair of brown leather sandals. I had a new, short haircut. He grinned and wrapped me up in a bear hug, lifting me off the ground.

I looked at myself in the side-mirror of the front passenger seat and noted that I looked older than I had when Dad had driven me to Brisbane three months earlier. I wondered if he thought so too.

The Holden rattled and throbbed along the red-dirt road. Outside, the clouds folded down over the undulating yellow fields and I inhaled the cool air rushing through the open window. I smelled dust and dirt and that familiar mix of animal dung and fertiliser. The road ahead quivered.

'You look different.' Dad smiled across at me. 'Older.'

So it wasn't just me. I felt kind of pleased that he had noticed.

'You've chopped off your hair.'

'Well, I had a haircut.' I laughed. 'I wouldn't use the word "chopped" myself.'

We drifted into an easy silence and I stared out the window and continued drinking in the familiar landscape.

It was almost lunchtime. The bus ride up the Range had been slow and steep. Out over the western hills, the sky was filling with braided clouds heralding rain. I could smell it, like metal in the back of my mouth.

Our farm, Tobermory, bearing that name on account of the small town in Scotland where my dad was born, was exactly five-and-a-half miles north of downtown Bandaroo Flats. There, we raised two hundred head of Black Angus cattle on seven hundred and eighty acres of land.

As we bounced over the cattle grids and headed through the wide gates, I was surprised to find that it was nice to be home. Agnes asked me all the time if I missed the farm and I always screamed *noooo* in response. But I did.

Instead of taking the car around the back to the garages, Dad pulled up at the front steps of the rambling colonial homestead as if I were royalty and needed to be dropped at the entrance. He leapt out and opened my door, grinning, bowing low. I laughed and slapped him on the back as I got out. A fat splodge of rain landed on my forearm.

'It's going to be heavy,' Dad called as he bounded up the steps with my bulging port to open the squealing screen door.

I gave a little yelp of joy as Oscar, our black labrador, came loping down the front steps to greet me. Falling to one knee, I rustled his fur and let him slobber all over me. His tail was wagging and he was as excited as a puppy, even though he was eighty-four in dog years.

'Settle down, Oscar.' I laughed and smiled up at Dad, who was holding the screen door open so I could go in ahead of him.

The central hallway that cut through the middle of the house was dark and cool, and I could smell meat cooking from the kitchen. I looked in at my old room. It was exactly how I left it, which was comforting.

I was excited to see my brother, Murray, so I hurried down toward the huge kitchen at the back of the house. As I walked into the dining room I stopped, mouth open, hands going comically to my cheeks. Grandma and Grandpa were sitting at the table with Murray and Uncle Jack, with my terrible twin cousins beside them, all dressed in their Sunday best. My grandparents had come all the way from Scotland. I hadn't seen them for years, not since I was little!

'Surprise,' they all yelled.

'Okay!' I squealed. 'You got me! I'm surprised!'

I wondered where Laura was. It was unusual for her not to be there; she and my brother were inseparable. Aunty Jan came in from the kitchen wearing a frilled apron.

The family all stood up and came shuffling over to me,

jostling for a hug. Grandma smelled like musky talcum powder and Grandpa smelled like the Brylcreem he lathered through his snow-white hair to stop it falling over his craggy old face.

'You look taller and skinnier,' Murray said, with a lopsided grin. 'You're wasting away. Might have to start calling you Bones.'

'I've missed you, Fi.' Jan smiled. 'No one to run across the fields and pinch the scones off my kitchen window sills and tell me stories over ginger ale.'

'I've missed you too.' I smiled back at her. 'And those scones!'

The men cracked the tops off their bottles of beer and Aunty Jan poured herself a tipple of her usual brandy and dry. Grandma frowned sternly at them all as she was a staunch teetotaller. I sat down at my regular place, poured a glass of lemonade and geared up, ready for Grandad's loud stories. Aunty Jan rolled her eyes and I could tell she was thinking the same thing.

Dad stood up and whistled for everyone to shut up.

'Now, now!' he said in his booming dad voice. 'We're here to welcome Fiona home after her first term of university, but we're also here to share some other family news.'

I raised my eyebrows, intrigued.

Dad gave a nod to Murray who was sitting at the table opposite me and my tall brother stood up, looking pleased as punch, with a stupid, big smile plastered across his suntanned face. He's going to ask Laura to marry him, I thought, imagining that she would suddenly appear, sporting a fancy engagement ring.

'I've been called up to serve my country!' he announced as if he had won the bumper meat tray at the pub. 'Got my draft notice a week ago.'

I felt sick. Dad was beaming beside him, banging Murray on the back. Grandpa roared as if he'd backed a winner at the races. Grandma raised her eyebrows, crinkling her forehead into a web of wrinkles. I looked at Aunty Jan and she had a smile painted on her face, but her eyes bore into mine and I could see exactly what she was feeling. Maybe it was a woman thing, a nurturing thing, but the idea of a young man going to war just summoned images of blood and death for me. For Murray and Dad and Grandpa it seemed they were just like small boys thinking about the 'heroics' of it all.

The twins, two milky-faced ten-year old boys, cheered. 'You can shoot up them Commies!' One of them, Billy or Bobby, I'm not sure which, laughed and followed the comment with a short, sharp clatter of noise that sounded like gunfire.

'You know you can get out of going if you take it to court,' I said, quite seriously. 'You can claim a conscientious objection if—'

'My son's not a coward!' Dad said down the table, his face darkening. 'Murray will proudly serve this nation.'

'Well, America,' I muttered, a little sarcastically.

'Yes, Fiona, our allies!' Dad snapped.

I shrugged and spoke into my chest. 'It's a bit different from the big wars, is all.'

'You do your old grampy proud, lad.' Grandad smiled. 'I served the Crown in the Great War.'

'Will you serve in Vietnam then, Murray?' Grandma asked in her thick accent. I could barely understand her.

'Don't know,' Murray said, sitting down as Dad headed to the fridge for beer. 'I have to pass the physical first before they'll sign me up and then it might be home service or Vietnam. I hope I get to see some action.'

'Murray. Action means killing or being killed,' I piped up. 'Don't glorify it. War's pretty serious stuff. I hope you get stuck behind a desk or something safe like that.'

Murray looked at me, confused.

'It's more honourable to go and actually do something and make a difference on the ground on the frontline. They need all the manpower they can get. I don't want a posting on Australian soil. Not even in New Guinea. I want to get into those jungles and fight the Viet Cong!'

'Just a question,' I said. 'If you wanted to fight, Murray, why didn't you enlist? Why wait for the draft?'

All eyes fell on me.

'Murray's been helping out on the farm,' Dad said, coming back to the table. 'It's all getting a bit much for me these days with my arthritis. We talked about it, didn't we, son?'

'Yeah, Fi.' Murray explained to me, 'We decided that I'd stay here, working, and if my birthday got called up, well then, I'd front up and if not, then I'd keep on working the farm. But I got called up so I'm going.'

'Only if you pass the physical and the other tests,' Aunty Jan said softly.

'Look at him.' Dad guffawed. 'You couldn't find a fitter specimen of a young man.'

'Fit as a fiddle.' Murray grinned, flexing his bicep muscle to prove it. 'If Walter Leary can get in, I can get in.'

Everyone fell into an uncomfortable silence. That was the one name that was never mentioned. Dad began fiddling with a stray thread on the tablecloth.

'And you can eat seven-and-a-half pies too,' I said under my breath.

Murray shot me a look and a frown and for a moment he looked small and vulnerable and I couldn't understand why.

'I'm just saying, Dad,' I looked at my father, 'that there are valid questions to be asked about both our involvement in the Vietnam conflict and the issues around conscription in this country. There's a lot of adversity about both. I'm just saying it needs to be looked at from all sides of the argument.'

'I can't believe this clap-trap rubbish coming out of my own daughter's mouth!' Dad slammed a fist on the table. 'Cowardly yellow-belly nonsense. Is this what you're learning at university?'

'Oh Dad, honestly.' I sighed and rolled my eyes. 'There are a million different points of view in the world outside of Bandaroo Flats. I'm out there in the real world, not this fishbowl and—'

'We need America and that's what friends do when an ally is in trouble. We stand beside them. You know that whole speech by Kennedy. Ask not what your country can do for you, but what you can do for your country or whatever it was.' My father's voice was passionate. 'My boy is doing something for his country and I am very proud of him.'

'Australians need to not just lazily tow the party line. Harold Holt said as much and he—'

'He got eaten by a shark,' one twin giggled.

I ignored this and kept talking.

'I don't want to get into a war around the table.' I sighed. 'It just feels a whole lot more real and dangerous when my brother is going. I don't want him to get hurt. I don't like the idea of Murray being involved in all that death and violence if it's not necessary.'

Dad downed his beer in a gulp. He was glaring at me from beneath his bushy eyebrows.

'Well, I don't want to argue either, love. Murray's been called up and it is what it is,' he said, and gave Murray a nod. 'Serving your country is an honour, Fiona.'

'Yes,' I sighed. 'I guess so.'

'Let's just have a lovely lunch and not talk politics,' Aunty Jan said, standing up and going to the kitchen. 'You can come and help me, Fiona.'

I grabbed the opportunity to leave the table without hesitation.

'Don't get those blokes riled up,' she said as she slipped on two stained oven-gloves. 'There's no way you're going to ever change their minds. They're as stubborn as mules.'

'But Aunty Jan,' I said gently, 'Mum's only been gone ... well ... not quite six years. Dad and I couldn't cope if anything happened to Murray. You wouldn't want your boys going off to war, would you?'

'They're ten.' She half-laughed.

'You know what I mean,' I said, stirring the bubbling peas. 'I've got a friend who is objecting to his draft notice. Another friend who is doing law is—'

'It's no use, Fi.' Aunty Jan looked at me, her eyes sad. 'Murray wants to go. Your Dad and Grandad are egging him on. We have to hope and pray that he comes home safely at the end of it. We're not special. We're not the only family having to make this sacrifice, to bear this cross.'

Silently we carved the roast beef, laid out the potatoes and pumpkin, buttered the peas and carrots, and made the gravy. The radio was murmuring in the background. Outside the rain had started beating down against the tin roof.

'Just don't mention it again in front of the men, okay love?' Aunty Jan whispered as we began to take the food to the table.

I kept my head down and ate my lunch without making too much eye contact with anyone. My reaction to Murray's news had surprised me. Now it felt real. It felt a whole lot different when it was affecting my own family, more so than the idea of Luke going. I felt a desperate need to stop my older brother, to chain myself or him to the house and scream and yell and make it all go away. We were a Catholic family and I wondered if I could talk Murray into arguing that he was against the very idea of war on the grounds of his faith. But as I listened to the men talk about battles past and the thrill of being on a frontline, fighting for your country, I began losing my appetite for the food and for the idea of conscription. I felt small and useless in the face of their military enthusiasm.

'So I got good marks for all my subjects.' I smiled, trying to change the subject.

'Good for you,' Grandma said in her gravelly Glaswegian voice. 'You got brains in your head, might as well use them.'

'Found yourself a doctor or lawyer to marry yet?' Dad asked with his mouth full. His wink told me that he was teasing.

'Haha, Dad.' I laughed. 'Very funny. I have no intention of getting married for at least ten years.'

'That's leaving it a bit late.' Aunty Jan smiled. 'You'll end up on the shelf if you're not careful.'

'Speaking of marriage,' I looked at my brother, trying not to imagine a bullet ripping through his temple, 'what's happening with Laura? Why isn't she here? I've missed her. She hasn't written for ages. I thought she would be here to see me too. What does she think of your call up?'

'Oh.' Murray shrugged uncomfortably and I felt the atmosphere turn arctic. 'We're off. To be honest, Laura got engaged to someone else ... Walter Leary ... just before he was shipped off to Nam.'

I nearly dropped my cutlery and tried to swallow that huge chunk of news. Laura and Walter? I suddenly felt dizzy. Laura had been my best friend since we were six. Murray and she had been dating seriously for years. I felt lost. Everything at home was changing and it was hard to keep up. How could Laura have dumped my brother for that horrible Leary boy?

'Oh God.' I wiped my lips on the starched napkin. 'Oh God, Murray, I'm sorry.'

He shrugged but couldn't look at me.

'Girls can't resist a bloke in a uniform and she accepted his proposal three nights before he left town. And then there's all the Leary money.'

Surely Laura wasn't so mercenary.

'There'll be plenty more pretty girls who like a man in uniform.' Grandad winked at Murray. 'Those Vietnamese gals are very pleasing on the eye.'

I shuddered at Grandad's comment. How had my homecoming lunch deteriorated into such a mess?

A week later I was digging a ditch near the fence by the dam when a police car rattled over the cattle grid. I looked up to see Constable Duggan behind the wheel. He'd been the local copper in Bandaroo Flats since I was a kid. Watching him pull in outside the house brought back a rush of terrible memories and I felt my legs go to jelly. I remembered the day he came to tell us about Mum's accident.

Something was going on so I walked to the back steps, wiping my hands on my jeans, and saw Dad flap out noisily through the flyscreen.

I went inside and saw Murray in the kitchen, standing at the open fridge, eating a bowl of leftover bread-and-butter pudding.

'Copper Duggan is out front,' I said, and Murray looked at me spooked.

'Don't know why,' he wondered. 'I haven't done anything wrong.'

'Funny that's your first concern.' I laughed and threw a tea towel at him.

'Have you studied any criminal law yet?' Murray asked mischievously. 'Murder trials. Anything really interesting?'

'Not really.' I grimaced. 'Most of it is pretty boring but first year subjects are more of an introductory and grounding. Brisbane's pretty cool though … well, not cool like in heat because it's very hot, but I've made some nice friends and—'

'Any good-looking ones?'

'Well, now that you mention it …'

Dad walked into the kitchen and the slump of his shoulders silenced us.

'That was Constable Duggan,' he said flatly, like all his energy had gone out of him.

'And?' I asked, sensing the seriousness of the visit.

'Walter Leary's been killed during a training exercise. His own gun went off … and there you have it. Duggan's letting everyone in town know so we can pay our respects to the family.'

I froze with the shock. The name Walter Leary had been a raw wound in our family for years.

'Oh God.' Murray coughed. 'Really? Oh my God. His own gun. So he wasn't in Nam, Dad?'

'No, son,' our father said, shaking his head. 'In Brisbane at the barracks.'

Walter Leary was dead. It just didn't seem real.

'I need to go to Laura,' Murray said, putting the empty bowl in the sink. 'She'll be distraught. Fiona? You coming?'

He looked at me. I was still dealing with the betrayal I'd felt that my best friend had hooked up with *that* boy and I hadn't seen her once since I'd been back. I didn't know if I could see her or offer the condolences that she needed. I didn't think I could be properly sincere.

'No.' I shook my head. 'No. I can't.'

And I went to my bedroom, walking quietly past my brother and father. I lay down on my old childhood bed where I had shed so many, many tears over the past six years. And it surprised me that some of the shock and grief I now felt was for Walter Leary and his family.

JEANNE

BEAUVAIS, FRANCE, 1472

'You can be sure that Charles the Bold has sworn an oath to his men that he will not end his siege until he has planted his banner on the walls of Beauvais!'

Madame Balagny was the sort of woman who held her chin high so that she might look down her long slender nose at people. Her hair was plaited and coiled in tiers on her head, giving her extra height, making herself appear taller than she was.

'You may have tossed one flag away, Mademoiselle Laisné,' she huffed, 'but you were simply lucky. I hear they have blasted a hole in the Bresle Gate and it is a burning inferno. The city folk are keeping it ablaze so that no man can breach it without incinerating himself but they will be inside within days. We four women are to leave for safety at nightfall. My husband has ordered it. The guard outside will accompany us.'

'But my cousin still ails,' I stammered. 'She is not fit for travel. Her burns are very severe and—'

'The girl is a peasant,' Madame Balagny said, pulling an ugly face. 'No. You, my daughter, myself and Liesel the maid to attend us. Not your lowly cousin.'

'Her mother was high-born and the daughter of a merchant and—' I began.

'No.' Madame Balagny spat the word at me. 'It is a kindness enough that the Captain has allowed you to come along when you are not yet married to the Lieutenant.'

'And my father? I cannot leave him behind to face the enemy. He can barely walk.'

Madame Balagny laughed and threw a look at her daughter, Giselle, who was sitting on a divan looking deflated and slightly bruised and battered, both from fighting on the city walls and the severe dressing down she had been given by Jean Lagoy and her imperious mother.

'The cheek of you,' the older woman said to me. 'To imagine that we owe you and your entire family safe passage … it's shameful. After your wilful escapade yesterday, I am amazed that the Lieutenant wants anything to do with you. I would have had you in the pillory for a week. It seems a suitable justice that Matthew the Coward should be left to face his fate alone, abandoning his wife and child as he did. Shameful. Shameful.'

'We can't leave the injured girl upstairs, Mother,' Giselle pleaded. 'She needs her wounds cleaned and dressed twice a day, although she is strong and healing well.'

I watched as the Captain's wife thought about that and nodded.

'Very well.' She sighed and turned to me. 'You can take two horses from the stable out the back.' Madame Balagny frowned at her daughter. 'Giselle, take Jeanne out and choose two horses for her. Then you, Jeanne, can take your cousin on one, while riding another, to the medics in the marketplace. Leave her there and return immediately. My husband will be enraged if he learns that you have borrowed the horses.'

'I can ride with her,' Giselle offered but her mother put up a hand.

'You will do no such thing,' she snapped. 'You have already been led astray by this unruly peasant and you could have been killed.'

'Mama,' Giselle replied boldly. 'If it hadn't been for Jeanne and the women she rallied to fight against the enemy we might *all* have been killed.'

I curtseyed to the woman, trying to contain my smirk. Giselle and I went to ready poor Aimee for the treacherous journey across town.

'We will leave tonight,' Giselle told me. 'Out through the tunnels that lead to pockets of thickets and then toward Paris. I am so glad you are coming with us, Jeanne. We will be safe. I like you so much. You are so different from the other women here.'

'While our sisters, the peasants and the farmers' wives are all out fighting alongside the men, braving the burning arrows and cannon balls?' I said angrily. 'I don't want to go!'

'If you don't go, then I won't either,' Giselle said, squeezing my hand.

Outside I could hear the continuing sound of exploding gunpowder and the thud of cannon fire that reverberated up from the floor, rattling the doors in the manor house. The smell of smoke and sulphur and dust sat in the back of my throat and my eyes constantly watered.

'The streets are full of people running to help keep the fire burning at the Bresle Gate and others are busy brick-laying and cementing rocks and stone into cracks and breaches in the city walls,' the guard told us as he helped put Aimee over the horse, his voice high with panic. 'It's a nightmare out there, Mademoiselles. The clergy are running ragged, tending to injured men, women and children. I tell you, every man or woman too old or frail to raise a pitchfork is on digging duty for the dead.'

'How do you fare, Aimee?' I asked and helped her lean down over the horse's neck while I took the reins.

'I am in awful pain but rallying,' she groaned. 'If I can get to the Cathedral, I will rest and have Mama to care for me. I will be all right. The wound is not too deep but the burns are raw.'

'Look out for my Papa, please,' I asked her as the horses moved slowly away from the Captain's yard. Our mounts were two tall, spectacular, matching grey-speckled horses, with neatly plaited manes and silken silver muzzles. The saddle was of the very best leather and as comfortable as an armchair. I turned and waved goodbye to Giselle.

The guard was right. The stench in the streets made me gag. Mingled with the smell of baking hides was the waste that was accumulating in gutters. And above all – the chaotic stink of choking smoke and gunpowder, dung and dirt – was the smell of death. It hung in the spaces between tightly wedged houses and between the rails of the fence posts. It wafted up over the high walls and burrowed into the dank spaces between shadows. Death hung like a storm cloud over Beauvais. I wondered how many more souls would make their final journey during this terrible conflict.

Aimee groaned beside me.

'Slower please, Jeanne,' she whispered.

We had tied her to the horse so that she would not fall and wrapped her legs and torso in a thick protective wadding of linen to reduce her pain and discomfort. I led her horse alongside mine, neck to neck. Most of the houses were empty. Gaping windows looked into dim rooms, evacuated and abandoned.

In the marketplace, tents and lean-tos were strung up to keep the sun from burning the wounded, as the nuns and doctors tended to the injured. The undertaker and gravediggers worked tirelessly in the stifling heat.

I found an old nun with a face covered in a labyrinth of wrinkles. She looked tired but kind.

'Please,' I begged her. 'Can you care for my cousin, Sister? She took an arrow in the side. She is badly burned and feverish. She is lucid and will live but she needs care. Here is a bundle of aloe to help with her burns.'

She nodded with pursed lips.

With some difficulty, I lifted Aimee from her horse and laid her on an empty stretcher. She winced with pain.

'Thank you, Jeanne,' she whispered, her eyes dilated with the pain. 'Go to Colin and flee. I will get stronger and care for your father. Love is everything.'

I left her in the nun's good hands and hurried to take the horses back to the manor house. The sky was darkening with smoke and an enormous boom shuddered through the streets. A wall must have taken the full force of a cannon ball. People everywhere began screaming and running in all directions like chickens. The horse I was leading spooked and reared up. I almost lost my grip but held tight, calling for him to settle. Although still early in the day, it seemed like dusk.

'*Calmez-vous. Calmez-vous.*' We had started heading back to the fancy quarter of the city when I caught sight of Jean Lagoy speaking with Colin down a side alley. I bristled and pulled up the horses, urging them into the small laneway between the inn and the cobbler. From there I could see the two men but they could not see me. I felt faint. What business was transpiring between my hated betrothed and Colin? Lagoy was looking around furtively as he handed a pouch to Colin, who quickly stuffed it into his shirt, also casting a nervous eye up and down the street. I watched as the tall Lieutenant put his helmet back on and disappeared around the corner to Gateway Road, which led toward the Bresle Gate. I pushed out of the shadows and clattered up behind Colin as he ran ahead.

'Colin,' I hissed.

I halted my horse and Colin turned, his face washed in guilt and surprise.

'What is going on?' I demanded, my mind racing over a hundred possibilities. 'Is that brute paying you to keep away from me?'

Colin's eyes skittered about and he looked afraid.

'No,' he said and took the reins of the horses, leading us further along the cobbled road and down the carriageway between two houses. 'You need to go, Jeanne. I've been given an important mission and it's dangerous. If Lagoy sees us together ... he's made some serious threats.'

'Lagoy gave you a mission? What mission?' I asked.

'I'm going out through the tunnels that lead to the woods by the edge of the river to spy on the enemy and to try to buy some of their Italian mercenaries. They are masters of gunpowder and have weapons we have never even heard of.'

'The Italians?' I asked, confused.

'The Burgundian army is so powerful because it pays mercenaries to boost its ranks. Some of the artillery men are from Italy and they'll fight for the highest bidder.' Colin held up the pouch that Lagoy had given him and shook it. It jangled with coins. 'Lagoy has a good load of silver for them if I can tempt them to come back with me to fight for us. With their help, we can keep up our defence.'

I tried to unravel his words from the jumbled and knotted ball he had presented to me into something understandable. My words came out as slowly as my unfolding thoughts.

'Why you?' I said, shaking my head. 'Lagoy has so many trained men and it is such a treacherous mission to go into enemy territory, unarmed and ...' And then it all began to make sense to me. Jean Lagoy was sending Colin Pilon on what could only be described as a death mission. He didn't care two jots for the Italian mercenaries. What he wanted most was Colin Pilon out of the way. No person, no citizen or serf of Beauvais could refuse such a mission during active military engagement. To do so would be tantamount to treason and punishable by death.

'You are being sent to your doom!' I cried. 'You cannot go, Colin.'

'I must, Jeanne,' he said, pleadingly. 'Get yourself to safety. I hear you are being evacuated south. Go. This is my burden but I am up to the task.'

'But Colin,' I said, my voice breaking. 'You can't do this.'

'I can and I will,' he said firmly. 'The Italians are camped not far from the old tunnels, beyond the brook that runs down past the quarry and the oak forest. I can lure them back here by offering them more money. This silver is just a small deposit. Lagoy will organise a payment from the King if they agree to fight alongside us.'

Colin was about to take a pouch of silver and head into enemy territory. It was like sending a hare into a huge den of foxes.

'We will see each other again,' he said and handed up the reins to me, then broke into a run down the street. He turned, calling loudly, 'I will bring back some soldiers. I will be a hero. Just like you were yesterday, Jeanne. Be safe.'

I watched him disappear around the corner and I felt numb. I was torn between following him and turning back to the manor house. My heart was leaden and I could not think properly. I needed to formulate a plan. Colin was in dreadful danger; Lagoy was a ruthless soldier.

Listening to the sound of cannon fire and muskets, I tried to come up with some kind of strategy, some way to make this wrong right. Arrows whizzed through the air like giant insects. It seemed as if Beauvais had descended into Hades and was being consumed by fire and brimstone. We were all doomed. I thought of the plight of my cousin Aimee and my father who was frail and defenceless. If Beauvais fell there would be nothing I could do to help them.

And then I was hit with a very tempting thought.

I had two good, strong horses. Colin had a pouch full of silver. I knew the tunnel exit well. It was wide and empty, built as an aqueduct by the Romans hundreds, perhaps thousands, of years earlier but long abandoned. It was only used for grain storage during the winter months. If I could manage to get in there unseen by Lagoy or his men I could collect Colin and we could escape from the city and make our way to some distant port. With enough money to fund a ship fare to England, we could start again, marry and live out our lives far from Lagoy and Charles the Bold and Beauvais. My imagination was sparking with dazzling and dangerous new possibilities. I knew now that Lagoy wanted Colin dead. Even if I married the Lieutenant quietly and obediently, Colin was a marked man and would never be safe. I was torn by loyalty to my father or to Colin.

I sat upon the restless horse, deliberating, unsure of what to do. I wasn't a bad person. I knew that to take the horses out of the city walls would open me up to a charge of horse theft. I might be considered a deserter or guilty of treason by leaving Beauvais. We could never return and I would never see Papa again. But he was old and not for this life for much longer and I had my whole life ahead of me. I knew that Papa would want me to take this golden opportunity. I shut my eyes and thought of Lieutenant Jean Lagoy and I knew that marriage to him would kill me – not necessarily in body, but in spirit. My Jeanne-ness, my soul, my dreams and wildness, would all have to be buried away. I would simply be a shadow of myself. A ghost.

Colin Pilon made me laugh. I loved him most for that. That and his broad smile and dancing eyes; his warm cheek and the way he held me that took my breath away and made me feel like I was a bird, flying through a sky full of nothing and everything at the same time. I was sure that I loved Colin. But how could a girl be certain? My mother had been taken from me when I was a babe. She had never been there to tell me about such things. Had she loved my father? I could tell that he loved her, by the way his face crumpled and his eyes grew wet when he spoke of her. Still, he had left her behind when she had been in grave danger. He had not been there for her. He had abandoned her. I would not abandon Colin. I would not let him die out there like my mother had. I loved him too much.

'Go on!' I called to my horse, digging a gentle boot into his side as I tugged at the rein of the other, pulling hard to get him to follow. I rode down the narrow streets, keeping my head down, trying not to meet the eye of any of those hurrying past. I was dressed in my dirty peasant tunic, which was covered in the blood of the man whose hand I had severed the previous day. And I was riding along with two fine Parisian horses. It looked suspicious. While I was within the city gates I could always claim that I was returning to the Balagny manor house upon Madame Balagny's orders but once I was in the old tunnels this excuse wouldn't work and punishment was inevitable if I was caught.

As soon as I entered the wide, old aqueducts, I breathed a sigh of relief that I had got this far without being questioned. It was cool and dark with only the distant glow of sunlight peeking through the hidden entrance at the other end of the tunnel to lead the way. The clop of the horses' hooves echoed through the chamber and the sound of dripping water was amplified. My heartbeat thudded in my ears. I could not see Colin.

The dim light in the tunnel had made me feel uncomfortable and I welcomed the view of the outside world when I got to the opening. I felt as if I was a budding shoot that had broken free of the earth. The woods were speckled with golden light and I stopped, pricking my ears for any sign of danger. Colin had said that the Italian mercenaries were camped close to the forest, beyond the aqueduct that spilled out onto a small tributary of the river.

I hung cautiously on the rim of the outer world, scanning the forest floor, the curve of branches and the fuzzy green ceiling of foliage above. I listened keenly for any noise that might herald danger but I heard nothing except the gentle hum of insects and the lilting whip of birdsong. My horse shook his head and stomped his hooves.

I moved him forward, leading the other horse beside us, and slipped quietly into the embrace of the woods. I knew them so well. Every moss-covered, rotting log was like an old friend.

It was further along past the first open grove that I came upon the one log that meant more than all the others. It was the one where my life had been spared. Dismounting, I went to it and sat, shutting my eyes for a moment, giving thanks for my small life. My gratitude went out to my mother and in this place I always felt her presence. When my parents had been accosted by bandits on the path so many years earlier, my father had fled in a panic and my mother ran, hiding me in the crumbling, damp, empty hollow of the log before running in the other direction to draw the men away from me. My father and a group of men from Beauvais had come back, fully armed, soon after, to search for us. They had found my mother ravaged and murdered. Eventually they found me, after hearing my sobbing from within the log. My father had cried that he thought his wife and child had a better chance if he'd gone for help. On that day he lost my mother and also the respect of everyone in Beauvais.

The horses helped themselves to small grassy knots on the ground. Being in the forest was a lovely reprieve from the city and I imagined I was much safer in the woods than in the city. I stood up and left the log. I tied up the horses down near the trickling brook so they could water themselves, and I went on foot, stealthy and fast, to trail Colin, my hand tracing the hard metal of my one remaining hatchet at my side.

I kept to the edge of the forest, following it around toward where Colin said the Italians had set up their camps. With a great deal of stealth, I scooted from one tree to the next, hugging the dim shadows, but I pulled up short when I saw a soldier relieving himself in the creek. I felt my stomach roil. He was dressed in a helmet of chain mail and the ducal colours on his tunic were emblazoned with the cross of Saint Andrew. I watched as he straightened and trudged back up the embankment. I gave a startled gasp as I saw Colin appear from the trees nearby, his hands raised in the manner of surrender as he approached the soldier. I watched, holding my breath, as they conversed awkwardly with much gesturing. I was close enough to hear that the man was speaking Italian. I knew well that Colin could not understand a word.

Colin pulled the bag of coins from his shirt and held it up. As he did, two more men appeared over the rise, coming down toward the water, shouting and waving their arms. I pressed back against a tree, my heart hammering wildly. I watched helplessly as one man took the bag of coins and the other two hog-tied Colin and carried him back over the hill. I could hear their cruel laughter. Fear snarled in my belly like snapped fiddle strings.

From the trees I followed them to the outskirts of their camp and watched as a man who appeared to be in charge of the Italians came out and spoke with Colin. I could just make out that they conversed in French but I could only snatch a word or two. The captain opened the pouch and counted the silver coins. I took this as a good sign. Surely the man must have been considering the proposal to jump sides and fight for us or he would have killed Colin on the spot?

Colin was tied to a post in a central area in front of the tents, which were arranged in the shape of a crescent.

I watched as soldiers came and went from the frontline, giving him nothing more than cursory glances. The Italian garrison seemed to have a steady stream of carts with all manner of strange contraptions – weapons I was not familiar with and a few others that I was. There were wheeled bombards and serpentines. Small cannons I could recognise, but others looked stranger and very, very menacing. Over in the far field I could see carpenters and masons with their tools, fashioning cart wheels and pick-axes to bolster their troops. It was a huge operation and it all seemed highly organised.

I couldn't be sure of what was happening. Colin was kept tied up in the hot sun, which beat down on him. I waited and watched. All afternoon, the sound of cannon fire and screams came from the two main gates nearby. I could see smoke filtering up into the sky and could not tell if it came from within the high walls of my city. As time passed slowly, I felt the dull ache of fear soaking into my bones. I had no clear idea about what I should do. I was beginning to panic, knowing that to stay would mean trouble but to return would have me in just as much strife. So I remained rooted to the spot, breathing in small, frightened gasps.

The Italians appeared to be ignoring Colin, apart from the occasional passing jeer. No one even offered him water. Messengers came and went on horseback, ferrying information, presumably from Charles and his men who were camped in greater numbers all around the eastern countryside surrounding Beauvais. I watched Colin sag at the post as if he was falling asleep in the heat. If they kept him there long enough, he would become completely parched and that could kill him. I slipped back to the horses and bent by the brook, cupping my hands to drink the water that tasted like dirt and grass. I picked some wild berries and ate them to quell the churning of my belly. The sun was moving west and the high part of the day was long over. It would soon be dark. I had been gone for hours. Madame Balagny would be getting angry by this stage, sending the guard out to find me. To return would mean certain punishment. But the capture of Colin by the Italians posed a serious threat to my plans of elopement and desertion.

The cannon and musket fire eased as the sun began its descent toward the Alps to the west, and the dense smoke started to clear. As the Italian soldiers filed back into camp, their swarthy faces masked with blood, sweat and dirt, the flagons of wine started to flow and the atmosphere became almost jovial, with the occasional drunken fight breaking out. Men in their hose and breeches and bare chests wrestled in the dirt and grunted, throwing punches. Fires were lit to cast light about the camp and I watched, hungrily, as three wild hares were roasted on a spit, the gamey smell of meat reminding me that I hadn't eaten anything apart from a few forest fruits. Night came swiftly and I felt even more alone and helpless in the dark. Young boys carried platters of food down to where all the weary men were seated at tables and chairs set up like a grand banquet on a flat embankment along the creek, which burbled over polished river stones, making a gentle gurgling noise.

Two men carried their crossbows to a tree close to where I was hiding and rested them there with a full quiver of bolts. I swung behind the trunk nearest to me and held my breath. They were speaking in their own tongue, which I did not understand, although it sounded quite melodic. When I peered around again, being careful not to be seen, the men were pointing to Colin and laughing. I felt a shiver of dread run down my spine. One man pointed to a spot between his eyes and the other nodded and chortled loudly. My blood ran cold. I pressed my back against the tree and tried to breathe slowly to keep my thoughts clear. It seemed that the Italians had no desire to fill their pockets further by jumping ship to fight for us. The invitation had been met with a refusal and Colin was a prisoner of war. Everyone knew that the Burgundian army took prisoners purely for sport. They meant to use Colin as target practice, pocketing the deposit of silver as a bonus.

Colin was awake and I could see by the droop of his head and shoulders that he had given up all hope of staying alive. The two archers left their weapons and went to help a troop rolling in from the frontline with kegs on the back of a cart. This bought me some time to do something, but in my panicked state I could not think what that might be.

They carefully unloaded the wooden barrels and I could smell the heady stench of saltpetre and sulphur. The kegs were full of gunpowder. This was what Beauvais feared most. We had weapons and boiling water and rocks and knives and heart and passion but we did not have the raw materials to make this powerful mixture, which could blow enormous holes in bricks and mortar. It made fire burn intensely and was the most destructive substance in all of Christendom. I narrowed my eyes and watched as they unloaded the kegs far from the camp and set down pails of water around them, with animal hides soaking nearby as a safety precaution.

When all the men went down to the great bonfire by the water and began singing battle songs and drinking skins of wine, my thoughts became clear. I knew what I had to do, although it was unthinkably dangerous.

I scrambled to remember the travelling jester who had shown the children of Beauvais his magic tricks. He had a pail of gunpowder and had thrown it into the fire, and we watched it fizz and pop, spitting fire like a flaming snake.

Under the shadow of encroaching darkness, I went over to the barrels of gunpowder. There was no guard. I supposed that the Italians thought it was safe to leave them unattended because the enemy was all walled up behind enormous stone battlements within the city confines of Beauvais, apart from the one slowly dying in their camp.

I moved down along the line of pines, toward the ring of kegs. I carefully wrenched open a lid and smelled the contents. It almost blew the top of my head off, it was so strong. I held my breath, blinked rapidly, and tried to see through my watering eyes, which were streaming as if I were weeping. I took a bronze ladle by its long handle and dug out a full cup of the light, soft powder. In the silver light cast by a half moon, I began to sprinkle a long line, like a white-grey mountain range, from the kegs to the row of weaponry carts and all the way back to the ring of large, colourful tents. Back and forth I went until my arm was aching. I had to press back into the shadows as a drunken soldier came up the embankment to find more wine, singing a slurring song as he struggled with a wheelbarrow filled to the brim with swollen wine sacks.

I rolled the last of the barrels of gunpowder all the way to the weapon carts and left some barrels there and others at the tents, sprinkling the last of the powder over them for good measure.

Pulling off my tunic, which was covered in the dust of the dangerous sulphuric concoction, I washed my hands thoroughly in a nearby bucket of water. I stood up and wiped my hands on my underskirts, feeling naked in my coarse cotton blouse with the hatchet exposed at my side. After taking another pail of water, I slipped between the tents, fast and soft on my feet, and went to Colin. He startled into wakefulness and hissed at me, his eyes wide in the silver light.

'Jeanne, what the devil?' He was so upset, he spat the words. 'You must get away from here. Oh Lord, if they find you … go … go! Get out of here. Now! *Va-vite*! They will tear you to pieces.'

'No, Colin!' I ignored his protests as I untied my hatchet from my side-skirts. 'Be careful or I'll cut off your hand.' I smiled. 'And you know, I'm quite capable of that.'

I had to make light of the awful events of the previous day or my dreams would be tied up in nightmares for a very long time. This was war. My life and the city were in danger and all was fair in such circumstances. Self-defence can bring out the monsters in our blood and steel us for brutality that would otherwise be unthinkable.

I managed to hack through the last of the ropes around Colin's hands and then his feet. I lifted the pail of water to his lips and urged him to drink. He slurped greedily and then nodded. I grabbed his hand and ran back through the maze of tents, grabbing a lit torch as I went, dragging him stumbling behind me.

'Don't bring a torchlight,' he gasped. 'They will see it bobbing in the darkness. No fire, Jeanne.'

'That,' I smiled, 'will be the least of their worries. Let them come. I want them to rush back to camp. All of them. Every last one of them.'

As we reached the outskirts of the encampment, I stopped at the head of my long, weaving line of white powder and looked back at it snaking about the ground toward the weapons carts and onto the tents.

'Now run. With all of your might. Run!'

And I dropped the torch to the ground and watched the powder catch and begin to sizzle and spark and race along like a streak of lightning toward my targets.

'Go!' I cried and together we ran back into the forest. We used our hands to feel our way, tripping over roots and rocks, making as much distance between us and the Italian camp as possible. My hands were scratched by trunks and branches and my chest was full and tight. I felt my clothes snag and tear on brambles.

'This way,' I panted as we reached the brook where the two horses stood quietly in a patch of bone-white moonlight, shards of diamonds catching in their big round eyes.

'What is this, Jeanne?' Colin gasped and bent down to catch his breath.

'I have horses, Colin,' I said. 'Good horses. And I thought with the silver that you ...'

'It's gone.'

'I know. I saw. But we could sell one of the horses,' I stammered desperately. 'And ride together to the port, catch a boat to England, start again, marry. Leave all this behind. But we must hurry now.'

In that moment a huge explosion ripped through the night. Sparks and flames shot up into the sky. Another and then another. It was as if the entire world was shattering and erupting. The sky was a crimson blush, and the sound of roaring foreign voices screaming and shouting filled the air.

Colin put his hands on my cheeks, coming close. 'I have my honour, Jeanne,' he said. 'I love you, but I would not have you love a man who steals horses from another and deserts his city in a time of need. You deserve better than that.'

'But Colin,' I stammered. 'If we go back ...'

'We go back heroes,' he said. 'Not me so much. But you! You just took out seven garrisons of men and the entire gunpowder artillery of the enemy. That was the core of their entire operation, Jeanne! You have single-handedly crippled Charles the Bold's entire campaign against Beauvais.'

I felt strengthened by Colin's words. He was a man of honour and wanted us to return to Beauvais to share our tale of victory. Taking his hand, we began to make our way home.

BETSY

COUNTY DOWN, IRELAND, 1798

By the time spring gave way to summer, the conflict between the rebels and the redcoats had been pushed to the level of war. There was tension in the streets and even more in the marketplace at Newtownards.

After the redcoats' suspicion following Jimmy's escape from the lock-up, George and Will had been making themselves scarce. And although my father was reluctant to let me go about on my own, he made an allowance for the Saturday market. With the summer sun high in the sky and the sound of voices filling my ears, I pressed through the crowded streets, which were closed off to horse traffic. Peddlers shouted and the fishmonger hollered over the briny stench of his slippery-skinned produce.

'Betsy!' I heard my name and looked around to find who hailed me.

Cousin Mary came pushing through the jostling bodies and waved. There was no sunny smile and a permanent crease was beginning to fold down in the middle of her forehead, making her look ten years older than she was.

'Where's baby George?' I asked, moving my heavy basket to my other arm.

'With me mam,' she told me. 'Any word from George? Or Will?'

I narrowed my eyes at her, overcome with suspicion.

'Who's asking? You or Connor?'

'Betsy! You don't think ...'

I gave her a look, pursing my lips and raising one eyebrow.

'Of course not Connor!' she pouted. 'George is my cousin after all. I was just curious. Although, to be honest with you, Betsy, the rumours going about are that the boys are hiding out, protected by the rebels.'

'That's nonsense!' I lied and tried my very best to look as innocent as a lamb. 'They are both living the life in Portsmouth and writing home is clearly the very last thing on their minds.'

'Well, I hope that Will of yours is staying true and not chasing English skirts. Funny place for them considering how much they hate the English!'

'It's a rite of passage, Mary.' I dug down deeper into the lie. 'All the young lads like to work the docks for a bit. It's a melting pot of cultures and you can make very good international connections.'

'Hmmm.' Cousin Mary leaned toward me. 'And Brigit? Any word from her?'

'You know we have no idea where she and Jimmy are!' I lied again, feeling like I'd have to spend a month praying to the Lord for forgiveness for so many untruths. 'None whatsoever, but I hope she and little Isabella are safe and far away.'

'Have you heard that Henry Munro is the new rebel leader?' she hissed close to my ear.

'What? The linen merchant? The handsome one? That Henry Munro?' I said, unable to contain my surprise.

'The very same,' she said, her eyes wide with the gossip. 'Lots of other local rebel-heads have toppled and been arrested down south. The rebels are losing their fire. You don't want to be singed by the dying embers, my dear cousin.'

This was worrying news but I tried to sound nonchalant.

'It's not my concern anymore,' I said, tossing my hair over one shoulder. 'George and Will have lost interest too. That's why they went away for a bit.'

'If you say so. How's your da?'

'He's fine.'

It was another lie because my father was not himself. He looked at me with an air of distrust and had done so every day since Brigit left for Scotland. The beating he'd taken from the Monaghan Men that terrible day had left him with no sight in one eye and a hip that had never been right since. The constant pain and frustration he found in doing the normal activities that he loved so much – the gentle walks over the hills behind our house and long nights of reading – had left him even more surly and ill-tempered than before.

'Pass on my regards to him,' cousin Mary said, over the din of the market.

Suddenly a voice rang out in anger and the crowd of people around us began to move and sway. An air of excitement and apprehension rippled through us as more shouting erupted and people scurried away from the noise like rats that have had light cast over them. I could see that the fuss was between two soldiers and a young man with a blue cap. It looked to me like one of the Ballenger boys. I recognised one of the soldiers as Mary's Connor.

'Oh Lordy.' Cousin Mary began to fuss. 'I should go. You should go. Go. Go. Go.'

She turned and hurried away without another word. I did the same and pushed out past the towers of chicken coops and briefly turned back to see that the young lad was lying in the dirt while Connor and the other soldier laid their boots into him, shouting the word 'Rebel'. I couldn't understand what would make an Irishman turn his back on his heritage and join the ranks alongside the English. Was it money? Fear? Or did it appeal to their base and bullying natures? It wasn't just Catholic versus Presbyterian versus Protestant. The United Irishmen were wanting all to live in harmony with equal rights in the law no matter what your faith. I couldn't understand the religious folk who couldn't see the sense in that. God was God. I'm certain He wasn't keen on all this fighting.

Sorry as I was for the young lad, I was glad there were no eyes following me that day. All through the spring, those mercenaries had kept our house under surveillance and did spot visits on a regular basis to try to catch known rebels in our house. The McCrackens were on their watch-list, as were all of Will's kin and poor Mr Jack Neale, who still kept looking for his precious Annie. None of these oath-sworn United Irishmen, or women, had stepped over our threshold in months and for the past two months, after someone had put forward their names as suspected rebels, George and Will had been hiding out in the hills. I maintained their lie to my father, who seemed to believe that they were headed abroad, to England. He believed they had gone to seek employment at the docks in Plymouth where there was constant labouring work servicing the convict boats that wove a steady ocean path to the faraway prison settlement of New South Wales. I knew Da was suspicious as he often wondered aloud why it was that George never sent mail or word when it would have been so easy to do so. I would shrug innocently and suggest that he must be busy or have fallen in love with some English rose. Which was a ridiculous suggestion because George loved the English about as much as he loved swarming hornets.

I waited until after lunch for my father to fall asleep, as he was accustomed to do of a late afternoon; the half-quart of whisky after lunch was always slept off deeply before he rose, ready for dinner. That June afternoon, I stood poised in the hallway off the parlour, looking at the family portraits, waiting for the sound of those first baritone snores. I smiled at Mam's picture, and for the one-thousandth time looked for similarities between us. Her twinkling, mischievous green eyes could have been mine staring back at me from a looking glass. I remembered so little of her, but I missed her so much that whenever I thought of her I got an aching pain beneath my ribs. I felt a warm rush through my veins as I examined the likeness of Katherine Campbell with her wild burgundy hair and a look that could fell an oak tree. I imagined it was a flame of pride running through me that I was related to her.

A rumble rolled out from Da's room and I was away before he took his next laboured breath. I ran down to the stables like a bolting yearling, my boots crunching on the gravel, my hair trailing behind me, loose like a flag. The sun stung my forearms and I felt free and wild, dressed in a pair of George's breeches with his white shirt tucked into them. If anyone spotted me galloping over the hills they would think me a boy, once I'd tied up my hair and tucked it under a riding cap.

Finn McCool was pleased to see me and gave a warm snort and nuzzled my palm.

'We're going to have some fun, Master McCool, indeed we are,' I said into his soft mane as he tossed his head and impatiently pawed the stable hay with his hoof. As I saddled him, he lifted his head and gave a loud neigh. He all but up and told me straight that he was excited and well pleased to be going on a jaunt.

I waited just behind the well, counting to four hundred, before taking to the back paddocks and leaping over the hedges into open country. I couldn't be too cautious. Every time I went riding into the wilderness I watched the gravel path from the road to make sure no one had me under surveillance. The coast was clear.

With the wind whistling against my face and the sound of Finn McCool's well-shod hooves pounding the warm dry earth, we sallied fast over three wide-sweeping hills, out past the abandoned dairy that used to belong to the

O'Sheas before Danny and his son had been found swinging from a tree near their front porch. It had been a tree old Danny had planted with his own hands as a boy, so the story went, and no one believed the pair had strung themselves up. There was the small matter of their hands being tied. Despite this, the English establishment found that the men had taken their own lives and they'd been denied a church burial. Poor Libby O'Shea and the seven little ones had been sent abroad to a convict settlement for cattle thieving. It was all a terrible set-up because they believed Danny O'Shea was sympathetic to the rebel cause. Everyone had to watch their backs carefully. The English were afeared that there would be an uprising and, to be honest, I hoped they were right. During the past months there was a heating up, like the head of steam about to escape from a kettle. The uprising was definitely a'brewing and while I'd kept my head low, I'd left my ears open and everything I heard I ferried back to George and Will at least once a week. The situation was fraught with tension and everyone was on edge. I felt it. The English felt it. Even Da felt it. There was too much cruelty, too much entrenched hatred toward the Irish culture. It made my blood boil. You wouldn't put a fox and a goose in the same pen – that's how it felt in Ireland.

From the top of the last hill I looked down over the pristine, verdant valley. By the edge of the burbling creek, under the shade of a big box tree, a young man was seated on a horse. He was tall and dark and looked toward the higher ground as if he was expecting someone. I was riding astride my horse. A woman riding a horse this way was widely regarded as an offence against decency but there was no one on the hills to see me and if there was they'd see my breeches and assume I was a youth.

I rode down the hill fast into the valley and drew my horse up to his. Will placed his hand on my horse's bridle and leaned over to whisper in my ear.

'A ghrá mo chroí.'

'Love of my heart, Will Boal,' I said, kissing his cheek and then I threw back my head and laughed up into the pale blue sky. 'I love it when you speak to me in the old tongue. And I love it out here. Let's live in a cave and speak true Irish and be as ancient druids, living off the land and having no beef with redcoats or the rebels. Let's live free.'

'If we can run the English devils from our fair emerald isle, my love,' Will said. 'Then we *will* be free. That's what we're fighting for. Liberty. I don't like it, the idea of fighting, but they're not going to just pack up and leave because we asked them politely, are they?'

Will led the way across the narrow, shallow creek and up the rise toward the yew-forest that covered the neighbouring hillside. We called this place the Red Deer Ranges. It was pastoral land peppered with scattered woods that had been abandoned during the last famine and had not yet been stolen by the Crown. In a clearing on the top of the rise, George and Will had been sowing a crop of mangelwurzel and barley for the purpose of distilling whisky. They were selling it on the black market to help raise funds for the United Irishmen to purchase weapons and favours from sympathetic Frenchmen and Scots who hated the English as much as we did. In a hidden rocky crop down by the creek, they had set up a still with a copper pot.

Further back was a fortress-like hut with log walls and small loophole windows. It was not weather-bonded with packed peat and whitewash, so they would not be able to sleep in it for the winter months but for the warmer months it was a habitable hideaway.

My brother greeted me with open arms. 'Ah, Betsy, my darling sister,' he shouted. 'I hope you've brought me sugar and flour and tea besides.'

I smiled and nodded, swinging a sack from Finn McCool's side-saddle. 'I don't think Da will notice this much.' I grinned. 'I did a big purchase up at Antrim last week and some more this morning locally.'

'Have you heard the word on the street, Betsy?' Will said, taking my goods and kissing me on the cheek. 'It's on!'

'What's on?' I frowned.

'The rising. It's been called. We are taking the towns and rising up against the English. Driving them from our shores! It's happening, Betsy. The rebels are intercepting the mail coaches to Dublin to send messages about the assembly points. This is war!'

I stared at him and then looked across to my brother, sure they were jesting me but their cheeks were pink with excitement and their eyes glistened with fervour. The redcoats were sludge-thick on the roads around these parts and most of the rebels had gone to ground like badgers. No meetings had been called for some time, unless of course they were very secret. I surely had not been invited along.

I'd heard not a word because I was so busy and isolated, holed up caring for my elderly father, cut off from the greater world, bored, housebound and dejected. My weekly trips out to visit the boys were the highlights of my dull existence. My only other outing was to the markets for produce and staples, and I knew that the yeomanry followed me because on more than one occasion I was stopped and had my satchels searched. The soldiers were everywhere like rats in the sewers; redcoats bobbing through the marketplace, striding through the busy streets like warning flags, congregating in huddles outside churches and overseeing funerals and weddings as if it was any of their business.

'Are you sure?' I asked. 'Because Da says that the support for the rebels is falling away. Many have renounced their oath and are being obedient and accepting of the Crown. Saving their own skins. And I was coming to tell you that Henry Munro is in charge of our chapter. Cousin Mary told me.'

'Damn them for that,' George cursed. 'Yes, we knew of Munro's promotion from Jack O'Neal. He's been bringing up weapons to us and he says we're assured of one hundred thousand Pikemen. That's enough men-at-arms to take on the dogs.'

'Well.' I huffed. 'Pikes are well and good but they are no defence against a violent army with cannon fire and muskets aplenty.'

'With enough muscle behind the pikes, Betsy,' Will said, tying my horse to an elbow in a tree branch, 'we can unsaddle the horsemen and give them a good walloping.

We have the numbers on the ground, we have passion and our Erin pride. We love our island, our language and they would steal one and stamp out the other. The English lack any motivation but greed for power. We have that over them.'

'You're right,' I nodded.

George weighed in, looking suddenly sombre, not like his usual cheeky self, and it made me wonder how he really thought this civil war might go.

'Half the bloody loyalists to the Crown these days have Irish blood flowing in their veins and stand by the English out of sheer terror for their own hides. We'll be uprising against some of our own in this battle. People like Connor Kelly.'

'How will cousin Mary feel about that? He's now a captain. But he's never said a word against you two. I'll take my cap off to him for that!' I said, thinking that Connor could have squawked on us at any time. 'Although I just saw him putting the boot into one of the Ballenger boys. I don't know how Mary puts up with the brute.'

'The Ballenger boys are tough and won't speak a word.' Will nodded seriously. 'But that Connor Kelly, I don't trust him none. He's got a wife and son. They can use them against him to get him to turn traitor.'

I did want to stand up for Ireland and I believed we could win. They had tried to bully the Americans but the American Revolution had put them in their place. After the French Revolution, our rebel leaders knew that it was possible to overthrow one's oppressors. But I was worried that we weren't quite ready.

'But we have no French support on the ground, no proper arms, no trained men to go up against the English. We'll be swatted like insects,' I said.

I was sounding like my father but I was concerned that the resistance was being far too hasty to call the rising for that summer. 'You must be joking with me, Will. Maybe this time next year we might stand a chance ... that's what I thought we were working toward.'

He shook his head and took my hand, leading me around the back of the cottage, explaining as we went. George traipsed behind us.

'Theobald Wolfe Tone has rallied some French troops, near a thousand, and they are sailing for a landfall in Mayo any day now. Our men are primed and already striking down south round Dublin way. George and I will be riding north to Ballynahinch in the days to come to call our men to stand up and fight alongside our comrades. We'll need you to rally a team of women to bring food to the troops.'

I felt a ripple of dread masquerading as excitement. Theobald Wolfe Tone was like a messiah to the rebels. He was a founding member of the United Irishmen and I'd heard his name but never laid eyes on him. If he was commanding it, then it really was going to happen. After all the talk, after all the years of ranting behind closed doors, after so long, suffering at the hands of our invaders, we were finally going to call the supporters to arms and take on the Crown. Foolish or not, I also felt proud to be a part of this. Perhaps we were ready. Perhaps we had always been ready.

We stood behind the shack and I surveyed the open field with amazement. The boys had been busy felling and clearing the land so that it lay bald and barren, all the way back to a line of trees, so neat and straight that they looked like fence posts. On the trunks of the pale-grey ash trees there were charcoal drawings of faces and other wedges cut into the tree flesh.

'We fire shot into them at twenty, then fifty, then one hundred yards,' Will told me, proudly. 'I have a good eye and great aim. George on the other hand ...'

George hooted and threw his head back. 'The man jests.' He laughed. '*I* am the hot-shot. Will is Lucky Larry with his aim.'

'You do me ill, Georgie boy.' Will sulked. 'I can shoot a red fox at a hundred yards with every shot fired.'

'Now you're just showing off, lad. Blowing your own trumpet.' George continued to tease. 'Trying to impress your betrothed. Why, I bet Betsy could outdo you in a target challenge. What do you say, Betsy?'

'You're on, boys!' I said, dancing and clapping my hands. 'I'm up for it. Hand me a musket. I'll blow the tree in two.'

'Easy up, lassie, it's not as easy as it looks.' Will frowned and went to fetch a weapon. He returned with a musket and pushed a shot ball into the barrel, pressing it in tight with a thin rod.

'We dig the shot out of the tree and reuse it because we don't have a lot and only thirteen muskets are stashed up here,' George told me as he cleaned his nails with a small paring knife. 'All pilfered from Jack's midnight raids on those English dogs in the barracks. He waits until they're dead drunk and then walks right in and takes them.'

'And they call us Irishmen drunkards!' Will laughed.

'Might I remind you that your entire little crop here is for making liquor?' I laughed.

'Jack O'Neal says the redcoats are our greatest customers.' Will grinned at me with his open smile, all teeth and eyes. 'He sells it from his back shed for a fraction of the full price of whisky. The bastards love it!'

'So they are funding us without knowing so that we can take them down,' George ranted triumphantly. 'The beauty of it. Ain't it grand, Betsy? The redcoats buy the grog and we pocket the lot to pay the smithies to smelt the pikes for us!'

I did see the rich irony of it.

'Mind you,' Will said, looking out over the distant, purple-dusted hills, 'those thirteen muskets are all we have by way of firearms for the whole brigade at Ballynahinch. The rest of the men will have to fight with pikes.'

'We have some grapeshot but can't waste it,' George told me as he carefully passed me the weapon. 'We are saving it for the hearts and heads and spleens of our English oppressors.'

Will stood behind me, pressed up close enough to cause me some warmth and showed me how to hold the long, awkward musket. It was much heavier than I had imagined.

'Be careful now,' he said into my hair, his breath tickling my skin. 'I stole this from an English soldier.'

I let my hand feel the wood and weight of the contraption and wondered if Will meant that he had killed the soldier for it, perhaps even with it. I felt faint thinking that I was holding an instrument of death.

'See that one there?' Will pointed. 'The charcoal face on the ash tree? There. The middle one. Go for that. The stock will jump back against your shoulder so hold tight and go with it. Don't drop it.'

I took the musket and held it high, aiming at the shoddy face drawn into the bark. I closed an eye and focused hard on the target.

'Look down the barrel,' Will said, stepping away from me and I saw that George stepped back even further, clearly wary of my capabilities.

With a gentle squeeze, I pulled the trigger and felt the click and then the roar as the beast reeled up against my body, pushing backwards as the shot flew out, so fast it was invisible and I heard it thud against something. I looked ahead, squinting so that I could see exactly what I had hit, if anything. George gave a whistle and Will trotted forward calling for me to secure my weapon. He inspected the tree and looked back at me with a lopsided grin.

'You took the English devil's head off, Betsy! You're a better marksman than your brother.'

'You have a fine eye, Betsy,' George said, coming to stand next to me. 'A very fine eye.'

I watched Will dig the shot out of the tree with his pocket knife, flicking his head of curls back out of his eyes. His broad shoulders were covered by a thin, sweat-stained grey calico shirt and his knee-high, green corduroy breeches were pulled down tight into his high boots, showing a nice long curve down over his strong thighs as he bent over.

'Yes, that I do, brother.' I smiled. 'A fine eye.'

After sharing billy tea and some venison jerky, I rode home alone at dusk, singing into the wind, happy to have seen George and Will. Will had kissed me hard and strong on my leaving, enough to make George blush. I couldn't wait to walk down the aisle and say a resounding 'I do' to William Boal. We'd postponed the wedding until the following summer and I wasn't sure I could wait all that long. Another whole year.

I galloped my Finn McCool and he loved the run, churning his hooves though the grass clods, kicking up a stream of dirt behind us. His strong haunches rose and fell as I sat high in my saddle. I felt the power beneath me as he bolted down the lush hills and up the other side until we stood on the final hillock, looking out over the valley, admiring our little farm that was nestled like a white pebble in a sea of green. A coil of thin smoke rose from the parlour chimney so I knew Da must have been up, trying to read by the light of the fire with his one good eye.

After settling Finn into the stable, I peeled off my riding cap, hung it on the hook and strode down the gravel path to the house, shaking my sweaty mane of hair out as if I was a horse myself. I decided I would slip in the back door through the mudroom, get out of my brother's clothes and tidy myself up before dinner. My father would disapprove of me riding in men's attire. As I walked, I whistled and planned an easy smoked-herring pie for our supper. Entering the dim doorway, I choked hard against something at my throat and stopped, gasping and startled, when out of the shadows a man's face appeared. He was fair and wore a red coat. He smiled down at me like a big fish, his eyes cold and his mouth like a thin, wet slice across his pockmarked face. His arm was stretched across the doorway and he lowered it as I coughed and rubbed my neck.

'Well, if it isn't the charming Miss Betsy Gray,' he hissed, and I felt a bead of his spittle land on my cheek. 'We've just stopped by to pay you and your daddy a visit, just to ask a few questions. Follow me, will you, lovely?'

Rubbing my bruised voice-box, I coughed again and walked behind him on legs that suddenly felt like they were made of wet sand. It was the rude soldier from the inn.

Inside the parlour, two more soldiers stood by the fireplace. My father was kneeling on the floor and my stomach rolled. I ran to him but was stopped by a firm hand around my arm. It hurt.

'Oh good.' The fat soldier laughed. 'Tommy Little's found your daughter, Mr Gray.'

'Yes, Jack,' Tommy replied, pushing me into the room. 'Sneaking around outside.'

'What is this? What are you doing?' I shouted.

'There have been uprisings all over the south,' Jack said through his yellowing teeth. 'And while we've squashed the rebellion down there, thanks to informers, we want to know if there are similar plans afoot in these parts. Thought your father might be able to shed some light.'

'I've told you we know nothing,' my father groaned.

'We have no knowledge of insurgent activity,' I pleaded. 'I swear. Let my father be. He is old and frail. And he is a loyalist. You know that! He has sworn an oath to the King.' I was sure my father had only taken that traitor's oath to save his children. Most people who had taken it had the same reason. Even though they resented the English occupation, self-preservation was a mighty incentive.

'Your son, George Gray?' the tall soldier by the fire asked, while taking a poker from the tray, reaching it into the flames. 'You say he's over on the Motherland? Working the docks?'

'I did, he is,' my father stammered. 'Gone for months now.'

'Along with my husband-to-be, William Boal,' I added.

The tall man with the thin moustache looked up from the fire, squinting across at me.

'Is he now? And your sister? Married to Jimmy Ballantine, wasn't she? Where is she now? Last I remember she was squeezing out a baby and you were sallying forth for a midwife.'

I took a sharp breath and glared at the soldier, my mind racing, my memory being kicked liked a recalcitrant horse. Yes. I remembered the seedy face. The tiny slash of hair above his lip. I went cold and looked at the other two soldiers: the one with the bulging belly, Jack, and the other, Tommy Little, behind me, with his pockmarked face. I shut my eyes and sent a prayer to heaven. These were the very same three that had taken Annie for questioning.

'My sister married a Catholic, Jimmy Ballantine, and we suspected he was a rebel,' I said carefully, slowly, measuring each word. 'Seems we were right. He was nicked, wasn't he, and fled, taking my sister along with him. We had naught to do with them and haven't heard a whisper of a word from them since.'

'So why was you caring to get a midwife for her?' fat Jack asked, narrowing his eyes.

'She was my sister and in need,' I said squarely. 'I am a good Presbyterian woman and could not stand by and do nothing. I am God-fearing and know the difference between right and wrong. We were at Connor Kelly's place, a good Monaghan man. We don't dice with the rebels, sir. Not my father, my brother, Will or me.'

The tall, moustached man paced up and down in front of the fire as if he were a general commanding his troops.

'See, Betsy,' he said in a voice that I did not like one little bit. 'There's been talk. People talk, you know, when pressed. And the talk on the street is that your brother and your lover are oath-swearing United Irishmen. Liberty Men.'

'It isn't true, sir!' I shouted.

'Well now, lassie, you are very pretty when angered.' He smiled.

I bristled, looking away as he raked his eyes over me.

'I don't care much for the boy's attire you are wearing.' He leered. 'Is that your riding gear? Where were you riding to this afternoon, Miss Betsy Gray?'

'Just out over the hills,' I said. 'My horse needed a run. His legs were getting bound up and I am mostly stuck here with my ailing da.'

'And a good thing that is too!' Tommy Little beamed, his face red and shiny in the glow of the firelight, lighting up his scars like milk pox.

'We are loyalists,' I said, standing tall, pretending to be brave. 'We cannot help you with your enquiries because my brother is in England. We know nothing of any uprising. We are farming people and care only for our cattle and crops.'

'Tell us where your son is, Mr Gray!' The tall man threatened, brandishing the hot poker from the fire dangerously close to my father's face. 'Tell us and we will leave you and your daughter be. If your son is carousing with the rebels, we will not blame you. Bad apples can fall from good trees. But if you are hiding anything, covering for him, you will be held accountable and so will Betsy.'

My father's eyes locked with mine and held fast. I tried to say one and a million things to him so he might understand but his eyes were bloodshot and I knew that one eye could barely see more than clouded shadows. As furtively as I could I shook my head very, very slowly from side to side. He could not divulge my brother's whereabouts, if he did indeed have an inkling that the Portsmouth story was a lie, otherwise George and Will would end up run though with bayonets, strung from the branch of an oak or simply disappearing like so many others, never to be heard from again.

'Betsy,' my father croaked. 'Elizabeth, darling. Go and put on some supper for these good men and leave us be.'

'No, Da,' I said slowly.

I did not want to be sent from the room so that he might betray George to save our hides. Da would do it for me, but not himself, and I could not let that happen.

'Where are George Gray and William Boal?' Little shouted from behind me.

I shivered with dread, but again, very carefully, shook my head, my eyes never leaving my father's face.

'In England. On the docks,' he told them, sadly.

'See, we know this is not true.' The one known as Jack laughed. 'We intercepted correspondence by his hand some days ago.'

'This is news to me,' my father barked, and coughed but I could tell he was not really surprised. 'I am a loyalist and my son knows it. He would never tell me if he was involved with the rebels because I would disown him.'

The three men looked at one another and something passed between them.

'Very well,' the soldier with the poker said, resting it back on the stone hearth. 'You are a man with many connections and are well thought of by the establishment. But your daughter is betrothed to Boal and knows more than she lets on.'

'I do not, sir!' I baulked. 'I have not seen nor heard from my brother or Will in months.'

'Take her,' the man directed Tommy Little and in an instant two strong hands had clasped mine behind my back, stringing my shoulders together tightly.

I winced and my father yelled. 'Unhand her!' he cried.

I was marched out the front door, my hair falling about my face and I went into a panic. From behind us I could hear my father begging for them to let me go, promising to tell them whatever they needed to hear, true or not.

Out in the courtyard I was spun around and the three men encircled me, smiling, grinning.

'We remember you well, Miss Betsy,' the man with the moustache leered. 'You wouldn't dance with Tommy at the Old Inn at Crawfordsburn ...'

Images of the soldier jamming the butt of his musket into Will's belly assaulted me.

'And your friend Annie O'Neal.' Jack laughed cruelly. 'I suppose you've been missing her. She just wouldn't play nice. Too surly and feisty for her own good.'

'You killed her!' I whispered.

'Oh, not straight away, love,' Tommy Little hissed into my ear.

I shut my eyes. I remembered Annie's intelligent face and the way she held onto me on the back of the horse, the way she stiffened against me when the soldiers appeared, the way her boots sounded as she dropped off the horse to the dirt below.

'We don't really want to know where your brother is anymore.' The tall man, who seemed to be the more highly ranked, smirked. 'It's too late for that now. What pretty yellow hair you have, Betsy.'

The man reached out and touched my hair and I recoiled, pulling a face and feeling like I needed to visit the privy.

'Oi there,' a loud voice called and I looked up, startled, to see a man in a large hat with a neck scarf concealing the bottom of his face beneath the eyes, sitting on a big black horse that I immediately recognised as Will Boal's. 'What business do you have with that woman?'

'Any business we like!' Tommy Little retorted as the other two went for the swords at their sides.

Will held up a musket and aimed it directly at the man who had touched my hair.

'Stand away,' he called. 'I am a rebel and I have a troop at my back. You walk away from this place and live or stay and we'll take you down. There's a firing squad beyond yonder trees with the three of you in their sights.'

'You won't get away with this,' Jack growled. 'You fools were stomped on down south. Informers squealing everywhere like little piggies. Your cause is lost, you Irish dog. You've already lost the battle.'

'Walk and I'll try not to shoot you in the back,' Will shouted angrily. 'This is not your woman, not your farm, not your land, not your nation. Now go.'

The soldiers gave me a surly look and nodded to one another. They were a marching trio and did not have horses with them or muskets, only swords. Foot soldiers. I hoped they would not challenge Will because George had said he was a terrible shot.

'You!' the tall soldier with the thin moustache levelled a cold stare at me. 'You're marked, lassie. You're one of them and we know that now. We'll be back and if you are still here, you will end up like Annie O'Neal: in several pieces at the bottom of a dam. You and your father.'

I gasped, tears springing to my eyes.

'*Go hlfreann leat!*' Will shouted and pointed the musket at them.

'Bloody language of savages.' Tommy Little laughed and the others joined in, and with a jaunty amble, the three men traipsed back down the gravel path toward the front gates. I waited until they were out of earshot before speaking out of the corner of my mouth to Will.

'Will,' I said, 'how did you know I was in trouble?'

'Oh, Betsy, love,' he said leaning down from his saddle toward me, 'I follow you home every time you come a'riding and stay here long enough to make sure you are all right. I've been watching over you and your da very carefully. I would never let anything happen to you.'

I smiled. Will Boal was a good man.

'Let's go and get you some clothes and pack your father up. It's not safe here for you. Tomorrow we ride to Ballynahinch to call our war.'

I thought about what the redcoats had said about Annie O'Neal. It broke my heart to think of how terrified she must have been in her final moments.

Inside the house I told Da straight. There was no time for lies anymore, things were dire. This was war.

'Da,' I said, helping him into his favourite armchair, the one with the elegant cabriole legs, 'I am helping George and Will to stand against these tyrants to take Ireland back for ourselves.'

'Oh no, no, no, Betsy,' he said, tears running down his cheeks as he stared at Will as if he was a ghost.

'They murdered Annie O'Neal, Da. They admitted it, and they would have done the same to me whether I was guilty or not.'

Will stood nervously by the door, kicking his boots against the stone floor, just missing the teetering plant stand.

'Hurry, Betsy,' he spoke low and sounded afraid. 'You have to understand English justice, Mr Gray. You are presumed innocent until proven Irish. Just being Irish is crime enough in their eyes, and cause enough to commit atrocities. We need to stand up and reclaim our heritage. *Éireann go Brách*!'

'They killed Annie?' Da blabbered. 'She was your mother's goddaughter. Did I tell you that?'

I nodded.

'We'll pack up everything of value and take you to cousin Mary's where you'll be safe during the uprising, Da,' I said gently.

He nodded, seeming to finally understand, and rested one hand on the mahogany desk beside him, drumming his fingers nervously against the leather top.

'May the road rise up to meet you, William Boal. You take good care of my daughter. I love her very much. But I'll stay here. This is my farm. My home. The land of my forefathers. I'll not be hounded from it. *Saol fada chugat*,' my father stammered, struggling with his pronunciation of the old words. 'I'm sorry. It's been so long since I spoke it.'

'Never mind, Mr Gray.' Will grinned. 'Broken Irish is still way better than clever English and a long life to you too, sir. We are no nation without a language and I for one will fight to keep it alive.'

My father had not spoken old Irish since my mother had passed away, but in those few moments when he tried to recall those words, I believed that he finally understood what it was that Will, George and I, and all the rest of us in the rebellion, were fighting for.

The freedom and liberty to be Irish.

FIONA

BRISBANE, AUSTRALIA, 1968

'I can't believe the turnout,' I said to Agnes.

The two of us stood on the edge of campus and watched as a swarm of students descended upon the Forum. A sea of white button-up shirts, the uniform of the general male body of the university, surged forward and then stalled as the crowd became denser. The throng was so large it spilled across the road away from the Forum, spreading back all the way to the library. I had my guitar slung over my shoulder because I'd gotten it restrung down at the music department.

'He walked me home last night and met my parents.' Agnes said, grabbing my arm and nestling into me.

'What?'

'Jeff,' she said, melodramatically rolling her eyes. 'Jeff met Mum and Dad. That's whole next-level stuff.'

'Hmmm,' I said, looking over my sunglasses at her. 'Yes. Is that ... Yes ... I think I hear wedding bells and hang on ... what's that? Oh yes ... the sound of squealing babies. A whole nursery of them.'

'I would so marry him,' she said dreamily. 'And have his babies.'

'Oh stop it!' I coughed. 'You are selling out. Agnes, you are here. That's really something. My mum would have jumped at the opportunity to go to uni. We're only here on the shoulders of the women who couldn't be. Don't throw it away. It's such an opportunity. You don't want to become the little woman who irons the shirts so that her hubby gets to go out into the world and have a stimulating life, do you?'

'Jeff? In an ironed shirt? Never.' Agnes pouted.

'Be warned.' I smiled sarcastically. 'It's just a ruse to lure you in. All this hippy, laid-back rubbish. The second he lands a job in a law firm the conservative tie-wearer will start emerging. Trust me. That guy is all show. No substance. And he's such a sexist bloke. He's so anti-feminist that it nauseates me.'

'Sexist? Surely not.' She frowned.

'Believe me, Agnes,' I said. 'That fellow is about as into the idea of female liberation as a turnip. But forget Jeff for now and focus. We're here to vote on whether or not to march. The police have refused to issue a permit for a demonstration. That's why we are actually here today! Not to play "he-loves-me-he-loves-me-not".'

'You're too serious sometimes, Fi.' She scoffed, putting her arm around my waist and hugging me to her side.

'This is serious stuff. If we march, Luke is going to burn his draft notice at Roma Street and Barton reckons there will be television people there. This is our moment to have our voices heard. The kids in America are shouting in the streets and people are listening! We can be the voice of change. We are marching for our boys' lives.'

'You sound like you've been infected by Barton germs.' Agnes frowned. 'I think he likes you. Have you been secretly pashing him in the library or something? Fiona the activist! Who'd have thought! You were sitting on the fence last time we talked about it.'

'Barton doesn't like me!' I scoffed. 'He's too self-absorbed to like anyone else and as for kissing him … well … ha … as if!' But as I said it I felt a weird sensation in the very lowest part of my belly.

'Seriously, Ag,' I sighed. 'Let's focus on this vote. Man, we could be a part of history here. Don't you feel it? Having my brother about to carry a gun and be a target changed everything.'

We went and sat at our usual spot under the Moreton Bay fig, nestled up against its solid trunk. I leaned my guitar against it.

'Walter Leary died,' I told her.

'What? *What*?' she gaped at me.

I shrugged and nodded.

'It's weird,' I said slowly. 'I've spent years hating him and now I feel guilty about it. I actually feel bad for him and his family. He was only twenty.'

'Heavy.'

'I mean, he was only fourteen when he made that horrible comment that started the fight with Murray, which now feels almost petty. Grief can blow things way out of proportion.'

'Dead or not, it was a really shitty thing for him to say to your brother so soon after—'

'But you know what?' I said, shooing a fly from my face. 'I forgive him. I know Mum would want me to. She would have if the tables were turned. She was like that. She was the best person. She would have shrugged off his comment and just laughed and said something terribly clever back at him. She was kind and so clever and she had the best comebacks.'

'That's so nice,' Agnes said. 'Your mum sounds great. I wish I'd met her.'

'She would have loved you, Ag. I hate that I'm forgetting little things about her, though. Like the edges of the memories are being sanded away.'

'She sounds like a strong woman and she'd be proud of you standing up and fighting for the rights of your brother and friend. I reckon she'd vote to march, hey?'

'She would.' I nodded. 'For sure. And that's the other reason I changed my mind. Whenever I'm not sure what to do, I just say to myself, "What would Mum have done?"'

I looked around the Forum at all the kids vying for a good vantage point so that they could see the speakers on the walkway with their megaphones.

'If it hadn't been for that draft, Walter's mum would still have her boy. He could have grown up, got married, lived a life, had kids and stuff. But the draft robbed him of that and he didn't even get to serve his country. It's so pointless. It could have been my brother or Luke. It still could be.'

And then I heard Barton's familiar voice floating out over the sea of people, loud, booming, passionate. The crowd cheered. They were like petrol on his fire and he loved it. After talking about the right to protest and march, the conflict in South-East Asia, civil rights and a general condemnation of conscription, Barton called for a show of hands.

'Raise your hands, people, if you vote to march next week.'

Hands went up like a giant collective jack-in-the-box. And the students roared their approval and began to chant: 'March. March. March.'

I even saw a few of the tutors and lecturers in the crowd with their hands up, too. Watching Barton, I was overcome with a flush of warmth that felt a bit like pride. His passion *was* contagious. I was really starting to like that about him. He had a fire in his heart and he was sincere. That was what made him stand out and shine. His sincerity and social conscience did not sit quietly, but roared. It was hard *not* being infected by his enthusiasm.

'Looks like a win for the affirmative,' Agnes said, beaming.

'Our trickle of discontent has become a flood!' Barton yelled at the crowd.

We listened and watched as the crowd cheered; it was an incredible thing to witness. After Barton stopped talking and the crowd began to disperse, I unzipped my guitar and checked the new nylon strings.

'Play me something.' Agnes smiled, lying on the grass beside me. 'I love your voice.'

'Hmmm.' I thought, strumming a chord. 'I haven't played this to anyone. It's an original. A Fiona McKechnie composition. I call it "The Sister Story".'

I closed my eyes and let the music carry me into the song and it was welling up from my heart, my core. I sang to the spirits of my mother and grandmother and all those women whose names were in the book at the top of my cupboard. I sang to Agnes, my honorary sister.

As I played the final chord, I heard a slow clap. I smiled and opened my eyes but was taken aback to see Barton McLeod leaning against the tree trunk, looking at me.

'Wow, Fi!' he said, nodding his head. 'You are incredible. How did I not know that we had a Joni Mitchell in our midst? Girl, you need to be on the stage. You need to be singing songs for the revolution.'

'I don't do audiences well,' I mumbled, embarrassed.

'Well, I'm impressed.' He grinned.

Despite myself I felt a tingle of a thrill at his genuine compliment. 'Thanks Barton,' I said.

'What a turnout, hey?' he said, sweeping an arm about the Forum. 'There had to be half the entire campus here. Maybe more! Even the teaching staff turned out in some impressive numbers. Nice to have their support! I tell you, we're the voice of the future.'

I nodded, still amazed by the reaction to the call up for a march against conscription.

'But, you know,' he went on, 'it's as much a march about the right to march, you know? Because they are trying to shut us down and we have the right to free speech, the right to say, "We are the young people and we are the ones on the frontline and we don't want to be target practice for the government's policies."'

'Hear, hear!' Agnes said.

'Yeah, I get it now.' I nodded and put my guitar down. 'I really do. It might be the law but sometimes laws get it wrong and the politicians kind of need to listen to the people, don't they? Otherwise nothing will ever change.'

'We have a convert!' Barton yelled at everyone and no one. 'Fiona has seen the light.'

'A girl can change her mind.' I laughed. 'Sometimes you just need to look at things from a different perspective.'

I thought about Mr and Mrs Leary, even Laura, and the terrible grief they must have been suffering. I'd been there. I was still there and I wouldn't wish it upon anyone.

'Do you reckon your boyfriend Luke's up for it?' Barton asked, kneeling beside me. 'I don't want to force him into this if he really doesn't want to do it.'

'Oh my gosh.' I laughed and it came out like a sneeze. 'Luke's not my boyfriend!'

'Oh, I thought ...' Barton looked surprised and I might have been imagining it but he seemed a bit relieved. 'Oh ... so you two aren't ...'

'No!' I said firmly. 'We're just friends. Nothing else.'

Agnes looked at me, then to Barton and then back to me, raising her eyebrow and giving me a cheeky smirk. I gave her a little snappy frown and a shrug that conveyed '*what*?'

'You know what?' I said, abruptly changing the subject. 'I was thinking. If we attempted to do something like this in the past ... you know like the French Revolution or in Ireland or America or any number of places in the past that needed a good shake up, we'd be facing death – execution or being burned at the stake or something horrific.'

'You're right, Fi,' Barton said, taking my hands in his. They were warm and soft. 'We are really lucky to be able to speak up and march and protest. It's our right. We can be the change. We can make our governments accountable to us. That's a gift and I'm going to use it well.'

'Me too!' I nodded.

'Me too!' Agnes said and rolled over and put her hands on ours.

'So let's march for liberty!' Barton said.

A week later we were marching. It wasn't a long distance to cover. The more timid, slightly reluctant students hugged the footpaths so that they were technically not marching, but spectating. Barton led the march like the Captain of the Cavalry, calling into his megaphone to keep our spirits up. He was wearing a huge National Liberation Front flag as a cape like some freedom-of-speech superhero.

Agnes, Jeff, Luke and I marched along the street as traffic was disrupted and car horns blared, some in support of our action but more than a few in anger at being inconvenienced. Jeff hummed to himself, keeping ever aloof, while holding Agnes's hand.

Luke and I fell behind and let ourselves be swallowed up by the crushing, swelling press of bodies all spilling like sludge through the inner-city streets of Brisbane. I was grateful that the day was cool.

'Barton reckons we'll run into the coppers at Roma Street,' Luke said, and I felt a flutter of nerves.

'We don't have a permit to march so I guess it's inevitable that we'll see the boys in blue.'

I tried to sound full of bravado but a little voice in the back of my head was telling me to go home and hide under my bed until it was all over. Barton had boasted the day before that he'd been arrested eleven times but had never actually been charged with anything other than a traffic violation for causing a traffic jam while marching. He told us this to convince us that there wouldn't be any serious repercussions if we marched and got taken in by the cops.

'I'm nervous about burning my papers in public, in front of the cops,' Luke said, and I gave his hand a squeeze.

'You don't have to do it,' I said. 'Barton would totally understand and the march is the important thing. It's your call, Luke.'

'I can't pull out now,' Luke said and I could hear the fear in his voice. 'To be honest, I'm more than nervous. I'm scared. But at the end of the day I'd still rather go to prison than war. Though neither would be my first choice, hey?'

I lost sight of Agnes and Jeff. A distant rumble suggested there was thunder approaching and I looked up at the pale blue, almost-white sky and then over my shoulder to the west to see a streak of gunmetal grey approaching.

Up ahead we heard a commotion and the march seemed to stall and simmer for a few minutes until the message came, shoulder over shoulder, shouted back to us. The police had formed a barrier up near Roma Street Station. I had that feeling in my lower belly that you get when you're in a car going over a bump at high speed.

'You ready for this?' I asked Luke breathlessly. 'I can't believe I am doing this. My father would kill me if he knew.'

Luke nodded. It was his turn to reassure me and he gave me a broad grin. 'You only live once. Might as well make an impact!' he said and pulled his draft notice out of his pocket and inhaled deeply, puffing out his chest.

Everyone was marching in rows, linking arms tightly, like we were stitches on a knitting needle all woven and connected. Slowly we pressed forward. One step at a time, carefully, like a choreographed chorus line. And then as we rounded the bend, all hell broke loose.

I was separated from Luke as kids started running helter-skelter all over the place, panicking. The happy dance was over.

Someone screamed.

I felt my chest constricting with fear.

'Sit down!' came a booming voice over the chaos. 'Everyone sit down peacefully.'

It was Barton on the megaphone. Around me, kids began dropping into cross-legged yoga poses on the road. As we sat, I could see the line of uniformed police ahead, their faces set like concrete. There were hundreds of them, all with truncheons at the ready.

'Golly,' I murmured because I couldn't think of anything else to say.

I looked around to see if there was any way I could escape and slink off into the city and run home, but I was hemmed in by hundreds of bodies. Barton came back to us, avoiding standing on anyone as if he was in a gauntlet university game challenge stepping between tyres. People leaned away to avoid being trampled by him.

'Luke! Luke!' he called.

I groaned as Luke stood up and waved. Some of my bravado had left me. I was scared too. I crawled on my hands and knees over to Luke and sat at his feet like a hypnotised devotee. Barton came over and took him by the hand and spoke into his megaphone again.

'Here's a young man, Luke Sheehan, who has his draft papers.'

Luke held them aloft and waved them to the crowd and then back at the police. I couldn't believe he actually said Luke's name. I could see people with television cameras up ahead and their big round lenses were trained right on us. I was sitting right beside Luke's leg.

'He doesn't want to murder innocent people just because they happened to be born in a certain part of Vietnam. He doesn't want to be Uncle Sam's foot soldier. He doesn't want to line the pockets of all those capitalists who get rich out of the spoils of war. He is not afraid to stand up and say so! Don't put guns in our hands against our will! Don't send us to war. This is a march for our lives. For Luke's life.'

Barton pulled out matches from his pocket and handed them to Luke who lit the papers and watched defiantly as they caught alight. He waved them around until the flames were high and then dropped them to the road before stomping out the ashes. I rolled into someone else's body just in time to clear a spot for Barton's shoe. I flicked light specks of ash from my jeans. I was acutely aware of the television camera getting closer so I tried to hide my face. The crowd roared its approval and Luke looked really pleased with himself.

The police surged forward and began to grab the student marchers in headlocks, pushing them down, screaming at them to lie face down on the road, pulling their hands behind their backs. I saw one girl get her hair yanked by a policeman. I hoped that the cameras were capturing what was happening because this response to a peaceful march wasn't right. I was iced by terror and I looked around frantically for Agnes.

Barton was running straight at the police while Luke was jack-rabbiting back through the crowd as he'd planned. He was now on the run from the law. The police were grappling with anyone they could get a hold of, dragging kids by their feet, their hair, their arms, off the road and dumping them like sandbags on the pavement.

Two policemen tackled Barton while he shouted out 'freedom' and 'liberty'. Handcuffs were clamped on his wrists.

I was so mesmerised by the interaction between the police and Barton that I didn't notice the policeman standing beside me yelling. I looked up too late and felt a boot in the back of my spine. Instinctively, I shouted in pain, then struggled to my feet to try to run away. The policeman grabbed me around the waist and picked me up like I was a stray dog. Flashbulbs exploded around me.

'You're under arrest,' I heard someone shout, and felt myself get dumped into the back of a truck along with a crush of other kids. I didn't recognise any of them. I fell back against the side of the vehicle and closed my eyes. My ribs hurt.

'What a buzz, hey?' Someone laughed near me. 'What a trip.'

'We really stuck it to them. One for us. Nil for The Man!' another voice shouted triumphantly.

I looked down at my ripped shirt and broken shoelace and felt like throwing up. I was awash with remorse and wished I had not gotten out of bed that day but as I looked around at the other students, all beaming and hugging one another, I began to rethink the situation. They *thought* they'd won. They *felt* like winners. And I let the regrets slip away. I'd made a point. I was only one little sardine in a sea of sardines. But we were swimming upstream and that was somehow really important in the grand scheme of things. I felt a bit taller, a bit stronger, for having done something so powerful and significant and defiant. I looked at one of the girls beaming at me and imagined my mother as a teenager. She'd looked a lot like me. And I thought about all the women in our bloodline who had fought, and to be completely honest, I felt a little bit like Joan of Arc, and I started laughing with the thrill and power of it.

'I'm Joan of Arc,' I said aloud.

'Damn straight, sister,' the girl on the other side of the paddy wagon said, and raised a fist. 'We all are!'

JEANNE

BEAUVAIS, FRANCE, 1472

We left the scent of gunpowder in the woods and clopped through the tangle of the overgrown entrance to the aqueducts. It was an in-between place, like purgatory, a waiting room, a place of purification and penance. Dark, damp and cool. I felt that I was no longer a part of the world but somehow removed from it, as if I was in a bubble with Colin. I was not in the crumbling, besieged city of Beauvais, nor was I in the woods. I was not betrothed in that place, nor was I free.

'Colin,' I spoke into the darkness and my voice echoed back, metallic and eerie. 'We could still go. These horses are fine creatures. Selling just one would pay for our passage to London. We can still be together.'

Silence. Except for the sound of dripping water.

'Jeanne.' Colin's voice bounced off the old stone walls. 'If we ran away, you would never forgive yourself for leaving your father. I would dishonour your family and my own.

If everyone disobeyed the laws and did whatever they wanted, everything would descend into chaos.'

Chaos sounded a lot better to me than being in a loveless marriage to a tyrant. 'I don't care about dishonour.' I sulked like a petulant child. 'I only care about you and escaping from my awful fate.'

I felt sure that Lagoy had deliberately sent Colin into the Italian mercenaries to have him killed. In my bones I knew now that my betrothed would stop at nothing to have Colin permanently removed from my life. Dead, he posed no threat for my heart. The only way that Colin could escape this fate was for us to flee.

'You will be happier with yourself if you do the right thing.'

'I will be miserable,' I said although I did not want to concern him with my fears of Lagoy's murderous intentions.

Our horses' hooves clipped in the darkness as we moved through the dense gloom toward the light ahead.

Outside the aqueduct, we stood our horses beneath a lamp-post, the lantern swinging and creaking hauntingly above us. The moon seemed to shine on only us, full and ominous.

'We don't choose our fate, Jeanne,' Colin said. 'It chooses us.'

He was right, but I wanted it to be different. If our fate was predestined, what was the point of life? To fulfil someone else's promise? Whose? God's? Captain Balagny's? Jean Lagoy's?

'But Jean Lagoy chose me,' I said, sniffing back tears. 'He gets to choose his destiny. His wife. His life. It's not fair.'

'No. Life isn't fair, Jeanne. It is different for different folks and the more things you have – land, standing, royal favour – the fairer it is,' he said. 'We are born where we are born and we must make the most of the life allotted to us. I am a chicken farmer. My father was a chicken farmer. You now have the chance to lead a life that I cannot offer you. Take it, Jeanne, make it the best life you can.'

'But I want you and the chickens and ...' I sobbed, lowering my head, feeling my chest heave with pain. 'I don't want finery and bone china and I don't want ... ermine gloves and ... and ...'

A whistle ripped through the darkness, so shrill it chilled me to the core. I heard the thud of footsteps, running, marching. And another short sharp blast of the whistle. I sat up straighter in my saddle, my ears ringing, stunned by the sudden noise.

'They are here!' a voice cried and I turned my head to see a group of men in uniforms heading toward us. 'I've found them.'

'It's all right, Jeanne,' Colin said in a soothing, calming voice. 'We'll explain and—'

They were upon us, surrounding our horses, swords drawn.

'Dismount,' one man commanded and from the dim shadows behind him I saw a figure striding along the street, his white ruffled shirt shining like the moon, the brass buttons on his coat winking like glow-worms, his hair an unruly mess, his chiselled jaw.

'I'll have you know that we have been on important King's business,' Colin said firmly to the townsmen who had formed a circle around us, but he obeyed the order and swung off the horse, reaching up to offer me assistance in sliding off my own horse.

'Unhand that woman!' I heard Jean Lagoy roar into the night. 'Let her be.'

My belly dropped as if I'd swallowed a stone and I slipped off the horse onto the cool street.

'Monsieur,' I stammered as he came to me, his nostrils flaring with anger. 'Good news. We have disabled the Italian stock of gunpowder and—'

'It is true,' another soldier stepped forward and spoke. 'From the eagle's nest on the battlements we saw the sabotage but did not know who was responsible. The entire northern encampment is obliterated.'

'Yes! Yes!' Lagoy tutted. 'We all saw it and certainly heard it! But there is no evidence that it was anything other than a fortuitous accident. To conclude that this pair were responsible—'

'I saw the line of fire,' another man said. 'It seemed clear to me—'

'Silence!' Lagoy shouted. 'You and you, Dupre and Berjot, arrest this man on the charge of kidnapping, horse theft and, Monsieur Pilon, pray, do you have my bag of silver?'

'No,' Colin said nervously. 'I was captured by the Italians and they took the silver but Jeanne, she took out all the barrels of gunpowder ... the explosions ... you must have heard. This was better than getting them to fight for us ... she took them out ... all of them ... it was incredible and—'

'And theft of the King's silver. Take him away,' Lagoy roared. 'Chain him up in the dungeon beneath the chapel of St Etienne. I'll deal with him later.'

My eyes grew as wide as saucers and my mouth fell open as I watched a pair of men take Colin by the elbows to lead him away.

'No, he was captured,' I pleaded. 'The Italians stole the silver. Colin only did what you asked ...'

My words sifted away into the darkness like smoke evaporating into the night. The Lieutenant looked down at my chest. I followed his eyes and gasped, reaching to cross both arms over myself. My under-blouse was ripped and torn and parts of my skin, scratched and bleeding, were exposed.

'You are an embarrassment, Jeanne,' he seethed. 'Look at you!'

Taking my upper arm in a vice-like grip, Lagoy marched me along the cobbled street, away from Colin, yelling back to his men. 'One of you come with me,' he called. 'The others take the horses back to the Captain's stables and see that you apologise to him. Tell them the culprit has been caught and will be dealt with very harshly.'

'*I* took the horses.' I corrected him, not caring if he threw me into the dungeon for it. I was hoping against hope that he just might. 'But I didn't steal them. I only borrowed them and I really did blow up the—'

'Shut your mouth, Jeanne,' Lagoy hissed, squeezing my arm harder as he all but dragged me down the street.

I felt the hatchet at my side, bumping against my leg as I walked. Part of me wanted to take to him with it but I gave a silent prayer of apology to the good Lord for having had that terrible thought. As we neared the poorest quarter of town, my quarter, the devastation from the siege became more apparent. Houses had been hit by cannon shot and were crumbled rubble.

'Where are you taking me?' I asked as I staggered beside him.

'Home to your father. He was brought back when the fighting stopped at sunset. There is no room in the Cathedral.'

My heart leapt and for a moment I thought he meant to return me to my father's keeping and break the betrothal contract, but he dashed that hope.

'You will begin to pack whatever you need and tomorrow I will have you interred at my residence, under lock and key, until we are married, which will be post-haste. Then woe betide if you ever get it into your head to disobey me again. I will break that will of yours, Jeanne. Mark my words.'

'If you don't like my will and my spirit,' I said brazenly, 'then why do you insist on taking me as a wife? Why did you not choose someone more meek and demure?'

We walked on for a moment and then Lagoy stopped and turned me around to face him. He glared into my eyes until I trembled.

'Because, Jeanne,' he smiled a cruel and cold smile, 'sometimes the unbroken horse is a challenge. Buying a tame horse is one thing but breaking one in yourself is so much more satisfying.'

He leaned forward and pressed his mouth against

mine, crushing my lips. I kept my mouth closed and shut my eyes, putting up a barrier of resistance between us until he pulled back. 'You will be my wife, Jeanne Laisné, and you will bend to my will.'

Never, I said silently to myself. Never would I ever be bent to suit Jean Lagoy. I would sooner snap in two.

We walked to my father's small house, which was mercifully undamaged, apart from the damp rot. The door was ajar. Inside, my father was lying on his bed in the corner, asleep. I could just make him out in the dim light from the candle burning low by the back door. It was sitting in a wide plate of molten wax.

'Who is it?' my father's voice came, cracking with sleep as the door banged shut. 'Who's there?'

'It's just me, Papa,' I called. 'I am safe. You go back to sleep.'

Shadows danced over the walls. I left Lagoy in the doorway and went to take the candle and a holder. I turned back to glare at him but said nothing, willing him to leave.

'I will return at daybreak to claim you,' Lagoy said roughly.

I watched my father struggle up onto one elbow, trying to rouse himself.

'Is that ... you, Lieutenant? So soon?' he stammered. 'You mean to marry Jeanne so soon? What of the siege? What of my bride-price? When will it be paid?'

Lagoy laughed, throwing his head back and tossing his dark hair from his high forehead. 'You stupid old man,' he snorted. 'Jeanne owes me a bag of silver. You won't be getting any bride-price. You owe *me* now. Twenty pieces of silver. Jeanne might be worth ten at a stretch, but you will need to work off the rest of it.'

My father looked at me, bewildered by what Lagoy was telling him. I could not believe my ears. Jean Lagoy was taking me from the slums as his wife and making my father indebted to him for the silver the Italians had stolen from Colin? It was an outrage, but I knew I had no recourse. I had no power and my father had even less.

'What of Colin Pilon?' I asked Lagoy. 'What will become of him? He tried to secure the Italian mercenaries. He did everything you asked. But you hoped they would kill him, didn't you? It was cheap at the price. Twenty pieces of silver to get the Italians to do your dirty work.'

Lagoy was smiling, his eyes flickering in the candlelight. 'There's no doubt about you, Jeanne,' he said slowly. 'You're as quick as a snake. But no mind. Your chicken boy will still end up like one of his little headless chooks in the square. Stealing silver and horses during a time of military engagement is punishable by death. The guillotine is too good for him. Ah, yes, you'll make a beautiful bride and I hope you'll come to see how lucky you are and be grateful one day.'

Lagoy left without shutting the door. I went to it, looking out at him speaking with the man who had accompanied us through the streets. Lagoy paid him a coin to stand guard outside.

I closed the door, bolted it, and went back to my father who was scratching his head.

'What did he mean, Jeanne, love?' he asked me. 'What was all that about not paying me my bride-price? He says I am indebted to him. I don't understand. Jeanne, what did he mean? Because as soon as we have it you can flee with Colin and start a new life.'

'Go back to sleep, Papa,' I said, the words sticking like dry bread in my throat. 'I will be up in the attic.'

'Jeanne?' he asked as I took to the narrow stairs, leaving him in the dark.

'Go back to sleep, Papa,' I soothed.

He did not need to be troubled by the news of what had befallen poor Colin. It would only scare sleep away from him. I postponed telling him that I would be leaving the next day. I could try to get a message to Aimee's mother to look in on him until I could make other plans for his care. Without me he would die.

Upstairs in the dusty, cluttered attic, I put the candle and my hatchet on the windowsill, watching a moth spinning outside. I sat between two heavy trunks, my knees pulled up to my chin, and I began to cry.

'Mama,' I sobbed. 'Where are you? I need you.'

There was no answer, only the screech of an owl in the distance. I curled up into a ball on the rough-hewn floorboards and let myself drift into a fitful sleep.

I dreamed of my mother. She was young and beautiful, dressed in a flowing white shift of chiffon. Over it was her red velvet cape. Together we collected berries in the woods while bumblebees buzzed by our heads. I smiled up at her as she wiped the purple juice from the corner of my mouth with one long, elegant finger. 'I am with you always, Jeanne,' she whispered. 'Me ... and your grandmother ... and your grandmother's mother and her mother and her mother before that, all the way back to the beginning of all time. You have no need to be afraid, Jeanne. We are with you always. We are you.'

BETSY

County Down, Ireland, 1798

The Rebel Army was assembling on a hill known as Edenvady, about half a mile south-west of the town of Ballynahinch. It was a high hill and well suited to the insurgency. Hundreds, maybe thousands of men were converging there, armed with whatever weapons they could get their hands on.

The sun was up and the day was promising a humid heat. Faint streaks of clouds gathered high in the blue sky. Down in the village of Ballynahinch, there was an air of simmering terror that was being glossed over with forced laughter and much convivial back-slapping and merry-making, not to mention whisky-imbibing despite the early hour. Behind the tight smiles was a township waiting in fear. All of them resented the English but even as the rebel troops marched into their town, promising salvation and liberty, many of the townsfolk were losing their courage, aiming to sit on the fence or pretend things weren't happening.

'Well, I don't know that it has to come down to bloodshed, is all I'm saying.' One old fellow at the bar shook his head and scratched his nose. 'The rebels have got thousands up there but they're like a field of plucked roosters, all crow and not much claw.'

Ignoring him, I dragged the plain wooden coffin into the inn's kitchen by myself. Mary Ann McCracken and I had bumped the cart carrying the coffin full of weapons over the back paddocks, gullies and creeks to get it up to town off the roads, which were being closely monitored by the yeomanry and various auxiliary commands. Finn McCool had been a good strong packhorse for us but we'd worn down the wheels and broken three or four cogs on the cart. Mary Ann was pleased with our effort. After I'd gone back outside and yarded my horse, I waved off Mary Ann. She was going on up to Antrim with her sister and two clergymen to begin rallying support closer to Belfast. I went back inside the inn, knowing no one, to organise supplies of sustenance for the men who were arriving from all over the countryside. I had received the secret call to arms at the assembly point of Ballynahinch the day before.

'My Irish sisters,' I called to the gathering of women, young and old, who'd come from out of town with their United Irishmen husbands, fathers and sons. I clapped my hands and gave a whistle through my two fingers until they quietened down and gave me their attention.

'We're going to sweep through the town with two tasks at hand,' I told them, taking charge. 'One, to gather provisions, anything at all. Donations that people might be happy to give up: foodstuffs, pies or pikes, muskets or any sort of weaponry, even kitchen knives. Anything will be accepted most gratefully. Our other objective is to rally some more manpower! Every rebel sympathiser should pick up a pike and speak with violence today. That is the only language the redcoats understand so let's take it to them and see some of *their* blood for a change. Manpower. We need a lot more of it!'

'Oh, I could with some more manpower.' One jolly woman roared with laughter. 'My Paddy's run out of steam, he has!'

Many joined her in laughter but I continued speaking.

'Our men on the hill need more muscle, more pikes, more men to stand alongside them! All we have on our side is our numbers. We are many to their few. Even hares can take down foxes if there are enough of them.'

I looked around the room at the rosy-cheeked women, the mischievous children and the elderly. A low rumble of talk rippled through the drinking house. It seemed that most of the folk present were there to provide solidarity to one another, and drink whisky and dark beer to numb the growing sense of discomfort and fear as the reality of the situation began to seep in. Someone had brought a fiddle and was tuning it in the corner and another colleen, already more than a little tipsy, was dancing a jig to music that only she could hear in her head. The room was strung tight with tension despite the attempts at light-heartedness. Blood *would* be shed unless one side or the other surrendered and submitted, and we all knew that was not going to happen. When English stubbornness came up against Irish pride, you had two stags with antlers locked.

I wanted the revolution. I just wasn't so keen on the blood shedding, although George and Will always told me that, 'Many may have to suffer, so that some day all Irish people might know peace and justice.' It was for the greater good and I understood that.

A large group of the women gathered out on the street and we carried baskets and pulled small, wheeled carts by hand. I blew a strand of hair from my face, rolled up the white buttoned sleeves on my blouse and gave a nod.

'Aye, lasses.' I smiled. 'It will be dirty work our men must steel themselves for and they'll be needing full bellies and peat-fire in their bones. Grab provisions and we'll meet back here at the inn in the kitchen for baking at high sun. Press upon their patriotism and make them give generously.'

Full of hope we set off through the narrow streets of Ballynahinch, door-knocking and requesting whatever the inhabitants could offer up. I collected beef and bacon and sacks of oats.

'Where are your menfolk?' I asked at the many doors that were opened by frightened women and children. 'They need to take arms and join the others on the hill. Have they left for there already?'

Most of those I asked dropped their eyes and then hurried to provide a generous proportion of food and produce, but were silent on the issue of their men. One woman was quite forthright with me and set me straight. I was not so happy to hear it, though.

'Most men in Ballynahinch have taken to the mountains,' she told me. 'With the yeomanry and the Monaghans and all the rest ready to march through our town, well, the nerve's gone from them. If they stand against the soldiers, we'll all be taken down. They'll burn the village to cinders. Some folks don't have the backbone for it.'

'But this place, Ballynahinch, was chosen because it is rife and ready with rebels,' I said, aghast at her words. 'I've seen you at a meeting, Madame, I'm sure of it.'

'Ah, love, it's not that we don't rally behind the cause,' she said, twisting her mouth around the words. 'It's just that we fear it will be the end of us. If the French were here with us, standing strong, then maybe, but we don't want to risk our children's futures or their very lives. I'm here to bake bread for those that want to fight but I'll not have my men slaughtered in a war they cannot win.'

I sighed and shook my head.

'What's your name?'

'Catherine,' she told me. 'And I've got seven wee ones under ten. We have nothing, but you can take all the food in the pantry, all of it, and we pray that the Rebel Army holds strong and all. The soldiers will leave the women and children well enough alone, we hope.'

'I wouldn't count on it,' I told her. 'You're best to take your young ones off to the mountains as well.'

Almost every cottage and farmlet had the same sorry story. They were all for booting the English from our shores but few were ready to risk their lives and those of their families for the cause.

Many of the women were eager to help at the inn and

had come to boil the salted beef and bacon, and bake oatcakes for the troops. I returned to the kitchen to find plenty of hands punching out dough on dusted boards. In the main bar of the drinking house, music was playing and the old men who had remained behind, too weary to flee to the mountains and too weak to join the rebellion, danced like calves taking their first steps on spindly, shaking legs. Children ran between their ankles, trying to trip them up, while their mothers gossiped and gabbed about how the day might unfold.

By early afternoon, the women had prepared a huge amount of food to be transported to the rebel camp and I nominated myself along with two other women from Ballynahinch to transport the carts up to the troops. I had not been to Edenvady Hill, but Will had drawn me a comprehensive map on a large piece of butcher's paper and I knew I would have no trouble finding it.

The women introduced themselves as Sarah and Eilish and with the help of some others we loaded up three carts full to the brim. Not scrimping on our menfolk, we packed ham and many oat-loaves, buns, boiled salted beef and bacon, and plenty more besides.

'Piking English dogs is hungry work,' Sarah joked but the younger woman looked away, discomforted by such talk.

As reality set in, I began to feel queasy at the prospect of having our good men, my own George and Will foremost in my mind, engaged in hand-to-hand combat with the redcoats. I had a vision of clashing metal and rivers of blood and shut my eyes, saying a prayer that it might all be over with as few casualties as possible.

'We've got thousands up there, so I've heard,' I said enthusiastically, trying as much to bolster my own spirits as those of the other women. 'A mighty proud and fiercely Irish army of men determined to sever Ireland from Britain and give her a place among the nations.'

'You sound like Theobald Wolfe Tone himself.' Sarah grinned as she threw the canvas tarpaulin to me and we secured it to keep the food shaded from the heat of the sun. 'Have you seen him in the flesh? Oh, he's lovely. Such a grand and handsome chap. I all but swooned, I did, when I saw him all those years ago. I was much younger then and might have turned his head if I'd had a mind to, but now I'm like a heifer put out to pasture. He's rallying the French for us.'

Sarah laughed a tinkling laugh and I smiled, but I saw Eilish close in on herself and go rigid. The poor thing was beside herself with worry.

'You all right there, Eilish?' I asked gently. 'Do you have menfolk up on the hill?'

She nodded stiffly. 'Me sweetheart, Donald. I didn't want him to go. I wanted him to head for the hills, go up with the rest of them till all the fuss was over, but he'd not hear of it. He wants to take down the English. It's foolhardy, it is. The yeomanry have got the whole King's force behind them. Our lads are just a ramshackle band of farmers with hayforks. They'll be crushed just like them down near Dublin. Bunch of foolish boys and men playing soldiers!'

That wiped the smile off Sarah's round face. Her expression changed and she spoke with the curl of a scowl.

'Where there's a will and a fire in the heart, there's a weapon more powerful than anything made of wood or iron. All those folks with ardour for the cause who up and ran away like rats on a sinking ship as soon as the call went out, they're cowards. Only those who are real Irish are up there on that hill, readying their pikes. I am proud of my man, Kenny, and my three sons. May God be with them. Now let's get this tucker to them and stop crying like babies.'

We took three of the packhorses tethered to the posts in the back paddock behind the inn and shackled them to three old block-wheel carts. I wasn't about to make my fine Finn McCool drag such a heavy load up the steep incline that soared from the other side of town. He was sore and tired from the cross-country ride and needed resting. It was going to be a long night and I wanted him ready in case I should need him for a speedy getaway or a lap of honour about Ballynahinch once we'd crushed our enemy the next day.

The ride through town felt like a funeral parade. Curtains hung like shrouds in the windows. Dogs poked about in puddles, their tails between their legs, bored and sniffing out some excitement: a cat or a rat or a forgotten bone. The flagpole bore the English flag but the flag hung limply, giving a half-hearted sigh with every breath of wind. There was no chatter. No laughter. No children tearing at breakneck speed through the narrow laneways, chasing kites or leather balls.

Ballynahinch was abandoned and any who remained must have been buried deep and quiet in the bellies of their homes. No smoke drifted up from chimneys. No fiddles or pipes played. Even the churches were shut.

'After the women and old men had given up their food, most of them hurried off to the mountains as well. Traitors,' Sarah said, bristling.

It was unnerving and despite the late sun and heat of the summer day, I felt a chill down my spine. We walked on with only the sound of the cart wheels on stone to accompany us. My thoughts were scattered and I tried to gather them. Many sympathisers were deserting on the eve of the battle. The horses pulled the front cart of food as we women walked beside it. I held Finn McCool's reins in one hand.

'It will be on their conscience when we liberate Ireland,' I muttered. 'We will all enjoy the freedoms that come with our victory but some will have greater earned them!'

Young Eilish looked to her hands, which she wrung nervously together. Above us a few soft clouds idled in the sky and I heard the gentle clang of a goat-bell from the back of one of the cottages.

As we left the town behind, the roads became more congested with bands of men riding toward the big hill. Most were travelling at speed and paid us no mind but a few doffed caps and called to us.

'God bless you, good women,' one man called and another whooped out some passing comment that was lost on the afternoon breeze. One well-heeled man wearing an impressive vintage cap rode beside us and gave us more detail on what was going on.

'They've had some heavy losses up Antrim way,' he said solemnly. 'That's why so many of the men from Ballynahinch have fled. General Nugent is leading the charge of British forces and from all accounts he put down the Rising in Antrim quickly and mercilessly. Those of us that fled unharmed are joining our comrades on the hills down here.'

'But my brother told me that the rebels have complete control of the north and middle eastern areas of County Down.' I questioned him as we began to climb the road up into higher country.

'True, true.' The man nodded, his mouth set tight. 'But for how long, hey? We needed all the men in this town to reinforce our troops.'

'My boys are up there,' Sarah said proudly. 'And same with Betsy's here and yours too, lassie,' she said, giving Eilish a stern look. 'It says it in the Bible,' Sarah continued. 'Every kingdom divided against itself is brought to desolation; and every city or house divided against itself, shall not stand.'

'Please,' Eilish said in a voice that warbled with fear, 'don't speak like that. I cannot bear to think of anything but victory. Our men are determined and they have fire in their hearts.'

I smiled at her and nodded. 'That they do.'

'We will rid this island of English just like Saint Paddy rid it of snakes and toads.' The man on the horse grinned, and gave us a friendly wink before cantering off to catch up with the men ahead of him.

The wheels of our carts rolled up the gravelly road,

playing percussion with the sound of our horses' hooves. I shut my eyes and listened to the beat as it pulsed in my blood and I instantly recalled a ditty we often sang at our rebel meetings. We called it the Liberty Tree. Slowly, in little more than a murmur, I began to sing:

It was the year of '93
The French did plant an olive tree ...

Sarah, obviously a grand supporter of our cause and a regular at meetings, took up with me, her voice rich and deep.

... the symbol of great liberty
And the people danced around it ...

Our voices grew loud and I smiled encouragingly at young Eilish as she meekly joined in and then gathered a little momentum, her chest swelling up with breath and song.

... that equality, freedom and fraternity
Would be the cry of every nation.

Climbing higher up the hills west of Ballynahinch, toward the ribbons of smoke and the sound of bugles and pipes, we sang at the top of our voices, our feet marching in the dirt, the sound filling me with hope, courage and great pride for our brave men. Men rallying to the cause, riding around us, joined in and it became a spontaneous battle song just like those sung by the great Irish kings and their troops going to battle over the many years, fending off those that would seek to claim our emerald isle for their own.

I was heartened to see the spread of our army on the flanks of the hill as we approached. Thousands had gathered and there was a sense of excitement and enthusiasm. The hill commanded a magnificent view of the country for miles around and the little town nestled at its foot. Men congregated in small clumps and some enjoyed the shade of thickets of trees, lying on the grass, resting in preparation for the battle ahead. Two stocky young men approached us with open smiles. The sun shone with a fierce brilliancy. County Down had suffered a long season of drought and the grass was scorched.

'Looky here.' One grinned. 'Are these angels come to minister to us from Heaven?'

The men took Finn McCool's reins and helped us unshackle our horses so we could lead them to drinking troughs, then insisted on unloading the food from the carts into the supply tents. Everywhere we went we were met with smiles of welcome and gentlemanly bows of gratitude. Someone somewhere was playing a concertina and tents were pitched between trees, behind which rose a gentle slope. I recognised some faces from meetings but felt enormous relief when Will came bounding across a patch of grass, waving wildly at me.

'Betsy, love,' he yelled. 'Betsy!'

He came to me and picked me up and spun me around making me giddy and my stomach lurch. It was no mean feat to lift me off my feet as I was a tall girl. I laughed and struggled out from his arms, landing my boots on the grass with a thud.

'They say many have fled to the hills, men who ought to be here fighting with you,' I said, catching my breath. 'Cowards.'

Will shrugged. 'Better they flee now than freeze on the field and let us down. We don't need them.'

I looked at Will in his dashing green tunic with polished pewter buttons, skin-tight white breeches, V-cut boots, and a small felt hat with a green ribbon tied in a knot sitting on top of his dark curls. He looked handsome and dressed to be taken seriously. Around his waist he wore a green silk sash and I noted that most of the others did as well.

'Are you afraid, Will?' I asked softly.

'No, love, no,' he said gently and pushed a strand of hair from my face, tucking it behind my ear. 'There will be ballads sung of these times and our children and their children will be free and it will be because of what we do here today, tonight and tomorrow. I am proud to be a part of it. Our dream of a republic is about to become a reality. I've waited my whole life for this, Betsy!'

'When will the British troops arrive?' I asked, breathlessly, feeling nervous but a little bit thrilled that the day of reckoning was upon us.

'They are almost here. We received word from Nugent, their leader, this morning. He plans to sack all four townships that have given us these brave rebel men,' he said, sweeping an arm around to take in the swarming rebels dotting the hills, more numerous by far than sheep. 'They have warned us that if we do not desist from our rebellious activities they will proceed to destroy the towns of Killinchy, Killyleagh, Ballynahinch and Saintfield. And any person found with arms will be put to the sword.'

His mention of arms took my breath away. I suddenly realised that I had forgotten the coffin of weapons on the kitchen floor that Mary Ann McCracken and I had risked life and limb to transport across rough terrain to the inn back down in Ballynahinch. I put my hands over my face for a moment and then looked back at him.

'The muskets,' I said to Will, my blood boiling with anger at myself. 'I … we … brought all the foodstuffs but the weapons are still at the inn …'

Will looked momentarily concerned but pushed it away and wrapped an arm around me, squeezing me tightly.

'The redcoats are some way off yet. I will ride back with you to get them. We need those muskets.'

Sarah and Eilish had been swallowed up by the rebel troops and I could see them laughing with some of the men. Eilish seemed to have settled somewhat. Perhaps the jovial atmosphere on the hill and the impressive number of men ready to fight had eased her terrors. I was a wee bit angry at the two women for also having forgotten. It had not been my sole responsibility yet I was silently cursing my foolishness.

'If we take my horse, we'll be there and back in the blink of an eye,' he winked. 'There is so much going on and I might have been distracted and forgetful too. Don't concern yourself, Betsy. You've been a pillar of strength to us and just look at the food you've brought. Think of the energy it will give us!'

'I feel right terrible, Will. I'm so sorry. It's something of a pattern for me. I forgot Annie O'Neal's plight and look what happened to her! Now, the weapons. I have a head of fluff. I was so busy with the cooking and packing of the food that the weapons had gone clean out of my mind. I get carried away by the moment and ...'

Will leaned forward and kissed away my words, consuming me with a marvellous silence.

'George?' I asked when we finally pulled apart.

'Oh, he's having a special meeting with Munro, going over tactics. He'll not miss me,' Will said. 'Let's get away so that we can be back before all that food gets gobbled up.'

Together we rode back to town downhill, fast. I rode astride the horse, behind Will, holding on tightly around his waist, pressing my body into his, my face buried beneath his shoulder-blades, listening to the gallop of his heartbeat. We pulled up in the yard behind the inn and at that moment a sound invaded my ears as I swung off the horse. It was a strange beating that came on the breeze and trembled up from the dirt underfoot.

'What's that?' I frowned, cocking my head toward the noise.

We listened, stopping still, searching, wondering. The sound came again. A solid, thudding distant drone, almost like thunder.

'Drums,' Will whispered, his face going white. 'Military drums.'

'The redcoats,' I said to him, gripping his hands in mine. 'Oh no, Will. They're here. They're marching into town.'

FIONA

BRISBANE, AUSTRALIA, 1968

That night in the Brisbane lock-up was one of the worst nights of my life. The holding cell stank of a heady mix of urine and vomit, and there was graffiti on the walls that might have been written in blood; swear words and offensive statements that I had never imagined existed. I was terrified, although at least I wasn't alone. There were three other female students in the same cell. I had no idea what had happened to Barton, Agnes, Luke or Jeff. The whole memory of the march became a blur. At least Barton had been right about one thing: the police did not end up charging us with anything and the only repercussion was a stern talking to.

Feeling dirty and dishevelled, I had to walk all the way home to Kelvin Grove because I had left the boarding house the day before with nothing but the key to my room in the pocket of my jeans. Out in the bright daylight it all seemed like a bad dream. Nothing had changed. People were going about their business, off to work as if nothing had happened. I scuffed down the street, kicking my sneakers against the kerb, feeling the autumn breeze through my hair. I licked my furry teeth, which were in desperate need of a toothbrush, and I began to wonder if any of it had really been worth it. We'd marched. We'd chanted. We'd carried placards. Luke had burned his draft notice. Some of us got arrested and then released without charge and then everything went back to normal. Walter Leary was still dead and my brother was still packing to go to war.

Back at the boarding house, I let myself in and walked up the stairs and along the hallway to my room. I felt a sense of relief to see my familiar mess. I was suddenly really hungry and realised I hadn't eaten since breakfast the day before. I wondered if Luke was back in the kitchen, preparing food just like nothing had ever happened. I lay on my bed, shut my eyes and tried to flush the past twenty-four hours out of my head. I was almost asleep when I heard someone whispering my name. I thought I was dreaming.

'Fi! Fi!' it said in a hoarse sort of whisper.

My eyes opened and I struggled to sit up. I looked down to see Luke rolling out from under my bed.

'Luke? What?' I said, still trying to wake up.

'Shh!' he said and put a finger to his lips, his eyes darting frantically to the door.

'What are you doing?' I said crossly. 'If Mrs Lotte finds you here she'll evict me.'

'Never mind the dragon lady,' he said, sitting beside me on my bed. 'It's the cops I'm worried about. They came looking for me first thing this morning and I managed to climb up the piping and crawl into your room.'

I looked across at my open window. The curtains were wet around the edges where the storm had crept in. Luke was wearing jeans and a white singlet. His arms were deeply tanned. His eyes were as wide as saucers and his hair was a wild mess.

'Shit!' I said. 'This is starting to feel way too real. Too serious. Too big. What the hell are you going to do, Luke? You can't live under my bed.'

'Well, obviously not.' He laughed.

We both smelled of stale sweat.

'Well?'

He shrugged. 'I'm considering my options. By the way, we were on the six o'clock news. It was the top story. I watched it in the common room and turned it off before my aunt came in but she is going to be ropeable when she finds out. And she will. The cops will be back. She was out this morning, thank goodness, but it won't be long before someone tells her.'

'Did they say your name or show your face?' I asked, alarmed that it had made such a splash in the media.

'Yes. My name. My face. Barton ranting into the megaphone and you sitting there like a stunned mullet.'

'You saw me?' I gasped. 'No!'

'Yes.' He nodded. 'Not a close-up or anything but it looked like you were clinging to my leg. Were you clinging to my leg?'

'No, of course not!' I said incredulously. 'Or at least I don't think I was.'

I let that bit of news sink in. I had never been on

television before. It felt pretty strange. I assumed my face was blurred in the crowd. There were so many of us and to the untrained eye I figured we all looked the same. I was extremely glad Mrs Lotte had missed it.

'You'll be out of a job when she finds out, I guess,' I said to Luke. 'Or will she cover for you? She's your aunt after all.'

He shook his head.

'Nah,' he said. 'She was just doing me a favour by giving me the job. She doesn't like me much. I'm going to catch a bus back home to Townsville. Probably today. Lie low for a bit.'

I felt a wave of sadness. I would miss Luke and his smile.

'I suppose you do have to get out of Brisbane,' I said, and pouted. 'But I wish you didn't have to.'

'Me either,' he agreed. 'But I'm still glad I did it. I really do believe in standing up for what I believe in.'

We sat there for an awkward moment and I don't know what possessed me, perhaps I could blame exhaustion or strained emotions, but I leaned across and kissed Luke on the cheek and began to inch around for a kiss on the lips. I hadn't kissed a boy since the year ten dance but it seemed like the right thing to do. Luke was so handsome. It took me about three seconds to realise that Luke was not only *not* kissing me back but was gently pushing me away.

'I'm sorry, Fi,' he stammered and drew back, taking my hand. 'I ...'

'No, no.' I gave an embarrassed laugh that came out like a snort. 'I'm out of line. I'm sorry.'

'I thought you and Barton …' he said shyly.

'Oh gosh, no! Barton! No way,' I erupted, shaking my head. 'Barton McLeod loves himself too much to let anyone else in for a shot.'

'Oh.' Luke nodded thoughtfully. 'I just assumed. He looks at you like … and I just thought. But, hey, Fi, it's not you. I think you are awesome. Really. It's just … I like you heaps, Fi. You're a great girl and if I was going to like a girl, you'd definitely be the one. I'm not … well … you know … into girls. Like that.'

He shrugged and his cheeks went a deep purple. It took me a few moments to understand what he'd said to me.

'Yeah,' he gave a tight smile. 'I haven't told anyone that before. I—'

'Oh my God, Luke,' I said, trying not to overreact. I patted his hand, nodding a bit too enthusiastically. 'Really? Hey, that's great. That's fine. I'm cool with that but you know … a bit … you know … embarrassed because I kissed you and …'

'Now, if you'd been Barton McLeod,' Luke laughed again, 'I might have kissed you back.'

I chased that image out of my head. It felt a bit weird. I had never met anyone who was open and honest about being a homosexual. I'm sure they were about, even in Bandaroo Flats, but no one ever actually admitted it. I thought it was pretty brave of Luke to tell me. I was surprised. Luke was Luke and I loved him. As a friend.

'You are one cool bird, Fiona,' he said, leaning in to my hair. 'I'm going to miss you.'

'Fiona!' A loud, angry shout bellowed from the

doorway. I reeled back, startled and filled with a creeping sense of dread at the sound of the familiar voice.

I looked, horrified, across to the open door to see my father. He looked like he was going to explode. I had never seen him so angry. He looked like a bull about to charge. And I realised then that I was sitting on my bed with dishevelled hair, cosied up to an equally ragged-looking boy!

'Dad!' I shrieked, leaping to my feet.

'What the devil is going on in here?' my father strode into the room, shaking with rage. I was really worried that he was going to thump Luke.

'Hi, I'm Luke,' Luke said, standing up and holding out his hand. 'I'm the cook here at the boarding house and I was just leaving. Like leaving for good and I was just saying goodbye to Fi because we're friends and—'

'It's not how it looks, Dad,' I groaned. 'Really. Luke's just a friend and he's leaving and I was just—'

'Pack your bags, Fiona!' Dad roared. 'I'm taking you home.'

'Why are you even here, Dad?' I stammered, confused. He hadn't once visited me in Brisbane since I had been at uni.

'I saw you on the telly,' he said. 'On the six o'clock news with the whole world watching. My daughter. A communist. A rebel. Marching illegally!'

Luke began to skulk out past Dad, giving me an awkward wave.

'And you!' Dad turned to yell at Luke. 'You should be ashamed of yourself. You're a coward and don't deserve to be called an Australian.'

'Sorry, sir,' Luke said sheepishly. 'See ya, Fi. I'll write.' Then he disappeared out the door.

My father continued to glare at me and his gaze felt like bushfire.

'Pack! Now!' my father ordered. 'This university caper is over. You are coming home with me. I would have driven down last night but I was too upset. It would have been dangerous.'

I looked around my disaster of a room. I'd come to love it. Even the tattered wallpaper. My textbooks were strewn about the floor.

'No, Dad.' I stood in front of him, defiantly. 'I'm not going home.'

'Yes, you are. It's an order.'

'No, I'm not.'

'Yes, you are, my girl!' he barked.

I began to cry. 'But I love it here. I love uni. I love Brisbane.'

'Yes, I can see what you love!' Dad growled. 'Half-naked boys in your room!'

'He's just a friend,' I said. 'He's not like a boyfriend.'

'You are down here in Brisbane, breaking the law, living like a pig and making out with boys in your room. Fiona, you are out of control.' Dad continued yelling, 'I thought you were mature enough to handle some independence but clearly you are not.'

'I'm eighteen!' I shouted back, losing my cool. 'You can't tell me what to do anymore, Dad!'

'Until you are twenty-one you will do as you are told.

Stop talking back to me, Fiona! Your mother would be ashamed of you today.'

I bristled. I thought about the book in my wardrobe. I thought about Joan of Arc. I thought about all those women's names.

'No, she would not, Dad!' I said firmly. 'She would be proud of me. She would not have wanted Murray to go to a war that doesn't involve us. Mum would have marched beside me. It felt like she did.'

'Stop now!' Dad seethed.

'*She* would have gone to university and done medicine if she could have. She wanted to be a doctor, not a nurse and even then, she had to leave to be a wife and mother.'

'There is no shame in that!' he argued back.

'No, there's not,' I said. 'But she wanted more. And she wanted more for me and she would have been proud that I stood up for what I believe in.'

'And she'd be fine with you having boys in your room first thing in the morning?' he growled. 'You know how that looks, Fiona?'

'Really, Dad,' I sighed, rolling my eyes. 'If he was my boyfriend I'd tell you. No big deal. But he's just a friend. He doesn't even like girls and—'

'Oh my God!' my father said, shaking his head. 'That's it. It's settled. I will wait downstairs. Not another word from you, young lady.'

We stared at one another in a silent showdown, both shaking with emotion.

'University has ruined you,' Dad said, his anger still high.

'You're wrong about that, Dad,' I said sadly. I was starting to feel defeated.

'Fifteen minutes,' he said, tapping his watch. 'I'll settle up the monthly account with the landlady when she gets back, and see you in the car. I'm parked out the front.'

Dad left me alone and I sat on the edge of my bed, sobbing. It felt like the end of the world. My life had become an enormous colourful balloon and my father had just come in and burst it. I thought about Agnes and wondered where she was. And Barton. I knew Luke would be packing downstairs. The house of cards had come crashing down and I wanted to be sick. I was trapped in a nightmare.

But my father was formidable and when he was angry he was like a big brick wall. There was no getting around him. I was just a kid and I didn't have the means to survive on my own and be independent. Perhaps, I thought, I'd just go home and things would settle and I could try to get back to university in a year or two. I knew that Dad needed someone to help him on the farm while Murray was away. I didn't think he could do 'alone' very well.

I wiped my face and pulled out my suitcase from the wardrobe and put it on my bed. I began to pack.

The last thing I put in, on top of my badly folded clothes, was the *Systir Saga*, wrapped in its red cloth. I put my hand on it and promised all the sisters that I would come back one day and I would be a lawyer and I would be a good one who made a difference in the world.

JEANNE

BEAUVAIS, FRANCE, 1472

Three days had passed since Lagoy forced me to forsake my place of safety, my refuge. I had been born in that small, damp cottage. I had been held and suckled as a baby by my mother, whom I could no longer remember. And yet those gentle embraces had seeped into my being and become a part of me. In that house, my grieving father had brought me up to be a good and decent girl. He had cooked me meals and told me stories. He had fashioned two little hatchets to keep me safe. He had stroked my hair when I was sick and cried with me on my final night at home as I packed up my meagre belongings, touching every surface of the house, committing it to memory. Three days and I missed my father immensely. The sorrow soaked into my bones, settling like a permanent ache.

In the fine home of my future husband, I sat in the window box and looked out over the rooves of the other houses in the best quarter of town. The air was much fresher in this part of town; a vase of roses on the side table sent wafts of perfume around me. The room taunted me with its prettiness. It was early morning and I looked at the tray of food that had been delivered. I could not stomach a morsel. I felt sick and knew that I should eat but I could not bring myself to try. Part of me wanted to never eat again. I could just waste away to nothing and disappear. It felt like a pleasant thought.

A gentle knock came at the door and it opened. Giselle poked her head in, smiling at me.

'Jeanne? May I come in? The Lieutenant sent me up to measure you for your wedding dress.'

I gave her a resigned nod. I felt like a prisoner in a tower in that room, despite its calico floral walls and a bed with coverlets that looked like clouds. Lieutenant Jean Lagoy had sent for me early on Tuesday morning, the day that the Burgundians had begun to retreat and march away westward, leaving Beauvais scarred but safe. A brutish, silent guard had installed me in the top room of Lagoy's manor house. My not-so-dearly beloved fiancé had not yet come to see me. That was one thing I could be grateful for.

'The enemy have gone and the peasants are returning to their villages,' Giselle said breathlessly as she came in with her sewing basket and a long roll of pearl satin under her arm. 'I can finally feel safe and sleep well.'

I shut my eyes and sighed, letting a small smile play on my lips although I cared not. Had the Burgundians continued their assault on the city, my impending nuptials might have been postponed, but now I was sitting in solitary confinement awaiting my fate like a condemned criminal facing execution. I was to be married to Lagoy by the end of the week.

'This is the very finest material,' Giselle said, going to the cedar bureau and laying the satin out for me to see.

I looked across to the corner where my old wooden trunk sat, the metal straps rusted and worn. Wearing only my plain cotton night-shift, I gave Giselle a tired look and crossed the room.

'I was looking through my mother's things,' I told her. 'And I wondered … what do you think, Giselle?' I opened the clasp and took out a folded lace dress and held it up. 'It's my late mother's wedding dress.' I felt the sting of tears and my jaw ached as I tried to hold back crying. I swallowed hard and tried to contain myself. 'She was a well-born woman who married down but I think it is fine enough for my wedding to the Lieutenant.'

Giselle came over to me and her fingers touched the delicate lace.

'It is beautiful.' She nodded thoughtfully. 'So intricate and elegant. The lace is exquisite.'

'It would mean a lot to me to be able to wear it,' I said softly. 'What do you think?'

'Oh, yes,' she nodded 'Most definitely.'

I had become fond of Giselle. She was tall and her skin was like bone china. The bruising on her face from our foray into battle had almost completely faded. She was a girl who had been born with a silver spoon firmly planted in her mouth yet she had a wildness of spirit simmering beneath the surface. Her bold defiance of her mother when she took up arms alongside me had forever bonded me to her. In my new life as the wife of a lieutenant, I knew she would be a welcome ally. In the previous days she had taught me so much: how to navigate my way through the proper cutlery and crockery during a banquet, how to breathe beneath a corset and many other foolish things that were going to be necessary if I was to not embarrass my husband. Giselle had instructed me in the basic poses, gestures and dance steps that I would need for my social debut at my wedding.

'The Lieutenant had the silk sent up from the haberdasher but I think this is far more special,' she said, taking the dress and holding it up in front of me. 'It looks like it will fit but I can make any adjustments necessary. It may need the hem taken up. Let's get you to try it on and we'll see.'

I felt the first flutter of happiness in a very long time. That I might be able to wear my mother's wedding dress was a beam of sunlight in my grey world. According to the sumptuary law, as a pauper it was forbidden that I wear such a dress, but as I was marrying up, and to a lieutenant at that, I was permitted to wear lace or satin or silk, even ermine. I undid the pearl clasp buttons down the back of the dress and Giselle helped me as I stepped into it. I held my breath, praying that it would fit and I felt a sense of relief wash over me as Giselle carefully buttoned up the dress. It fit me perfectly, almost as if it had been cut to my shape.

My mother had been the same age as me when she married my father. Almost seventeen. I wondered how she must have felt when she put the dress on for the first time.

Had she been excited? Nervous? She had married for love. It was a rare thing and something most young girls could only dream about. I was flooded with thoughts of Colin's smile and his embrace. To think of him wallowing in a dungeon while I dressed up in fine lace made me feel ill.

'Ohhh!' Giselle smiled as I turned around to show her. 'You look beautiful.' Her face was glowing and her words made me feel a little brighter.

'I wish my mama could see me,' I whispered. 'But, Giselle, I know she would have hoped for me to be happy and I am not.'

'But Jean Lagoy is so handsome and–'

'I care not for his good looks,' I said sullenly. 'I do not love him.'

'I did not love my husband when we were first married,' Giselle said, straightening my collar as she spoke. 'But he is a good man and I have come to care for him. As you become more familiar it will grow on you.'

'Like a wart!' I groaned and we both laughed.

'You look like a princess,' Giselle said, more seriously, after we had calmed down. 'Let me braid your hair for you.'

I sat again at the window and watched the pale blue sky playing host to a feathering of white clouds. I rested my hands on the delicate lace embroidery in my lap. Giselle brushed my dark hair and I let myself enjoy her touch as she wove my hair into place.

'Can you read?' I asked her dreamily.

'That is a strange question.' She laughed. 'Yes. Of course. Why do you ask?'

'Well, I was never taught,' I told her, a little ashamed. 'My father did not know how and could not teach me and with my mama gone ...'

'I could teach you!' Giselle said, sounding excited by the idea.

'No,' I said. 'Well, I suppose you could. Though, I've never thought to read and yet I have a book. Let me show you.'

I went to the trunk, rummaged around and took out an old book. It was bound in some kind of skin, softer than leather, and had strange markings on it that looked like a bird had walked across it before it had set, like plaster.

'This belonged to my mother. She could read but I don't know what all the words say. It is very strange.'

Giselle and I sat on the end of the bed, the book between us, and I watched as Giselle took it and began very gently turning the pages.

'They are names,' she said, sounding amazed. 'All names. All women's names.' Her fingers traced over the words running down the pages, branching out like the limbs of a tree. She came to the final page of writing although there were more pages left blank after it.

'Here is your name: Jeanne Laisné. And above it, Alice Fourquet.'

'My mother's maiden name,' I said, biting my bottom lip to stop it from trembling.

Giselle went back through the names, each one written in different ink and different handwriting. Some letters sloped forward, others back. Some of the names were written in small, dark, neat letters and others were scrawled in a large and flamboyant hand.

'This looks like your mother's family, running back through the female bloodline. Jeanne, darling, this is incredible. Here is your cousin Aimee's name as well, on the same line as yours. Look back here. Isabelle Romée. Jeanne d'Arc. Oh my, Jeanne. You have the blood of heroines in your veins.'

I put a hand over my mouth for a moment, thinking of the stories my father told me about being related to the French heroine Jeanne d'Arc. I'd never really believed it deep down. I spoke in a halting voice, choked with emotion. 'Read me the names. All of them.'

Giselle read them aloud. Starting with my name. Then my mother's. Then my grandmother's. And on and on backwards and I let myself bathe in the glorious names of the women who were the threads that were sewn together with stitches of time and blood to make up the garment that was me. Beautiful names, strange-sounding names. All the way back to the first one, which was written in letters that Giselle could not understand.

'These first ones are such ancient markings that I cannot decipher them,' Giselle smiled. 'This must be a very old book before common writing or letters came to be. See, beside some names is a place. Beside your name is Beauvais.'

I marvelled at the markings in ink. Each name represented a life. A woman. Every one of them had lived and loved and eaten and cooked and sewn; some had daughters and those names rolled on like roots, seeding other lines. Some names stopped. I supposed that some of those lives had been cut short or perhaps had simply not borne female fruit. But where a line finished, a new one sprouted, perhaps with a sister, cousin or aunt.

'Yes, I do want you to teach me to read, Giselle.' I nodded. 'I want to be able to read these names for myself and one day I will put my own daughters' names in here and I will pass this book on to them.'

Giselle closed the book and touched the markings on the cover.

'Systir Saga,' she read. 'Perhaps it means the sister story? Yes, Jeanne. I will teach you to read all these names.'

I looked at the markings and let my finger reach out to trace them. I pushed away the sadness that engulfed me to think that my daughters, should I have any, would wear the surname of Lagoy. I comforted myself that they would be a part of my mother's bloodline and that was blood that I was very proud to have running through my veins.

'I would have loved to have had a sister.' I smiled to myself.

'Let us be as sisters,' Giselle said, squeezing my forearm. 'Secret sisters. I have never had one either.'

I leaned forward and kissed her cheek and she kissed mine.

'Sisters.'

Through the window the sound of a trumpet reverberated up from the street. It startled me and I felt my belly leap in surprise. Giselle gave a little jump as well and we both fell into a fit of giggles.

'What on earth was that?' She laughed.

'I don't know but it certainly gave me a fright.'

Another burst of noise filtered up to us. This time it was more of a heralding tune. We frowned at one another and a few moments later we heard footsteps running through the hallway outside and a serving girl burst through the door without knocking.

'Liesel!' Giselle said, standing up, looking cross. 'How dare you enter Jeanne's room like that. Out!'

'But Madame—'

'No, Liesel,' Giselle ordered the girl, pointing at the door. 'Go back outside and do that properly. Go. Now.'

We waited as the girl gave a nod and a curtsey and went back out of the door, closing it behind her. We waited. Nothing. A knock sounded at the door and we both giggled again.

'That's better!' Giselle cried. 'Now you may enter you naughty, naughty girl!'

The door opened and the maid, Liesel, re-entered the room. 'Your ladyship,' she said, dipping into a deep curtsey before standing, red-faced. 'Mademoiselle Jeanne has a visitor asking after her.'

I frowned. A visitor? For me? I couldn't think who might come knocking on Jean Lagoy's front door looking for me. Giselle shrugged her shoulders at me as a very well-dressed man in a fashionably curled white wig stepped into the doorway, bowed to us, then stood aside and to attention, his arms held stiffly by his sides.

'May I present Mademoiselle Jeanne Laisné, also known as Jeanne Hachette, the maiden who conquered Charles the Bold.'

Before I could even wrap my thoughts around the words, a tall, imposing man entered my room. He was dressed in a blue silk coat and a white surcoat with a mantle of scarlet satin. He wore a cap with peacock feathers. His brows were low and tight and he had a prominent nose.

'Mademoiselle Jeanne,' the man said gently as he lowered his head and bent low, taking my hand. 'I am indebted to you.'

Beside me Giselle gasped loudly and fell into a curtsey that had her almost on the floor. I stared at the man, unable to move, my face prickling as if it were overrun with ants.

Standing before me, bowing to *me*, was King Louis XI.

BETSY

County Down, Ireland, 1798

I will never forget the feeling of when I first killed a man. I fired and he fell down dead. I shook all over and couldn't stop my teeth from chattering. I heard myself saying to Will, 'Oh look what I've done. I've killed the poor man.' But it was easier the second time and by my third I had almost become deliberate and callous about it. It was hard work, loading the gun, fixing the priming, looking to the flints and adjusting the locks. Will and I had dragged the coffin of weapons into a small hedge behind the inn and hid them there. We'd taken our horses, a musket each and some ammunition and holed ourselves up in a small natural trench in a thicket just outside of Ballynahinch. We were not alone. The woods were thick with rebels who had seen the approaching King's men from the lookout on the hill and had swarmed down in the shadows. The order had come from Munro that we were to take down every redcoat we could.

Long afternoon shadows crept out over the fields and the temperature dulled to a pleasant and tolerable warmth. Three small regiments of British soldiers had marched along the road and we had made good account of ourselves. My mark had been hit first and while I recovered, Will continued the assault. My soldier had fallen, his blood leaking out in a thick stain in the dirt on the road. Once I had composed myself and readied my weapon again, there were three bodies on the road and many injured, limping away as fast as they could, back toward the township. No sooner had another band of the King's forces advanced within range than we peppered them with shot. The ground on each side of the road was divided into small fields with fences rising one above the other, forming a kind of amphitheatre. Here, ambuscaded behind the cover of fences, Munro had posted some of his best musketeers. Will had insisted that I be included, remembering my fine aim back in their hideaway.

A lanky young officer named McCance was in charge of our division and had directed us to our places, ordering us to shoot redcoats on sight.

'War is a dirty business,' Will had told me, sombrely. 'We have to do terrible things. If we don't kill, we will be killed.'

For almost an hour we kept the British advance in check and we were encouraged and emboldened as Nugent's men went down in great numbers while we sustained not a single injury, tucked behind the safety of our fence-trenches, our horses hidden on higher ground. Gradually the onslaught discouraged the redcoats from taking that particular road and our targets dried up. By the time they had fully retreated I had taken three of them down like sacks and grazed a few others who'd staggered back down the road, leaking from the holes I'd put in them.

'If only we had more cannons to fire at them,' Will complained, wiping the sweat from his brow as he reloaded his weapon. 'These few guns will not do us if they come at us in any great number.'

George came up behind us as jittery as a headless chook.

'The scouts are back and say that there are about seven hundred infantry, a hundred and fifty cavalry and five pieces of cannon down in Ballynahinch proper.'

'Heavens above!' Will exclaimed. 'We've only got a few small ship guns, some six or eight, mounted onto country carts! And perhaps six medium cannons on rolling carts.'

'Munro has ordered us to stay out of Ballynahinch as the English have seized it,' George muttered. 'We've been commanded to retreat from this hill because Nugent has changed tack and is sending covert troops out to surround us and isolate us here on Windmill Hill. So back up to Edenvady now. To regroup and plan.'

Corporal McCance came up to us, loosening his neck-tie before using it to wipe the perspiration from his cheeks.

'Hey,' he said, grinning. 'We've got word back in, fellows, that the bulk of the British troops left down in town are busy looting and plundering and burning cottages for sport and drinking the town dry! Most of them are already at the inn having a jolly party! Dusk is rolling in so we need to away. You did good, Betsy Gray! Nice marksmanship. Not just a pretty face, eh?'

I smiled at his compliment.

Night swallowed us up as we hurried our mounts back over the fields to the high hill of Edenvady. Darkness was dotted with so many lanterns that they looked like a scattering of tiny yellow stars. After I helped the other camp women prepare great vats of food, heated up over wild and open fires dug into the turf, I forced myself to eat some bread and meat to give me strength. I breathed in the smell of burning peat and took my food to the oak tree where Finn McCool was tethered and let him nibble some bread from my open palm. As I ate I saw some men shirt-fronting one another further along the rise, their voices raised and heated. Curious, I wandered over closer to see what was transpiring. It looked like a fist-fight was brewing between our own men. I could see that Will and George were in the affray and I wanted to know what it was all about. It would not do at all to have us infighting.

Many of our men it seemed, including George and Will, were urging Henry Munro to let them filter down through the dark night into the town of Ballynahinch to pick off the drunken soldiers.

'Our scouts have told us that many troops have taken advantage of the empty cottages and have made themselves right at home,' George said, sounding impassioned and enthusiastic for the plan. 'They are sleeping in vacant beds and draining the cellars. We could torch the buildings and take down any that flee, picking them off as easy as rabbits. We'd only need pikes and swords. They are in a right sorry state down there and will put up no steady defence.'

'No! Absolutely not!' General Munro argued forcefully.

'We would dishonour ourselves by taking advantage of the cover of darkness and their inebriation. No. We will meet them in daylight on the morrow and fight them like men, not alley cats.'

The argument escalated with more and more men taking one side or the other. It seemed to me that most of the men were for doing night raids. It made sense to me too. The local men knew the layout of the town and while the King's men were making merry and had their wits dulled we could strike fast and hard. I had already killed three and I was surprised to feel the urge to take down more of them. As I had pulled the trigger, each time, I had thought of poor Annie O'Neal, taken by the likes of those men who saw us Irish as foxes in blood sport, not worthy of respect or equal standing. It felt good to turn the tables on them. But Henry Munro was resolute and adamant. We would not take them down in darkness and drunkenness. As soldiers we had to obey our captain. That was the first and most important rule of combat.

Later, as the moon reached high like a skull in the night sky, I tried to catch up on some sleep, with George and Will on either side of me, all of us lying in a state of discomfort upon the cool grass. I saw many shadows slipping away from the hill. Men, and *lots* of them, were deserting us. I had not slept well for many days and I felt sick with tiredness but my mind would not calm enough for slumber. George and Will had predicted that Henry Munro's stubbornness in refusing to take advantage of the cover of darkness and the King's men's inebriation would result in many desertions. I couldn't believe that Munro had not jumped at the plan. It did seem foolish and yet he had been elected leader for a reason. Many said he had an unsurpassed tactical intelligence.

I rested my burning eyes by pressing my face into Will's shoulder. He rolled over and kissed me. I wanted to cry but I was too tired to weep as he rocked me in his arms, squeezing me so tightly that I thought my ribs and spine would crack.

'They are skulking away, deserting us,' I moaned as I saw over his shoulder another small huddle of shadows seeping away down the hill.

'We still outnumber the British, my love,' Will whispered. 'But when the sun comes up you must ride away from here and take cover far from the town. There will be a good deal of hand-to-hand combat.'

'I will stay and hang back as a marksman!' I told him.

'Well, markswoman.' He laughed.

'The bullet shot that hits isn't any weaker for it having been shot by a woman's arm,' I chided him. 'Don't worry, Will, I'll have your back.'

'Shut up and let me sleep,' George groaned, rolling.

I nestled beneath Will's arm, and the rise and fall of his chest, his warm breath on my face, lulled me into a light but fitful sleep. I dreamed of blood and carnage and the roar of men's voices.

Morning brought with it another day of brilliant sunshine and a sore back. My eyes were caked with crusted sleep and I had to stretch myself to iron out the kinks. Henry Munro was already darting around the men, shouting orders and slapping backs, giving encouragement but we could all see that our numbers had dwindled. Corporal McCance came over to us as we were sheltering under the shade of the oak, readying our horses, and told us that an early head-count had put the deserters at about seven hundred. It was a shocking loss of manpower.

'That still leaves over six thousand of us and more than enough to resist and repel the redcoats,' Will said breezily. 'More than enough to secure Ballynahinch and then on to Lisburn. The battle in County Down will go down in history as the one that took back Ireland for the Irish!'

Oh, how I wanted to believe him. All the men around me and the few women who had stayed to support their men were all glowing with smiles and whistling patriotic ditties as if they were off to an enormous grand fair. But I had been persecuted all night with thoughts of the men I had shot. They must have had families and women who loved them. I had shot at the redcoats as if they were simply targets, symbols of my discontent, and had thought little of the flesh and blood of which they were made. I'd asked God to forgive me in the depths of the night. Will often told me that the rules were always different during war, particularly wars when someone was fighting for freedom because God was all for freedom.

We readied ourselves for battle on the steep slopes of Edenvady. Before us was spread a valley several miles wide, made up of gently rising hills and further away a ridge of slate grey mountains. The broad bowl of the valley was covered with fields and crops and although the sea was still some way away, we were high enough that I imagined I could smell her salty breath. A mild haze lay like a glass bell over the lowest paddocks. We set off and my heart was equal parts on fire with the passion of what we were about to do, and terror, also for what we were about to do.

The British troops were ready on Windmill Hill, the same place where I had hidden behind fences to take my aim the previous day. I was frightened because I knew that the forces of the King were trained in the ways of warfare while we amounted to thousands of poorly armed and untrained men. But we had patriotic men and a small smattering of women who were prepared to do battle unto the death for the land and the people that they loved. Below us, in the valley, slumbered the pretty little town of Ballynahinch, deserted of her inhabitants but suffering a hangover from her unwelcome guests, I warranted.

'Musketeers will stay high and back,' Munro shouted as we assembled, a motley crew of Irish all dressed in our Sunday best with dyed green feathers in our hats and green ties about our necks. I wore my best green velvet dress, even though the day was far too hot for it. I had been wearing the same outfit for three days. My dress was sweat stained under my arms, had dirt about the hem, and my boots were scuffed. But from a distance it still looked grand. I tied my hair into a plait and secured a matching green velvet ribbon about it. The front of our cavalry had four men carrying our United Irishmen flag, with the yellow harp and our beloved green. Behind them were the battle drummers and a row of rolling cannons on carts. I counted eight.

'Let's march for Ireland,' General Henry Munro shouted and I fancied I could hear a quiver in his voice and I looked at his open, handsome face and wondered if the linen merchant from Lisburn, a good Catholic man with a family and a grand sense of humour, had ever thought he would lead an army against the Crown? He was our own great Finn McCool, small in stature but a giant character in our cause, who would no doubt go down in Irish history as a true hero. Munro led a column of men down the hill and I steadied myself on my horse with the other musketeers beside me.

'You're not letting your sister come along, are you, George Gray?' one surly middle-aged man armed with a pitchfork called up at us, spitting on the ground.

'She's the best shot I know, Seamus, and took out a handful of English dogs yesterday! I'd sooner let her have my back than you!' Will retorted, giving me a wink.

The drums beat and rolled, and the men marched in time with the thumping cadence. We rode our horses far behind the sweeping sea of footmen as we descended toward the township. We stopped when we reached a point with a wide, open view of Windmill Hill, where the slick and uniformed wash of redcoats waited for us. For some tense minutes we waited in the sunlight and squinted in the glare as both sides prepared themselves for battle. The British troops were drawn up in a solid square. Munro gave the first order and our cannons fired, hitting the front row of redcoats in a wave of destruction. The noise was deafening and I felt my ears ring as if there were bells in them. The main officer commanding the British Army in the frontline was down, clearly dead, and this threw his troop into a panic. They dispersed, running in confusion, some of them injured. Two more shudders of cannon fire and the King's men were making a hasty retreat back into the cover of the town of Ballynahinch. A cheer went up among us, rolling into one enormous voice of victory. The Irish had taken the first approach and had driven back the foe. I could see that it encouraged the men who all seemed more fired up and ready for battle with an early win under their belts.

At the call from Munro, we began to spill down the hill. Our men marched and chanted as the drums gathered momentum and I felt the noise rumble through my bones. We forced entry into the town with our advance guard raising their pikes, dragging soldiers from their horses and finishing them brutally. The sound of clashing metal and screams of pain filled the air.

Cannons smashed into the sides of houses, as men went flying and cottages began to blaze so fiercely that soon the air became thick with smoke. I coughed and blustered and felt my throat tighten, but hung back watching the spectacle unfold as if it wasn't real but some dream. I saw a number of our men stagger and fall under a sweep of grapeshot but they were quickly replaced by another wave of Irishmen storming the redcoats as they hurried to reload. Injured men were picked up and hurried out of town, dragged and carried back toward the open fields where some of the women had come to tend to them. I had seen both Sarah and Eilish among them with water flasks, salves, bandages, and twine for suturing wounds.

Our pikemen charged to the very muzzle of the guns, the sheer overwhelming numbers quickly overcoming the enemy and making away with a good, heavy piece of artillery. It might have been a cannon. Munro led them all boldly and Will motioned for me to take to an alley where we could see a group of redcoats pushing a cart full of swords.

'Take them, Betsy,' he shouted, pointing and then nodded a head to George. 'You, George, round out about the square and cut them off at the other end.'

I led Finn McCool to the corner and readied my musket, took aim around the edge of a whitewashed cottage, then fired. I hit the cart but scattered the soldiers, who turned and began running angrily at me.

'A woman!' one yelled. 'Take her down.'

They laughed and I felt my blood boil and bubble. I did not have time to reload and they were bearing down on me, jeering. There was no sign of George at the other end of the street.

'Come on, come on,' I muttered, and with some measure of trepidation I took the musket in my hands, ready to bring it down on the men.

As the men neared, a sound exploded near me and I saw one man fall, an enormous gaping black hole appearing in his chest that began to pump out dark blood as he hit the stones on the road. Over my shoulder I saw Will on his black horse, with a musket to his shoulder. The other soldiers were in a panic and immediately raced off, swords drawn, into abandoned cottages, each to a different one, their purpose surely to lure us into hand-to-hand combat.

'Leave them,' Will said as he pulled up beside me. 'But we'll take as many of those swords as we can carry because Munro's ammunition is being fast exhausted. He's gained the centre of town though!'

We clattered down the road and Will dismounted and passed up a medium-sized thin sword to me. I brandished it high and it glinted in the sunlight. The din of musket fire, and the clashing, clinking of steel against steel filled the streets alongside guttural moans and blood-curdling screams of panic.

George cantered up to us, breathless.

'Munro's pushing into the redcoats with bayonets and pikes but he's being badly raked by their artillery,' he said. 'How much ammunition do you have, Bet? Will?'

I checked and shook my head.

'Not much,' I said.

'Come on!' Will cried as another loud cannon burst through the town, shaking the eaves of the cottages in the narrow street. 'Let's charge them! For the honour of County Down!' He leapt onto the back of his gelding.

Turning our horses, we galloped toward the main body of our army. I threw down my musket to one of our men who ran by, along with a bag of shot. He was headed straight for a wild throng where men were wrestling and stabbing, blood spilling down the streets, English and Irish mixing together. A man in uniform began tugging at my leg, trying to dismount me, but I kicked at him, getting him hard in the head with my boot, which saw him reeling until he shook his head and came back again. This time I took the sword and sliced, making a nasty gash across his cheek, his hand went up and the blood oozed out between his fingers. It was enough to frighten him and he ran back into the scrum of men.

A loud bugle sounded and it startled many into a sudden moment of stillness, a pause in the fighting. It came again. A clear call. Corporal McCance looked back at us, his face covered in blood and his eyes wide; he had a pike in one hand that still had flesh hanging from it.

'Retreat!' he yelled. 'It's the call to retreat. To the hills again. Away we go! To Edenvady. Retreat. Retreat!'

I watched, amazed as he dropped his pike and began running like an injured rabbit back up the street, his shirt torn and flapping behind him as he screamed like a madman from the public house of the insane: 'Retreat! Retreat!'

The crowd began to disperse, dazed and disoriented. I saw Munro at the other end of the street waving his two arms in huge sweeping motions. I could just make him out through the clouds of smoke that hung in the town like choking fog.

'Munro is calling us to retreat!' I shouted across to Will and George who were looking confounded.

'But we are winning.' Will shook his head in disbelief. 'We've all but taken Ballynahinch for ourselves. Look at the mess.'

In the street lay tens, maybe even hundreds of dead soldiers, the red of their coats matching the blood that pooled in the puddles between the stone and dusty pebbles on the road.

'Look!' I pointed. 'The King's men are retreating. See?'

The British were marching, broken and injured, many leaving their horses behind. And they were heading out of town. The King's men were retreating. Again the bugled call went up but through the dense veil of smoke we could not see who was playing it.

'It's definitely a retreat,' George said, and pulled his reins and turned, calling over his shoulder. 'Come on, Betsy. Will. I for one have had enough for now! We are alive. Let's regroup and see what Munro's plan is from here.'

Along with many men on foot, tired but marching, running and tripping out of town, and some few others still on horseback, we moved like a muddy river through the streets and out onto the open roads.

Tired and drenched in sweat, we began to climb our horses up Windmill Hill. As we made the rise, we heard a shout and suddenly our men on foot began to stop and turn and run back toward us like salmon swimming against the tide, falling over one another.

'Ambush!' they screamed.

Up ahead, with a sense of dread and a sickening terror, I saw that a whole battalion of light dragoons was charging our fleeing troops. This new outfit must have been marching into town from another direction to offer reinforcements. I recognised some of the men as being from Downpatrick and they appeared refreshed and armed with a full artillery. With vigorous shouts, they were cutting down our men like wheat chaff as we began pressing back toward Ballynahinch.

General Henry Munro came riding up behind us,

shouting and waving his arm. 'God save our souls!' he thundered. 'It was the redcoats call to retreat! Not ours! We had the town but we are lost! It's all lost.'

I felt my face go numb and for a moment all the noise, the noise of death and horror and pain and bloodshed, evaporated. Everything began to move slowly. And then the sound of my own heartbeat returned and my breath came like rushing water in my ears. I heard Munro shouting at us. His eyes were ablaze and I looked into them and I saw everything. I saw what was happening. The Irish had given it their all but we had failed. We had lost this battle and every last one of us would be cut down.

'To the hills, to anywhere!' Munro screamed at us! 'Go. Hide! Save yourselves. Scatter. It's every man for himself!'

I looked to Will and George.

'Ride!' Will shouted frantically as the sea of men around us churned and bubbled. 'Ride. Head north for Ballycreen Road and we'll meet at the intersection, then we'll try to take the fields up to Bangor and jump a ferry! Ride, Betsy!'

In the swirling chaos, I nodded, stabbed the sword into its sheath to secure it and pressed Finn McCool out from the crush. It felt like I was forcing the poor beast through thick human mud. I could feel his panic between my thighs as we watched a swarm of my beloved countrymen being butchered further along on the road, their desperate, pleading screams coming like the lashes of a belt over my heart. I reined my horse away, alongside my lover and brother, and I galloped like the wind to escape.

Behind me the town of Ballynahinch burned, and with it, all our hopes of a free Ireland.

FIONA

DARLING DOWNS, AUSTRALIA, 1968

'Thank you so much for coming,' Mrs Leary said, dabbing at her eyes with a lace handkerchief. 'It means so much to our family, Fiona.'

I nodded and shook her husband's hand, walking out into the churchyard and the brightness of the morning sun. It had taken weeks for the government to release Walter's body after the autopsy and inquest. In the end, it was ruled to be an accident but talk about town was that Walter might have taken his own life. I was glad for his parents' sake that they'd ruled it an accident otherwise the priest might not have given him a church funeral.

I walked over to Laura and stood there waiting for her to look up at me. She kept looking at her shoes. I looked down at mine. The black patent leather shoes I'd bought for my first day of university.

'Laura? Hey, I'm so sorry,' I said gently.

She had a small black pillbox hat with a net hanging over her face.

'Fiona,' she whispered, and reached out a hand and held mine. 'Walk with me.'

The two of us walked past the open hearse, past the shiny cedar coffin, which was covered in flowers and draped with the Australian flag, sitting on a silver trolley ready to be wheeled over to the cemetery. Laura stifled a sharp noise from the back of her throat. She sounded like she was choking with grief.

'I'm sorry I didn't write to you more when you were in Brisbane,' she said. 'I thought you'd hate me for falling in love with Walter.'

We walked on for a bit before I answered. 'I didn't know for ages until I came home at Easter,' I told her. 'Just before the accident. I was confused at first but not angry. I should have come straight around to see you that day after we heard. I'm sorry. You must be so, so sad. I'm so sorry, Laura.'

The cemetery next to the church had one gaping open hole and a little mountain of dirt beside it. I looked to the far-eastern corner and thought of Mum over there. I could see the flowers that Murray and I had put there a few days earlier.

'I … I … we …' Laura stammered. 'We had our whole lives ahead of us. We were going to get married when he got back and … oh Fi,' she looked up at me, her eyes stricken behind the dark gauze, 'I'm pregnant.'

I gasped and stopped, still holding her hand.

'Oh,' I said because I couldn't think of anything else to say.

The two of us went over to a fallen log just outside the cemetery. We sat there in silence, listening to the carking of crows and the low sombre rumble of conversation from the mourners.

'What are you going to do?' I asked. 'I'll help you as much as I can. And your parents ... the whole town will rally behind you.'

'Murray asked me to marry him,' she said almost inaudibly.

I took in a sharp breath. 'What? My brother?'

'Yes,' she said. 'He is such a good man and although I was with Walter, I still care very deeply for Murray and when I told him, when he came to see me the day we got the news, well, he said he wanted to do the honourable thing because a child needs a father and ...'

I let my mind take all that in as I looked across to my brother, who was in his best brown suit, talking with the Leary family. It was a strange thing. I wasn't sure it was a good idea but at the same time I wasn't sure it wasn't. I knew that Murray really loved Laura. He had for as long as I could remember. But to raise not only another man's child, but Walter Leary's child, that was something different altogether.

'That's ... um ... and you said yes?'

'I did,' Laura said softly. 'Murray can apply for a deferment of his service. We've talked about it a lot these last few weeks and we're certain. He won't have to go away. We want to get married as soon as possible.'

I felt the relief flood through my veins. That was one positive to the strange arrangement.

'Anyway, I'd best get back,' Laura said. 'Murray and I are going to talk to your father tonight. The Learys have been wonderfully supportive.'

I nodded mutely and watched her walk back to the people congregating around the grieving family. I sighed and felt a breeze blow over my skin, giving me goosebumps. I'd been back only a week and already it felt like my term at uni was a distant dream. Agnes rang me every night crying, begging me to come back. The cows lowed outside my bedroom window every morning. I baked bread and biscuits. I stripped the sheets and did all the laundry. I helped Murray pull dead birds from the guttering. The rain filled the dam. Murray rode out on the plains with Oscar racing beside him to herd the lower paddock of sheep. Life went on in Bandaroo Flats like it always had. Round this part of the Darling Downs nothing much ever changed.

I stood up and began to walk through the dried grassy aisles between the headstones until I came to Mum's.

'Hey, Mum,' I whispered.

I looked at the headstone, so new compared to those around it.

Lillian Daisy McKechnie (nee Fergus)
Beloved wife of Alistair McKechnie.
Adored mother of Murray and Fiona.
Real love stories never have endings.

'I miss you so much,' I said, bending to arrange the flowers and trim the yellowed petals. 'I know you'd be sad about

Walter. I know you thought the best of everyone, even nasty people.'

A huge rolling bank of clouds was clumped against the horizon and I wondered if we would get another afternoon storm. I looked over to the churchyard. Almost every single resident of Bandaroo Flats and the surrounding district was there. All except one. My father.

'Try to get Dad to forgive him too, Mum,' I whispered. 'It'd be good for him.'

I smiled, remembering all the times that Murray and I had gone to Mum to get her to intercede on our behalf with Dad. She always knew how to talk him around. It had been Mum's intervention and persuasiveness that had made my father soften and let me attend high school. She'd been so good at that.

'And maybe talk him into letting me go back to uni,' I said.

I wondered how Dad would react to the news that Murray had asked Laura Bell to marry him.

'Thank you for the sister book, Mum,' I said, kneeling down, talking to the headstone as if she were sitting there, smiling back at me. 'It's amazing. I didn't mention it in front of Murray the other day because it's our special book, isn't it? I can't get over the names. The places. The history. We are part of something special, aren't we? A real bloodline of the sisterhood. And I've also been reading your stories. The ones in the suitcase. You could have been a writer, Mum. They are so good. They say I'm a good writer at uni. I guess I got that from you. And so much more.'

I wondered what Mum might say back to me about the book, her stories, about Walter, about Dad, about Murray and Laura. I imagined she might have asked me what I missed most about university. I imagined I might have answered that I missed the intellectual stimulation, the social scene, the Foco Club, Agnes, Luke's meatloaf and potato chips, Brisbane's sultry heat, and even Barton and his megaphone. Yes, I missed Barton's fire and passion. It made me feel alive and part of something important. But what I think I missed most was the climate at uni that allowed me to think for myself, to use my own voice and to make sense of my place in the world.

'I love you, Mum,' I said and stood up. 'I'll come by again soon.'

I walked back to the others as they began to stream into the cemetery. I linked arms with my brother and pressed my cheek into his strong shoulder.

'I love you, Murray,' I whispered. 'You're a good bloke.'

And we went and buried Walter Leary and I laid to rest a great heaviness in my heart, feeling so much lighter and freer for it.

When I got home, Dad was sitting on the front porch. An orange and white dusty Kombi van was parked behind the Holden. I walked up the long driveway, more than a little surprised to see Barton and Agnes sitting beside Dad, drinking ginger ale. They all waved like it was the most natural thing in the world. I pulled off my hat and laughed and, whooping with joy, broke into a run. I whispered, 'Thanks, Mum.'

JEANNE

BEAUVAIS, FRANCE, 1472

I gasped. It was as if the presence of the King had altered the air in the room. I knelt into a deep curtsey to match Giselle's.

'Mademoiselle Jeanne,' the King said to me, his voice like treacle. 'Rise. Let me look at you.'

I rose and stood there in my hose with slippers on my feet, wearing Mama's fancy lace dress. I felt like a child who has been caught dressing up in her mother's clothes but no one in the room seemed to notice. The King's man stood with his back straight, his eyes trained on a spot high on the ceiling; he was as still as a statue. Giselle stood with her head down, her gaze on the floor, and the ladies' maid, Liesel, gaped like a fish. Behind Liesel, I could see the rest of the household pressing up in the hallway toward the doorway.

Jean Lagoy pushed his way in, coming up behind the King, his head reaching higher than the monarch's wig.

'I beg your pardon, Your Majesty,' he said breathlessly. 'I was out in the stables when you arrived and I hurried straight upstairs. We can retire to speak in the parlour.'

'I have not come to speak to you, Lieutenant, though we will discuss the unsuccessful bid by Charles and his Burgundians to take Beauvais. It has been a deep wound to his pride and he marches on with a little of the wind taken out of his sails. Beauvais did very well.'

'My men fought tirelessly and—'

'You did well Lieutenant, but I have not come to speak to you. So, please. Leave us,' the King commanded.

'Leave you? Leave you where?' Lagoy stammered and looked to me, a glimmer of surprise registering on his face when he saw me clad in wedding attire.

'Leave me here to speak with Jeanne,' King Louis said, dismissing Lagoy with a raised curl of his hand.

'My betrothed is just being fitted for her vestments for our marriage, perhaps she can meet us downstairs in—'

'*Au revoir,* Lieutenant,' the King said with a tap of his walking cane, which I had not noticed until that moment.

His manservant sprang to life and with a guiding hand led Giselle and Jean Lagoy from the room but not before the Lieutenant shot me a look of daggers. I wondered what he meant by it. He looked angry but I could not see why it was any fault of mine that the King of France had appeared, rather surprisingly, in my new bedchamber and was standing before me with a warm smile. The door closed and the King gave a long, loud sigh of relief, pulling off his wig and cap and throwing them on the dresser beside him.

'Too hot for such formalities.' He laughed and went to sit in the brocade armchair by the window, leaning his cane against the wall. He motioned for me to sit in the matching chair inclined toward him. 'Please sit, my dear.'

I walked across the room and sat, although my legs could barely function. I had never seen the King so close except for the unflattering side-on silhouette portraits that were hung in the manor house and the featureless statue at the city gates. Looking at him front on, the King was much more handsome and normal. He was swarthy with severe eyebrows dividing his forehead from the rest of his face, but his deep-set eyes were gentle and held a hint of mischief.

'Your Majesty,' I mumbled, tripping over the words. 'I think you mistake me for someone else. I am simply Jeanne Laisné, daughter of the widower Matthew Laisné and I—'

'Single-handedly drove away the Burgundian army led by my nemesis, Charles the Bold, a most ruthless and vile adversary. Yes. That Jeanne Laisné. Charles the Bold. Charles the Bold. Hate him. Always have. Since we were children. He tortured cats.'

'I did not know that,' I whispered, folding my hands in my lap and staring down at them.

'How old are you?'

'Almost seventeen, Your Majesty.'

'The tales of your bravery, first in taking up arms with your army of recruited women and then boldly sabotaging the gunpowder stocks, have spread far and wide,' the King smiled, leaning back in his chair, his belly rising up as he did. 'I am indebted to you. A girl. And so young. You are something of a David to the Bold's Goliath, *oui*?'

I laughed with embarrassment and covered my mouth as it was not seemly to be laughing in front of the King. It was all I could do to resist looking him in the eye.

'I saw you once,' I said timidly. 'When I was about ten years old. You had just been crowned and you came through Beauvais on a great golden chariot with white horses. I imagined you had flown down from Heaven. I thought you were an angel.'

The King roared with laughter.

'Many a king has thought himself as much and more,' he chortled. 'But I assure you, Jeanne. I am nothing more than God's servant and a brutish man of flesh and blood who feels fear and anger and can be moved by a sunset like every other person on this earth.'

My eyes met his and I could not bring myself to look away. This ageing man with tufts of hair about his protruding ears and a mean slit of a mouth had the kindest eyes that I had ever seen, other than my papa's. Again I thought he might perhaps be an angel in disguise.

'They call you Hachette.' He laughed. 'Jeanne Hachette. Tell me how you came to wield a weapon so well.'

I gave a small smile, stood and went to the chests carrying my belongings, opened one and lifted out the one small hatchet I had managed to save after my foray into the woods, the subsequent wrath of my husband-to-be and my luxurious imprisonment. I went back and knelt before the King, offering the little hatchet into his hands to inspect.

'My father crafted it,' I said. 'He made two for me when I was very little, as my mother had been murdered by marauders many years earlier and he taught me to protect myself.'

'Very wise.' He nodded, turning the handle over in his big hands, letting a finger test the blade.

'I have practised my aim and delivery for many years,' I told him, warming to the conversation, feeling the knots of shock and amazement unravel from me. 'Never did I think a day would come when this little axe might become a symbol of resistance and victory. It saved my life. The other … well … it took one.'

The King nodded and patted the top of my head.

'You saved your city, Jeanne,' he said softly. 'Your courage was the flame that fired them into action. Your actions, rising up and defying conventions, defying your superiors, sometimes these things are more important than being obedient, *oui*?'

I shut my eyes. I had never heard someone tell me that it was a good thing to be disobedient, to do what you felt was right in your heart, turning away from what was prescribed to be the correct course of action.

'You are to be married?' he said softly. 'It is a good marriage for you, I hear. Lagoy is a lieutenant with great prospects.'

I looked up at him and into his face and my eyes brimmed with tears.

'*Non?*' he frowned, and all I could do was shake my head very gently from side to side, dropping my eyes, not wanting him to see my sadness and terror.

'Ah, Jeanne,' the King smiled, putting a hand under my chin, lifting my face to his. 'You are not happy? You do not love the Lieutenant?'

I shook my head, feeling raw and vulnerable to be sharing such intimate truths with the regent of all of France.

'Let me tell you a story, Jeanne,' he said. 'Take a seat, wipe your eyes and listen.'

I did as I was asked, blinking rapidly to dispel the tears and I sat, adjusting my mother's lace dress around my knees nervously, wondering how it came to be that King Louis XI was sitting with me, about to tell me a story. No one but my father had ever told me a story.

'When I was thirteen, my father forced me to marry,' he said.

I looked up at him quickly. 'Thirteen?'

'Yes.' He laughed. 'My bride was nine years old. It is a strange thing when you are royal. They would have you exchanging rings in the womb if they could. It's all about geography and gold, my dear. Love never ever enters the equation.'

'Nine,' I whispered, still reeling from the information.

'Of course, it was just a marriage of political convenience,' he explained. 'Not a real marriage. I barely, if ever, saw the girl. She was ensconced at court like a porcelain doll and treated as one, while I went on and lived my life, fighting, playing, travelling. She died some years later and I could feel no grief because she was little more than a stranger. I had a true love, a Spanish girl name Patricia, but she was a commoner and ...'

He looked sad. I gave him a small smile to ease his pain and let him know how very much I understood his words. Louis then looked up at me sharply, the sadness suddenly clearing like the evaporation of storm clouds from the sky, spontaneously and surprisingly, and the sun came out, spreading over his ruddy cheeks.

'Tell me, if you will, Jeanne Hachette,' he said, leaning forward, his eyes glinting from unspilled tears. 'If I am out of place to ask tell me so, but are you reluctant to wed the Lieutenant because your heart sings elsewhere?'

I took a sharp intake of breath, unnerved. It was almost like the King could see right through me as if I was made of gauze. My mouth went dry and it took three attempts for the words to come.

'Um, yes ... yes, Your Majesty.'

He clapped his hands. He made me laugh. He was so very theatrical and dramatic as he spoke.

'Jeanne, my dear,' he said. 'I came here today to ride through the town to congratulate Beauvais on her marvellous courage and fortitude but as soon as I cleared the city gates, all I heard was Jeanne Hachette, Jeanne Hachette. The heroine. Jeanne d'Arc come back to earth. And I thought then that I must seek out this girl and reward her handsomely.'

'It is not necessary, my liege,' I whispered, feeling once again overwhelmed by his enthusiasm.

'All my life,' he said, walking around the room, touching ornaments, running his hands over the furniture, stopping to look out the window as he spoke. 'All my life, I have been inspired and humbled by the courage and strength of my subjects, people like you, Jeanne: peasants, farmers, the salt and bone of our great France. My life is so much pomp and ceremony and yet even I cannot, and never could, marry for love. What a world! We sing songs and odes to love but it is out of reach for most, *oui*? Even for me. I chose my second wife for political reasons and almost lost the throne for it. And she turned out to be … well … let's just say I did not marry for love!'

I nodded.

'But I have the power to choose and permit or deny marriages other than my own,' he said kindly. 'It is just one of my many pointless privileges and yet …' He stood still for a moment before turning around to face me with a smile. 'And yet, perhaps, by way of thanks, I could grant you the gift of happiness.'

I put a hand over my mouth and the tears came, feeling hot against my cheeks.

'Who has stolen your heart, Jeanne Hachette?' he asked.

'Colin … Colin Pilon, Your Majesty. A simple chicken farmer. He's in the stocks in the dungeon of the Cathedral.'

'Oh,' the King said, raising his eyebrows. 'Now that's interesting. I believe that is a story that you might wish to tell me. Start at the beginning Jeanne and tell me all about yourself.'

And so, in a strange and unusual diversion from the reality of my small life, on that gentle summer's day, I sat with King Louis XI and told him my story. From the time when I was a babe and my mother wrapped me in her red velvet coat and hid me in the old tree trunk to save my life, to the time Colin was dragged away and imprisoned after I had taken out the Italian mercenary garrison.

And the King listened, entranced.

The first spectators had arrived by midday the next day and secured themselves places. They brought chairs and footstools, pillows, wine, food and children with them. Even the peasants from the surrounding countryside streamed in through the still smoking city gates. The King had ordered a parade to march through the town and he had asked the women of Beauvais to march ahead of the army. This was unheard of and there were a lot of miserable-looking men on the streets, but I had never seen the womenfolk so joyous and rowdy. Everything hummed and shimmered; it was like an enormous country fair. I watched it all from the carriage window as we began the most celebrated guild procession Beauvais had ever seen. People stood on balconies and hung from signposts, and middle-sized children squatted precariously atop walls. Townsfolk were pressed ten or twelve to a window. The strangest thing of all was that I was travelling with the King as the most honoured citizen of Beauvais. I looked across at the head of France in his fine white wig, his face touched with rouge, and smiled at him. He had assured me he would insist upon the release and pardon of Colin and that my father would be seen by the King's own physician. Louis was a kind man.

As we turned into the main street leading to the hub of the city, the clatter of horse hooves on the cobblestones was swept away by the applause, which roared like a wash of raging flood water through the city streets. I was bedazzled by the spectacle of it all. I had never been in such a fancy coach, never mind a gilt-edged coach with a driver in a silk coat, liveried footmen and a mounted guard. The King waved to those who pressed close for a glimpse of him as he made a grand tour of the streets of Beauvais. The children and men cheered as the women who had fought led the parade. And it wasn't the finest and most cultured women up front but the peasants and the working women.

Captain Balagny and Lieutenant Jean Lagoy were at the head of the guard, leading the army behind the women, alongside the best of the King's men.

'Where are we heading, Your Majesty?' I asked again, hoping that he might enlighten me but he gave me the same cryptic smile. 'Is there some ceremony or just a parade?'

Giselle and her servants were travelling in another small carriage at the rear of the cavalcade. She had set my hair in ringlets, with a smattering of tiny white baby's breath dusted over it. A hint of rouge and a touch of peach paint on my lips had left me feeling soft and pretty. I wore my mother's lace dress but had exchanged my slippers for a pair of satin ribboned shoes, which were uncomfortable as I was used to a pair of worn boots or bare feet. Over my mother's lace dress, the only decent garment I owned, I wore the red cape.

'We shall see, Jeanne,' he smiled and winked at me like I was a good friend.

'I assume your front guard knows where he is leading us,' I smiled. 'Or are we simply travelling around in circles so you can wave to every man, woman and child in Beauvais?'

The King winked again and went back to waving to the clamorous crowds.

The carriage stopped midway between a makeshift grandstand in the wide, fragrant park that was protected by what must have been a hastily constructed barricade, and the magnificent Cathedral, looming up like a palace of stone and stained glass before us. I could see that the grandstand was beginning to fill with rich gentlemen and beautiful women wearing big hats and shimmering clothes. It seemed as though the entire nobility from both town and country, far and wide, was on hand for the victory celebration. I saw a priest dressed in black stockings and a black hat running across the open expanse to the Cathedral, his black frock coat flapping so that he looked like a fluttering raven. A burst of music filled the air and all eyes were turned our way as the footmen opened the doors of the carriage.

King Louis accepted a helping hand down the three small steps to the red carpet that had been laid out for him. 'We will have a victory Mass to praise God for the delivery of Beauvais, followed by a huge feast of celebration.'

I was completely surprised as he turned and held up his hand to help me down, steadying me. The entire crowd inhaled and gave a loud murmur of surprise to see the King of France make such a gesture to a common woman. Stepping out into the blinding sunlight, I blinked and then carefully walked in my uncomfortable shoes down to the carpet. A roar went up from the crowd. My surroundings were a blur and I felt as though I was dreaming. Everything around me was swirling. I felt dizzy.

With a herald of French horns, I walked with my halting little steps beside the King down the red carpet, smiling and nodding to the sea of faces screaming and shouting at us. I just managed to put one foot in front of another without falling over and was grateful for the King's arm, which steadied me.

And then the noise seemed to be sucked away into a spiralling eddy, disappearing and yet still humming on the periphery of my hearing. At the top of the stone steps that led to the enormous arches of the doors of the Cathedral was Colin.

I stopped and held my breath, trying to wake myself up from this strange dream.

'Jeanne,' the King whispered and untangled his arm from mine. 'A king may not be God, but sometimes he can make miracles happen.'

I shut my eyes, then opened them. Colin was still standing in front of me. He was wearing a blue frock coat, a white shirt, white silk stockings and black shoes with silver buckles. He was not bound. He was a free man.

'But before the Mass,' the King said, leaning toward my ear, 'before the feasting, we are to have a wedding. And what a thing, Jeanne Laisné, *ma petite* Hachette, because this one will be born of love! Your father is waiting inside. My men dressed him up and brought him on a cart.'

I looked at King Louis, a man of such infinite benevolence, tenderness and compassion, then back to the crowds, to Giselle waving at me, to Jean Lagoy glaring from atop his horse, and then to Colin who looked so small framed by the entrance to the Cathedral. With the voices of my fellow Beauvaisi in my ears, raised and hollering in celebration of courage and valour and honour and love, I shouted, too, with joy and relief and disbelief, as I ran, trying not to trip over my dainty slippers, wearing my mother's lace wedding dress and her red cape, to Colin.

To my chicken boy.

BETSY

COUNTY DOWN, IRELAND, 1798

As we rode into dusk we climbed and crossed the darkening fields, sheltering behind farmhouses and small shadowy thickets. Gunshot and smoke and the sounds of clashing metal and men's shouts rang out through the air whenever we neared the roads. As soon as we heard human noises we veered back into the darkness, like night creatures, and waited until they passed before we moved again. Each time I shut my eyes hard as my heart hammered in my chest, and prayed that we would make it to Bangor safely.

'They will maraud through the night, chasing down the rebels,' George said as we converged on a small thread of shepherd's tracks. The moon was dusted with bruises and looked angry, shining down from above. A wood hen stirred and clucked, running from the undergrowth, startling us all.

'I know a family along Ballycreen Road,' Will told us,

his voice betraying his feelings of desperation. 'The Armstrong family. They are mindful of the cause but Samuel's wife is an Englishwoman and they are under no suspicion. They may let us rest in their stables until morning.'

'But we cannot travel through the day,' I worried aloud. 'It will be too dangerous and there are many miles to cover to get to Bangor. And I want to say goodbye to Da on the way.'

'No, Betsy,' George said. 'I'm sorry but that's out of the question. Da will be safe on the farm so long as we are not there. They will be watching him. We've all been seen fighting. The masks are off. They know who the rebels are now. They have names and faces all confirmed. Henry Munro must be running scared. And I heard they got Henry Joy McCracken up in Antrim and he's going to hang.'

I thought of his sister, Mary Ann. My heart broke for her. She was the strongest, smartest woman I knew and she'd ridden north to support him.

'How long must we stay in Scotland?' I asked, forcing myself to think of practical thoughts like the small matter that I had not packed any clothes or belongings at all. 'I am empty-handed and what of our horses?'

I reached down and gave Finn McCool a rub over his mane. He had sustained some cuts and abrasions during the battle, but nothing that could not be patched up with some vinegar and rest.

'I say we leave the horses to themselves,' George said softly. 'And travel on foot. We will be less conspicuous that way and can hide in smaller spots.'

'We'll travel slower,' Will said, thinking carefully, running his hands through his unruly hair. 'But you are right. All our rides have telltale nicks and grazes. Perhaps if they are found and identified, it will be assumed we have met a dastardly fate. Yes, this could be a good ruse.'

The thought of setting Finn McCool loose to paddock to perhaps be recruited by the British broke my heart.

'Just let them go to wander?' I said, beginning to cry. I felt as fragile as blown glass that was beginning to crack.

'They are good strong stock and will be well cared for, wherever they end up. You know that, Betsy,' Will said gently. 'They will be safe. It is our hides I am more worried about.'

In a gently sloping field, under the uneven shadows of a clump of fir pines, we dismounted, took a sword each and nothing more. I walked Finn McCool away to the cool and darkest recess of the grove, with tears rolling over my dirty cheeks. I could see the glint of his eye in the moonlight and I put my forehead to his, the warmth of his head against my own.

'We've been together for a long time, boy,' I said softly, feeling his breath come in warm gusts against my chest. 'You were with me today and every day and no matter where I go I will never forget you. I love you, Finn McCool. Be safe and strong. I am letting you go for your own good ... not because ... I'm so sorry, Finn.'

I just couldn't say any more words. They clenched up in my throat. I was bereft. It wasn't fair. I didn't want to run away. This was my Ireland. Why did I have to run? The tears came like a torrent. I wanted to put my arms around the neck of my horse and never let go. Da had brought him home to me after Mammy passed away. Finn McCool's mane had soaked up my tears then too. For ten years he had been my very best friend; the beast had loved me unconditionally for most of the life I could remember.

'Come on, Betsy,' Will said, walking over to us, rubbing my shoulders. 'We will let them graze and roam together. They all know each other well.'

I clung to my horse for a few more moments and pulled back, still crying, as Finn gave a long whinny and shook his head and shuddered. He nudged my hand and knocked it up so that I could rustle his long white hair one last time.

'I'll find you again, Finn McCool.' I sobbed as Will led me away. 'I promise. I will come back for you.'

I cried quietly as the two boys led me away, each holding one of my hands. In the darkness we travelled over hill and dell. We crept through thickets and under bushes, sticking to the undergrowth and the most inaccessible spots. If we heard the sound of angry men's voices or marching or violence, we rolled our bodies up into balls like animals and wedged ourselves up against boulders to blend in. The moonlight knew no colours, which made it harder to trace the contours of the terrain we crossed. It covered the land with a dirty grey, strangling me with its monotony. The world was moulded in lead. Nothing moved but a light breeze and there was no scent but that of the naked earth and the distant hint of smoke.

Silence lay upon us as we wandered north under the blanket of darkness, each of us wrapped in our own thoughts. I thought of my good horse and hoped he understood why I had abandoned him. He was intelligent. I had always seen that in his eyes and I liked to believe he understood everything I said to him. It must have been as traumatic for him as it was for me, being caught up in the battle that day and then the violent ambush that we'd only narrowly escaped. He was tall, strong, an asset for any man, soldier or farmer, and he would be well nurtured no matter where he ended up. People often cared more for horses than they did for folk.

'There.' Will pulled us up and pointed to a deep purple coiling cloud of smoke that was lit up in the glare of moonlight. 'That's the Armstrong farm.'

The cottage was nestled into a valley and beyond it I could see a stretch of road cut like a scar into the land, winding up to the north.

'That's Ballycreen Road.' Will gestured. 'If we can take rest for a day and keep out of sight, then travel by night off the main roads, and keep heading north past Newtownards and up to Bangor, we should be on a boat to Scotland by Wednesday.'

'I've never been to Scotland,' I whispered. 'Is it like Ireland?'

'It's the same,' George said wearily. 'Less green, fewer Irishmen, less good ale, but more nooks and crannies to hide in. From there we will plan a route to France. There they welcome the Irish.'

The thought of all that travel made me feel exhausted and a sudden wash of weariness flooded me. I felt myself sink to the cool ground and lie there, looking up at the moon and the smattering of stars that winked and blinked down at me. At least, I thought, in Scotland, I could be with my sister once again. But with my father old and frail, I wondered if I might ever see him again. I looked over at my brother and Will standing there in the moonlight, two tall young men, and I thanked God for them.

'When France comes to our aid with shiploads of re-inforcements, we will rise again,' Will said aloud into the night sky. 'With the French behind us we will succeed. We will take Ireland back.'

In those moments, I no longer cared. I just wanted to go home to Gransha and put the fire on and walk my hallway, gazing upon my ancestors, the wall of portraits. I wanted Brigit in the rocking chair knitting a cap for her daughter, her husband playing a card game of Switch with Da and George, all friends, no wall of religion or politics between us. Mammy in the kitchen cooking my favourite pie. And Finn McCool with his head poking in through the back kitchen door, looking for a vegetable peeling or a handful of sugar.

'Come on, Betsy.' Will came over and laughed, reaching out a hand to me. 'Get up and we'll rest once we have some safe shelter. They'll give us a blanket and a cup of broth for sure.'

'Start down the hill, you boys, and I'll roll on down after you. I just want a moment.'

Truth was, I needed to water myself and didn't want an

audience. I didn't have to explain. I waited until I saw them edging down the embankment before going to the darker area beneath a tree where I could tinkle in private. It was some sweet relief as I'd been holding on for the last mile or so. I breathed out, pulled off one glove with my teeth, used a leaf from the ground and tidied myself up before straightening my torn and dirty dress. I started after Will and George and that is when I heard a shout. The blood in my veins turned to stone and I stopped breathing.

'Halt! Who goes there?'

Silence. A sudden rummaging through the grass, a thud, then silence. My heart shuddered and I stood as still as a statue, listening, poised, ready to run but unable to.

'You there, stop or we'll shoot.'

I groaned and began to shiver as if it was cold, although it wasn't. It was a second voice and English and that meant there were two of them. I heard the thump of footsteps on the ground, running. I tried to peer into the darkness to see what was happening but all I saw were shadows, flitting, rearing up, blending and disappearing. Figures loomed and vanished and as I took a shaky step forward in the grass, I could see two figures bounding down the incline and three others in pursuit. I held my breath and did not know what to do.

Realising that I could not stand there doing nothing, I dropped to the ground, feeling for my sword but then remembered I had laid it against the tree. I was missing one glove, which must have fallen when I'd heard the noise. I was too afraid to stand again so I crept like a badger through the grass, down and toward the road where the shadowy figures were stumbling and tripping. I was tasting grass and the fingers of my bare right hand were digging into the dusty dirt as I pulled myself down the hill, splitting my fingernails.

Near the road I heard voices raised and a heavy slap of fist on flesh and the guttural moan that comes from being winded. I was up on my hands and knees like a cat, peering into the dimness, breathing with a crackling wheeze, wanting to empty my bladder again.

'You dog-meat Irish rebels,' a voice growled. 'I'm gonna enjoy disembowelling you little bastards.'

Another thud.

'You can go to hell.' I recognised Will's voice but he said it breathlessly as if all but a little of his wind had been knocked out of him.

'Here, let my sword show us what you ate for your last supper, eh?' Another voice sliced through the darkness. I felt like I had been stabbed as I struggled to my feet and saw the flash of metal and heard Will's cry of surprise and shock.

'Noooo!' I screamed and began running and falling further down the hill toward the sorry party of men.

I could feel them all look my way and heard a burst of laughter and another shout of horror that I knew spilled from my brother's lips.

'Betsy! Run!' he cried. 'Go!'

'Yes!' I yelled. 'Come and get me, you English dogs.'

I turned and began to run, hoping they would follow, giving George time to grab Will and escape. I was blind with fury and fear and my hair was in my mouth and I was coughing it out and my boots were snagging against small rocks. I fell and hit my shoulder hard, wincing in pain, but struggled up again, hearing shouts and grunts in my ears. Then a heavy arm wrapped around my waist and pulled hard and I was off my feet and running in the air.

''ello lovely,' a voice oozed into my ear and I knew it straight up. Tommy Little. 'And from the glint of golden hair I'm thinking I've just caught me a Betsy Gray.'

Struggling like a mackerel on a hook, I kicked and lashed out, trying to find the fellow's face that I might gouge at his eyeballs, but he held firm and bounded back toward the road with me like a sack under his arms, my boots dragging in the grass. I dug down, trying to plant my feet into the earth and slow his progress but he was strong and angry, which is not a good combination in an English soldier. On Ballycreen Road he threw me to the gravel and I banged my face hard, knocking me reeling for a few moments as my head steadied.

I looked across to see that Will was on the ground nearby, his eyes catching hold of mine. 'Will,' I called but my voice had no sound.

'Betsy Gray, Betsy Gray,' a man said as he stood in front of me. I could only see his black boots and could smell them, a blend of dung and coal. 'See lads, we always knew she was one of 'em, eh? A rebel colleen.'

'Eh, Jack, we was almost right here where we first met the pretty lass. Remember? At the Old Inn.'

'Ahh, you're right, Tommy Little, right indeed you are.' He laughed cruelly. 'You wanna dance with us now, Betsy Gray?'

'Over my dead body,' George growled like a beast and shook off the man holding him down and took a full-bodied run at the two men standing over me, growling and ready to take them down.

'As you wish,' one man said as I rolled up onto my side and staggered to my feet.

'Stop,' I shrieked again as I saw the man with the moustache pull a sword on George and lunge so that it was aimed right at my brother's belly. I fell forward, my right arm outstretched, to either push George out of the way or force the sword out of range but the man slashed backwards at me and I looked in shock and stunned amazement as it cut straight through my one gloved hand.

It took a moment to register that the man had taken my hand clean off my arm and there was a moment, suspended like a candle flame, upright and unmoving, and then the blood came in hot spurts and I gasped.

'Lordy lord, I've taken off her little hand,' a voice said, and the English brute dropped the sword.

I heard George groan again and, grasping at my wrist, holding it tight, I spun to see them take him down and begin laying into him as if he were a sack of flour they wanted to bust.

'Betsy.' I heard Will croak out my name and I crawled to him. I could feel the blood soaking into my skirts as it ran down about my ankles. I was light-headed and not sure what was happening, thinking perhaps I had fallen into some terrible nightmare.

'I love you, Betsy,' Will whispered. 'Fight them. Don't let them toy with you. Fight with your last breath.

Éireann go Brách.' He shuddered as the light left his eyes.

I groaned and let out a wail of pain. I stood, angry, raging and I summoned up the spirit of my womenfolk who came before me. I let them fill my heart and my belly. I watched the life-force float away from my beloved brother and I picked up the sword on the road that had taken my lover and my hand from me and I shouted, my voice sailing out into the darkness like that of Ireland herself.

'*Éireann go Brách*. You will not mess with me. I am Ireland!' I staggered toward them with the sword wavering. My eyes were half-blind, my breath was a sirocco, my feet failed me. I heard them laugh like crows as I saw one, Tommy Little, raise his musket and press it against my eye.

'See that, Betsy Gray?'

'Yes,' I said, spitting on the dirt as I stood up straight and let my one eye meet his. 'And it looks like freedom.'

FIONA

BRISBANE, AUSTRALIA, 1968

My mother always said that if you wished upon a star, the first one – the evening star – on the night of a full moon, then that wish would come true. That was obviously a lot of nonsense but I did it in Bandaroo Flats one dusky evening as a kid. I wished that one day I would make a difference in this world in memory of my mum. And as I stood on the stage and accepted the First Year Academic Prize, I saw my father sitting proudly in the front row with Murray and a very pregnant Laura beside him, and I knew I was on my way to making that wish come true.

I'd taken part in three marches by this stage and had joined the university magazine team as a reporter. Every time I had a political or legal article published, I snipped it out and put it in a scrapbook and marvelled that people, strangers, were reading my thoughts on the page. I did have something to say and was really pleased that people wanted to listen.

After the morning tea to celebrate my prize, my family headed back to the hills and I kissed Laura and wished her well.

'Next time I see you, you will be a mother.' I smiled.

'Yep.' She grinned. 'When will you be home? Because I am going to need all the help I can get from Aunty Fiona.'

'In a few weeks,' I told her. 'Before Christmas. But I've still got some things to do here. We are taking a petition to Parliament House and I've got the final magazine to edit.'

'You did good, Fi.' Dad nodded gruffly. 'You're a good kid. Get home soon, hey? The bottom field needs some attention and I miss your cottage pie. You might be a budding lawyer during the school year but on the holidays you're my chief cook and bottle-washer.' That was Dad's way of saying he was well-pleased with me.

The rec area was chockers with kids and the vibe was pretty upbeat. Although the state election had come and gone and most of us were too young to vote, we were still putting pressure on the legislators to dump the policy of National Service on a federal level and had rallied our hopes behind Gough Whitlam.

Barton had graduated with honours and I wondered what options he was considering. I watched him handing out placards and was certain he'd miss uni life. Out in the real world he'd just be another graduate, but while he was at university, he was something of a messiah.

'Hey, Fi,' Agnes called, waving frantically as she pressed through the crowd.

She had just performed in a lunchtime pantomime as part of the end-of-year festivities and was dressed in period costume. She was also carrying my guitar case.

'You look like you just stepped out of *Wuthering Heights* or something.'

'I'm Nora from *A Doll's House*,' she replied.

'Ibsen.'

'Correct. Thanks for lending me the guitar. I don't think I was very good though.'

'I did not realise Nora played guitar.'

'We did a weird blend of modern and traditional. It was kind of a mess really. *A Doll's House* did not translate well into a musical. Let's just leave it at that.'

She passed me the guitar and we went to our favourite spot beneath the fig and sat down on the grass.

'Only three more years till you get to wear a silly white wig and black cape like a crow,' she said, arranging the folds of her long dress. 'By then I'll be taking Hollywood by storm.'

'That wouldn't surprise me, Ag.' I laughed. 'But I'm not sure your lover-boy Jeff will let you fly too far away. What's he doing next year?'

'He's asked me to drop out and follow him to Sydney. He's been offered a job at a law firm down there.'

'You wouldn't!' I gasped.

'It's tempting,' she mused. 'Sydney. He'll be making good money. There's a great theatre scene down there. Television studios. He's dropping hints about engagement rings.'

'You dare!' I glared at her. 'I can't let you leave. You are my honorary sister!'

'We'll see.'

'Ag, you aren't even old enough to vote. I hardly think you are mature enough to make a life decision like that.'

'We could live in sin.' Agnes wiggled her eyebrows.

'Your mother would disown you!'

'True.' She nodded.

I stopped and cocked my head. I recognised the voice blaring out over the Forum. Barton was at it again.

'Listen to him.' I smiled. 'Does he ever let up? For a minute? He's graduated now. You'd think he'd retire the bloody megaphone.'

'Someone told me he's coming back next year to do some post-graduate degree in politics.'

'Really?' I said, kind of impressed, and surprised to note that I was also feeling pleased to hear that he would still be around because, to be honest, I knew I would miss Barton. Campus wouldn't be the same without him.

'I reckon it's a strategy to avoid being conscripted.' She smiled. 'As long as he keeps studying he can keep the wolf from the door.'

'No.' I disagreed. 'I reckon it's because he really does plan on being prime minister one day and then God help the country! He'll turn the tables upside down.'

'Well, we're sure due for a good shake up.'

I was wearing a new orange crocheted blouse with an olive green skirt. My hair had grown out again and was sitting in two plaits on either side of my head. There was a welcome cool breeze whisking through the quadrant.

'Do you like my new top?' I asked, striking a pose.

'I do.' Agnes nodded thoughtfully. 'It makes a real statement. I don't know what that statement is but it says something. Maybe … I'm a life-raft.'

I unzipped the guitar from its case, thinking I might have a little play on the strings. I was in an excellent mood and thought a bit of music might be appropriate, a bit festive, but I felt my toes shrivel up inside my new brogues as Jeff the jerk came across the grass toward us.

'You ever hear anything from Luke?' Agnes asked as Jeff dropped down beside her and kissed her ear.

'Yeah.' I confirmed. 'We're regular pen-pals. He's doing seasonal work, moving about the place. I last got a postcard from Charleville. He's loving the life. The coppers gave up looking for him eventually. Too much bother, too much paperwork and he's as slippery as an eel. Barton has kept in touch with him as well.'

'Steal that blouse off your dead granny?' Jeff pointed at me.

I got the impression quite often that Jeff felt the same way about me as I did about him. We just didn't warm to one another at all. All the other kids were well-dressed for the graduation and academic ceremonies, but Jeff was in a tattered singlet with his signature peace symbol painted on his chest.

'Fiona McKechnie!'

I heard my name blasted all over the courtyard and looked around in a daze.

'Barton's calling you,' Agnes said, pointing over to the walkway.

I frowned, confused.

'What? Why is he saying my name?'

'I don't know,' Agnes was wide-eyed, but for all her theatrical skills, I could tell when she was lying.

'What are you guys up to?'

'Nothing!' she replied.

'After lunch, Fiona is going to sing us a song,' Barton called out.

'I am?' I muttered under my breath. 'I don't think so.'

'Looking forward to hearing from you later, Fiona.'

I felt so angry. Barton McLeod had no right to do that and I was not going to play. I hated singing to an audience. I'd done it one time at the Foco Club after Agnes and Luke hassled me to do it. I'd sung Bob Dylan's 'Blowin' in the Wind'. Barton had told me I was a better singer than Joan Baez but I think he'd been hitting the punch pretty hard that night.

'You are in on this, aren't you, Agnes?' I growled suspiciously. 'That's why you asked for my guitar. You didn't make *A Doll's House* a musical at all, did you? Because that is kind of ridiculous. Am I right?'

'Maaybee,' she replied slowly.

'You can't get up there and sing a song about women's lib stuff, though.' Jeff laughed. 'Not unless you burn your bra and stop shaving under your arms.'

And that was the straw that broke the camel's back. I'd had it with Jeff the jerk. I really did not know what Agnes saw in him other than the obvious good looks.

I stood up and glared down at him.

'Jeff,' I challenged him, hands on hips. 'Stand up.'

'Oh God, here we go.' He staggered to his feet.

'What, you gonna fight me?' He began bouncing on his feet like a boxer, hands balled up into fists in front of his face.

'Don't tempt me, mate,' I said seriously.

'What?' He sulked. 'What, Fiona?'

Out of the corner of my eye I could see Barton approaching us with his megaphone hanging by his side. I was surprised to see that he'd had a haircut and was wearing a clean, white button-up shirt. The transformation from upstart to prime minister had begun.

'For your information, Janis Joplin is a goddess. And what's wrong with a girl having armpit hair anyway?' I challenged Jeff.

'Are you serious? It's gross.' He laughed awkwardly. 'It stinks and—'

'It's normal. Humans have armpit hair!'

'Not girls,' he grimaced. 'That's revolting.'

'Why?'

'Because it is. It just is.'

I looked at him. His blond hair was glistening in the sun. His baby-blue eyes were looking bored with the whole thing and he was smirking at me. Agnes was squirming uncomfortably on the grass. Barton had arrived and was trying not to laugh. I was getting really worked up.

'Put your arms up, Jeffrey!' I demanded.

'Why?'

'Put them up.'

He did.

'Look at that,' I said, pointing and some of the kids around us looked over and started to laugh. 'You look like you've got wombats under there. You stink, Jeffrey. I can smell you from here. That is gross. What are you, a gorilla?'

'Cut it out,' Jeff bristled, putting his arms down, looking uncomfortable.

'Does Agnes have hairy armpits?' I asked him.

Agnes dropped back onto the grass rolling around with her hands over her face in embarrassment.

'Stop it, Fiona!' she moaned.

'No,' Jeff said, indignantly.

'Would you go out with her if she had hairy armpits?'

'Oh seriously, Fiona? Give it a rest, you annoying freak,' Jeff snapped. 'Barton, call off your red setter bitch, would you?'

'Oi, mate! You are out of line!' Barton stepped forward and frowned at his shorter friend. Agnes sat up, shielding her eyes from the sun, looking very upset.

'I'm right but thanks, Barton,' I said firmly, my eyes not leaving Jeff's.

'What if Agnes asked you to shave your armpits, Jeff? Because she finds the stench offensive? Would you do that for her?'

Agnes stood up beside me, copying my Peter Pan hands on hips. 'Yeah, would you, Jeff?'

'Oh, gang up on me, why don't you?'

'I'm serious.' Agnes glared at him. 'I want you to shave your armpits for me. Will you?'

'No!' He made a nervous grimace. 'Of course not. No way.'

'Then you're dumped.' Agnes smiled.

‘Hahaha, Agnes,’ he said sarcastically, with a roll of his eyes. ‘Yeah, right.’

‘I’m serious, Jeff,’ Agnes replied, raising her voice, talking him down. ‘Nobody calls my best friend a bitch. I’m a red-head, too, so you can get stuffed on that count as well.’

‘Your loss,’ Jeff shouted, picking up his books and pushing his way through the crowd.

I looked at Agnes and let out a whistle. ‘Are you serious, sister? You just dumped Jeff because he wouldn’t shave his armpits for you?’

‘Yeah, sure.’ She shrugged. ‘He was starting to get on my nerves anyway.’

We all laughed. Barton laughed the loudest. He suddenly wandered off, leaving Agnes and me alone.

‘Sorry about that with Jeff,’ I apologised.

‘It’s cool.’ She smiled. ‘I was never going to go to Sydney with him so it had to be done. And no one calls my sister a bitch. Nobody.’

After lunch I did it. I got up on the raised bench on the walkway with my guitar and I sang ‘Blowin’ in the Wind’. I could see Agnes singing along. By the end, all the kids were singing and it kind of felt like an anthem for our generation. It was nerve-racking but I did it and as all the kids applauded, I felt really good. Strong. Proud.

‘You were awesome,’ Barton said, catching up to me. ‘If you ever get sick of law, you’ve got a career as a folk singer waiting for you. You’ve heard of the Singing Nun. So why not the Singing Lawyer?’

'Thanks.' I nodded. 'I can't believe you made me do that but … thanks. It was fun. The Singing Lawyer? Hmmm. It has a certain ring to it.'

'I was wondering …' he said, and I looked at Barton with concern because he had suddenly stopped talking and was looking uncharacteristically unsure of himself, 'I was wondering if you wanted to come out for a bit of dinner and maybe to the pictures tonight.'

I looked at him as I cocked an eyebrow. 'You don't mean like on a date, do you?'

The poor guy looked a little deflated.

'Oh, yes like a date?' I said, guiltily. 'Sorry. I mean … really? You and me?'

'Sure,' he said hopefully. 'I've never dated a fresher but you're officially a second year now.'

'Hmmm,' I said, buying some time while I thought about it. Barton McLeod. Cute. Tick. Ambitious. Tick. Politically literate. Tick.

'And just in case you were undecided …' He grinned and I stepped back, not sure where he was going with it as he started to unbutton his shirt, 'I thought this might seal the deal.'

I stared. I gaped. I had never seen anything quite like it.

Barton McLeod had shaved his armpits. 'You have no idea how hard it is to find a razor on campus at short notice!' He laughed.

My mouth fell open and I didn't know whether to laugh or cry or a combination of both.

'What do you say? You wanna risk a date with me?

I smell real nice,' he said, leaning down and taking a big sniff of his armpit.

'Ahh, like roses,' he said, rolling his eyes skyward.

What could I say to that? I liked Barton. I couldn't help it. Everyone loved Barton McLeod. 'Sure.' I smiled. 'Sure. But only because of the armpits.'

We walked to the cafeteria, me carrying my guitar strung across my back, Barton with his megaphone on a strap around his neck. I was feeling a smorgasbord of feelings. Elation, after my public performance. And a hint of those silly girl tingles you got in the pit of your belly when you suddenly realised that you liked a guy and that you'd liked him for a really long time but had refused to admit it to yourself.

'So do you think you can see me as a lawyer now, Barton McLeod?' I asked with a wry grin as we stopped by the coffee depot.

'Well, yes, but actually there's this other thing,' he said, putting a hand on his chin, appraising me, staring deeply into my eyes.

'This other thing?' I frowned.

'Yeah, this other thing.' He grinned. 'Hmmm.'

'And what, may I ask, is this other thing?'

'It's something else I can see when I look at you.'

'And that thing might be?' I asked in a sing-song voice, coaxing it out of him.

'Well, Fiona from the Darling Downs,' he said, looking at me seriously, 'when I look at you now, I see a girl who might just change the world.'

AUTHOR'S NOTE

The characters of Jeanne Laisné and Betsy Gray are based on actual historical figures, although there is little recorded evidence of the details of their lives outside of the events for which they became renowned. They have, however, become the subject of legends, songs and local folklore. Given that these were young women, it is likely that their stories were overlooked by writers of history who during that time were almost exclusively male. For this reason, I have pieced together remnants of information and evidence still in existence and, using a blend of my own imagination along with my research of those specific times and places, I fleshed out the circumstances and family histories that saw these heroic women become legends. Fairytale stories where real girls are the heroes. *Liberty* is my own way of telling these 'herstories'.

JEANNE LAISNÉ

(Born 1456, date of death unknown)

In 1472 Charles the Bold, Duke of Burgundy, along with his army, sacked the French town of Roye before moving on to the fortress town of Beauvais. Over the course of the siege, a woman named Jeanne Laisné organised a contingent of women who loaded the town's cannons, delivered arrows to the archers and dumped scalding oil over the walls onto the attacking Burgundians. As the siege progressed, the Burgundians got up onto the walls and were about to take the town. Many of the French defenders began to lose hope. However, the seventeen-year-old Jeanne grabbed a hatchet and launched herself at the Burgundian officer about to plant the Burgundian flag on the wall to claim the town. She threw the flag and soldier from the wall. Charles the Bold gave up after night-time spot attacks on his troops and the sustained defence from the townspeople and marched on, leaving Beauvais alone.

King Louis XI, upon hearing of Jeanne Hachette's heroism, allowed her to marry any man of her choosing, which was unheard of for a woman in the 1400s. She married a man named Colin Pilon. Jeanne was also granted tax exemption for the rest of her life, as were her descendants. Every year the town of Beauvais holds 'The Procession of the Assault' where the women of the town march through the streets. Colin Pilon died only a few years after the pair were married. No more is known about Jeanne.

BETSY GRAY

(Born 1778, died 1798)

Betsy Gray was a young Presbyterian girl from Northern Ireland, killed during the 1798 Rebellion of the United Irishmen. She fought in the Battle of Ballynahinch with the United Irishmen (also known as the Liberty Men) against the English and was killed the next day, with her brother, George, and lover, William Boal, having her right hand cut off before being shot in the eye. Much of what is known of Betsy was passed down in her family through oral history. There is some debate about her gravesite. The storyline of her older sister Brigit is fiction.

My own family lived on a farm not far from where the Grays lived, outside of Newtownards, and my great-great-great-grandmother was Isabella Ballantine who returned to the area from Paisley, Scotland, around twenty years after Betsy's death. (Thanks for helping me stumble upon the story, Granny Ballantine.)

FIONA MCKECHNIE

While Fiona and all the characters in her story are fictitious, the University of Queensland's student protest movement was one of the most vibrant of its time and it could be argued that the marches and rallies helped to sway the government and society at large to give up on the policy of conscription and withdraw Australian troops from the Vietnam conflict. The student march depicted in

Liberty was based on the 'Big March' of 8 September 1967 when up to four thousand students, teachers and activists marched from the University of Queensland to Brisbane City, illegally, to protest involvement in the Vietnam War. Conscription in Australia ended in December 1972. The marches and protest movements rising around the world today – demanding fairer treatment of women and minorities and bringing attention to issues such as gun control and climate change – show that grassroots activism through taking to the streets is still a valid and effective way to spread the will of the people.

ACKNOWLEDGEMENTS

This book is for my daughter, Mia, and her friends – Taliah Miller, Mia Fulham, Levi Lund and Freya McCowan Pearson – and my son Thomas and his sidekick Eric Ridley.

Thanks also to Anne Powles, Gary and Julie Mason, Louise and Steve Rayner, Becc O'Neill, Sam Barker, Taylor and Elvis Goodwin, Lisa Standish and baby Ivy, Fiona McCowan, Jo and Graham Ridley, Peter Miller, Adelene Liu and Donna Cameron. To Rhoni Stokes for shouting me a tart at The Haven! Alison and Merril from Bookface Erina. To the lovely Pip Harry for her kind words and to Maria Lewis for hers (black cats and broomsticks forever, coven-sister). To Gemma Ward for being a warrior woman. And comrade Mandy Beaumont.

To the kids from Book Bazaar Umina's Junior Book Club. You rock!

To my family. Dad. Mum. The sibs. The nephews. The cousins. The kids and kids-in-law. My precious grand-bibby. And the beloved Outlaws.

To my friends. You are many and loved. Amanda Fullarton – sorry for the misspelling last time.

All at UQP, thank you. Most of all, thank you to Kristina Schulz for helping me bring all my girls to life. Vanessa Pellatt, thanks for smoothing, tightening and tweaking me line by line. Jean Smith, you are wonderful at getting my words into people's eyes! An enormous thanks to Jody Lee who is very much the godmother to *Hexenhaus* and *Liberty* and *Saga*. You are a great partner to have. And Jo Hunt – I love your beautiful cover so much!

Of course none of my books would be possible without the mighty power of the beard of Zeus. Love love.

Liberty. Equality. Sorority!

May the Sisterhood be with you.

COMING SOON

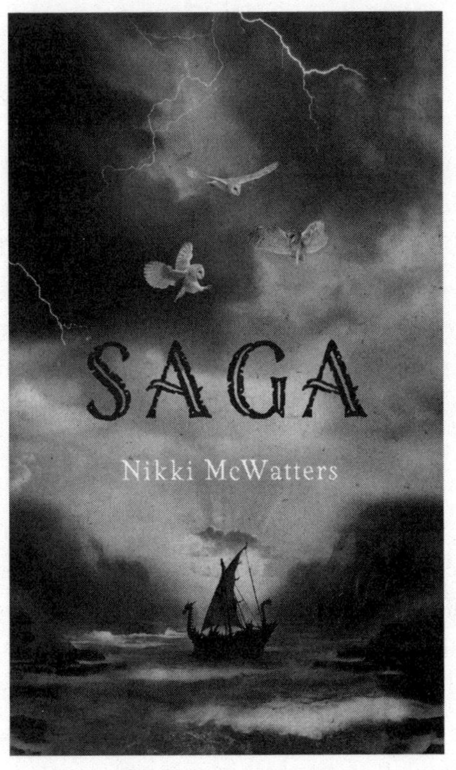

Available 2019

Saga

In the last years of the Viking Age, as traditions and old wisdoms are being replaced by those of the Roman Catholic Church, Astrid, a skáldmær from Norway, takes on the task of writing the *Goddess Book* so that the True Things are not forgotten. When she realises that she must protect her baby daughter, Freyja, from the king's men, Astrid stows away on a Viking ship to the Orkney Islands.

Mercy escapes the harsh conditions of a Victorian orphanage in Glasgow to take her chances as a street urchin. She is taken in by Ann Radcliffe, a successful but reclusive author of Gothic horror novels, and taught the art of storytelling. After she leaves to become a nursemaid, Mercy tries to find her true identity by deciphering an ancient book left to her by her mother.

At her cousin's funeral, Mia, who lives in the Blue Mountains, is given a centuries-old book. With the help of a university research assistant, she manages to decipher the early rune symbols and discovers that it points to an even more mysterious book buried somewhere in the Orkney Islands. Mia travels to the windswept Scottish isles to discover the true secret of the *Systir Saga*.

ALSO AVAILABLE

HEXENHAUS

A powerful novel about three young women caught in the hysteria of their own times.

In 1628, Veronica and her brother flee for their lives into the German woods after their father is burned at the stake.

At the dawn of the eighteenth century, Scottish maid Katherine is lured into political dissent after her parents are butchered for their beliefs.

In present-day Australia, Paisley navigates her way through the burning torches of small-town gossip after her mother's new-age shop comes under scrutiny.

'A gripping tale rich with demons and bigotry, potions and politics, *Hexenhaus* draws a sharply observed line between modern-day prejudice in Australia and the paranoia surrounding the European witch trials.' Nicole Hayes, author of *One True Thing*

'*Hexenhaus* entwines the past and the present in three compelling narratives that will keep readers on the edge of their seats.' Kate Forsyth, internationally bestselling author

'A riveting novel inspired by the true
history of witchcraft and witch-hunts.
Unputdownable!'
Kate Forsyth
HEXEN
HAUS
Nikki McWatters